"I don't know what all this fuss is about anyway. I was just inviting you up for cookies." Ronni shrugged naively and they both laughed. Jeff started picking at the crease in his slacks. "Besides, aren't you the one who's always giving me the—" Ronni raised her eyebrows twice to indicate his sexual teasing.

Jeff smiled and leaned in to raise his eyebrows at her right then. "Yeah—I'm good at that, huh?"

Ronni gently punched his shoulder and then opened her hand to soothe the area she'd struck. His biceps were rock-hard and his body threw off a sultry heat that the fine fabric of his shirt couldn't possibly contain.

Jeff's familiar, handsome face was extremely close to hers. She watched his deep brown eyes as they darted back and forth between both of hers. Her hand firmly gripped his shoulder and squeezed. She then slowly, smoothly slid her hand to the back of his neck. There, her fingers played with the line of his freshly cut hair while her thumb found the earring intriguing. Now there was nothing but pure desire behind Jeff's hooded eyes as he pressed his lips tightly together and swallowed hard. He closed his eyes, as though the absence of her visual stimuli would stop the overpowering hunger he was feeling.

With Jeff's eyes closed, Ronni found more confidence and her lips faintly connected with the small cleft in his goateed chin before sliding up to the corner of his mouth. She felt Jeff release a deep sigh from his nostrils, the breath brushing her cheek. Eyes or no, his hand deftly found her waist. He pulled her closer to him and his mouth skillfully took control of their kiss. First he kissed her lips full on, their mouths closed. Next, they peppered each other's lips with small, wet kisses. Then, all tension replaced by passion, they both explored each other's mouths with willful abandon, tongues pressed together and caressing.

ALL OR NOTHING

Crystal Downs

BET Publications, LLC
http://www.bet.com
http://www.arabesquebooks.com

ARABESQUE BOOKS are published by

BET Publications, LLC
c/o BET BOOKS
One BET Plaza
1900 W Place NE
Washington, DC 20018-1211

All Kensington Titles, Imprints, and Distributed Lines are available at special quantity discounts for bulk purchases for sales promotions, premiums, fund-raising, and educational or institutional use. Special book excerpts or customized printings can also be created to fit specific needs. For details, write or phone the office of the Kensington special sales manager: Kensington Publishing Corp., 850 Third Avenue, New York, NY 10022, attn: Special Sales Department, Phone: 1-800-221-2647.

First Printing: February 2005

10 9 8 7 6 5 4 3 2 1

Printed in the United States of America

To my parents, Charles and Queen, who are not only the wind beneath my wings, but the ones who attached them to my back and convinced me I could fly.

ACKNOWLEDGMENTS

Creating is such a collaborative process that anyone who has ever put anything creative out there in the world—be it a book, painting, play, dress, or even a great meal—knows the creation wasn't produced in a vacuum. For that reason, I would like to thank God and those individuals who were with me as I leaned over the keyboard well into the night. I couldn't have created without my precious little faces, Immanuel, Daniel, and Linnea. Those who have my back, unconditionally, Chuck, Carla, Craig, Dwayne, Vanessa, and Patrice: I love you all.

Thanks to my girls, who provided much-welcomed distractions, Tricia, Melody, Connie, Nicole, Faye, Darlene, and Sheree. To my writing buddy and supportive friend, Patty, thanks for making sure I didn't give up. Thanks to my loving aunts, Ruth and Daisy. And I can't forget Toni, the first fan I ever enjoyed as a wee writer. Finally, I'd like to give a special, heartfelt thank you to my editor, Demetria Lucas, who showed me how it's supposed to be done.

Chapter One

Veronica Hampton was on the elevator swiftly climbing the ninety-five floors to the famed Signature Room on the top floor of the John Hancock Building. She knew this fine old downtown Chicago building like the back of her hand—she had been going there since she was a little girl. It was where she first developed her love of the "ladies' lunches" she shared with her mom. When she was little, these outings had always made her feel grown-up. Now Veronica really was grown-up, and being on her own had lost its luster long ago.

She stared at her reflection in the elevator walls, thinking it was inconsiderate on the architect's part to subject people to having to view themselves when there was nothing else to look at in such a confining space. Nevertheless, she transferred her shopping bags to one hand and straightened the hem of her black knit halter-top, which had crept up the side of her cream-colored slacks. That accomplished, her eyes met her reflection again and two words sprang into her mind: *idle rich.* Just thinking about how her girlfriend Shelly Jones had called her that earlier really ticked Veronica off.

Besides, Shelly had a lot of nerve. She'd done twice as much buying on today's shopping spree as Veronica. Plus, while Ronni perused the sales racks, Shelly was hunting through pricey designer duds just yards away. As far as Veronica was concerned, summer clothes were summer clothes. You didn't have to pay hundreds of dollars for a halter-top and blue-jean shorts just because they had somebody's name on the label.

To her, the words "idle rich" applied more to those who belonged to exclusive country clubs, vacationed in Saint-Tropez and considered Fashion Week in New York an opportunity to fill out their wardrobes. Veronica had neither the time nor the money to waste on such extravagant indulgences. She guessed that Shelly's characterization, though meant in a friendly way, was more about Veronica's not working than about her being a wealthy socialite—which she by no means was.

Besides, she wasn't raised that way. Thinking about this, she looked at her watch. The shopping date with Shelly had made her a little late for meeting her mother.

When the elevator doors opened on a floor she hadn't chosen, a fine and professional-looking light-skinned brother with pretty curly hair and an even prettier blue suit got on with an older white gentleman. "I'm working hard and you're out shopping," the brother joked, pointing to Veronica's array of bags that represented some of the finest stores on Michigan Avenue.

His colleague laughed. "Women have the good life. You probably ran into my wife out running up our credit cards."

Veronica chuckled briefly, indicating her annoyance that her thoughts had been interrupted and not really feeling like flirting. The men seemed to take the hint easily enough and proceeded to talk solely amongst themselves.

A pleasant *bing* signaled that she had arrived at her floor. As Veronica exited, she quickly spied her mother across the spacious dining room. Approaching, she watched Beverly Hampton languidly gaze out the restaurant's picture windows and was a little troubled by the portrait of loneliness she exhibited.

"Hi, Mom."

To Beverly, it was as though Veronica had suddenly appeared in the booth across from her in a whirlwind of shopping bags and a mildly fragrant vanilla-based perfume. She observed that Veronica's hair was freshly cut and her nails, though short, were neatly manicured. After collapsing in the booth like a weight, Veronica remembered to stand back up and kiss her mother's cheek.

"Hello, Ronni. Don't you look nice," Beverly said, accepting the kiss with a warm smile. She was proud of her child of twenty-seven years. Veronica was smart and confident and seemed relatively happy. Beverly would have to remind herself to resist the temptation during this lunch to start in on the fact that she longed for grandchildren. The last thing she wanted to be seen as today was a meddling old mother. The second to last thing she wanted to do was drive a wedge between Ronni and herself. Since Beverly's divorce, they were all each other had.

"Thanks, so do you. You didn't order already?" Veronica grabbed a menu while signaling for one of a group of waiters. "You should've ordered."

"No, I thought I'd wait for you. . . . That's not our waiter . . . the other one."

"Oh, whatever. One of them should come."

When a waiter finally arrived, Veronica took charge in her usual style, ordering a nice domestic white Riesling and the grilled chicken salads she and her mother typically enjoyed as their entrees. The Signature Room was her mother's favorite restaurant and Veronica knew exactly what Beverly wanted. Her mother certainly didn't mind. She was embarrassingly pampered that way and made no apologies for it. Someone had always taken care of Beverly. First her father, then her husband, and now her only child.

After thanking them for their order, the waiter, a cute—but young—white guy, left the table. Veronica fixed the woman across from her with a serious look. Despite her own assessment from across the room and her mother's offhand greeting earlier, Beverly really *did* look good. Her brown skin had a healthy-looking glow, her eyes suggested feistiness and her hands, which always made Ronni jealous because of their effortless femininity, featured neatly polished fingernails. Always preferring suits, her mother wore one of her Chanels—the beige one with the signature black trim that flattered her figure well. Beverly was a little hippy with a tummy she couldn't get rid of and had long ago given up trying.

Veronica leaned forward on her elbows and gave a brilliant smile. "So, Mom . . . how's it going? You're almost glowing. Spill the beans . . . is there a new man in your life?"

Beverly nearly blushed and threw off the telltale response with a quick gesture of her hand. "Thanks, honey."

"No. Really. So, is there a new man or something?"

Beverly fidgeted with her fork, and, though their food hadn't arrived yet, she placed her napkin in her lap. "No. No. Nothing like that."

"Why do you say it like that? It's not totally beyond the scope of imagination is it?" Ronni pressed lightly, taking a sip of the water with lemon wedges the waiter had poured. She knew she needed to tread carefully to get her mother to talk.

"Yeah, but it's not the main focus of my life either." This was the part of their lunch dates that Beverly had come to dread. Since she'd started to pester Veronica about finding the right man and possibly settling down, she'd unwittingly given her daughter carte blanche to do the same.

It was easy for Beverly just seven years earlier when she was married to Benjamin, Veronica's father. Then she held the status of a mother, not a girlfriend. She was a real matron of society. Mrs. Benjamin Hampton, wife of the owner of the first black-owned Cadillac dealership in the nation. Back then, she would sell the most tables to the various galas any of her boards organized and she threw grand parties and mentored young women.

Now, belonging to all her social clubs and serving on her various philanthropic boards didn't bring her any joy. As a divorcee, she wasn't comfortable on her committees anymore. Beverly had lost the security of a husband and didn't feel she carried as much influence with her colleagues as she used to. Some of the women showed serious discomfort with her around their husbands—after all, she was a single woman, and though they were loathe to admit it, she was still quite attractive. Beverly actually stopped attending most of the societal events for fear that Tamara, Benjamin's new wife, would want to claim those perks as the "new and improved" Mrs. Benjamin Hampton.

And to think, Beverly had brought that snake into her own home. Tamara's way was just to push forward and claim anything she wanted. Beverly couldn't believe she had hired the girl as her personal assistant to help her organize a schedule full of those very same activities she was now too embarrassed to attend. Right from the start, Tamara was overly solicitous of everyone in the household. Yes, she was a hard worker who came in the morning to help, then would stay late to finish her tasks. Beverly had never really looked at her closely enough to consider her attractive or even interesting, for that matter. For a while, she thought Tamara had set her sights on Benjamin's lawyer, Tyler Washington, and was going to warn her off for Ronni's sake.

Beverly also was pretty sure Tamara conveniently became pregnant from the affair with Benjamin so it would force his hand in having to tell Beverly. At one time, Beverly felt strangely sorry for her poor husband . . . he hadn't needed to think about birth control for years. Hell, he was probably shocked that the little suckers were still swimming upstream. She could kick herself for being so gullible back then, but now, she was no longer the clueless doormat she was then.

Ronni watched as a wave of emotion washed over her mother's face, settling into sadness. She wanted to back off, but she also wanted to see her mother move on with her life.

"I wasn't saying it was your main focus, Mom, but it should figure somewhere in the scheme of things. You and Daddy have been divorced for seven years now. Have you even seen one man in all that time?"

Their drinks arrived along with a breadbasket and Beverly immediately drank a sip of her wine, then stared out the window at the beautiful Chicago skyline. When it became obvious that she wasn't even going to acknowledge the question, Ronni insisted.

"Mom, you're a very attractive woman. You have a nice figure and men are always hitting on you or inquiring about you down at the club and at nearly every social event I've attended lately. You could have a man if you wanted to."

That was the last straw. Beverly had heard enough. "Look, Ronni, I know I could have a man. Been there, done that, as they say. My child is grown. I've been married. I've been through a divorce. I'm over all that and I am happy." She caught Ronni's questioning eyebrow. "I reiterate, I *am* happy. Now, what about you? You're in the

prime of your life. Talk about attractive—men nearly
stop and stare at you everywhere we go." She jerked her
head toward a group of waiters standing by their station.
"That group over there is congratulating our waiter for
having the good luck of serving your table. They're
probably harassing him to get your phone number."

Ronni rubbed the back of her hair and casually took
a peek. Her mother was right. They were all looking at
her. A few of them smiled broadly.

"Lord knows why. You're a bald-headed, four-eyed,
skinny, freckled thing," Beverly teased. They both
laughed at this oversimplification of what were really
Veronica's very good looks.

Ronni's "bald-headedness" came in the most stylish boy
cut accentuated by natural dark, black, shiny hair. Women
approached her all the time asking for the name of her
hairstylist. With her evenly shaped head and cinnamon
skin, short hair looked perfect on her. Ronni's "four eyes"
were prescription glasses with elegant frames and thin
lenses. She'd noticed that her eyes almost always attracted
men's attention as an afterthought. Usually they were already caught up in her overall beauty and then they'd get
this glazed look in their eyes before commenting, "Did
you know you have some beautiful eyes?" Actually, Ronni
did know. Not that she was conceited, but she considered
them to be her best feature.

As many times as she might be complimented on her
neat hands, her beautiful feet, or her gorgeous shape, it
was when someone noticed her eyes that she stuck her
chin out proudly and smiled. It wasn't because they were
the hazel or green or gray coloring, so prized in the
black community. In fact it was just the opposite. It was
her eyes' almost complete lack of any color other than
pitch black against the whitest white eyeballs that made
everyone take notice. Then there was the almond shape,

outlined by thick lashes and surrounded by naturally arched eyebrows. Her onyx eyes combined with the color of her skin gave her an exotic look which sometimes made strangers guess at her ethnic makeup.

And the "skinny"? Her mother was referring to the fact that Ronni's body-fat percentage had been greatly reduced after college, and she was now more in line with her ideal weight. In college, she gained the usual "freshman fifteen" and then about ten more. She was very close to her mother and missed her so terribly that she found herself eating lots of comforting foods while she was away at school. Then, with her parents going through marital trouble and, later, getting a divorce, eating was almost her only joy. After she graduated and saw that the weight she'd gained wasn't helping to solve the problem of her parents' divorce and was heightening her insecurity, she decided it was time for the extra pounds to go. One year under the instruction of a rather tough personal trainer gave Ronni the body she craved, and the renewed closeness to Beverly gave back some of the self-reliance she needed to survive.

Much to Ronni's dismay, when she lost the weight, she also lost her boobs. Though she missed her D cup size, she had nice, small firm breasts and more hips than anything else (she could thank Beverly for those). Her booty was round and high—what she considered perfect—and complemented long legs that had grown shapely from daily lunges and serious time on the treadmill.

All in all, Ronni was quite an all-around package, although she really was just getting to the point where she could appreciate this fact herself. Sure, she was in Jack & Jill as a child, in all the popular clubs in high school, and joined the premier black sorority in college, but she still had some nagging self-doubts.

Though her friends probably wouldn't concur, Ronni often saw herself less as a participant and more of an observer. When she was out with them, she followed along and enjoyed herself, but it was as if she were experiencing everything through an impenetrable glass. She was never part of the late-night party-hearty crowd in college and often retired to her small off-campus apartment, wondering what her roommate was up to when she was out until the wee hours of the morning. In college, she had a reputation for being inaccessible and she guessed that there was a bet out on who would be the first to bed her. So, rather than suffer the embarrassment of being dogged, she kept her distance from the boys.

She still had the social anxiety thing, but she was fairly content with herself and accepting of her looks, whether they were the best or not.

She smiled at her mother and pointed a finger at her face. "Don't start on me." As far as relationships went, Ronni currently wasn't in one, and though she felt some twinges of longing, she didn't consider herself to be looking either. She was solely concentrating on taking more responsibility in her father's auto-dealership business.

"Oh. It's okay to pick on me, but you're off-limits?" Beverly said, laughing as she prepared for the salads she could see were on their way from the kitchen.

"Sorry, that's the way it is," Ronni said, sitting back as the waiter placed her napkin in her lap with a great flair intended to attract more attention to himself than the occasion called for. Beverly winked at her.

"Will there be anything else, ladies?" he asked, looking only at Ronni.

"No, thank you," Beverly said, raising her hand dismissively at the waiter. Ronni stifled a snicker at her mother's antics and began eating her salad without acknowledging him.

"All right," Ronni said. "Let's call it a truce. I won't pick on you and you don't pick on me."

"No. It's my prerogative to pick on you. I'm the mother. I want grandbabies."

"Huh! Grandbabies who can't call you Grandma?" Ronni feigned incredulity.

"No. They can call me Nana . . . or maybe Beverly. Oh, I don't know. It's all theoretical at this point anyway, isn't it?" Beverly began to feel like her old self again when she realized Ronni was falling into the daughter role without a fight. "By the way, Tyler asked me just the other day if you were in town. Haven't you called him?"

"Tyler." Ronni said his name in a British accent and stiffened her back as though the mere mention of his name required her to sit up straight.

"Tyler is a very nice young man and your father trusts him and likes him a lot," Beverly pressed, knowing her words were falling on deaf ears. Ever since the divorce, Ronni and her father's relationship hadn't been the same.

"Tyler just wants to get in better with Daddy. I don't think he really loves me. Hell, I don't even know if he really likes me. He's in love with Daddy."

"Just like everybody else," Beverly said, and thought, *Including me.* She didn't dare tell Ronni that the primary reason she hadn't moved on in her romantic life was that she still loved Benjamin. He was the first and only man she'd ever loved and she was afraid he would be the last. "But I think Tyler's genuinely hooked on you."

Ronni gave her mother a raised eyebrow in warning. "Can we change the subject?"

Beverly obliged, moving to many other topics, including her home remodeling, politics, books she'd read, and Ronni's search for a new condo. After they finished their meal and while they were waiting for the waiter to return with Beverly's credit card, they enjoyed their view of the Chicago skyline. The day was picturesque, offering the bluest sky and the most serene water. Boats were out in full force, trekking very slowly across the lake.

Ronni had always thought that the best thing about Chicago was its summers. Sure, most cities had great summers, except for maybe Las Vegas and parts of Texas and Arizona that were battered by a relentless heat, but Chicago summers were something of a study. The bleak, cold, gray city was transformed, like its own Brigadoon, rising from the gloom and blossoming into a world-class city full of greenery, multicultural faces, and life everywhere.

If you knew your way around, you could find hidden areas and open spaces that reminded you of any of your favorite places. There were parts that mimicked Paris, some like London, others you would swear were slices of Italy, and others dead ringers for New York. And the people—these were no urban-hardened tough talkers like New Yorkers. The exuberant friendliness of the people was a testament to the fact that everyone had made it through that grueling journey of winter to this fantastical time. Most Chicagoans enjoyed the sights and sounds of their summers so much that they preferred to vacation in May, November, or December rather than miss out on all the fun of the vacation spot that came right to them.

The waiter returned and leaned in conspiratorially. "I'm sorry, Mrs. Hampton. There's a problem with your card. Would you like to try another one?"

"What? There must be some mistake," Beverly said, shock evident in her voice. "That one has no limit. Try it again."

"I'm sorry, ma'am, but I've tried it three times already." The waiter looked seriously pained to be giving trouble to the mother of the woman he was trying to impress. "You could call the customer-service number on the back and see what the problem is. I'll bring you a phone."

"What?" Beverly took the extended card and was beginning to get annoyed. "That won't be necessary."

"I'll get this one, Mom," Ronni said, reaching for her purse.

"No, no. I've got it." Beverly reached into her purse and fished out the appropriate amount of bills, plus a generous tip, and dropped them into the check folder.

"Thank you. I'm sorry about the inconvenience." For the first time, the waiter scurried away without attempting to make eye contact with Ronni.

Ronni frowned, placed her elbow on the table, and rested her chin on her hand. She watched as Beverly dialed the number of the credit card company on her cell phone and talked with the customer-service department. Ronni only half paid attention. She stared out the window at the beautiful day, trying to decide whether to hit some of the great shops on Oak Street or head home.

Being a child of privilege, she wasn't overly concerned about her mother's situation. Last year, Ronni's father's auto dealerships had sales exceeding seventy million dollars. In the late eighties, Benjamin had had the foresight to expand his business to include more luxury cars from several foreign automakers. When he saw the trend of upwardly mobile African-Americans expanding into the south suburbs, he was the first to open branches in locations like Country Club Hills, Matteson, and Flossmoor. Most recently, he'd added a couple of northern suburban locations. All seven of his places in and around the Chicago metropolitan area were quite profitable and Ronni couldn't remember a time in her life when her family didn't have money.

When her mother turned the phone off and put it back in her purse, Ronni looked at her and felt her blood run cold. Beverly looked stricken, the color gone from her face.

"Mom, what did they say?"

"Um, my card has been canceled," Beverly said, talking breathlessly as though the wind had been knocked from her lungs. She could barely speak.

Ronni sat straight up in her chair. The words didn't make any sense to her. It was almost as if her mother were speaking gibberish. "What? I—I don't understand," she said, leaning forward. "Canceled?"

"Ronni, that's all I can tell you myself." Beverly placed the strap of her purse on her shoulder, preparing to leave.

Ronni touched her arm to stop the action. "Mom. Aren't you paying the bills? What do they mean canceled?"

Beverly was on the verge of tears at the thought of having to explain her situation to Ronni. She stopped fiddling with her bag and turned to her daughter.

"When your father and I divorced, I took a lump-sum settlement of five million dollars with no monthly alimony payments. You remember how upset I was at that time and just wanted everything over with as quickly as possible? But Ben, I guess feeling guilty about breaking up our marriage, told me privately that the American Express card would serve as my alimony. He said since the card had no limit, I could determine what monthly amount would keep me in the lifestyle to which I was accustomed. It's the only one I carry with me. The only one I use, really. For everything."

Beverly's tears were flowing and she reached into her purse for a handkerchief. Ronni moved to her mother's side of the booth, putting an arm around her shoulders.

"Oh, Mom," she said, feeling her pain.

"He's paid it faithfully every month for seven years. I don't understand what would make him change his mind now. They said there hasn't been a payment in more than six months." Her shoulders shook in a quiet sob.

Even as Ronni felt herself tearing up, she also felt anger rising. "I think I have an idea of what changed his mind, and its name is Tamara," she said stiffly.

Beverly dabbed at the corners of her eyes and sniffed. "But surely she's known all this time. She would've complained before, don't you think?"

Ronni shrugged. "I wouldn't put anything past that cow." She glanced around shrewdly, catching the eye of the waiter by the computer station. He quickly looked away. "Come on, let's go. Do you have enough money with you to pay for your parking?" Beverly nodded. "You go home and I'll go have a talk with Daddy." Ronni hugged her mother protectively.

Beverly's hand suddenly gripped Ronni's arm in a clutch that was almost painful. "No, Ronni." Her mother looked very firm on this point. "I don't want you going over there making trouble. This is between me and your father. I can handle this myself."

"Mom," she said, prying off the death grip, "I'm not going to make trouble. I'm just going over to talk to him. See why he's changed his mind."

Beverly gave her a suspicious glance.

"Really," Ronni urged, hoping her face looked calm enough. She could feel an angry heat under her skin but hoped it didn't show.

"Calmly," Beverly stressed.

"Calmly."

Chapter Two

Ronni was annoyed with so many things as she drove to her father's house. She didn't look forward to this confrontation, but she didn't appreciate that her mother had been tossed aside like funky laundry either. She was also under the distinct impression that if she wasn't so much older than her father's only son, Benji, she too would be cast out like yesterday's news. Tamara, Benjamin's newer, younger wife, was extremely proud that she had borne Benjamin's first son. *Son.* Even the word seemed to carry so much more weight than *daughter.*

Truth be told, Ronni had never felt anything less than loved by her father while she was growing up. She'd always been a mama's girl, but she had a special relationship with her dad. He was proud of her and attended all her track meets, spelling bees, and district science fairs. He encouraged her in school and helped her with her homework. And being part of a fraternity himself, he understood what she was going through when she pledged her sorority. When her mother asked her ceaseless questions as to why she couldn't be reached in her room even at one or two in the morning, her dad ran interference on the home front to allay her mother's fears. He kept Beverly from calling the sorority's top brass, who were friends and acquaintances of hers, during that final hellish week of pledging.

But with the birth of Benji, Ronni saw a whole new

dynamic in her father. He gazed proudly at his son and stuck his chest out. *Did he do that with me?* Ronni wondered. Also, he was home more for Benji. She didn't know if that was because he was in his early sixties now or because Benji was a boy. One of her girlfriends had declared that she was glad she had a boy first because men were much more attentive with boys. Her theory was that men seemed not to know what to do with baby girls. Ronni wondered if that had been true with her.

Benji was the first person she spotted as she turned her car into her father's driveway. He was on the front lawn, batting a ball tethered to a pole. When he saw Ronni, he turned with a big smile and ran to her car. He was pulling on the car door before she shut off the engine, as though she couldn't get out fast enough for him.

"Ronni! Hey, Ronni!" he called out to her.

He was really a sweet boy and she couldn't help but smile and give him a big hug. He molded his small body into hers, leaning on her as they walked. Ronni felt her hostility leaving. *Who could be grumpy in the face of such a beautiful smile?* In spite of the fact that his face was a male copy of Tamara's, Benji always made her happy.

"Hey, guy. What are you doing?"

"Playing baseball. Come on, play with me. You can be the next batter up." Benji pulled her hand, dragging her toward the array of toys spread over the lawn. Ronni slipped out of her stylish low-heeled sandals, and actually took a good twenty minutes out to play T-ball, catch, Frisbee, and, finally, chase with Benji. Benji moved her quickly from one activity to the next, chattering and directing her the entire time as though he rarely had an adult playmate with such enthusiasm. Winded, she eventually told him against his protests that she had to go inside.

"Noooooo," he whined, pulling on her arms. When that didn't work Benji grabbed her tightly around the waist. Ronni laughed and tried to pry his arms loose. This was another game for him.

"Benji! Honey, let go! I've got to go in and talk to Daddy." She couldn't help giggling as he swung her around with all his strength. They tumbled onto the grass. She got up first and ran up onto the huge porch. He came after her and she screamed. Ronni caught his arms before they latched on again in the bear grip she had just escaped. "No. I have to go see Daddy. I'll come back and play with you afterward. Okay?"

"You promise?" he asked, excitedly bouncing up and down.

"I promise." Ronni let his arms go and he ran back into the grass, choosing a tennis racket and ball to play with. Walking into the foyer, she could hear the tennis ball thunking against the wall. Ronni was smiling absently to herself and brushing the grass and dirt off her slacks when she bumped into a large object. Her hands ended up pressed against the rock-hard chest of a man. Even under the casual blazer and polo shirt he wore, she could feel thick muscles and a chiseled body. Powerful hands gently encompassed her shoulders, steadying her on her feet.

"Ho . . . watch yourself," a deep voice rained down on her. The voice was smooth and the diction refined. Ronni looked up into the most perfect mouth and teeth she had ever seen. His lips curled up into a deliciously generous smile, framed by a very closely cropped mustache and goatee.

When her eyes rose to meet his, Ronni gave a startled jump and backed away. He was gorgeous and in just the way she liked—clean-cut, sophisticated, with the chiseled chin and pointy nose. He was an almond color with piercing brown eyes that featured tiny smile lines right in the corners. His eyebrows were thick and expressive.

Right now they registered amusement. His hands were still "steadying" her, so he must have felt her jump.

"Uh . . . thanks. I'm okay," she said, stepping farther back to get out of his grasp. He was still smiling at her. She noted again that the teeth were perfectly straight and brilliantly white, before looking away. "I—uh—sorry." She didn't know why her old shyness was kicking in again, but she was feeling too nervous to even take another good look at him. She started to go around him when she felt him gently touch her arm.

"Ronni, don't I get a hug? A hello? Anything?"

She looked around, at a loss for words. A hug? Did she know him? She smiled unsurely. "Wha—?"

"You're Veronica, aren't you? Ronni Hampton?"

He held out his arms in a kind of *it's me* gesture. Something about that smug and teasing smile did look familiar, Ronni thought, staring at him openly. He put his hands in his pants pockets, cocking his head and silently refusing to help her with any references as to where they'd met. It was the bold confidence that gave him away. In her lifetime, Ronni had never encountered another man who was so frankly self-assured.

"Jeff Conley!" she shouted, pointing a finger at his expansive chest.

He laughed and reached for her. Before she knew it, all his hard, fragrant, and vigorous body was pressed against hers. She thought she felt a jolt of electricity pass from him to her and back again. Ronni didn't even know Jeff Conley knew her full name; now he was in her father's foyer.

Ronni had only had a crush on this man for as long as she could remember. It became stronger in college when he'd dated her roommate, Stephanie. Ronni seemed a dowdy, fat wallflower next to Stephanie, who was a size four and wore makeup and dressed to the nines for classes every day. Jeff and Stephanie went out for five grueling months and Ronni would hit the books harder whenever he came by. He would attempt small talk while Stephanie made him wait—doing Lord knows what in their small bathroom—but back then, Ronni could barely look at him. His relationship with her roommate had seemed fine until one day Steph was crying her eyes out, claiming her relationship with Jeff was over.

Jeff stood back and his eyes slowly crept over her body. He liked what he saw. "Last time I saw you, you were just a little freshie at Columbia."

She could see his eyes roaming freely over her face and body as if there were going to be a quiz afterward. "Yeah. You were a big-time senior," she joked. Her eyes narrowed at his handsomeness as though it were too much for her brain to process. He hadn't sported that mustache and goatee in school; he wore dreadlocks in college and was a lot skinnier back then. Now, he had developed a man's body, filled out in all the right places: chest, arms, shoulders, and thighs.

"Yep, junior, actually. To think, I knew you when you were just one of the little kids in Jack & Jill. Now, you're all grown up." There he was again, taking in her firm breasts, small waist, and womanly hips.

What she didn't realize was that Jeff couldn't help it. The woman he was staring at now had been the object of his desire back in the day. When she was one of the little kids in Jack & Jill, he barely noticed her during the group gatherings. But by the time she arrived at Columbia University, she was the girl most of his frat picked as the one they wanted. Not just to knock boots with like Stephanie and some of the other fine girls Ronni had pledged with, but for a serious girlfriend. Yet she was such a hard nut to crack, most of them opted for easier prey. The closest you could get to Ronni was a near-weekly report of her political activism and academic achievements in the university's newspaper.

She crossed her arms self-consciously over her chest. "What are you doing here?"

Jeff snapped out of his indulgent gaze at the question. He looked her directly in the eye. "I came to see your father. I wanted to get his business advice on something." He pulled her sleeve lightly. "So what are you up to these days, little girl?" The smile returned to his lips. He positioned his body closer to hers and unconsciously mirrored her stance.

"Oh, not much. You know, working at Daddy's business. And you?"

"Just a drifter."

She noticed his expensive watch, custom-tailored designer slacks, imported Italian shoes, and manicured hands. *Some drifter,* she thought.

She knew that Jeff's father, Aaron Conley, had been one of her father's peers. They had money, but Ronni wasn't sure of the source. Aaron Conley was one of the first African-American state senators in Illinois. He'd led a faction of black leaders who'd put pressure on the automakers to have more minority representation, and he'd helped her father find funding to acquire his first dealership. He'd retired a few years before his death almost three years ago and Ronni didn't know what he'd done as a private citizen. However, she did know the senatorial salaries weren't that high, especially back then. She wondered if Jeff had found a way to describe a comfortable life without working the way she had not.

"A drifter, huh?" She started to follow that comment with something witty when Jeff abruptly looked at his watch.

"Look, if you're not doing Daddy's business tomorrow, why don't you meet me at the South Lake Shore Tennis

Club? I have some court time and we can hit a while." He started to walk away. Ronni thought his retreat was awfully presumptuous, as if she'd already agreed to go.

"Sounds good. Depends on what time," Ronni called after him. She couldn't resist. For one thing, she couldn't believe this was happening, and she really didn't have anything else planned.

"Eleven," he threw back over his shoulder.

Ronni took him in, thinking the back of him was just as pleasing as the front. She really liked the way his pant legs fell on his calves. She'd always liked his walk; it was more of a stride, really. And his broad shoulders worked easily under the linen blazer. He turned back to look at her, spinning on his heels and she flushed. *Busted.*

"Oh, yeah, and don't be showing up there dirty like you are now," he teased.

Her eyes widened with embarrassment and she lunged at Jeff like she was going to hit him. He moved nimbly for such a tall and tightly muscled man, avoiding her swing. He was on the porch yelling back, "And I'm gonna whip your butt, too," by the time she caught her balance.

Ronni watched Jeff through the glass door as he took a moment to scoop up Benji and swing him around as he walked to his Lincoln Navigator. *The biggest car he could find,* Ronni thought. She hadn't noticed it when she'd pulled up, but because her father was an auto dealer, it wasn't unusual to see unfamiliar cars at his house.

Suddenly, Tamara ran through the front door, nearly knocking Ronni's shoulder off as she passed by. Waving her hand at Jeff, she ran to the driveway. "Jeff! Jeff, hold up!" she called in her annoying schoolgirl voice. Tamara was wearing high-heeled sandals, Daisy Dukes, and one of those fitted button-down tops with the last three buttons unbuttoned so everyone could see her flat, brown stomach.

Ronni shook her head in disgust. Even after seven years, Tamara and her father just didn't seem to go together. Ronni watched Jeff's face turn somber as he placed a giggling Benji on the ground and patted his butt to send him on his way. They talked closely, with Jeff leaning against his car and Tamara talking animatedly, extending frequent touches to Jeff's arm.

"Veronica—hi, sweetheart," her father greeted, coming from his office down the hall. Ronni tore her eyes from the interesting scene on the lawn and focused on her dad. His arms were outstretched and she fell into them coolly, allowing herself to be hugged.

"Hello, Daddy."

"Hello, Daddy? Is that any way to greet your old man?" He knew he'd caught her cold mood, but put his arm around her shoulders and led her into his office anyway.

Entering the room, Ronni was struck by the amount of disarray. Papers were strewn across his desk and his file cabinets had been left open. There were lots of scribbled-upon legal pads he must have started to write on and then abandoned. There were even some balled-up papers that missed the garbage can. Usually, her father was meticulously neat when it came to his surroundings and his person. Ronni noticed he looked sort of scruffy, too. His hair was a bit long, he had a five-o'clock shadow, his nails weren't manicured, and his shirt was tucked but a bit wrinkled. On anyone else, this wouldn't have been a big deal, but on her father these things were significant.

After playing with Benji and running into Jeff, some of her anger over her mother's anguish had dissipated. All Ronni felt now was a little friction. She sat in one of the huge leather chairs facing her father's desk and he sat next to her in the other. She watched as he moved some paperwork from his chair just to sit.

"How's my girl?" he asked, reaching for her hand and

holding it lovingly. He had that admiring look in his eye that she'd just convinced herself was reserved for Benji. Ben's gaze turned to concern. "Why are you looking so mean?"

Ronni swept her free hand in the direction of the mess. "When was the last time you let Angie in here to straighten up?"

Angie, a "Tamara addition" to the household, was their live-in housekeeper-slash-cook-slash-nanny. When Ronni was a child, Beverly had always managed to take care of the house and cook the family meals. Twice a week she hired someone to tidy, but the woman usually found herself polishing the silverware, dusting hard-to-reach places, organizing her mother's knickknacks, or some such busywork. Ronni's mother certainly never needed a constant companion to wait on her.

Benjamin looked at the junky office as though he were seeing it for the first time. The smile fell off his face. "Oh, yeah . . . I'm looking for some receipts. She can't come in here until I find them." He looked around the room again. "I guess it is a bit junky, huh?"

"Yeah."

"So, kiddo, what's on your mind? How are the NADA classes going?"

NADA was the National Automobile Dealers Association. Ronni was halfway through a twelve-month academy program that taught prospective dealers all aspects of managing a dealership.

"Classes are going fine. I've passed every test so far with top scores and gave a couple of presentations on consumers," she said quickly and matter-of-factly.

"Fantastic. I'm not surprised."

Ronni let go of his hand and turned to face him fully, looking very serious. "Daddy, that's not why I'm here."

"What's on your mind, honey?"

"Daddy . . . have you just moved on with your life and completely forgotten about Mom? What you're doing is hurting her."

Benjamin frowned, totally oblivious to what Ronni was referring to. "What do you mean?"

"Why did you cancel her credit card? Mom was humiliated at the Signature Room." When Ronni got mad, her words were slower and more carefully chosen. She could feel the anger returning now that she was talking about the restaurant incident.

He sat forward, looking alarmed. "What? Canceled?"

"You reneged on your promise to take care of her."

"Honey, I never! I—I'd never hurt your mother. There must be some mistake."

"Daddy." Ronni sighed, sitting back in her chair and folding her arms across her chest. She felt tears trying to surface and mentally pushed them back, looking out the window past his desk. Benjamin seemed so genuinely surprised and hurt at this accusation that she wasn't sure how to proceed.

"Listen, Ronni. Listen to me." He touched her knee, but she still wouldn't look at him. "I wouldn't do that to your mother."

Ronni turned her head slowly. "Then, what happened?"

He removed his hand and looked down at his lap. "I don't know, but I'll call and take care of this. Tell Beverly not to worry."

"She's *not* worried. She's *hurt.*"

"I know, I know, Ronni. Trust me. I'll get this straightened out as soon as possible." He stood up and gazed out the window. It overlooked part of the backyard, which provided a view of the gazebo. He saw Tamara and Benji sitting on the bench, sharing a book. Benjamin rubbed his hair backward and let out a long sigh.

"I'll take care of this," he said again almost absently.

Ronni stood up and fidgeted with a paperweight on her father's desk. She saw what her father was looking at.

"Could Tamara have canceled Mom's card?"

Benjamin turned around, looking astonished and a little sad at the suggestion. Ronni looked at the floor. He shook his head. "No, Ronni. I know what you and your mother think about Tamara, but she wouldn't do anything like that."

Ronni stepped forward and looked out the window, unconvinced. Her eyes narrowed and her father caught her skepticism.

"Look," he said, going toward her and putting an arm around her shoulders. "As long as Tamara's credit cards are paid and I keep her in jewelry and shoes, she doesn't give a damn what I do with the rest of the money. I promise you, it's probably some glitch at American Express. I'll get it straightened out today, okay."

Ronni nodded and pressed the side of her face into his chest. His hug was welcomed now. "All right. I'll tell Mom it's okay." He gave her one big squeeze before letting her go. She had another question she wanted to ask. She supposed now was as good a time as any. "Oh, I ran into Jeff Conley in the foyer. Are you doing some sort of business with him?"

Just for a second, Benjamin looked startled. He tried to recover quickly, but Ronni spotted it. His eyes were shaded and defensive. "What? You know him?"

"Yeah, Daddy . . . you know, from growing up and stuff. . . . He was at Columbia, too. . . . " She trailed off. She hadn't expected this reaction.

Benjamin still seemed to search her face before answering. "Were you talking to him?"

Still, with the questions, Ronni thought, keeping her hands busy by straightening the stacks on her father's desk. "Well, just now. I haven't seen him for years. He dated my college roommate. He said he was here for some business advice?"

Benjamin appeared to relax and went to the seat behind his desk. "Yeah. His father was a real help to me when I was starting my business. I keep up with Jeff from time to time and see how he's doing."

He was talking about Senator Conley like Ronni didn't know who he was, though he and his wife had been to their house for lavish dinner parties many times.

"How's he doing with what? What kind of business is Jeff in?" She didn't meet his eyes as she spoke, but when she glanced at him, he wasn't looking at her anyway. He was sorting through papers. Suddenly Benjamin sat back in his chair with a sharp eye on her.

"Why all the curiosity about Jeff? You're not interested in him, are you?"

"Daddy, I barely even know the guy. I ran into him in the hall; we haven't seen each other since college and he was in a hurry. I didn't have a chance to catch up on his life. I just asked what he was up to, okay?"

"Well, he's not right for you. You should take more of an interest in Tyler. He'd make you a much better boyfriend or husband than that Jeff," her father said, and the way he put on his reading glasses and went back to his paperwork, it seemed this was his final word on the matter.

That Jeff? Ronni didn't know what to think about her father's aloofness. As far back as she could remember, he'd never meddled in her social affairs, even when she was going out with that creep Terry, one of his employees at the main Chicago dealership. If he was going to warn her off anyone, it should've been Terry. *Tamara's not right for* you, *but that didn't stop you,* Ronni thought. Feeling her anger rise, she knew she needed out of this conversation, and fast. "I have to scoot," she offered, heading for the door. "Right now, I've got a play date with a four-foot-tall cutie-pie."

"All right, honey. Tell your mother I said hello and not to worry about the card."

Ronni went outside and looked at the abandoned toys on the front lawn. She stepped around the side and saw Tamara chasing Benji across the expansive grounds. He was screaming, laughing, and having fun. She had no desire to come in contact with Tamara, so after watching them for a few minutes without their noticing her, she decided to leave. At her car, she reached inside to get a sticky note off her dashboard. Ronni dashed off a short note to Benji, promising to play with him some other day and telling him to call her. Knowing that Benji would have to pick up all his toys before he went in, Ronni stuck the note on his baseball glove.

As Ronni drove away, she wondered about this attitude her father had toward Jeff. Did he really think he was a poor choice for a boyfriend, or was it just that he and her mom would prefer to see her with Tyler?

Jeff's conversation with Tamara contained all its usual tediousness. After repeatedly thanking him "for helping us out," she gave her weekly report on how difficult Benjamin was to live with at the moment. Jeff never said much in response and all but ignored her constant touching. He wasn't helping *them* out; he was helping Benjamin and himself, too. He'd only been to the Hamptons' house three times, but he was already sick of encountering Tamara.

Unfortunately, he knew her before she'd married Benjamin. Not very well, but enough to speak to in passing. Several times he'd suggested that Benjamin meet him at his place or downtown, but the man seemed reluctant to leave the house. He'd seen cases like this before. They start to get themselves in trouble and they think everybody secretly knows or is judging them. *How did he get involved with a woman like that?* Jeff wondered, turning out of the gated development. Jeff didn't want to devote any more of his brain matter to thinking about Benjamin Hampton's scheming wife. If he was going to be distracted while he was driving, he would prefer it to be because of Ronni.

"Veronica Hampton," he said aloud, a grin crossing his face. He couldn't believe his luck. Sure, he knew that the elusive Ronni was Benjamin's daughter, and that he was bound to run into her eventually, but he wasn't prepared to meet her so soon in his dealings with her father.

She'd crossed his mind quite a bit over the years—usually after he'd suffered through another failed relationship. Ronni was the one who got away. Frankly, the one who wouldn't give him the time of day. But the woman he'd just run into far surpassed his memory. It was like the difference between a photograph and a Technicolor movie. This time there was real eye contact and they'd actually shared more than twenty words. Jeff would have killed for just that back in his college days.

Jeff knew why he hadn't come clean with Ronni about his real reason for meeting with Benjamin, but he wasn't sure why he'd been so vague about his profession. Maybe it was that he felt it would raise other questions regarding his visit and he certainly didn't want to get into that. He didn't know how much Ronni knew about her father's business dealings, or how close the two were—especially considering the second-wife thing. Jeff knew better than to go running off at the mouth about what he was doing.

Still, he was surprised at himself for asking Ronni out. He shook his head. No, actually, he wasn't. He'd botched it in college by dating Stephanie when he'd really wanted Ronni and he wasn't going to miss his chance again.

Chapter Three

Indeed, Ronni's father was as good as his word. The morning after their talk, she had checked with her mother and found that her father had Beverly's card reinstated. With that squared away, Ronni was free to enjoy her day.

It was also one of the most beautiful summer days she had seen in a long time as if it were prearranged for her appointment with Jeff. The sun was shining, the birds were chirping and she had a good-looking man to meet.

Ronni also felt nervous. Usually, she would play tennis wearing comfortable shorts or sweats and an old T-shirt, but she'd gone out and bought a tennis skirt as soon as she left her father's house. Now, stepping timidly out of her car in the parking lot of the country club, she worried that this was trying too hard to impress her date. As she leaned over her trunk to pull out her racket, her heart jumped when she heard a catcall and a whistle.

"Yeah, baby! Look at those fine legs!"

The deep voice was coming from far across the parking lot, closer to the door of the club. She turned slowly, trying to look cool. She hoped it wasn't Jeff. *Thank God for sunglasses,* she thought, adjusting them on her face. At least she could hide some of her embarrassment. Now she was sure the skirt was too short.

"Could this be the same Ronni? Miss Frumpy herself?" the voice asked.

Ronni turned again and watched as the man approached with a sashay in his walk. She knew who it was and smiled.

"Cornell, if you don't shut up . . ." It was her first cousin on her father's side. He was her favorite relative, and Ronni saw him or talked to him on the phone at least twice a week. He hugged her hard and then stood back, looking her up and down.

"Shut up," she warned again, sensing his next sarcastic remark.

"Girl, why are you looking so fine? And you are wearing that funky attitude well. I was checking you out," he teased, following her to the entrance. She wished he wasn't so loud. The tennis courts were close to the parking lot and she didn't dare look in that direction. In her peripheral vision, she thought she could see someone who looked like Jeff near the fence.

"None of your business. Now beat it," Ronni was thinking of a way she could ditch Cornell without being overly rude. There was no way she was going to walk out on the court in the company of the very embarrassment she feared; someone pointing out to Jeff that she'd made a special effort to look nice.

"Ooooh, touchy. I guess it's true what they say. It's better to look good than to feel good."

Cornell was still following her. She stopped walking and turned to look at him coolly.

"Cornell, could you excuse me, please?" she said, clearly annoyed.

He looked sort of wounded. "All right, all right. I'll chill," he assured quietly, catching up to Ronni who had walked away. "You going to hit?" he asked, attempting casual conversation. Ronni didn't budge. "Okay! Good Lord. Who is it you're looking so nice for anyway, by the way?"

"Look, if you beat it, I'll tell you all about him later," she said, poking him with the head of her racket.

"Are you ashamed of me, your own cousin?" He gestured to himself with a hand splayed innocently across his chest. Ronni just cocked her head at him stonily.

"Fine, I'm gone. Carry your stank butt on in there. I'm telling Aunt Bev," he quipped, heading toward his car quickly.

Ronni breathed a sigh of relief as she watched him go. Cornell was halfway to his car when he turned around and yelled. "We're here! We're queer! Get used to it . . . Ronni!"

Playfully rolling her eyes, she laughed as she ran through the doors of the club and quickly hurried past the front desk. She didn't want that bubbly receptionist Melody making a big deal out of her short skirt. She dashed past a large group of people she knew and said a quick and generic "hi" before running up the stairs toward the Platinum Members' locker rooms.

Ronni was in such a hurry that she almost ran into Tyler.

"Slow down, gorgeous. What's your hurry?" His voice was velvety, clipped, and a bit nasal. He was looking very good, but in typical Tyler Washington fashion, it was over the top. He had on an entirely preppy tennis outfit. The white V-neck cardigan vest rimmed with blue and green stripes over a white polo shirt, white pleated shorts, white socks, and white court shoes. Of course, the clothing had the appropriate designer symbols in all the appropriate places. And, naturally, he was wearing his prized possession, his Patek Philippe watch. It looked plain and simple to the inexperienced eye, but Ronni knew it didn't sell for anything less than twenty thousand dollars.

"Oh, hey, Tyler." Ronni tried to keep walking toward the women's locker room. The section of the club they were standing in was glass-walled, overlooking the entire club. The location was in clear view of the front desk, the lounge area, and the row of treadmills. Ronni knew Jeff was waiting for her somewhere and she didn't want him to see her talking to Tyler.

Tyler held her arm, not forcefully, but not lightly either. Ronni stopped and looked at his hand on her arm. Tyler quickly let go but remained beside her.

"I haven't seen you in weeks. Where have you been hiding?"

"Well, you know I've been busy with my NADA classes and other things."

"Did Beverly give you my message?" he asked, gazing at her intently.

Ronni hated the way he called her mother by her first name and addressed her father formally. Sure, her mom had told him to call her Beverly, but her dad had given up coaxing him to call him Ben or Benjamin ages ago when he saw that Tyler would never do it.

"My mother told me you'd asked about me."

"What! I did more than that. I told her her daughter was breaking my heart. I barely see her and she won't even let me take her to dinner." He smiled and laughed after he spoke in an attempt to be funny. Humor didn't come easily for Tyler; he was too stiff and practiced.

Ronni glanced at him sideways. She felt a little sorry for him, but not much. He was extremely handsome, tall, and on the lean side, but hard and strong. Very neat in appearance, with a full mustache, burning hazel eyes, and milk-chocolate brown skin; he had a few razor bumps right at the crease where his head met his neck, but otherwise his skin was unblemished. His hair was a study in conservatism—not really short, but not really long either. She guessed it was purposefully just right, so as not to offend any potential clients or judges.

Tyler was ten years older than Ronni and as a lawyer with a large clientele of successful African-Americans like her father, was able to afford the finer things in life. He only needed someone to share them with, who could also produce the prerequisite number of offspring. A lot of women would have been honored to do the duty.

As a matter of fact, Cornell had told her stories of how some of the women who belonged to their neighborhood gym had been hounded by Tyler. These were women whose rumored naïveté she was surprised to hear about: Jennifer Mangus, who always held herself above everybody else and didn't even talk to anyone at the club, and Shirley Bassinger, who usually only dated older white guys. It was even whispered that Yvonne Massey was pressed by Tyler to get an abortion after a booty-call fling they'd had during the winter of 2002.

Of course Ronni and her family never witnessed this side of Tyler, not even remotely. Her parents weren't on this malicious grapevine and had never heard anything but good things about him. Ronni really didn't know what to believe. The women involved in the gossip were not the type to talk to people about their personal lives. Some sources claimed to have witnessed various fights in a darkened car or to have seen the interested parties dining together at some out-of-the-way place all cozy or vacationing or at a certain doctor's office. It was all conjecture and hearsay. Just because it came from her very own cousin Cornell didn't make it the Gospel. He was a notorious gossip and Ronni suspected he was a bit of a troublemaker, too.

If she hadn't heard about these trysts, she would've been wondering if Tyler were gay, but Cornell also dispelled this notion. Tyler was overly neat, his car meticulous, his briefcase well organized. The only woman she'd actually seen him date was Catherine Jacobsen. During Ronni's last two years of college and that following summer, Catherine had been Tyler's official girlfriend. Together, they'd attended a lavish Thanksgiving dinner at Ronni's parents' house.

And as far as Ronni could tell, Catherine seemed to be happy during their courtship, and came out of the relationship unscathed. She went on to marry Kevin Roberts, a movie producer who was based in Chicago and moved to California once he achieved some success.

Despite his good looks and her parents' blessings, Tyler just didn't appeal to Ronni. She knew he was willing to support her financially; she just got the feeling it would be in a hands-off way. She could imagine him calling AAA if her tire had a blowout, arranging for landscaping if she said she wanted to start a garden, contracting an exterminator if she saw a spider, and, worst of all, signing her up for a masseuse or a spa day when all she really wanted was a neck rub. She knew that some women would kill for that kind of life, but Ronni was looking for a lover, a best friend, a man—not just a good provider.

"I'm sorry, Tyler. I just don't have time for a lot of things, dinner being one of them." She tried to put a light note on it, but knew it came out flat.

"Well, what about right now? What about lunch?"

"No, I came to get a workout. Y'know, hit a few games."

"Fine. I was just about to leave, but we can do that, then have lunch." They'd made it to the women's locker room and now Tyler was standing slightly in front of the door, blocking her clear escape.

She shrugged her shoulders and avoided his eyes. "I'm hitting with someone already. We'll probably just play through lunch."

Suddenly it dawned on Tyler that Ronni was on a date. He looked at her hard from head to toe, thinking she looked good—very sexy. He took in a lungful of air and caught the scent of her perfume. She even smelled nice. "Oh? Who's the lucky guy?"

Ronni looked up, smiling easily as she tried to look casual about the whole thing. "What? It's not a *guy*. Not the way you mean it. It's just Jeff. You know, Jeff Conley. Senator Conley's son." She was talking too much.

"I know Conley," he said dryly, with emphasis on the "con."

"Yeah. You did his father's estate?"

"Yes. So you two are . . . what? An item?"

"No, no. We're just hitting together. I know him from college. He dated my roommate. You remember Stephanie?" She realized he'd never met Stephanie and she was still sharing more than the necessary amount of information. She had to ditch Tyler, fast. "Hey, look, I'll see you around. Call me tonight, maybe we can meet for lunch tomorrow or something." *Damn.* In trying to get out of Tyler's scrutiny she'd given him an opening. She saw the immediate spark in his face and the straightening of his spine.

"All right. I'll call you tonight," he said, reaching over and brushing her shoulder.

She could've cringed when he touched her. *Damn. Damn. Damn. Why did I have to run into him, of all people?* She walked into the locker room and took a deep breath as she opened her locker and checked herself in the mirror. Tugging on the skirt, Ronni reached into the locker for lotion.

"Hey Ronni-girl. You missed your cousin," a gravely woman's voice said behind her. She turned to see her mother's friend, Miss Lavonne, struggling with the laces on her athletic shoes.

"Hey, Miss Lavonne. No, I saw Cornell," she said, quickly applying lotion to her legs.

"Oh? Is he waiting for you downstairs?"

She checked her teeth in the mirror and put on a fresh coat of lipstick. "No. He left."

"Yeah, 'cause I was going to say, you two are as thick as thieves, but you don't look like you're getting ready to hit with him." Miss Lavonne was openly staring at Ronni's very short skirt.

"Yeah, well, I'll see you later," she replied. Refusing to supply Miss Lavonne with the information she wanted, Ronni threw the lotion and lipstick back into her locker and slammed the door. *Why did I agree to meet Jeff here?* People at the club were so nosy and everybody was always there.

Ronni picked up her racket and headed toward the exit with Miss Lavonne calling after her. "Tell your mother I said hi and she *could* come up and have lunch with somebody sometime."

Ronni waved a hand in acknowledgement.

Exiting the locker room, she saw Jeff at the bottom of the stairs. He was talking to someone out of her view and didn't see her. He looked really good, Ronni thought, exactly Tyler's opposite. Jeff wore the new baggier-styled men's tennis shorts and a big tennis polo shirt in the same colors the pros were wearing: blue, black, and white. On his feet were running shoes and white socks that were bunched low, allowing Ronni a glimpse of his fuzzy, muscled calves. Ronni forced herself down the stairs, noticing the black sports watch on Jeff's arm and the sweatband on the other. *Now that's what I'm talking about.*

As if on cue, Jeff turned his face up to see her descending the stairs. She could tell that the person he was talking to must still be there, and Jeff wasn't hearing a thing they were saying. Jeff didn't mean to be rude, but he just couldn't tear his eyes away from Ronni. His head was stuck in a captivated position, his eyes engaged.

"Here's the lady I've been waiting for," he said hoarsely as if his throat was dry. He turned to face the stairs, completely dismissing the person he'd been speaking with.

When Ronni got to the bottom of the stairs without

tripping, he held out his hand to her. Ronni could see now that he had been talking to Amanda Wordlaw, a magazine publisher's daughter.

Amanda gave Veronica the once-over and hesitated a bit. She knew Ronni and initially wasn't sure whether to stick around and make conversation. Finally, something about the way Jeff was looking at Ronni made Amanda decide to take her leave. She quickly excused herself.

Ronni took Jeff's hand, admiring its large, square shape. It made her hand feel incredibly small and delicate. She was trembling, but hoped he couldn't feel it. To her amazement, she thought she could feel his hand shaking, too. That took the edge off her nervousness.

"I thought I saw you coming from the parking lot," he said, leaning to plant a burning kiss on her cheek. It was so close to her mouth that she felt a tingle in the pit of her stomach. He smelled good, like the freshest ocean-breeze soap. "I guess I had to wait until you got through greeting all your other men before I got my chance to claim you," he teased.

Men? He must have caught the whole scene with Cornell and her walking with stick-in-the-mud Tyler. Well, at least he hadn't been close enough to hear anything.

Staring at her appreciatively, Jeff gave her hand a small squeeze before letting go. Feeling her nerves begin to take over just like a high schooler, Ronni was eager to get out of his too-direct gaze. It was like she could read his mind and she was both flattered and insulted by what he was thinking.

"So, are we gonna hit or what?" she asked. Ronni didn't know what else to say as she squeezed by him and headed for the courts.

"We're on three." Jeff hung back, enjoying the view. He watched her hips sway, noticing the extra bounce the tennis shoes gave her. Ronni wore cute ankle socks, giving him clear view of her perfectly smooth, long, shapely legs. He was staring at his favorite part of a woman's anatomy—when Ronni turned to see why he was so quiet. Busted or not, his eyes lingered on her legs and took a leisurely trip up to her face. His smile crept up slowly.

"You serve first," Jeff said, taking his side of the court.

Seeing them, a young man from the club placed two bottles of water on the table adjacent to their court.

"Let's hit a while to warm up," she said, unzipping her racket and collecting the balls left near the net.

"I can't get any warmer than I already am," Jeff said, leering.

Ronni caught the sexual innuendo but chose to ignore it. She could hear the murmur from the bleachers as the other club members were trying to figure out who was out there. They were a bit hard to identify, especially since Jeff used to sport dreadlocks and had been living in another city for years—only returning to Chicago after his father's death. Ronni, on the other hand, had never looked this good when she played—mostly with Cornell—and she usually came in the evening.

She placed the tennis balls in her skirt pocket, stretched her arms, and sent an easy one over the net. Jeff almost missed it—he was so busy concentrating on the beautiful physique of the woman opposite him. But he recovered quickly. He, like Ronni, had been playing since he was four or five. They enjoyed easy volleys for about seven minutes until they were ready for a set.

Their play was competitive, yet fun, and each was impressed with the athleticism of the other. Jeff won the first two games easily, but when Ronni grasped his style, she took Jeff to match point five times during their third game before he won. They went to the table, collapsing hard and drinking their water before speaking.

"Whew. I wanted to work up a sweat with you, but not

like this." He winked, holding her gaze with narrowed eyes. Ronni was feeling more comfortable and looked at him openly, not sure if her thoughts were being projected. As if by invitation, he moved his chair closer to hers. "You ready to go again?"

Ronni's heart raced and she realized she wasn't as self-assured as she'd thought. Restlessly, she started to get up, but Jeff stopped her easily by putting his hand on her forearm. She felt her blood rush to meet his fingertips.

"Slow down, Tonto. The sun is high in the sky. There's plenty of time for me to kick your butt." She punched his arm. He smiled. She could feel his leg lightly touching hers. "You want to go into the club and get some fruit smoothies or something?"

Ronni glanced toward the restaurant lounge and shuddered at the thought of all the busybodies inside. "No, let's stay out here in the fresh air."

Jeff looked in the direction of the clubhouse, too. Even through the smoky glass, he could see that more of the regulars had started to gather. "I know what you mean. Plus, we can guard our court. I wouldn't put it past the old-timers to come out here and play, even though they know we have the court time. Then we'd never get back on."

Jeff leaned into her even more and sighed. Ronni didn't move away. This was perfect, she thought, inhaling Jeff's cologne. *Am I crazy?* It seemed like the hotter and sweatier he got, the more fresh and manly he smelled.

"How come we never hooked up in college?" Jeff surprised Ronni with this abrupt question.

"Probably because you were way out of my league, didn't know I was alive back then, I was fat, and you dated my roommate," Ronni said matter-of-factly, ticking off each item on her fingers before taking a sip of water. "Take your pick. Oh, and you broke her heart, by the way."

Jeff sat upright, his leg pressing into hers more noticeably. That small touch was sending heat up Ronni's legs and making her feel flushed. "Fat? You? You were *fine*. Frat was always talking about the fine sistah whose face was buried in the books. I definitely knew you were alive." He grinned roguishly, glancing at her cleavage in the V-neck tank top, and was rewarded with another solid punch in the arm. "Ouch. You're dangerous, girl." He rubbed his arm and then looked at her squarely. "Of course, I always thought of you as one of the little kids from around the way."

Was that longing she saw in those mischievous eyes? Maybe she was projecting her own thoughts onto him.

"If the brothers were looking at me, it's news to me. No one ever told *me* I was fine. Almost all the calls to our apartment were for Stephanie," she said, and then realized that Jeff had been dating Stephanie at the time. *Uh-oh.* Maybe she'd said too much. She backpedaled. "This was after you guys broke up, of course."

Jeff gave her an easy curl of a smile, shaking his head. "No sweat, it was college. You know . . . sow your wild oats and all that. Besides, I think she was more into my Mustang that she was into me."

He was wrong. Yes, lots of guys called Stephanie and she'd dated a lot during her four years of college, changing boyfriends almost as frequently as she changed her hair. Sometimes she juggled several at a time. But when Stephanie was seeing Jeff, she was only into him. She would've been a fool to do otherwise.

At Columbia, Jeff was the stereotypical Big Man On Campus. He was not only academically accomplished, he was the star player on the baseball team. The team had gone to their division finals all three years under his leadership, winning twice. Attending the games suddenly became *de rigueur* for a lot of her sorors. It was a great chance to see the fine first baseman with the dreadlocks, and if you were lucky you might even get to talk to him afterward. That is, if he wasn't busy talking to the scouts. Everyone just knew he would turn pro, including Stephanie. She would irritate Ronni day after day with her musings on the fantasy life she had planned for her and Jeff after he went to the majors. Now that she was thinking back, Ronni remembered how he had surprised the masses by quitting the team after his junior year and transferring to a college with a better law program.

Jeff bumped his knee against her leg to get her attention. "So who were you seeing on the yard? You kept your stuff under wraps. Stephanie told the brothers you were stuck-up and only liked white boys."

"What?" Ronni was genuinely taken aback and hurt. "Stephanie said that?" She searched Jeff's face to see if he was lying. "You have got to be kidding me." He shook his head.

Ronni was outraged. This was the kind of pettiness she could usually spot in a woman and avoid like the plague. She had very few friends, but she prided herself on finding the ones she could really trust.

Though Stephanie was the kind of woman who had little use for girlfriends, Ronni had taken a liking to her. Stephanie's parents were jet-setting, affluent retirees who were glad to finally have time to themselves with their youngest child out of the house. Her two much-older brothers had their own lives with wives and children. Ronni often took Stephanie home with her over the holidays, rather than have the poor girl go home to an empty house. She would help Stephanie decipher her marketing homework and let her use a lot of her nice things. In fact, Stephanie got more use out of Ronni's diamond tennis bracelet than Ronni ever did and she'd logged the most miles in Ronni's small, used Mercedes in college—traveling up and down the road to see her friends at a college upstate.

It wasn't so much that Stephanie had talked about her that stung, it was the vicious characterization and lie that came along with it. If anything, the description fit Stephanie to a tee, just substitute the word *rich* for *white* and you'd have her mind-set.

"You didn't believe that, did you?" she asked, hoping he didn't.

"Of course not," Jeff said so quietly and earnestly that she almost didn't hear him. "A lot of guys thought it was true because they'd tried to approach you and got shot down. The others probably found solace in the lie because they found you so intimidating."

"And you?"

Jeff sat back and drank some water, his leg losing contact with hers. "I found solace in the lie for two reasons. One, it kept the brothers away," he said, raising his eyebrows and smiling slyly. "And two, it gave me another good reason to break up with that game-playing gold digger." Casually, he examined Ronni's watch, picking up her wrist and turning it so he could look at the time. His leg moved snugly back to hers.

"Huh? You didn't break up with Stephanie because of me!"

He nodded slowly. "Mm-hmm. Partially. I would always ask about you. I'm sure that really got on her nerves." He glanced over to see how Ronni was taking this new revelation.

"Yeah, but your asking to include her bookish roommate on a few outings couldn't have caused a breakup. Unless she was an even worse self-centered lunatic than

I'm now finding out." Ronni was beginning to feel real affection for this man. He'd seemed so unattainable in college, she had no idea he could've been so considerate.

"Well, it was a little bit more than that," Jeff said quietly, cocking his head and assessing her to see if she was worthy of hearing the rest of his tale. He breathed a sigh before continuing. "I would ask her if you were seeing anybody, what classes you were taking, what kind of things you liked to do for fun. Of course, not all at once, and always under the guise of one of my boys wanting to know."

Jeff thought about how his evenings with Stephanie had been intense in the beginning. At first Stephanie was enjoyable-enough company, her mindless chatter distracting him from having to really think about anything. After about two months of this, he was hooking up with her later in the evening, *after* he'd hit the books. By the third and fourth month, though, Stephanie had dropped the pretense of being a nice person and her most malicious comments were focused on her roommate. Jeff would take Ronni's side, arguing, "I thought you said she . . ." And in response, there were lots of "Yeah, but she . ." Then she started trying to run his life. "Honey, I know you're interested in the Yankees farm, but don't you think you should enter into the league in California? Minor leaguers don't make any money, blah, blah, blah," she whined. By month five, it wasn't even worth the sex to him. He could find that anywhere on campus—and he did.

"She would fume if she told one of her crazy stories and I asked, 'What did Ronni say about that?' I think she figured out I was interested in you when I would invite you to come with us," Jeff said, chuckling to himself. "Then she wouldn't speak to me in the car, would pull an attitude, and didn't want me touching her."

"Well, I'm sorry you didn't get any on those nights because of me," Ronni said flippantly, having gotten over the sting of betrayal. She sipped her water again, not knowing how to react to his surprising confessions.

"Whoa, I didn't say all that. You didn't know Stephanie that well, huh? She was always going to kiss and make up so she could get on with her extracurricular activities. The girl was a taskmaster." He shook his head, remembering their times together.

After all these years, Ronni's greatest suspicions had just been confirmed. Stephanie really was sleeping with guys all those nights she was out. Stephanie always used to label so many of the other girls on campus as *easy* and *out there* that Ronni assumed Stephanie herself wasn't fooling around. Ronni could kick herself for being such a Pollyanna. She had convinced herself that maybe Stephanie and her boy toys were studying together, or out at the pizzeria, or . . . or whatever. While she was thinking back on the fact that Stephanie was out nearly *every night,* her hand stopped in midair on its way to bringing the water to her lips again. Her thoughts and prudish disbelief were interrupted when Jeff leaned closer to her and looked into her eyes. He was taking in her whole face, his questioning eyes searching every inch.

"You're genuinely shocked, aren't you?" he said, the reality of her innocence dawning on him. He laughed again from the belly, seriously tickled.

She snapped out of her daze and took a long swallow when she felt her face redden.

"So you were really a baby in college, huh?" Ronni knew he was referring to her virginity.

She stood up, suddenly uncomfortable with the direction this conversation was taking. "Look, are we going to sit here all day reminiscing about our college days or are we gonna play?"

Jeff stood, too, and wrapped his arms around her back, encompassing her shoulders, swaying them both back and forth. "Aww, it's cute," he said in her ear, his deep voice tantalizing her eardrum. At first she stiffened defensively, then relaxed into his embrace. His body against her back felt extremely good, tight, and strong. His head against hers felt so right. She knew it was a cliché, but her knees felt weak. She hoped he would let go soon, or they might give way. At the same time, she hoped he would never let go.

"Veronica Hampton, the little college virgin," he teased, kissing her ear.

Ronni struggled to resist the urge to turn around and kiss him squarely on the lips. Mercifully, he let her go and picked up his racket. It took a moment and two more sips of water for her to compose herself and join him on the court.

They played another friendly set and, surprisingly, Ronni managed to squeak out a win, though it didn't escape her attention that there was the possibility Jeff had let her. This time, they were both sweaty when they came off of the court around two o'clock.

"You want to stick around and have some food?" Jeff suggested. "Or maybe we can shower and change and we could go to that new calypso restaurant in Hyde Park."

Ronni looked at her watch. "No, I've got to run. I have a class tonight."

"Class?" Jeff was certain Ronni had her master's degree . "How much schooling are you going for, girl?"

"Hmm? Oh. No, this isn't college. It's specific training for auto dealers. I won't be through with this for a while." She found a fresh towel, left by the table as a service for members, and wiped the back of her neck. The

upward move of her arm made her top raise just enough
for Jeff to get a glimpse of her stomach. He had seen it
during their play, but up close it was even more impressive. Tight. Flat. Cut. Even-toned.

"Oh, right. Your dad told me about that. What time do
you get out of the class? Maybe we can get together
later," he asked, putting her racket back in its jacket and
then taking care of his.

Jeff's passing mention of her father jolted Ronni back
to reality. What was up with Jeff and her dad, anyway?

"I don't finish that until nine-thirty tonight, which
isn't that late, but I'm usually so beat after that boring
class that I do good just to get in the door and pore over
my notes."

They walked toward the lounge and Jeff held the door
as Ronni walked through. As they stepped inside, she noticed Amanda Wordlaw was still there, sitting at a table
with some girlfriends. Her eye was right on the hand Jeff
placed at the small of Ronni's back to guide her through
the dining area. Ronni wondered if they'd caught the action on the court. *Crap!* Ronni saw that one of the
women with Amanda was Alicia Davis, a member of the
catty bunch Cornell liked to hang with. Now she would
have to fill her cousin in on her date once she got out of
class—maybe even before class. Ronni hoped none of
the gossip about today's outing would reach her father,
especially since he seemed so opposed to her seeing Jeff.

They made their way to the front of the club and
found Tyler leaning over the reception desk, talking to
that Melody girl. *He said he was leaving. Did he hang
around this whole time, trying to get in my business?* Ronni
wondered. God, this club worked her nerves. Tyler
would have gladly pretended not to notice the two of
them, but the bubbly Melody couldn't resist speaking.

"Hey, there, Jeff!" she yelled toward them in her

squeaky-yet-cigarette-rusted voice. She moved from behind the counter, leaving Tyler leaning over it. "Were
you gonna leave without giving me a hug?" Fixing her
eyes on Jeff, she waved her long, artistically decorated
fingernails in Ronni's direction. "Hi, Ronni."

"I was trying to," Jeff shot back, playfully. He fell easily into the gregarious role Ronni remembered. He
handed Ronni her racket and obliged Melody amiably,
wrapping his arms around her and smothering her in
a sweaty embrace.

Apparently Melody thought better of having approached him once she was in his wet hold and tried to
escape. "Eww! Let me go!" she squealed in delight, her
ample butt jiggling in too-tight Lycra leggings as she
pushed against his chest. Ronni smiled gently. Although
she couldn't pull it off herself, she had always liked carefree personalities like Melody's.

"No. You can't go now. You wanted your hug." Jeff
played captor, moaning, "Mm-mm," as he smushed her
closer.

Tyler nodded at Ronni and started toward her. Ronni,
who had been waiting to probe Jeff about his relationship with her father, headed for the door.

"Ronni! Get him off me!" Melody laughed and vehe-
mently threw a head full of blond microbraids around in
protestation.

"Can't help you. You're on your own, girl," she said,
waving her hand at Melody and Jeff before pushing the
door. Just as she stepped out, Ronni turned to see Jeff
break the hug to shake Tyler's hand. Ronni didn't even
know Tyler could do a black-man's handshake or at least
she'd never paid much attention to him to notice how
he acted around guys who weren't her father's age.

As she made a beeline for her car, she could hear Jeff
at the door. "I'll catch you later, man," he said to Tyler.

"I got to catch up with this pretty lady who's running from me."

"She's afraid, man! You got a reputation, man!" Tyler called after him, trying out his *just one of the guys* persona. Ronni was sure the reputation reference was said for her benefit.

"Is that what it is?" Jeff called over his shoulder as his footfalls closed in on her. He caught up with Ronni as she was fumbling with the keys to her car. Jeff quietly took her keys, located the right one, and opened the door for her before he handed them back.

"Thank you . . . thanks," Ronni said, tossing her racket on the passenger seat and sliding under the steering wheel. Why did this man make her feel so flustered? He closed the door on her and she rolled down the window. Those piercing eyes were locked on hers, his expression expectant. Ronni looked at something on her dashboard. She supposed it was up to her to say something. "Well, I'd better go. I have to shower and change before class."

"So when am I going to see you again, woman?"

Jeff stood with his arms crossed loosely over his chest, looking so serious. She was thrown by his composed manner and the intensity it seemed to convey. Did she affect him as much as he affected her?

"I don't know, I've got a pretty full schedule and—"

"What's your phone number?" he asked, cutting her off. She noticed he wasn't taking out any paper. "What?"

"Your phone number," he repeated.

Ronni rattled off her home and cell-phone numbers. Jeff nodded. "I'll call you tonight."

"I don't finish class until—"

"Nine-thirty," he finished, nodding slowly. Obviously, he had been paying attention. "Yeah. I'll call you."

She didn't know if she was annoyed by his coolness or his forwardness. Or, if she was angry at herself for being so unnerved by his presence and not taking charge of the situation. Ronni decided to put him off. "But I'm so tired and I usually just want to go over my notes after class."

Jeff leaned in the car and ran his hand over her short, moist hair. Starting from the front, his thumb trailed her head enticingly until it ended at the back of her neck where it rested a beat, supporting her head like one of those airline pillows. Shivers went up and down Ronni's spine. "Ten, okay?" Jeff persisted in his raspy voice.

"Ten-thirty," she said. She wasn't even sure she had spoken the words. Ronni felt as if he'd drained all her resistance away with the meaningful placement of his hand. For coming up with the right answer, her cheek was rewarded by the wet warmth of his lips as they softly pushed against her face. This time, they were so close to her lips that they caught the corner of her mouth. Butterflies fluttered to the top of her stomach and set down at the bottom of her esophagus, turning into a frog in her throat.

"All right, lady. I'll talk to you tonight." His brown eyes bore into hers before he stood up and backed away from the car. Jeff left no doubt in her mind that today's outing was no "just hanging out" diversion. He gave her one more look as if trying to create a mental photograph before he headed back toward the club. "Nice car," he called, walking backward. "It suits you."

Ronni smiled; the frog wouldn't let her say anything anyway. When he turned around, she put her forehead on the steering wheel. *Oh. My. God. This man is so beautiful, I don't know whether I'm coming or going.* She just couldn't get her mind around the idea of Jeff, let alone Jeff in the flesh. In so many ways, he was so different from the other men she knew. Other guys had always commented on her silver Audi TT once they saw it. A sporty two-seater, it was generally considered a man's car. The vehicle was also a lot sexier than her conservative manner conveyed, and every guy, with the exception of her father, had expressed surprise that this vehicle belonged to her. Jeff mentioned it as a postscript, like, *Screw the car, I'm into you.*

During college Jeff was always a fantasy figure for her, but the reality far surpassed her most imaginative days. Ronni blew out a breath and backed out of her parking space. *Get it together, girl.* As she steered her car onto Lake Shore Drive, her cell phone rang. She answered with her standard greeting. "This is Ronni."

"No, you didn't just make out with Jeff Conley on the tennis courts!" It was Cornell. His sources had already been at work.

Ronni laughed. "Cornell, I'll call you back when I get home."

Ronni entered her large apartment, flipping through the mail as she walked. But her mind was on the conversation she'd had with Cornell before she went to class. She dropped the mail and her keys on a table in the entry hall and kicked off her shoes. When she got to her living room, she plopped onto the comfy brushed-suede sectional sofa without turning on the lights. She let out a huge sigh before removing the leather briefcase strap from her shoulder and placing the case on her glass and wood coffee table. Despite her earlier assertions that she needed time to digest her class notes, she didn't feel like working on anything. She had to admit that Cornell's information was disturbing.

While he pumped her for information about her rendezvous with Jeff, Ronni tried to get the four-one-one on her date and what exactly he did for a living. Cornell admitted that he didn't know for sure, but he also shared that his friend Randy Marshall hated Jeff Conley because he was confident Jeff had stolen his parents' business and killed his father, George.

Ronni couldn't believe her ears. *Murder?*

"Well, not that he *murdered* him," Cornell rambled, telling the story in the most dramatic fashion possible. "But Randy thinks his father died of a heart attack the next year from the grief of losing a business that had been in his family for three generations." Had Cornell been present, Ronni would've slapped him. It was okay for him to add flair to his anecdotes about other people, but this involved her life and the man she was interested in.

According to Cornell, George Marshall's carpeting business had been failing for several years before Jeff stepped in to "help." Randy said Jeff talked his father out of obtaining another bank loan to revitalize the business but had convinced George to accept a low-interest loan from him. Jeff advanced them a lot of money, which at first seemed a gift from heaven. Staff paychecks were on time again, the Marshalls were able to remodel all three of their stores, and customers were rediscovering the neighborhood staple.

After just two short years, Jeff called in his loans. Randy said this was much earlier than his parents had agreed upon and they weren't yet in a position to repay such a large amount. Jeff was adamant, which forced the Marshalls to file bankruptcy and liquidate their assets. According to the rumor mill, all the money wound up in Jeff's pocket. George died a year later and his wife, Ruth, was left with just enough money to get into a senior residence near Randy in Nevada. That is, only after Randy sold his parents' house. Cornell ended with the declaration, "Randy says he's a snake, Ronni."

She thought about this on her way to class, while she

was there, and now as she relaxed on her couch. But a loan couldn't be what Jeff and her father were meeting about. His dealerships were doing exceedingly well and her father was one of the most astute businessmen in the city, and one of the best African-American businessmen in the country. He was always featured in *Black Enterprise*'s Top 100, and several feature articles specifically about him had been done over the years. No, her father wouldn't fall victim to a swindler. But this meant she still didn't know what the connection was between the two of them. She intended to find out, though.

Glancing at the clock, she saw it was ten-fifteen. Ronni peeled herself off the couch and checked her caller ID. Tyler had called three times. Typical of him, each was exactly on the hour: seven, eight, and nine. She was glad she wasn't home. She'd forgotten about running into him, and she guessed he didn't remember she was taking NADA classes.

Ronni decided to relax with a glass of wine and a nice herbal bath. But just as the wine, the candles, and the massaging jets were beginning to work their magic, the phone rang. The phone on the wall by the bathtub read: CONLEY, JEFF. Ronni took another sip of her wine to calm her nerves and lifted the receiver before the voice mail grabbed the line.

"Hello?"

"Hello, may I speak to Veronica, please?" Jeff's deep, sexy voice was still a pleasing sound to her ears.

"Hey, Jeff." She didn't believe in pretending that she didn't know who it was. Everybody had caller ID these days, and anyone who didn't probably didn't know it was the twenty-first century either. Ronni slid down in the bathwater until she touched the pillow behind her head.

Jeff's ears were keen. "Where are you, woman? In the tub?"

"Yep." She drew out the tiny word and took another sip from her glass. She was going to take this inquisition slow and easy.

"What are you trying to do to a brother?" He moaned the words as if he were in pain. "You knew I was going to call. Did you set this up just to tease me?"

"You're early. I said to call at ten-thirty. Besides, I couldn't break my routine just because some guy says he's going to call. I probably wouldn't have even heard from you if I were sitting by the phone, waiting."

"On your first point, I couldn't wait. And on your second, that's not me." He sounded as if he was in some sort of relaxed position himself. She allowed his voice to roll seductively into her ear and get inside her head.

"What's not you?" The timbre of her voice was dropping too, each word a slow dance.

"Some guy who just *says* he's going to call. I only say what I mean."

"I don't know," she said in a singsong tease. "That's not what I heard."

She could hear him shifting his weight as if he was giving the phone his full attention. "Hmm? What did you hear?"

Ronni hummed the musical equivalent of "I don't know."

"You mean from Stephanie? I thought we already established she was a liar."

Ronni could hear the breath being released through his nostrils. He was still having fun, but obviously this was not the direction he wanted the conversation take.

"How do I know you're not the one lying?" She was still flirtatious, but closing in on her target.

"I'm the good guy in this tale. You'll just have to trust me on that. You could always ask Stephanie, but I doubt you'll get a straight answer."

"Maybe I'll ask Daddy." She raised a leg out of the water and looked at her toes. *Got to get a pedicure,* she thought. She was enjoying this tête-à-tête.

Jeff was silent for a moment. "Ask Daddy what?"

Did she detect a little tightness in his voice? "If he trusts you." Ronni freshened her glass with more wine. "If Daddy says you're trustworthy, then I can take that to the bank."

Jeff gave a provocative chuckle. "Bit of a daddy's girl, huh?"

She heard the tension leave his voice. He was relaxing again, maybe even settling back into his bed? Couch? Chair? Wherever he was. "Well . . . you gotta do what you gotta do. But I'm pretty sure I'll get the thumbs-up from Mr. Hampton. He'll say, 'Ronni, I've never . . . in my life.' "

His words were interrupted by two muted beeps, indicating a call on Ronni's other line. She couldn't believe it. She sat up and glanced at the clock. *Quarter to eleven.* "Hold on a minute, Jeff, I've got another call." She stared at the phone, waiting for the caller ID to show her who it was without switching over. Finally, the screen flashed Tyler's name and number. *What in the hell? Why is he calling at this hour?* He'd never done that before.

If Tyler was calling this late, he was probably wondering how far off court she and Jeff had taken their game. Ronni didn't want Tyler to think she was still out on her date. The last thing she needed was Tyler "innocently" stirring up trouble by asking her parents if she was dating Jeff. She deduced all this within a matter of seconds, and decided to let Jeff go. "Look, Jeff, I'll have to call you back," she said.

"While you talk to some other dude? I don't think so. Get rid of him."

Ronni's mouth flew open in a gaping smile. "What makes you think it's a guy?"

"If it's your mom or one of your girlfriends, tell her you'll have to call her back. If it's an emergency, click back over and tell me. But if it's some hard-legs, tell that knucklehead you're talking to me."

"Jeff, I—" she started to protest.

"I'll be waiting."

He'd dug in his heels and Ronni had to admit that she admired his pure male nerve. Too many men hid their natural reactions in deference to females—*and then we demand they share their feelings, on our terms.* Ronni had no choice but to switch over before Tyler got any ideas.

"Hello," she said briskly.

"Well, hello. I thought for a minute there I was going to get your voice mail again. This is Tyler." He paused uncertainly. "Were you on the phone?"

"Hi, Tyler. I'm . . . in the middle of something." She moved around to produce splashing sounds.

"Oh. Are you in the bath? I'm sorry, I—" He cleared his throat. "I'll let you go. I was just following up on our little chat today. To make arrangements for lunch."

She stuck her tongue out in a gag. *Chat?* "That's fine, but I'm really beat and I'm just getting home from class. So, why don't I call you tomorrow so we can set a date?"

"Oh, I—uh—" Ronni knew Tyler wouldn't have the nerve to remind her that the date had already been set. It was now just a matter of time and location. "Okay, well, use my cell-phone number. I always have it with me."

"Okay." She was keeping it brief. "Talk to you then."

"All right. I'll let you go ahead and enjoy your bath."

"Okay. Bye-bye."

"Bye. Don't study too—"

Ronni clicked back over to Jeff. Now she had completely lost her groove and didn't feel like getting it back. "Jeff?"

"That took longer that I'd liked. Was it your man?"

It was his voice. It was soothing and easy to get lost in. Her head fell back onto the welcoming pillow. "Your penance for my compliance is that you'll never know," she said.

"Did you tell him you were talking to me?"

"Yeah. I gave him your address. He's coming over to kick your ass."

"I hope you said your good-byes. 'Cause I got his ass-whooping," he said in a way that assured Ronni there was no doubt of his strength.

Ronni couldn't trust the big smile on her face or the surrender messages coming from her body. She knew she should run from this man, and run far, too. But she kept feeling drawn in by his overriding masculinity. He was the salve she needed on a wound she had just discovered. "Look, Mike Tyson, it's late and the bathwater is getting cold. I've got to get off this phone."

"I'll come over and warm you up."

I know you would. "Don't you have to get up and go to work tomorrow?"

"I don't work like that, baby." His voice was so growly and enticing.

"Oh? How do you work?" *Ha!*

"Have dinner with me and I'll tell you all about it." Who was weaving a web around whom? Ronni wasn't so sure she hadn't played right into his grasp, but she so desired to be there.

She stepped out of the tub and wrapped a towel around herself. "Tell me now."

"Sorry, babe. I talk business by appointment only. Did you just get out of the tub?" Jeff's mind was racing with the visual images.

"What's it to you?" she asked, thinking how this man brought out the real naughtiness in her.

"I couldn't care less. It's my little friend here who's curious."

Ronni's jaw dropped. Apparently she brought out the raunchiness in him.

"Jeff Conley! You'd better not be trying to have phone sex with me!" This time, she really was outdone.

"No. Relax. Nothing like that, just creating a narrative he and I can share later."

"You. Are. Bad. I'm getting off the phone."

"Dinner . . . when?"

"It'll have to be tomorrow. I have classes every other night this week."

If Jeff picked up on clues—and he did—she was really saying that she couldn't wait three days to see him again. Ronni tried to convince herself this was just because she wanted to get to the bottom of his work thing. Both she and Jeff knew better.

Chapter Four

Ronni woke up thinking about Jeff. Indistinguishable from the rays of sunlight that found their way past mini-blinds to touch her, these thoughts crawled over her, warmed her body, and teased her out of bed. It wasn't until she'd stretched and placed her feet firmly on the floor that her misgivings about him came into play.

They'd agreed to meet at eight o'clock at Charlie Trotter's. Although Jeff wanted to pick her up, Ronni insisted they meet at the restaurant. If she was going to discuss what he did for a living and his relationship with her father, she needed to have her own avenue of escape, if necessary.

But the day was early and she had a lot to do before dinner.

After a full morning of running around, which included working out at the YMCA, yeah, she was paying for an expensive athletic club downtown. But the community Y was a great mix of black people, and she'd become addicted to an exciting gospel aerobics class after attending once with her friend Macy. Stopping by her mother's to help her select wallpaper patterns for several rooms, getting a pedicure, and begging off from lunch with Tyler, she arrived at her father's original dealership, where he still maintained an office.

Ronni had stopped by to get some paperwork that

could help her with an upcoming presentation on fore-casting consumer trends. As she walked through the showroom floor, she greeted the salesmen and steeled her-self for the inevitable approach of Terry. She hoped he was with a customer and wouldn't come over with his usual snide comments. As she headed for the file storage room that held the information she needed, she could see out of the corner of her eye that he was in his office.

Just as Ronni settled down at the small functional desk to sort through the reports from the eighties that detailed how Benjamin had planned to expand his dealerships, Terry came through the formerly *closed* door. It seemed he couldn't resist the opportunity to pester Ronni. Although he was married with three children, he still harbored bit-ter feelings toward her from the way she had summarily dismissed him after only three dates.

"Well, look who the cat dragged in. Hello, there, Miss Ronni Hampton," he said, leaning in the doorway. The room was small and crowded with file cabinets, and he was a big guy, built like a football player, but not much taller than Ronni. Always a little bit on the heavy side, he had more of a gut, now that he was married. Terry had a shaved head and his most striking feature was his mouth, complete with cute teeth and dimples. She did recall a couple of nice kisses coming from that mouth, but the bad attitude had spoiled the chances of their exploring anything more.

"Hi, Terry," Ronni said, glancing up for a second, but making it quite clear that she was busy.

"Weren't you even going to speak?" He toyed with his tie and adjusted his jacket. All the salesmen were required to wear suits.

"I spoke to everyone when I came in, weren't you there?" She knew he wasn't, but what the hell.

He waved a hand in the direction of the showroom.

"You didn't speak to me and you know me better than all these guys."

Don't remind me. "Well, I'm speaking now. What's up?" She really was concentrating on trying to locate the right paperwork. It wasn't just an act to get rid of him.

"Must be old-home week around here," he said. When she didn't bite, he continued on without any prompting. "First Tamara was in early to check out the new Cadillac SUVs, and then the old man came in, and now you."

She looked up. "Daddy was in today?" This news was surprising. Jim Mitchell managed the office, and Benjamin was comfortable meeting with him at home or out at a restaurant.

"Oh? Now I got your attention, huh?" Terry said, with a grin big enough to show all his teeth. "Yeah, *daddy's* in. You didn't know? He's still here, with that guy."

"What guy?" This was such good luck for her to run into her father, he barely came to the office anymore and here she was at the dealership at the same time as he.

"Your boyfriend. The lawyer." Every word from Terry dripped with resentment. He resented her and he plainly despised her father, but he was such a consistently good salesman that Benjamin chose to ignore his surliness. For a minute, Ronni wasn't sure who he was talking about.

"You mean Tyler?"

He snickered. "How many boyfriends you stringing along, woman?"

Ronni found Terry so exasperating that his question and his assumptions weren't even worth commenting on. She gathered her papers so she could get some direction from her father about which year's reports would be the most relevant to her lecture. She could figure it out herself, but firsthand knowledge was always more valuable. Terry wasn't exactly moving out of the doorway as she approached. It wasn't until she was right upon him that he grudgingly stepped aside to let her out and then followed along.

"So, when are you gonna get married? You're not getting any younger."

"I'm waiting for you to leave your wife," she said glibly.

"Aww . . . you don't even want to go there," Terry said. He dropped back, losing interest in this pursuit and heading for his office. "Plus, I can't have no high-maintenance woman. My wife is cool. She's a Christian woman who places her man and her family above herself," he said rather boisterously so the other salesmen could overhear.

"You're a lucky man." Ronni didn't really care what his problem was and had heard this yarn about his wife being a good Christian woman ever since he'd married her.

"Yes, ma'am. I know I am. My wife is a beautiful and loving woman and I thank God I found her," he said on his way back to his office. It was all background noise to her now because as she turned the corner in view of her father's office, she stopped in her tracks before slowly resuming her step.

The office walls were glass and she could see Tyler and her father facing each other in a rather heated argument. So involved in their quarrel, they didn't even see her approaching. When she got closer to the office door, she could hear their raised voices.

"Mr. Hampton, it's not a matter of something being taken away from me," Tyler said, his hand jabbing his own chest. "I don't give a damn about that. It's a matter of what you are getting yourself into. What do you know about Conley? What are his intentions?"

"No, Tyler! It's a matter of you doing what I ask!" her father shot back. Ronni was close enough now for her father to notice her. He visibly calmed himself. Tyler followed Benjamin's eyes and looked behind him to see

Ronni. He too dropped his hostile position and turned to get his blazer, which was neatly folded over the back of a chair.

Were they arguing about Jeff? She would have thought it was centered on her if it weren't for Tyler's words. Ronni placed a shaky hand on the doorknob. Though she didn't know if she wanted to go in, she knew she couldn't exactly turn on her heels and leave either.

"Knock-knock," she said, entering the room and looking curiously from one man to the next. Neither of them would meet her eyes. In all the years she had known her father and Tyler, she'd never seen them fight with each other like this. Of course, the secret life of men is oftentimes concealed from women, so this kind of thing could've happened all of the time. But for some reason, she didn't think so.

Clearly, it was Jeff who'd brought them to this point.

"Hi, sweetheart," her father said. He gathered the papers on his desk, a frown creasing his brow. "What brings you here?"

"Hi, Ronni," Tyler said solemnly, picking up his briefcase. He managed a smile in Ronni's direction, but his face was still clouded.

"Hello, gentlemen." She cursorily touched Tyler's arm and kissed her father's cheek. "I came to get some reports for a presentation I'm doing on forecasting. What's going on with you guys?"

"Oh, Tyler and I were discussing a few things," Benjamin said, shoving some papers into his attaché case.

"Discussing? It sounded more like arguing to me." After getting no response and no eye contact from either, she continued. "Something I should know about?"

"No—no. It's all in a day's work. Just the price of doing business with someone as accomplished as your father,"

Tyler said lightly and put his hand on the doorknob. "All right, Mr. Hampton, I'll get back with you."

Benjamin looked at him sternly. "Tyler, work on that tonight."

"I'll call you later." Tyler and Benjamin held each other's eyes a moment, their disagreement continuing silently. "See you later, Ronni."

Benjamin watched him leave, then prepared to go himself. "What kind of presentation?" he asked distractedly, trying to pick up on her conversation.

"What's going on with you and Tyler?" Ronni inquired. "He never disagrees with you." She trailed behind her father as he locked his desk and turned out the lights in his office. They walked through the showroom together.

"I'm gone," her father yelled in the direction of Terry and the other salesmen. They waved back and said goodbye. Ronni waited silently, in step beside him. "It's nothing. You'd be surprised at how often Tyler and I disagree on certain things."

"I certainly am surprised," Ronni said quietly, following behind him.

They'd reached his car and he opened the door. "Did you need me for anything? I have to go pick up Benji from his baseball game."

"Not really. I can figure out these reports on my own."

"Take whatever you need, just bring it back." He sat in the car and closed the door. The window had been left down earlier. "Call me if you have any questions."

As he started up the car and put it in gear, Ronni saw her opportunity slipping away. "Daddy, were you two arguing about Jeff Conley?"

Benjamin's head jerked toward her and he scowled. "Were you listening in on a private conversation?" Ronni was taken aback by the severity of his face and tone.

"I—no—I came up to say hi and I heard the mention of Conley," she said nervously. She had never known her father to behave this way. "That's all I heard. Then I—I opened the door." She felt like she was under attack. Benjamin must've realized he was overreacting and decided to back down.

"Ronni, listen. I'm making a few changes. It's nothing for you to concern yourself with, and I'll let you know what's going on on a need-to-know basis." Though his words were supposedly softened, to her ears they were still harsh. "Look. I've really got to go, sweetheart."

He didn't wait for her agreement, and began to leave. "See you, Ronni."

"Okay. Tell Benji I said hi."

"All right," Benjamin said, pulling off.

Ronni was stunned as she went to her car. Now more than her gut instinct was telling her Jeff was bad news. He was the cause of all this strife. There was no way she was going to sit down and break bread with him tonight.

When she got in her car she dialed Jeff to call off their date, but the cell phone wasn't getting a signal. She was about to turn it off when she heard a baritone "Hello? Hello?" coming from the phone.

"Hello?" she said.

"Hello? Ronni?" Incredibly, it was Jeff. He must've been calling her at the same time she was calling him.

"Jeff? How did you get this number?"

"I have my sources. Look, there's been a change of plans for tonight. Why don't you meet me at my place instead? Let me cook dinner for you."

Smooth move. "Jeff, I was just trying to call you. I have a change of plans myself. I can't meet you tonight."

"Oh." He could tell she was being short with him. "Something wrong?"

"Something came up. Nothing I can get into at the

moment." She was trying to decide if she actually *did* want to get into it now.

"What's wrong? Talk to me, lady," he said. Ronni noticed that he sounded like he was calling from someplace very noisy at first and now had moved to a quieter location.

This was exactly the case. Jeff was downtown at City Hall with a client. He was on a break from the proceedings and his assistant was briefing the client on her deposition until Jeff's return. He'd said he had to make a quick call, but now that Ronni was acting funny, he was willing to spend some time to feel her out. He'd moved from the hallway to a quiet unused courtroom.

Jeff had been looking forward to his evening with Ronni all day. He woke up thinking about her, thought about her during his run, thought about her while going over his brief, while conferring with his client. When another lawyer was interviewing prospective jurors, Jeff had the idea to move the dinner to his house. Ronni would have a chance to see his place and he could show off his fabulous lemon chicken piccata with angel-hair pasta.

Besides, he nixed the Charlie Trotter's idea because he knew she had a tendency to be somewhat skittish around him. Since she insisted on driving her own car, he didn't want her to bolt right after their dinner and he didn't want to have to try to convince her to come back to his place. Not that he was going to try to get her into bed. He just really, really wanted to kiss her. He could almost see himself holding her small face in his hands, kissing her, then wrapping her up in his arms and holding her for a lifetime. He'd be damned if this was all going to slip away within a matter of seconds without a fight.

"I'll have to call you back," she said, deciding she would have to sort out all these things in her head before confronting him or even seeing him.

"Ronni, wait," he said, pausing to compose his thoughts.

He still wasn't sure how to close this deal. "Whatever you have to do, you can come over afterward. I'm usually up pretty late. Let me give you my address." She gave no verbal response. "I'm at four-eight-five-five South Woodlawn."

His voice was, even during her misgivings, having the same hypnotic effect on her it always had. She couldn't reconcile the things she was hearing about Jeff with the Jeff she talked to. She had to withstand the temptation to confront him in person. She remembered that much like Jeff on the phone, in person Jeff was nearly irresistible. "Jeff, I really can't see you tonight. I'll call you later."

Before he could protest, she hung up. Jeff looked at the phone in his hand and nearly threw it across the room. He slumped down on a cold, hardwood bench. Now he had to return to his client and the courtroom in one of the worst moods ever.

Ronni had decided it was time to have that lunch with Tyler. He was surprised to receive Ronni's call, but he wasn't going to miss his opportunity. Tyler arranged for them to meet for a late lunch that same afternoon. In spite of herself, Ronni was impressed by the location—Stella's—which was nearly impossible to get into on such short notice. When she approached the host to say she was meeting another party and gave Tyler's name, she was shown to a table with a great view of the room.

Tyler rose to greet her as she approached. Obviously, he had more connections than she'd given him credit for. Ronni allowed him to kiss her cheek. This wasn't the time for her usual aloofness.

"So, this is a treat. I get to see you twice in one day," Tyler said when they sat down.

"Yes . . . well . . . to tell you the truth, that's actually what I wanted talk to you about. Seeing you at Daddy's office earlier this morning . . ." Ronni was unable to put off her interrogation. She was dying to find out what was going on with her father.

"Oh, yes. Well." Tyler was visibly disappointed and looked overly interested in perusing the menu. "They have an excellent Caesar salad here. I know how women love salads." He chuckled, obviously trying to stall for time with dull jokes.

Ronni glanced at the menu and set it aside. "Yes. That'll be fine." She watched him as he continued to ignore her inquiry.

"I think I'll have the . . . a rather large lunch, I'm afraid. I don't think I'll have time for a proper dinner. I'm going to get—"

This stalling was excruciating for Ronni. Finally, the waitress came to their table.

"Oh, I see your lady friend has arrived. Are you ready to order or do you need a few more minutes?" she asked.

"Yes, we're ready. The lady will have the Caesar salad and I'll have prime rib with no potatoes and extra vegetables." Tyler also ordered iced tea for himself and Ronni nodded for the same. After the waitress left, Tyler took his time placing his napkin in his lap before turning his attention to Ronni. She felt no need to fill the silence with idle conversation and just looked at him. "So, how have you been? I never get the chance to see you."

This was ridiculous. "Tyler, what's going on? Why were you and Daddy arguing this morning?"

He cleared his throat. "Oh, that—that was nothing, really. He's making some changes I don't really agree with. But Mr. Hampton is the boss." His smile didn't reach his eyes.

"Tyler, what changes?" Ronni said, remaining serious. After waiting a couple of beats and seeing his discomfort, Ronni touched his hand. "We've been friends for a long time. I know you would tell me if Daddy was in some sort of trouble."

He looked down. She could tell he wanted to tell her something. "You know I can't really discuss the specifics of it with you. Your father is my client."

She fidgeted with her utensils. "But, you *are* concerned about something."

"Yes, frankly, I am," he said, returning his eyes to hers. "Maybe I shouldn't be telling you this, but . . . as you say . . . we've been friends a long time and I've known your father for years. But lately, I am a little worried about his actions."

The waitress returned with Ronni's salad, a side salad for Tyler, their iced teas, and a basket of bread. Ronni ignored her food as Tyler spooned dressing onto his appetizer.

"Does it have something to do with Jeff Conley?" Ronni concentrated on placing her napkin in her lap, hoping that less scrutiny would allow him to open up. But when she glanced back up at him, his face looked stonier than before. He cleared his throat again.

"What is your relationship to him exactly?"

"I told you, I knew him in college. He dated my roommate. When you saw us at the club, that was the first time I'd seen him in years. We were just catching up."

Tyler looked at her for a second and took a bite of his salad. Ronni decided to do the same. After all, she did lure him there with the promise of lunch. "You're right. This is an excellent salad," she said.

"I knew you would like it." He looked pleased with himself. "This is one of my favorite places." He gestured to the room and added unnecessarily, "They all know me here."

"Well, Stella's is nice. I've only been here once before . . . a while back . . . with my father."

"Yes, so we have that in common. It was also Mr. Hampton who introduced me to Stella's. Now I'm a regular." He gave another self-satisfied smile, which waned when he noticed it wasn't returned. "But to your question. You may not want to hear the answer, but it has everything to do with Conley."

"Oh." Her shoulders dropped. She was actually kind of disappointed that her suspicions were confirmed. "How?"

"This is absolutely confidential, Ronni. You can't go to your father with what I'm about to tell you." Tyler eyed her seriously.

She nodded. "I understand."

"Well, my concern is that your father wants me to hand over all his past and present legal files involving accounting, finances, and taxes to Conley." He paused for effect, but he didn't need to because Ronni was stunned. Her throat felt dry. She opened her mouth to speak, but no words seemed to spring forth. "Yes . . . well," Tyler continued, "I can see you're as uncomfortable with this arrangement as I am. But you saw him. He was adamant that I do what he said—despite my protests."

"Wh—what do you make of this? Why would he want Jeff to handle that stuff? Is Daddy in some sort of trouble?"

Tyler shrugged and continued to eat his food. Ronni had no appetite. This scenario pretty much fit into the bad things she'd heard about Jeff's tactics. She drank a big gulp of her tea and waited for Tyler to wipe his mouth, select a roll, and start buttering it before he elaborated further. "Well, his new location is not performing as well as it could. There is a matter of some missing funds and we suspect one of the location managers. But my assessment is that his business is pretty sound. He took me off his personal accounts a couple of years after he married Tamara, so I'm not too sure what's going on there. The last thing I worked on personally was revising his—"

"Revising his will," Ronni finished for him. She wasn't really concerned about that. Arrangements had to be made for Benji and she knew Tamara had a prenuptial agreement that should limit her ability to wipe her father out in the event that their marriage dissolved or he died. But she appreciated Tyler's delicacy in trying not to bring up anything too sensitive. "But what does Jeff do exactly? Have you heard anything about him?"

Tyler looked surprised. The waitress came back with his entrée, asked if they needed anything else. Receiving no further requests, she left.

"I thought you two were rather . . . friendly. You don't know what he does?"

"Well, I know he's a lawyer, but what is his specialty?" she asked, embarrassed at what little knowledge she had of Jeff.

"Financial matters and contracts, I would assume." Tyler ate some of his steak and marveled at how good it was. "This is delicious, Ronni, you should really have some." He tried to feed her a bite, but she shook her head.

"Have you heard anything improper about his practice?" Ronni didn't meet his eye, but before she could decide on whether to bring up the rumors she'd heard from Cornell, Tyler beat her to the punch.

"You're not listening to idle gossip, are you?" Tyler raised an eyebrow as he cut more bites of his meat. "I hate to say this," he said, swallowing and pausing to wave a fork at her, "because Conley is obviously my competition for your affections."

Ronni nearly choked trying to utter a protest, but Tyler held up a hand that it wasn't necessary. "But you shouldn't believe everything you hear about someone's dealings with clients. Early in my career, I was the victim of the negative, gossipy set. You were probably too young to remember that. Actually, I was maligned by a man I considered a mentor. But a lot of these business deals are pretty complicated, involving a lot of inner workings the general public just doesn't understand."

This was the thing Ronni kind of liked about Tyler. He wasn't prone to be a follower and was unbiased in his professionalism. "Fair enough, Tyler, but that doesn't explain why you were so upset with Daddy handing over these files to Jeff."

"Well, that's more personal, obviously. I've always handled his accounts and Jeff Conley is not nearly as qualified as I am, or as up on the issues concerning your father's dealerships. I don't understand why he would make this kind of move. And I fear there must be some sort of problem he's not sharing with me."

Ronni took a moment to consider this by picking at her salad. "And what do you suspect that problem is? Who else has Jeff represented and what were their problems?"

"I don't have a clue what Mr. Hampton's reasons could be for these document transfers. I was hoping you could shed some light on that. And as for who Conley represents, I've lost out on attracting a few prominent people in our circle to him, but I can't say for sure what he's doing with them. From what I've read in the papers, his name has been linked with those in the more desperate situations, but that might not be his full client base. He and I aren't exactly friends, and despite popular belief, we lawyers don't share our cases with each other." Tyler chuckled, another flat attempt at humor. "Has your father ever mentioned to you that he was unhappy with my work?"

Ronni shook her head, bit her lip, and glanced around the crowded dining room. She inadvertently caught the eye of a woman whose face she knew, smiled, and nodded a greeting to her. "No. He's always spoken highly of you. That's what doesn't make any sense. What did he say when he asked you to transfer those responsibilities to Jeff?"

"As you know, Mr. Hampton can be direct and to the point. He just said he would like for Conley to handle some of his legal matters."

"Maybe he just wanted to throw a little work Jeff's way. He might feel he owes it to Senator Conley for helping him start his dealerships."

"I also considered that possibility. But the thing is, he's transferred everything financial. That *is* a cause for concern. We've got a big audit coming up. You don't change horses in the middle of the race."

"Yeah," Ronni said and pushed her salad aside.

Tyler, finished with his meal, also pushed his plate forward. "Why don't you just ask him what's going on?"

"I tried to after I saw you guys arguing, but he shut me down. I just hope I'm not taking these NADA classes in vain. I hope there'll still be dealerships for me to take over." She hadn't meant to say this out loud, but there it was. Her worst fears put to voice.

"I wouldn't worry about that, but I do have other reservations about Conley."

Ronni was fiddling with her fork, but now gave Tyler her full attention. "Oh?"

Tyler smiled and leaned forward as if to create intimacy. "Well, this may be none of my business, but you should be careful. I've heard he's a bit of a lady-killer."

It definitely is none of your business, Ronni thought, wondering how she could end their lunch as soon as possible. Ronni muttered a noncommittal response, changed the topic, and, after a while, made her excuse to leave. As she drove home, she thought the lunch had been a revelation. Although he didn't have all the specifics about what her father was doing, Tyler told her what she wanted to know about Jeff's involvement in his business. Unfortunately, due to Tyler's insistence that she not betray his indiscretion, Ronni couldn't confer with her father about her apprehensions.

When she got home she concentrated hard on completing her work for the next night's presentation, but all the data kept mixing in her head along with her thoughts of Jeff. Even after four hours, she wasn't making much progress. Finally, she picked up the phone and dialed Cornell, the only person with whom she could share everything she was thinking. Coincidentally, Cornell also had bad news to relate. He'd heard that Jeff had been seen with Mrs. Cathleen Winters, a prominent maven in the beauty-supply industry.

After they discussed the seriousness of Jeff's involvement with Cathleen, Ronni told her cousin all about her own reservations over pursuing a relationship with Jeff. Despite his partiality for gossip, rumors, and speculation, Cornell advised that the most sensible thing to do was to stick with her original plan and go straight to the source. "We can keep talking about this until we're blue in the face," he said. "But we'll only keep coming up with the same ole, same ole."

"But it doesn't make any sense either. I know Daddy can't be in any financial trouble, so Jeff can't be hanging around him for that."

"You have to go over there, Ronni. And do your *own* investigation," he said firmly. "My sources are weak. Brenda told me she thinks he's a lawyer. Randy, I have to tell you, girl, is kind of crazy, and you don't really know why your father was yelling at that stupid Tyler, despite what he said. Maybe he was screwing up or something."

Ronni didn't believe that about Tyler. He was one of the most dedicated and by-the-book professionals she knew. Her father had relied on him for years, and he always came through with the right approach on his business deals and contracts. Plus, Cornell hadn't heard the real concern in Tyler's voice, even as he protested.

Yet, she appreciated her cousin's opinion. Yes, he was sending her into the lion's den because he too really wanted to get the scoop on all their questions, but he also really liked Jeff.

The night Ronni officially entered in her sorority, Cornell had come up from Xavier University with some of his friends to attend her line's debut party. He and his friends brought her tons of Greek paraphernalia. They also drank and partied all night, finally crashing on the floor of her and Stephanie's small living room before driving back to Louisiana the next afternoon.

When Cornell arrived at the party, he told Ronni to introduce him to this "fine" Jeff she was always e-mailing him about. He knew the whole back story—about how just seeing him nearly every day was torture and how she would sometimes hide in the library until she thought Jeff and Stephanie had gone from the apartment before returning home.

Ronni had been too scared to approach Jeff at the party, saying, "He barely knows *me*. I can't just walk up and introduce *you*." Cornell, who fortunately didn't have one shy bone in his body, rolled his eyes before he marched into the group of frat brothers Jeff was standing with and introduced himself. Jeff was cordial, even going so far as to get him a beer and talk to him about his school and major. Most impressively, Jeff ignored the looks and mocking behavior of the goons around him who were hung up on the fact that Cornell was so obviously gay. When he got back to his own dorm later that week, Cornell called Ronni to say, "Screw that Stephanie. She's a first-class bitch. You should go ahead and jump on her man!" Cornell had been an advocate for Jeff ever since then, and in the back of his mind, he too wanted to believe the best about Ronni's latest crush.

"You think I have to go over there, huh?"

"What have I been saying all this time? You've got to get your ass up, put on something sexy, and go see the man. You can't find out what's up sitting over there, talking to me for hours," Cornell said, going into advice overdrive. "If you don't do it, I'll do it myself. And you know I will."

Ronni felt butterflies in her stomach at the thought of going to see Jeff. But Cornell was right. There was little choice, *other than not going and forgetting about him and this whole thing*. Her mind offered her this alluring out. But she knew her body—which had so enjoyed the sexy talk on the phone, the way he'd held her, touched her, and kissed her at the tennis club—would never put him out of her mind.

"I know, I know," she said, letting out a big sigh. "Okay, I'm going to call him."

"And go over," Cornell insisted.

"That's what I meant. I'm going to call him and tell him I'm coming over."

"Tonight," Cornell added emphatically. He knew of Ronni's tendency to talk herself out of things.

"Cornell, I said I'm going, okay. I'm going."

"Good. Call me when you get back and let me know what happened," he said, clearly satisfied. Another guidance session completed.

"All right. Bye," she said and hung up. She considered the phone in her hands. She flipped through the caller ID until it showed Jeff's number, but her thumb hovered over the DIAL button. It was nearly eight-forty. She guessed she'd better just do it and pressed down on the button. As it rang she felt like hanging up. *But you can't get away with that these days,* she reminded herself. He picked up during the second ring.

"Hello?" His deep voice sounded raspy and rushed. She panicked. *He's with somebody.*

"Hello, Jeff? Did I catch you at a bad time?"

"Hey, lady," he said. She could hear him shifting position. "No, I fell asleep at my desk. I was poring over some boring transcripts. What time is it?"

She heard him take a deep breath, trying to shake off the drowsiness. She smiled to herself. He just seemed so *normal.* Not like a snake at all. "It's twenty minutes to nine." There was amusement in her voice. Why did her mind always go straight for the worst-case scenario? She didn't know why she was so relieved he was alone. She didn't have any claim on him or his actions. "Too late for you?"

"Oh, no. I'm glad you woke me up." He yawned. His next words sounded clearer. "Did you finish whatever it was you had to do?"

"Yeah. I was working on some pretty boring stuff myself," she said. "I would've worked on it all night, but I just couldn't concentrate." *For thinking about you.*

"I know what you mean, neither could I," he said pointedly, his words echoing the same unspoken reason. She wouldn't have believed how much her call had lifted Jeff's mood. He said a soundless thank you to God for answering his pleas that she would call. "So, are you coming over?"

"Does the invitation still stand?"

"Hell, yeah. How quickly can you get here? I'll even come and get you if you want." He fell into his flirtatious role, but he was deadly serious.

"I think I can make it on my own. Is there still going to be any dinner?"

"It won't be what I planned, but I can whip you up some vittles. What time do you think you'll be here?"

Ronni was surprised at how easy this was, as if they regularly made plans to meet each other. She was still edgy, but this was more like nervous anticipation. "Give me half an hour."

"That means an hour in woman time, right?" he teased.

"I'm not that bad. Maybe forty minutes." She looked down at her beat-up T-shirt, cut-off sweatpants, and socks and realized she didn't know what she was going to wear.

"All right, Ronni. Call me when you're outside so I can open the gate for you."

She loved the sound of her name rolling out of that deep, sexy throat. "Okay. See you soon."

After he said good-bye, she looked around her apartment, alarmed. Despite the fact that this was supposed to be an information-gathering session, she was about to meet one-on-one with her former dream man—at his house. She wanted to take a quick shower, decide what she was going to wear, slap on some makeup, and get over there. *Thank God I got that pedicure today!*

Chapter Five

As instructed, Ronni called Jeff when she was minutes away from his house. He was waiting in the driveway when she pulled onto his property. In his khaki shorts and blue short-sleeved knit top with soccer sandals, he was dressed perfectly for a summer night. Ronni had a small grin on her face as she watched him close the gate behind her car. She hadn't followed Cornell's advice and opted for a more casual than sexy look, choosing to wear well-fitting blue-jean capri pants, a fuchsia short-sleeved silk blouse that tied at the waist, and matching flat sandals with thin straps.

Jeff was at her car door as she exited and held it for her while she gathered her purse. She was a bundle of nerves that were only heightened by his appreciative smile as he assessed her from head to toe, stopping to admire her painted toes.

"Hey, there," he said, kissing her cheek and closing the door. "You're looking casually fine."

"You look nice yourself."

"Thank you." He started toward the entrance to his home and she followed. His house was one of those modest, old brick mansions, but, typical of spaces in the city, it didn't have much yard. "I told you it would be an hour," he called over his shoulder, making a big show of looking at his watch and then back at her.

She chuckled easily. "No, it's not. Forty-five minutes. I was only off by maybe five minutes."

"More like fifty minutes. That's almost an hour." As she came through the door, he leaned in close to shut the door behind her. As usual, he smelled good.

"Fifty minutes is fifty minutes. You should just be glad I'm here." She moved into the house. Lights led her from the foyer and into the living room. She was impressed with his style. She had pegged him for a modern, maybe techno-style guy. But his place was cozy and decorated in an eclectic mix of traditional yet modern furniture with lots of African influences. The atmosphere was made even better with the silky jazz of Joe Sample, one of her favorites.

"Oh, I'm *very* glad you're here," he said, his voice slow and full of meaning.

After Jeff had gotten off the phone with Ronni, he'd sprung into action himself. He'd shaved, showered, and hunted through his closet before deciding on his own casual look. He rushed around the house, cleaning up the little messes he'd left in various rooms and profusely spraying air freshener to get rid of the lingering scent of the cigar he'd smoked when he first got home. He hoped she would be later than planned so he would have time to prepare something for her to eat.

Jeff watched Ronni as she strolled through his living room, trying to see it through her eyes. He had second thoughts about dimming the lights so low, hoping she didn't think he'd tried too hard to create an overly romantic mood. The lighting was actually the way he typically liked it. It was welcoming, with an amber feel when lit like this. His living room was filled with African and African-American artwork and Egyptian-inspired detailing in the woodwork with coordinating patterns in the pillows and generous fabrics as throws and window coverings. None of the walls were white; Jeff used blues, deep yellows, and greens to warm up the space. A lot of the possessions in his place had meaning for him— things he'd picked up in his travels or were given as gifts or inherited from his parents and grandparents. He smiled to himself when Ronni settled into his favorite spot in the vast living room.

"Can I get you something to drink?" he asked.

From her seat, Ronni was still looking around approvingly and steered her focus back to him. "Whatever you have. Wine, please." She knew she'd pay for it in the morning when she had to peel herself off the bed, but she needed something to help her relax.

"Coming right up," Jeff said, heading in the direction of the kitchen. You couldn't knock the smile off his face. Sitting in his spot on the couch, looking fine as she wanted to, Veronica Hampton was there, in the flesh. His hands were a little shaky as he poured wine into the glass meant for her. He had to reach back to high school to bring up images in his mind of the last time he wanted a girl so much. And back then, his infatuation had been driven further by his inexperience. It could be dismissed as the frivolity of puppy love, high school sweetheart, and first love. Now, having been a sought-after athlete and an eligible and handsome black man, there was no shortage of women who'd shocked him with their sexually aggressive pursuits.

Some of these occurrences he'd found downright insulting. He didn't enjoy being reduced to a sexual conquest any more than women who complained of males behaving like pigs. He recalled an attractive, bright sister who was a partner in the law firm where he worked as a neophyte lawyer. He was startled when, working late with her one night, this older married woman's head fell toward his lap, her hand stroking. It wasn't the first time a woman was willing to perform the act she thought every man most wanted with no prompting or commitment on his part. It was just that he'd presumed that this sort of thing didn't happen in the professional business world.

His naïveté was further shattered when, despite his reflexive arousal, he'd rejected her advances and suffered retaliation in the form of poor performance evaluations. It was like reliving that Michael Douglas movie, *Disclosure.* Yet, unlike Douglas's character, there had been no point of trying to fight this dynamic lawyer—or, for that matter, her prestigious firm—in a sexual harassment lawsuit. So he did his best until he could finally move on. But even as he gained his own power and prestige, women shamelessly tried to seduce him.

Though all his encounters with women hadn't been demeaning, he still didn't know another woman who'd stirred his desire to pursue and make an impression like Veronica Hampton. When he was leaning past Ronni to close the door, his lips wanted nothing more than to connect with her smooth, fragrant neck. He had to resist the urge to just grab her around her small waist and kiss her luscious mouth. Jeff was certain that sort of impulsive behavior would not be tolerated by Ronni.

He knew she was shy back in college, but now he saw a confident, intelligent, and beautiful black woman who'd truly grown into herself. What he was dealing with currently wasn't the young, voluptuous coed who could barely converse with him, but an intellectual and physical equal whose apprehension was the result of overly protective walls. It was his newfound mission to break down those barriers and enclose her within the confines of his affection.

"Ah-ha! The big chef is really a phony," Ronni said, coming up behind him as he pulled some containers out of the stove. She couldn't sit still in the living room any longer. Out of his presence, her nerves tried to take over her evening.

He smiled to himself, but continued in his actions. "You didn't leave me any choice," he said. He handed her the glass of wine he'd poured for her. "First you said you weren't coming, and then you said you'd be here in half an hour. I had to get some help from Dixie Kitchen."

"Mmm. Dixie Kitchen. One of my favorites," she said, watching as he opened an array of entrées from the soul-food restaurant. "So, can you really cook?"

"You've heard of Real Men Cook? Well, that's me, I'm a real man."

He liked having her standing next to him at the center island. He could imagine what it would be like if she were there all the time.

"Oh, a real man, huh?" Ronni enjoyed seeing this side of Jeff. He moved easily around his kitchen like he was accustomed to doing things for himself. Plus she needn't have asked about his ability to cook. He had a fully equipped kitchen that would make even Paul Prud-homme proud. And the way he readily opened cabinets and put his hands on exactly what he was seeking proved to her he was no stranger to this area of the house.

"Was there any doubt?" He looked slyly at her as he placed their plates, napkins, and utensils on a tray. "What do you want to eat?" His hand fanned over all the selections.

"This is enough stuff to feed an army. How hungry do you think I am?" She knew she was here on a mission, but she may as well enjoy herself in the process.

"I might only get this one opportunity to impress you. I didn't want to mess it up—have you going back to your girlfriends saying, 'Girl, he served shrimp. And you know I'm allergic to shrimp.'" He did a pitiful falsetto imitation of a woman that made Ronni laugh. She marveled again at how easy he was to talk to. "So, what'll you have . . . since I bought out the place?"

Ronni sipped her wine and considered the entrées. "I'm sorry you went through all this trouble, Jeff," she said, rubbing his arm in consolation. The muscles and heat she felt underneath the thin fabric of his shirt made her nearly choke on her next words as she spoke them quietly. "I'm not really hungry." Truth was that she was kind of hungry, but the way her stomach was doing flip-flops, Ronni knew she could barely force a bite past her lips. "Let's just relax with the wine and talk for a minute."

"All right," he said easily. This sounded like a good idea to him, too. He wanted nothing more than to get to know her better. If that would take food, fine. Wine? Fine. A back rub? Hey, a guy can hope for the best. "The living room or the deck?"

Ronni looked to where his hand was gesturing past the back door. "The deck looks nice." Even though she'd familiarized herself with the living room and was at ease there, Ronni could see the seating area through the glass doors and it also looked inviting. Plus, she could use some fresh air. As Jeff replaced the covers on the food, she spied a state-of-the-art mixer in the corner of one counter and smiled to herself at the image of Jeff baking a cake. He took their glasses and the bottle of wine and led her to the couchlike benches that surrounded the deck. He sat and Ronni settled in next to him, but not too close. She remembered her prime directive: to find out what this man was all about.

"So, you wanted to impress me, huh?" she teased.

Jeff looked surprised. "Did I say that out loud?" He grinned and settled back on the bench, watching her as she looked out on the Japanese-styled landscaping of his backyard.

Ronni sipped her wine. "You certainly did, mister. So let's start with what it is you do for a living."

Jeff stretched out his legs and eyed her, considering her question for a second. "Would that impress you? You don't seem like the materialistic type to me."

"It's not a material thing, although you obviously have the trappings of a man who knows no limits. It's more about how you are contributing to our life here on earth." This was truly her philosophy. What a person chose to do in life said a lot about them.

"I'm contributing to society as a lawyer . . . and I do have my limits," he answered as if under cross-examination. But he smiled, scooted down in his chair until his head touched the back and looked at her for her next question. He found her direct manner refreshing.

"A lawyer?" She watched as he nodded. "I thought I'd heard that, but you really don't seem like a lawyer."

"Oh? What does a lawyer seem like? Tyler Washington?" He casually threw that name out there. He wanted to get to the bottom of a few questions of his own. He watched as the color in her face heightened and she stared into her wineglass.

"No," she answered too quickly, feeling the heat in her face. "Well . . . yes. S—sort of." She still didn't meet his eyes.

"He's a bit high-strung, huh?" He chuckled, sipped his wine, and watched for her reaction. Getting a shrug in reply, he pushed on. "Tyler's more successful than me." She noted that Jeff was comfortable without having to play up his self-importance. "I take clients only occasionally, only if I can really help them out. Is Tyler more your type?"

"What?" Ronni had heard him, but she was supposed to be in control. She decided to ignore his question and press for more answers of her own. "So where do you practice?"

"Here. I'll show you my office upstairs during the grand tour." He knew she'd changed the topic intentionally, but he wasn't going to let her off that easily. He knew that as fine as she was, there had to be a brother lurking in the background somewhere. "So, is he your man?"

"Who?" Ronni's voice showed great agitation as her head snapped toward him. Why did her name always get linked romantically to Tyler's even in the most unexpected circumstances? She had never even dated him. They'd gone on a couple of lunches when she'd first graduated from college, but even if it was what Tyler wanted, they'd never ventured into anything romantic.

"Tyler . . . Washington," he said slowly, amused by her embarrassment. He didn't know if she was annoyed that he knew about Tyler or if she didn't like the reversal of questioning, but he was having fun toying with her.

"What?" Ronni found herself saying this a lot in his presence. She watched a sly smile creep over his face and thought he was playfully trying to get on her nerves. "Anyway . . . so . . . you said you only take cases if you can help out."

Jeff nodded. A little smile hadn't left his face since she'd arrived. He tried to keep his eyes from appraising her body or focusing on her cute feet.

"Help out how?"

He brushed away something barely visible on his shorts. "Any way I can."

"You make it sound like they're in trouble or something." She didn't know if she was being too obvious here, but her future was potentially on the line. Besides, he didn't seem to be fazed by her persistent questioning. He appeared to be rather enjoying it.

"Some are. Some aren't. It's the nature of my business." He drank his wine. "So, you and Tyler on a break or something? Is it because of me?"

Ronni was ready to slap him. Instead she gave him the evil eye before answering. "For your information I don't have a man and I'm not looking for one. I'm too busy for relationships right now."

"Too busy for a relationship?" Jeff sat up. "That doesn't make any sense," he said, looking at her with an unguarded frown. Ronni could see a muscle working in his jaw. She was puzzled by his unmistakable annoyance.

"Sensible or not, it's true," she shrugged.

"You're here now. You were with me at the tennis club. We talked on the telephone last night. Other than a couple of dinners and . . ." He had gone too far now to back down. ". . . and maybe a few sleepovers, that's all a relationship takes. With a little commitment, you have time for a relationship."

Ronni was surprised by his evident emotional investment in the topic—and by the way he so obviously interpreted her antirelationship comments about the possibility of the two of them having a relationship. She had imagined him to be a bit more suave, a bit more of a playboy. Ronni hadn't expected him to be so emotionally vulnerable toward her. She specifically remembered Stephanie saying she wished Jeff would open up more, tell her what he was thinking.

Now that she observed his countenance in relation to his surroundings, she saw that the exact opposite was probably true about him. Where she'd come in expecting his place to be modern, minimalist, and cold, she'd found a home with overstuffed seating and warmth.

She had noticed that the pictures on his wall leading from the living room to the kitchen were sepia photos of generation after generation of his family. Lovely babies in white christening gowns. Men and women with caps and gowns from a time when most blacks couldn't even dream of college. Boys with short pants at their fathers' knees. Stern-faced men and women looking out across the ages to say, "You are our progeny, make us proud."

That gauntlet of photographs, along with his other personal touches, were in stark contrast to the modern sterility and remoteness of her place. She had meaningless art photographs on her walls, lots of open hardwood floor space, cool black marble countertops, miniblinds, and square furnishings. No pillows, no expressive fabrics, and, most telling, no family photos.

The fact that his space was a house and hers was an apartment also spoke volumes about who was declaring, "I'm approachable and ready for a family," and who was hiding in the anonymity of a huge building, declaring, "I want my personal space and you can't come up unless I see you on the monitor and you check in at the security desk." Here he was, broadcasting his intention to take this night much further and here she was with Plan of Attack in the back of her head. But she couldn't change who she was—or had become—over a glass of wine, even if it was with a man to whom she was drawn.

"I think relationships take more than that, Jeff," she said softly, returning her eyes to her drink.

"Like what?" Not waiting for her response, he continued. "What's been a major issue in your relationships?"

"Well, trust, for one thing." Ronni gulped on the words. She couldn't tell him that she hadn't been in that many relationships. In actuality, she hadn't been in a real adult relationship. Ever. She had had some dates and spent some time with men she was only half interested in, but her big secret—and her secret embarrassment—was that she had never been intimate with any man. Of course she blamed herself. First it was her shyness that made her keep her distance from men, but as she grew older it was an issue of not letting her guard down. She didn't wear her virginity as a badge of honor like some of the women she'd seen on reality shows, who would proudly proclaim that they were saving themselves for marriage. She saw it more as a failure on her part to allow anyone to get close to her.

Jeff, who'd been watching her face as though he could read her thoughts, placed his drink on the deck floor and turned his body to fully face hers.

"Yes, trust is a serious one." His solemnity was unnerving, the same way it had been when he'd followed her to her car at the courts. "What is it that you feel you can't trust about me?"

"I wasn't talking about *me* trusting *you*," she lied. "I meant trust is a serious thing in relationships in general." Under his searching eyes, Ronni tried to keep it light and maybe work back to this topic at a later time, more indirectly. There were issues of trust she wanted to bring up, just not now. Not like this.

He moved closer and took her drink from her hands, placing it on the floor next to his. His voice was soft and his eyes demanded hers. "Yeah . . . well, I'm talking about *us specifically*." His large hands enclosed one of hers. "What can I do to ease your doubts about me?"

"Jeff, really . . ." She pulled her hand back, uncomfortable with the intimacy. "I barely even know you. This is . . . a bit premature, don't you think?" She smiled, trying to lighten the mood and stood in reflex to her tenseness. He caught her hand again before she could pace around the deck.

"Why do you always do that?" he said.

She looked back and saw his furrowed brow, his rising anger. "Do what?"

"Pull away, put distance between us. You did the same thing today when you canceled on me. No explanation, just 'Jeff, I'm not coming. Good-bye.'"

"I'm not. I didn't. You're just . . ." She shrugged. She

didn't have words that would effectively fight off this intrusion on emotions she was not ready to admit to.

"Getting too close? Getting too real?" He stood to look down on her face, his hand still firmly holding hers. Well, that wasn't exactly true, his thumb was gently caressing the sensitive skin on the back of her hand. Jeff took a step closer. Ronni wanted to back up, but his admonishments made her stand her ground. Her only defense was to stare at the wood floor. Jeff took even this security away by lifting her chin with his free hand.

"Ronni, I know you like me. I can feel it when I'm with you. I can feel it when I touch you. And I sure as hell know I like you. Why are you holding back? Why do we have to play these games?"

"What games?" Her voice was barely a breath. Ronni had never considered herself a game-playing female. She felt a tear tracking down her cheek from her left eye. Where was that frigging guard who was supposed to be standing at the gate of her heart? She cast her eyes downward and felt the hand that was holding her chin turn over to wipe the small tear away.

"Ronni." His voice was hoarse as it broke and he bent to kiss her lips. She stiffened and drew back, but his lips softly found hers and closed over them. The sensation was so warm and so much of what she wanted that she closed her eyes and let out a small stifled whimper of pure desire. She relaxed and slightly opened her mouth to his.

His lips pressed harder and his mouth opened more greedily. Jeff moved his full body against hers. The fingers on their connected hands intertwined and she put her free arm around his neck; his firmly encircled her waist. His tongue cautiously explored her smooth teeth, but hers, having none of that tentative stuff, met his and invited it to come in. Their bodies were responding so passionately to their moist kiss that they broke the hand clasp and fully encircled their arms around each other. His hands roamed up and down her back as he probed her mouth, and her hands roved Jeff's face and the back of his hair like a blind person trying to determine his looks. Their breath was rapid and each one's heart pounded urgently on the other's chest. They had to come up for air and stared into each other's face, both of them caught in the same caress—one hand on the face, the other holding the body. He leaned in to nuzzle her cheek.

Ronni was surprised that a fresh tear had once again made its way down her cheek and was thankful to press her face into his shirt. She suspected that her crying must be her body's instinctive response to losing some of its long-held defenses. He kissed her neck with little wet kisses that left heat wherever they landed.

"I just want to hold you." *Forever.* He only considered adding that last word for a second. But telling her what he'd wanted her to know from the moment he saw her at her father's house might scare her right back behind those damnable walls of hers. His body already told her what she wanted to know about how much he wanted her.

"Jeff, I—" She wasn't sure what she was going to say, when she heard a noise behind her and gave a startled jump, looking around quickly. Jeff looked calmly to the source of the scratching noise. He gave her a squeeze before breaking their embrace and heading over to the patio door.

"Hannibal, you picked a crappy time to show up, buddy. I'm not even going to lie to you," he said hoarsely, letting a fat, black pug out onto the deck. Hannibal moved slowly, favoring one hip as his nails made a faint clicking noise on the wood. They could tell by the little black eyes staring right at Ronni that the dog was interested in checking out the visitor to their home, but he decided to pause and yawn first, then stretch his back.

"Oh, he's cute." Ronni stooped down to be more accessible to him. Hannibal finally reached his target and was rewarded with the pleasurable scratching he was hoping for. "And old," she added when she spied his gray beard and the gray rim around his irises.

"Oh, yeah. He was old when I got him, and he's still hanging in there." Jeff squatted over his feet and patted the dog's back. "I figure him to be about a hundred and twenty-five in dog years."

"Aww, you're not that old, are you?" Ronni was given a loud asthmatic-sounding pant in reply. "Well, not *quite* that old, huh?"

She looked up at Jeff. "I didn't even know you had a dog. Where was he when I came in?"

Jeff shrugged and smiled. "Who knows? Upstairs sleeping. Downstairs sleeping. Wherever he was, I can tell you he was sleeping. That takes up, like, ninety percent of his time these days."

She gave the pug's smiling face another friendly rub and stood up. "Stairs! You still make him go up and down stairs?"

"Make him? Who can stop him?" Jeff stood, too. "I thought he was getting too old to tackle the stairs and I put one of those baby gates in front of the steps. But when I went to bed, he would nearly break his neck climbing over the thing to get to his room, even though I moved all his bedding and stuff onto the first level."

They laughed and looked at the old fellow, who was proving Jeff's words true by gingerly taking the five steps from the deck to the backyard. "After three nights of waking up to find him asleep on the floor upstairs, I figured he must've pulled the gate down with his teeth because it was pretty damaged. I gave up and took it down. As you can see, he takes his time. The vet says he'll let me know when he can't make it anymore."

"Yeah, by tumbling back down," Ronni teased.

"That's exactly what I said. I have a retired neighbor come in to check on him during the day when I'm out." They both watched Hannibal disappear into the darkness of the yard, but they could still hear his labored breathing.

Jeff looked back at Ronni. He walked over to her, took her hand, and led her back to the cushioned bench. When they were seated, he put his arm around her shoulders. Ronni reached for her wineglass. She needed a crutch. Not the alcohol, but the comfort of something in her hand. It had been a long time since she'd kissed or even amorously touched a man and she was still unsure of her ability to relax.

"But enough about him. Back to us," he said.

"Us," Ronni repeated.

"Yeah. So, you know where *I* stand. But from your perspective, is there going to be an us, or are you gonna bolt on me?" His tone was lighthearted, but Ronni saw frank earnestness in his eyes.

"I don't want to *bolt,* as you say . . ."

"But?" She could see his face becoming heavier as though steeling itself for the blow.

"But I have reservations." *Not the least of which is that Randy says you're a snake.* It appeared that her internal defenders were regrouping.

Jeff let out a deep sigh. "What reservations? Just tell me."

"Well . . ." She sipped some wine. Her throat was dry, but the liquid wasn't helping. She could use some water. She felt Jeff kiss her forehead and take in the fragrance of her hair.

"Tell me, sweetheart," Jeff said. Ronni relaxed back into his arms with a sigh of her own. It would be so easy, so wonderful to just let go and let this thing happen without her mind constantly niggling at her.

Even though she didn't need a psychiatrist to tell her that her father was the major source of her distrust of men, she couldn't shake the feeling that if she put her heart out there, it would definitely get stomped on. When she was growing up, her father had been her example of the perfect man. He could do no wrong. And as she got older, she knew she wanted a man just like Daddy. When her father had the affair with Tamara, he not only broke her mother's heart, he broke and damaged Ronni's as well. She cried for days and wouldn't talk to her father for months. She was barely civil to Tamara and the first time she saw her after hearing the news of her parents' divorce, she tried to scratch her eyes out. Her father had to pull her off Tamara and calm her down.

Now all Ronni knew was that she couldn't stand not knowing the connection between Jeff and her father. It would mean another secret her father kept that she didn't know about. And if Jeff were involved, what did that say about him? Her emotional wounds were deep. They had healed on the surface but were tender underneath. What if her dad was doing something that was going to diminish her inheritance? The true object of her mistrust was Benjamin, but being unable to express that to him, she took her misgivings out on Jeff.

Jeff's thumb rubbed her forehead where he'd recently kissed it. His leg gently bumped hers. "What's going through that head?"

Ronni turned her face to him. She wanted to kiss those lips that had just given her so much pleasure a moment ago, but she had business to take care of. "Jeff. What's your relationship with my father?"

Jeff inhaled and exhaled deeply. "Is that what's troubling you?" He watched as she nodded. Her eyes dropped for a second and then returned to search his face. "Ronni, it's nothing. He has me looking at a few of his legal things. You know, double-checking on stuff."

"Double-checking on what kind of stuff? Is our business in trouble?"

"Of course not. Is that why you were asking about clients being in trouble?" He saw her nod, then rubbed her arm protectively and pulled her closer to his body. "Your father is really a shrewd businessman. I've always admired him."

"But what about Tyler? He's always relied on Tyler's advice and trusts Tyler." Ronni could feel the tension in his body. She glanced up and saw that telltale muscle working in Jeff's jaw. He held her hand and played with her fingers. Ronni thought it was in an attempt to calm himself on a topic he didn't really want to get into.

"I guess this is something he wanted to get a fresh opinion on." He stared at her fingers longer than she would've liked, especially since she was now watching his face for clues. He finally looked at her and just blinked, waiting.

"*What's* something he wants to get an opinion on?" There was no cause for timidity now. Jeff was definitely keeping something from her.

"Well." He sighed deeply. "You'll have to talk to him about that. Lawyer-client confidentiality and all." Jeff looked pained to have to say it. He was beginning to understand that his connection with her father was the major cause of the distance between them.

"So you're really his lawyer?" She didn't know if she liked this. She moved away from him to get a better look at his face. Ronni could hear Hannibal coming back from his backyard exploration. They watched as he tentatively approached the steps before finding the energy to dash up them as best he could. The dog, apparently not interested in engaging them anymore, stood waiting at the back door for Jeff to let him in the house.

"On certain matters," he said as he stood and opened the door for Hannibal. He returned to the bench, but this time he sat apart from Ronni and crossed his leg over his knee. To her, he looked like a little boy who was required to endure a lecture from his mother before he could go back outside and play.

"Financial matters?"

He nodded silently. "Is this going to be a problem for us?"

Ronni stopped looking at him and looked in her glass. "I don't know," she said truthfully, with a barely visible shrug. She wanted to let this go. She knew it was non-sensical. Why should her father, and whatever his issues were, keep her from becoming involved with a man she could really like? More honestly, a man she could envision herself falling in love with?

Jeff was more comfortable expressing his emotions. He moved forward and allowed his fingertips to graze her knee. "I don't want it to be. I want us to be free to like each other . . . to fall in love if we want to."

She looked up into that face she knew so well and re-connected with the young woman who had imagined this situation so many times during her college days. Even after he left campus, she would have this fantasy where Jeff just happened to stop by the campus for a visit and they would see each other, strike up a conversation, and fall in love. Her younger mind hadn't really worked out the specifics of how all that would happen, but it was her favorite fantasy back then. Her favorite part was imagining the reaction of all the other girls, whispering viciously about what he saw in her while she held her chin up proudly and held his arm.

The girl she was would've loved to be listening to Jeff

Conley say he wanted to be with her, wanted to *fall in love* with her. Ronni found, in her heart of hearts, that she wasn't so far removed from that coed.

"I want that, too."

"Then let go. Let it happen." He put his hands on both of her knees. "There's nothing keeping us from being together but you. Your brain is working overtime, baby. It's as simple as this." He kissed her forehead, then her nose, and finally her lips. This kiss was lighter and less demanding than their previous one, but it carried much more weight. It took all her inner strength to break the kiss and push him away.

The expression on his face was one of confusion and hurt. He knew she wanted to kiss him as much as he had just wanted to kiss her, but he couldn't figure out what was holding her back. If what she said about her reservations was true, then he had only one solution. "All right, if my working with your father is going to be a problem, then . . . I'll tell him I can't take him on as a client."

Ronni lowered her eyes. This is what she thought she wanted, but upon further consideration, what right did she have to encroach upon her father's business dealings—especially when she didn't even know what they were? But if Jeff was the cunning snake she had heard, he was hiding it quite well, because this was the perfect solution. "No, Jeff. I don't want you to do anything that drastic. Just assure me that it's nothing that's going to hurt me . . . or my father."

Now a deep frown creased Jeff's brow as if he didn't understand her words. "I can't promise you it won't hurt you . . . if I don't know what your issues are with him and me." He waited a beat to see if she would further explain her opposition to Benjamin being his client, but when she didn't, he continued. "I haven't really done anything for him yet, so I can just get out of it and return the files to Tyler."

Ronni was relieved, but she didn't say anything. If Jeff and her father were truly involved in an innocent legal arrangement, why did they both hide the purpose of their meeting when she first saw Jeff? It was definitely better that he not be her father's lawyer.

"Is that what you want?"

She shrugged and looked at her hands.

"You liar," he said, pulling her toward him by placing a hand at the back of her neck and giving her forehead a kiss. "You look happier already."

She smiled now at his brutal honesty. This was the quality of his that most refuted the image of him as a conniving swindler.

"This is quite a sacrifice, woman. I've waited years to land a client as big as Benjamin Hampton." Even as she chuckled, Ronni had to wonder, *Land him, why?*

He stood up in front of her and offered her his hands. When she took them, he pulled her to a standing position. He led her into the house. "Come on. I've got all this food. We'd better heat it in the microwave, unless . . . you want to have it for breakfast?" His eyebrows went up to match his roguish smirk as he moved in closer to her.

She pushed at his chest. "Calm down, buster. You'd better make mine to go."

"What?" He feigned innocence, but turned to open the containers. "We're going to be an official couple now, aren't we? I've made a gesture to move us toward the trust part. . . . Now, what else did we agree that relationships take?"

"I didn't agree on anything." She smiled and shook her head in disbelief as he pulled real Tupperware from a cabinet to place her food in. "You have such a dirty mind. Is sex all you think about?"

"No. I also think about . . . well, come to think of it, sex is pretty much it." They both laughed. Jeff continued to smile to himself as he packed up a little bit of everything for her.

"Don't forget johnnycakes," Ronni said, not wanting to miss out on the small, circular cornbread pancakes.

"Oh, no doubt." His answer seemed to emanate from far away as he opened the tinfoil and added two johnnycakes to her plastic dish. Instead of enjoying her company in the flesh—which he naturally was—his mind was racing ahead to when he could present her to the world as his woman. *His.* He knew he was taking a chance in simply declaring like a schoolboy that they were an official couple, but he couldn't resist. He wanted to lock this woman down.

That old tune "If My Friends Could See Me Now" rang through his head so vigorously that he almost started to whistle it out loud. He thought of all the brothers who would've patted his back and given him vigorous dap at appearing on the yard with the unattainable Veronica Hampton. Now, he simply imagined a future meeting of her and his mother. His mom often complained that he never brought any of his "lady friends" home to meet her and frequently stated that she'd probably never get to see any grandchildren before she left this earth. *Mom will definitely like Ronni,* he thought. He was vaguely aware that he was grinning like a fool and he didn't care.

Ronni's locking the lid on the Tupperware into place snapped Jeff out of his daydream. He looked freely into those beautiful onyx eyes and, for once, she looked back unguarded.

"What are you thinking about?"

"What do you think?" he said. Jeff considered himself to be in touch with his emotions, but he was just as afraid of being hurt as the next guy. Playing the rascal was his crutch.

"Mm-hmm. Well, stop thinking about it, 'cause it's not going to happen," she said with a playful lilt to her voice as she gathered up the plate. He followed her as she snaked her way back through the house to the foyer.

"Oh, yes, it is," he teased, really thinking about the future meeting between her and his mom. He became distracted by Ronni's walk, which reminded him of all the reasons he loved black women.

"Not tonight it's not." She stopped at the front door where a snoring Hannibal was blocking her exit. Jeff had to muster all the strength in his body not to clasp his hands together and declare *There is a God* when he heard the small promise in her response.

"Look, he's old. I can't wake him. You'll just have to stay."

"I'll go out the back door then." Ronni said, turning on her heels before being caught by Jeff's tightly muscled arm.

"All right. All right. If you insist on getting away from me as fast as you can." He nudged the old dog with his foot. With that, the dog woke with a start, but finding that the source of his disturbed nap was only Jeff, he rested his head on his paws and remained fixed in place. Jeff nudged him again and Hannibal indignantly got up and walked away. "Sorry, bud, the lady insists on leaving," he called after him as he opened the door for Ronni.

"Sorry," Ronni called after the dog.

At her car, Jeff took the keys from Ronni and opened the driver's-side door. He took the food out of her hand and placed the dish on the passenger's seat, then closed the door and returned the keys. She leaned against the car with her back to the door and her arms crossed.

"Well—"

"I guess this is good night then," he finished. He put his hands on the roof of the car on both sides of her, enclosing her frame within the boundaries of his masculine body. She was surprised at how nonthreatening this felt, even as he towered over her. With any other man, she would be ready to run away, but with Jeff she actually felt safer here. He reminded her so much of her father—of the stories her mother told her about how her father behaved when they were courting.

"Jeff, look—"

"I'm looking," he said and nuzzled her neck—first sniffing, and then kissing the sensitive skin there. Ronni pushed gently at his shoulders so that she could see his eyes.

"Don't tell Daddy I'm the reason you can't take him on as a client."

"Of course not." He sighed, removed his hands from the roof, and took a step back. He was thinking about how difficult it would be to get out of his deal with Benjamin— and if he really wanted to.

Ronni noticed the sudden distance between them and the coolness in his posture. Just a second ago, she was churning up her nerves to give him a big hug, but now she decided it was best to leave. "Thanks . . . for everything. Well . . . good night." She turned to her car, and, as usual, he held the door for her. Jeff had fallen into that maddening silent role again and she was stammering to get the words out. After she was seated and turned her face to say something about when she would see him again, she noticed that he was gone and was opening the gate for her. As she backed out she rolled down the window and said "good night" again and watched as Jeff waved.

He was reacting strangely. *Did I say something wrong?* She thought about the point at which he backed off. *Was he thinking she had manipulated him just to get him to leave her father alone?*

Chapter Six

"And if you want it, you got it forever, this is not a one-night stand, bay-bah," Jeff strained his voice, trying to match Smokey Robinson's high notes as he drove his car onto Benjamin's property. Lately his every waking thought was filled with memories of the night Ronni came to his house and he'd held her in his arms and kissed the woman he'd fantasized about for so many years. To finally have broken down some of Ronni's defensive walls was a major feat for any man. For Jeff the accomplishment produced a ready smile that was quickly becoming the default setting for his face. Once he reached the head of the driveway, the smile dropped from his face and he switched the radio off. He turned off the engine and sat looking at the ornate wood and glass door to Benjamin's home. It was early evening and the sun had receded slightly. The soft glow from the windows signified a warm, cozy home, but he knew turmoil really lay inside. "I promised Ronni I'd do this," he muttered to himself and reached for the documents on the seat next to him.

He got out of the car and briskly strode to the door. As Jeff rang the doorbell, he hoped he wouldn't encounter Tamara first. He was in no mood for small talk, particularly her singular sort of chatter. *Let's just get this over with.* Fortunately, answering doors was not the new Mrs. Hampton's style. The housekeeper greeted Jeff and asked him to wait in the foyer while she fetched Benjamin. Jeff had never toured their home, only met Benjamin in his office. The house was massive, with a large entry hall decorated with an étagère full of exotic knickknacks and framed photos of Benji at various stages of life. There were also side tables displaying fresh flowers and a large curving staircase. Jeff was peering into the great room to his left when he heard Benjamin's voice behind him.

"Jeff, my boy, this is a surprise," Benjamin said, approaching and shaking the young man's hand. "I didn't expect to hear from you this soon."

"How're you doing, Ben?" Jeff said with a mild smile. He wasn't comfortable with how pleased Ben was to see him.

"Fine, fine. So, to what do I owe this visit? Have you found something already?"

"No, actually, I came to tell you—"

Tamara's complaining voice interrupted Jeff's words as she climbed the stairs from a door left ajar to the right of the hall. "Ben, you can't blame this one on Benji. What's happened to our good merlot? How many times do I have to tell you—"

The two men were watching her as she emerged from the wine cellar with two bottles of wine in her hands. She had been shouting because she figured Ben was in his office. When Tamara saw Benjamin was in the foyer with Jeff, her entire demeanor changed. "Jeff, hi. I didn't know you were coming," she said sweetly, placing one of the bottles on a table, rubbing her hair and smoothing her midriff-baring shirt. Tamara wore leggings and high-heeled house shoes that clicked on the floor as she approached them.

"We were just headed for my office," Benjamin said, watching her eyes fix on Jeff and unguardedly appraise his body.

"Stay for dinner," she said, reaching out to touch Jeff's arm. "We always have plenty."

Jeff adjusted his weight slightly and switched the folder from one hand to the other to avoid her contact. "No, I really can't. I—"

Benjamin made Jeff's excuses for him and moved the younger man toward the office. "He just came to talk to me, but he has to get to something else."

"That's too bad. You've got to promise us you'll have dinner with us sometime." Not so easily deterred from her prey, Tamara followed them a step or two before they entered the office and closed the door.

"Sorry about that," Ben mumbled, embarrassed. It was a while before his eyes met Jeff's.

"No sweat," Jeff muttered back.

Benjamin settled in the chair behind his desk and indicated for Jeff to sit opposite him. Rubbing his hair, Ben's face turned grim when he saw the serious look on Jeff's face. "What have you found? Is it bad news already?"

"Well, yes." When Jeff saw Ben's eyebrows crease into a frown, he amended his answer. "I mean, not in your documents. I actually just dropped by to return these." Jeff held out the papers, and when Ben didn't reach for them, he placed them on the desk. "I won't be able to take your case. I would've sent them back to Tyler, but since my agreement was with you, I—"

"Wait a minute," Ben said, confusion evident on his face. "Return it? Why?"

"I won't be able to work on your case."

Benjamin sat forward in his chair and leaned an elbow on the desk, scratching his head. "You already said that. But what I want to know is, why?"

Uncharacteristically, Jeff avoided Ben's eyes, rubbing his eyebrows as he spoke. "I just have a really full work-load and your case is gonna take up a lot of time." He finally looked at Ben and offered feebly, "I could refer it to someone else if you want."

Benjamin sat back in his chair and stared at Jeff. "That's bull." Ben angrily stood and turned to stare out the window behind him. Jeff stirred uncomfortably in his seat.

Turning back to the younger man, he spoke quietly and apprehensively. "If you've seen something there that's going to land me in . . ." Ben tugged up his pants, not wanting to complete that thought and his eyes bore into Jeff's. "Don't play coy with me. Tell me what you've found."

Jeff stood too and walked over to a file cabinet. He picked up a glass paperweight and studied it. "Honestly, I haven't even gotten into looking them over yet, but I know it's going to be more than I can handle right now," he said, feeling like an idiot to offer this pathetic excuse. He hadn't thoroughly developed a strategy to get out of working for Benjamin without revealing that Ronni was behind his decision. He turned to Ben, reaching for his wallet. "Look, if you don't want to use Tyler, I think I've got a guy you'll like."

Ben's patience had run out. "You can't *seriously* be suggesting that I take this to someone else," he said, raising his voice as he came around his desk. He jabbed a hand at Jeff's chest. "You know my situation, and you said you'd handle it. Now you come to me with this garbage about not having enough *time* and suggest I hand my life over to a complete stranger?"

"Or Tyler," Jeff said composedly, not appreciating Ben's sudden aggression.

"I didn't give this to Tyler! I gave it to you and I don't give a rat's behind what kind of schedule you're facing. You're working on it." Benjamin turned to his desk, picked up the folder, and thrust the package at Jeff.

Jeff's eyes narrowed. The testosterone running through his veins told him to act aggressively in response. He held the older man's eyes for a long time. It was only after he saw fear behind Ben's posture—not of Jeff, but of the potential loss of everything he'd worked so hard to build—that he backed down. Jeff still didn't accept the folder, but he returned to his seat.

Benjamin tossed the folder onto Jeff's lap as he walked to his chair. "I already owe you money, is this some sort of trick to see me fail? To be unable to settle my accounts with you and everybody else?"

Jeff cut his eyes at him. "Why would I do that? Does that even sound like me?"

"To be honest, it doesn't. But why would you pull a stunt like this?" Ben asked, sitting down. He gestured at Jeff. "Here I am thinking you've come up with a solution to my problem and you're trying to back out of it, leave me to expose myself to Tyler or—or someone I've never even met. You said you'd handle this matter. I'd pegged you as a man of your word."

Jeff was stuck now. He wanted to respect Ronni's wishes, but honor amongst men was important, especially in the situation facing Ben. Besides, how could he have a happy life with Ronni if he'd left her father high and dry? If anybody was going to handle Ben's case and handle it right, Jeff knew it had to be him. "I am a man of my word, it's just that . . ."

"Well, spit it out," Ben said, growing impatient again.

Leaning forward in his chair and waving the folder at Ben, Jeff said, "Look, if I do this, you can't mention my involvement to Ronni. Even after it's settled."

"Ronni? What's she got to do with anything?" Benjamin was at first confused, and then his face became angry. "You haven't shared my business with her, have you?"

Jeff shook his head, annoyed at Ben's recurrent false assumptions. "Of course not."

It finally dawned on Ben. "Then what . . . oh, are you seeing my daughter?"

Relieved to have it out in the open, Jeff nodded slowly. "You think you'll have a problem with that?" He raised questioning eyebrows at Ben.

Benjamin leaned back and laced his fingers behind his head. He blew out a deep breath before resting his hands in his lap. "If she likes you, you have my blessing. But I'm more concerned by your behavior. You're about to pull out of our deal because of . . . what? Something you two discussed?"

"She doesn't want me to work as your lawyer," Jeff said wearily.

"How did she even know you were working for me?"

Jeff shrugged. "Ronni asked me, point blank. She must've been suspicious since the day she saw me here."

"And you told her?" Ben's voice was rising again.

"I didn't tell her the context. She's not a stupid woman, she already knew. She must have heard something," Jeff said evenly, ignoring Ben's anger.

Benjamin then remembered that Ronni had caught part of the argument he'd had with Tyler. She had asked if they were disagreeing about Jeff. "Tyler," Ben said under his breath.

"Excuse me?"

Ben sighed before admitting that Ronni's interest had been piqued by his own actions. "Ronni came by the dealership and I was telling Tyler to hand over the documents to you. We got a little loud and I think she heard us mention your name."

That explained the meeting a colleague of Jeff's had casually mentioned about Ronni and Tyler dining together at Stella's. Jeff hadn't liked what he'd heard about the way they were huddled together in deep conversation. "They had lunch together at Stella's." Jeff shared his information with Ben. "What does he know?"

Ben shook his head. "Nothing. Just to hand over all those documents to you." Another thought occurred to Ben. "Do you think she knows it's financial?"

"She knew," Jeff said, scratching at his five-o'clock shadow and looking distractedly around the room. Suddenly he looked at his watch and stood up, holding the folder. "All right, I'm going to work on this, but you've got to tell Tyler to keep his big mouth shut."

"He doesn't know anything, and I can imagine that the only reason Ronni had lunch with him was to pump him for information about our argument. She doesn't like him enough to stay in contact with him," Benjamin said, standing to show Jeff out. "Tyler won't be a problem."

"He'd better not be," Jeff said emphatically and opened the door onto the hallway. He felt Ben's hand on his left shoulder and turned back to look at him.

"And, Jeff . . . don't do that again," Ben said, fatigue showing on his face.

He raised an eyebrow, surprised at the older man's words. "What's that?"

"What we're involved in is too serious. You know that better than anyone. You've got to keep me informed about everything that's going on." Ben's hands dropped from Jeff's shoulder when he felt him tense up.

Jeff snickered derisively, turning his full body to the older man. "So let me get this straight: lie to your daughter, but never lie to you?"

Chastised, Ben looked at the floor. "Right now, it's for her own good," was his meager reply.

Chapter Seven

As usual, Ronni arrived early for her NADA class. Twenty minutes before the five-thirty time, she set up her laptop and tugged at the jacket of her Nicole Miller suit. There were only nine people taking this class and an instructor, Lance. It was set up like a boardroom, complete with comfy executive chairs, coffee service, and an automated projection screen. The class attire was casual, but the participants could usually tell which people were giving a presentation because they wore business suits. The ones who came from work and weren't presenting removed their jackets or switched to comfortable athletic shoes.

Today Ronni was thankful for the few extra minutes to herself so she could think about Jeff. She had been famished when she arrived home after their date and heated up the plate once she got in the door. Now, Ronni smiled to herself, thinking that she was going to have to learn how to eat in front of the man. She hadn't really had a clear chance to think about him since she'd left his house because she had so many more statistics to pore over, notes to write, and then had to try to turn the whole thing into a PowerPoint presentation. By the time she went to bed after two A.M., her evening with Jeff had felt like another of her schoolgirl daydreams. In the quiet, empty classroom, Ronni amused herself by recalling Jeff's wake-up call.

"Good morning, sleepyhead. Are you still in bed?" the rich male voice asked her. When she realized it was Jeff, Ronni tried to rouse herself. She cleared her throat; she was caught off guard by the ringing phone and hadn't checked the caller ID.

"Good morning. Yeah, I was up all night."

"Oh? You couldn't sleep. Thinking about me?" Jeff asked. His voice was flirtatious and Ronni thought he was pretty cocky for so early in the morning.

"I was studying for class. It's ten o'clock already?" Ronni reached across her bed and turned the digital clock around. Without either glasses or contacts, she squinted at the numbers.

"Mm-hmm. . . . Well, I was up all night . . . thinking about you."

She smiled. "Liar."

Jeff aimed for innocence. "It's true. I even dreamed about you."

She pressed her ear into the phone, turned over on her back, and toyed with the buttons on her pajama top. "Really . . . what was I doing?"

"You were over here . . . at my house," Jeff said, pausing to tell his dream at a leisurely pace. "And you were fixing dinner for me."

"Mmm . . . that sounds tame enough," Ronni allowed in the space he provided.

"And you were naked," Jeff added, laughing before he could even get out the words.

She laughed, too. "Oh, brother. For some reason, I knew it would end that way."

"No. I'm just kidding. Really, you were screaming at me," he said quietly.

"That doesn't sound good. What was I screaming about?"

"Kidding again." He chuckled.

"You know, Jeff, you're a lot goofier than you appear from a distance."

"That's not good, huh? I'm wrecking my reputation." Jeff's voice seemed to sink into the background of people gabbing right next to him.

"Big time. Where are you? It's noisy over there." Ronni sat up, feeling insecure about having a sexy conversation while other people were in the room.

"I'm at work. Hold on," Jeff said and Ronni could hear him moving around, then a door shut and the people's voices were gone. "There, I closed the door."

She frowned, wondering who the people were at his house. "I thought you worked from home."

"Unless I have to come downtown. I keep an office for the clients I don't want to meet at home. It's pretty small," he said in his typically honest fashion.

"So did you really dream about me, or is the whole thing a lie?" she asked, wanting to steer the conversation back to them and having forgotten she'd even asked a question.

Jeff sighed, and she could hear him adjusting his weight. "Seriously, I did. But I shouldn't have told you."

"Why not?" she asked, teasingly.

"Where did I get this reputation for being a liar?" He sounded serious.

"Did I say you were a liar?" she backtracked, not wanting to change the mood. "I meant you have a tendency to embellish the truth."

"The truth is, I wanna see you. Is tonight a class night?" Jeff hadn't really been irritated; he was still coming across as playful and sexy.

"Yeah," she said sadly.

He moaned, disappointed. "And afterward? Come over."

"No, no. Not another late-night tryst," Ronni said, sitting up and placing her feet on the floor.

"Is that what we had? A tryst?" he said gravely.

She could imagine the naughty grin on his face. "Whatever it was, I can't do it again. I need my beauty sleep." She stood and put on her glasses.

"Girl, you don't need any more beauty sleep in life!"

Ronni placed her hand on her hip and laughed at his silliness. "Shut up. Don't try to flatter me. So what was the dream about?"

"Come over after class. I'll tell you in person." He cleared his throat. "Better yet, I'll show you in person."

"Persistent, aren't you?" she asked, walking into the bathroom.

She could hear Jeff blow out a breath. "Then when will I see you again?" he asked with barely contained patience.

"Let's do something tomorrow," she offered.

"Mental note to self: I'm doing all the work here."

She smiled at her reflection in the mirror and cocked her head. "I'm saying we'll get together tomorrow!"

"True, but I want to see you tonight and I have to face your rejection," he whined, trying to manipulate Ronni to change her mind.

"It's not rejection, it's delay. Besides, that's the male's role, isn't it? Woo the female?" she teased.

"Oh? Is that how it is?" Jeff sounded clearer, but she could also hear a knock at his door.

"It's biological," she explained like a professor.

"Oh, she's pulling the science thing on me," he said before she could hear him talking to someone else. "Hmm? Okay." Then he was back to her. "Look, Ronni, I've got to go. Liz is telling me I gotta be in court in fifteen minutes."

"Nooo, don't go. I was having fun," she whined shamelessly, resting her butt against the sink.

"Yeah. I'll bet you were," he said, laughing. "Actually, I do have an event tomorrow night I'd like for you to accompany me to. . . . I really better go. I'll call you tonight."

Ronni's reminiscences were interrupted when someone opened the door to the classroom. "Hey, girl," the entering classmate said breathlessly. Ronni glanced at her watch. Right about now, she would usually be stuck in a stilted conversation with Lance. Ronni was surprised to see that it was Theresa Posner, the only other black female in the class—it was obvious that Theresa was coming from work: she was wearing a blouse and slacks with gym shoes. She chose the seat next to Ronni and placed her briefcase, purse, and jacket down before heading straight for the coffee.

"Hey, Tee. You never arrive early," Ronni said.

"I know. Girl, I left work early. I was ready to go off." Theresa picked up the empty pot. "Nobody made coffee?" She didn't wait for an answer and began to open a package of French Roast. "I'm going to need coffee if Eric is presenting tonight. He is boring as hell. Girl, at work today I was like, 'Y'all gon' make me lose my mind up in here.'"

Ronni laughed. "They still giving you grief?"

"I told you, those stupid guys I work with are worse than my boys. Wait until I finish this class, get my certificate, then go and apply at another dealership. They'll look like some damned fools. Every time a customer comes on the lot, the manager, Jay, is always like, 'Uh, Theresa, let Jim get this one. He needs to get his numbers up.' Then got the nerve to rag me about my numbers at the end of the month." She sucked her teeth and rolled her eyes, turning her attention back to the coffeemaker.

Theresa was naturally crude, but Ronni liked her. Ronni

was certain she was probably the brunt of some of Theresa's venom before the woman got to know her. She could just imagine her calling her a stuck-up, wanna-be-white, bourgie bitch. But they had avoided that path in the fourth week of the class when Theresa approached Ronni afterward to ask her if she was related to Benjamin Hampton. When Ronni responded in the affirmative, they struck up a conversation on their way to the parking garage. Ronni had agreed with and laughed at Theresa's characterizations of the other class members and they exchanged phone numbers.

Since then, if Theresa was struggling with some of the assignments, she would call Ronni at home to pick her brain. It was during one of these first phone calls that Theresa dropped her pretenses and just said what she wanted to say, the way she wanted to say it. Ronni admired her story. Theresa Posner was only thirty-eight, but she was a single mother raising three teenage boys by herself. She had gotten off welfare twelve years ago by getting a job as a cashier at her neighborhood auto dealership. She'd kept trying to move up to salesperson at that first location, but when they didn't take her seriously, she studied the way the salespeople operated, went to community college at night, and applied to other dealerships. Three years ago, she finally landed a job as a salesperson at a Toyota dealership in a south suburb, but now she had her eyes set on becoming a manager.

"The only time Jay lets me go out on the lot without opening his big mouth is when he's out of the office, it's a brother, or it's a single woman." She ticked off these conditions on her fingers. "Unless the single woman is fine—then they trip all over their stupid asses trying to get to her first. I'm telling you, girl, you should come on my lot to buy a car and request me. That would really piss them off, especially since you're cute. Plus, you're the only girlfriend I know who has enough money to actually buy."

Ronni didn't feel put on the spot and adjusted the screen to her laptop. She knew Theresa would be on to the next subject in a second. She threw out this idea to Ronni at least twice a month. Ronni thought she probably would have done it if she hadn't just bought her TT. "You've got to show me how to hook my laptop into the screen," Ronni said. This was the first time everyone was required to present their ideas in PowerPoint.

"It's easy, there's a plug right in front of it. What time does Lance usually get here?" Theresa tapped her feet as she looked from the dripping coffee toward the door.

"He's usually here by now. He must be running late. What did he say about your presentation?"

"Awww, the same old bull. I need to dig deeper into my statistics. But he said I came across very professional." Theresa's annoyed neck roll ended in a haughtily thrust chin. She walked to the front of the room and gestured for Ronni to come over. When Ronni got up, Theresa eyed her from head to toe. "You look really good."

"Thanks."

"Here. You just hook your computer into this jack."

They both headed for the coffee. "Cool. Now I'm totally ready. Didn't I e-mail you the link to the site with the statistics you would need?"

"Yeah, girl. I included some of that stuff, but I was working on it at the last minute. You know how I am." She nudged Ronni with her elbow. "And my youngest, Stevie, was like, 'Ma, I need to use the computer, Ma, I need to use the computer,' until I just said screw it, I've got enough stuff. You know, Stevie can act like a six-year-old sometimes."

Lance came through the door with two other students he must have met on the elevator. They were already talking and set their bags down before saying their hellos and heading for the coffeemaker. Within five minutes, the entire class was assembled, and Norma Clark would present first, followed by Ronni and then Eric Schlesinger.

Ronni was very proud of the report she'd prepared. Unlike her other classmates, she never took the safe route. Tonight she was forecasting that although most consumers in the United States said they cared about the environment, they were buying sport-utility vehicles in increasingly larger numbers. She was predicting that the American public would like more hybrid cars—either hydrogen cells or electric—but that, so far, they only came in smaller vehicles.

The risky part of her proposal was that the automakers needed to start making hybrids in designs more to Americans' tastes, but these SUVs would require more fueling stations. Instead of modifying gas stations, Ronni's solution was that dealerships would also act as recharging stations, thereby satisfying the growing consumer demand and creating an additional source of revenue for the auto dealerships. They already competed with service stations for mechanical repairs. Why not enter into the energy market?

As they watched Norma's presentation on the rising older population and the need for more luxury cars and wheelchair-accessible vehicles, Theresa nudged her and whispered, "Damn. Why couldn't it have been my night to present? I could've been looking good."

"Why? What do you mean?"

"You see the cutie-pie at the door?"

Ronni looked behind her to see Jeff at the door window, straining to see through the darkness of the room. "Oh! Jeff?" she whispered, mostly to herself. She ignored Theresa's question about who Jeff was, got up as quietly as she could, and went out the door. After she made sure the door closed silently behind her, she turned to Jeff and saw a big cheesy grin on his face.

"Jeff . . . what are you doing here?" She didn't realize she was still whispering. She hugged him and then it dawned on her they were still in front of the window. She moved him down the hall a bit.

"Hey, Ronni. I thought I would drop in on you before heading home."

She was still touching his arm, actually happy to see him. "How did you know where to find me?"

"I looked it up on the Internet." He looked really pleased with himself.

"I thought you were going to call me tonight."

"I couldn't be denied my chance to see you in person. And I must say, my instincts were well rewarded. You're looking mighty fine. Mighty fine," he teased, saying the last bit like an older black man as his eyes took her in appreciatively.

"I have a presentation tonight." She glanced at her watch. "Actually, in a few minutes." She noticed he looked pretty good himself. Ronni had never seen him dressed for work, but she could see why anyone would hire him to represent them. "Did you talk to Daddy yet?"

"Yeah," Jeff said with a sigh. Ronni rubbed his arm.

"How did it go?"

"It's cool."

"Cool? How did he react?"

Before she could receive her answer, Lance poked his head out the door. "Everything okay?" he asked. Ronni was startled, and, truthfully, a little annoyed to be questioned as though she might be in trouble. Lance hadn't heard any yelling coming from them, had he? So what was with the overly concerned face?

Her brow was creased with a frown. "Am I up now?"

"Norma's wrapping up. You'd better come in."

Who do these instructors think they are? This wasn't high school or college. She was a grown woman talking to her boyfriend. "I'll be there in a minute." She couldn't believe it when Lance looked pointedly from her to Jeff before going back inside.

"I guess you better go." She noticed the irritation on Jeff's face, too, but neither of them commented directly on the intrusion.

"Yeah. I'll talk to you later."

"Oh, wait a minute. I have this for you." Jeff opened his suit jacket and pulled out a single white rose.

"Jeff, how sweet. Thank you," she said, sniffing the beautiful flower. She wondered if Jeff knew the meaning of flowers. Her mother had taught her about them while gardening when she was a little girl. She glared at him playfully. "Why was it in your jacket? You too cool to be seen carrying a rose downtown?"

He laughed. "You caught me. Yeah, in case I couldn't find you. I didn't want to walk away looking like the most dejected dude in the history of the earth, carrying his little flower."

"Please. The way you look, people would just assume you were on your way to meet a lady."

"I couldn't take that chance." He smiled and wrapped his arms around her waist. "What's your presentation about?" They both glanced up when they saw the lights go on in her classroom.

"Hybrid cars. I'll tell you about it later. I really better go before he sends out the SWAT team." Ronni kissed him quickly on the lips. "Thanks for my rose."

"All right, baby, I'll talk to you later." Jeff stuffed his hands in his pockets and watched Ronni dash back to the classroom door. She took a moment to wave at him before going inside, mouthing, "Talk to you later." He

waved back and stood a while before going to the elevator. As Jeff pushed the DOWN button, he rubbed his eyes
and let his hand drag down his face to linger on the five-
o'clock shadow that had grown there.

Ronni ignored the knowing smile on Theresa's face
when she placed her rose on the table, gathered up her
laptop, and moved to the front of the class. She had
extra confidence about this presentation and couldn't
wait to take command of the room.

Jeff looked toward the heavens, which, in this case, was
the ceiling of the elevator, and knew he didn't have a
right to ask, but he wanted this relationship to have a
chance. He had no idea how he was going to answer
Ronni's question about her father the next time it arose.
How could he say how Benjamin reacted, especially
when the truth was that he hadn't broken off anything?
He couldn't tell her her father had pitched a fit and
made accusations about Jeff being a fake who never really planned on bailing him out. Benjamin had accused
him of wanting to see him fail. Recalling this spat, Jeff
shook his head and looked at the floor. If Ronni found
out, they would be through before they'd even really
began—that's why he had broken his second promise to
her. He needed to elicit a guarantee from Benjamin that
he wouldn't tell Ronni he was still handling his financial
accounts and to tell that pompous fool Tyler to also keep
his mouth shut.

Chapter Eight

Wham! Stars filled Jeff's eyes and he crumpled to the ground, noting to himself that a powerful whack on the head truly did sound just like comic books depicted, even if it was delivered by a relatively soft volleyball. He fell to grass as lush and full as carpet in the makeshift backyard. The victim of a mean spike, Jeff considered jumping right back into the brutal game for about two seconds when his throbbing head let him know *it ain't happening*.

"Ouch!" Jeff yelled out in mild agony, managing to chuckle as his young teammates towered over his body, blocking out the sunlight. "That's it. I'm out," he said, grabbing someone's offered hand and pulling himself to his feet. Jeff waved his other hand in the air, defeated.

"Come on," said one of the teenagers he was playing with, heartily patting Jeff's back and trying to convince him to hang in there, "Don't quit."

"Nah, I know when I'm licked," Jeff said, scrutinizing the young men with a fresh respect for bodies at the peak of their physical strength. He guessed that the boy who encouraged him had extremely good manners. The way the others averted their eyes, Jeff knew the rest of his team had calculated their chances of winning to be roughly the same without the "old" dude in the game.

Staggering away from the match, Jeff put on his cockiest face and prepared for the ribbing he was sure to receive. As predicted, the guys closer to his own age didn't bother to hide their amusement and heartily laughed at him when he came within a few yards of the barbecue grill where they were gathered. Jeff walked past them to rifle through a large blue gym bag situated on top of the small cooler he'd brought with him.

"Man, I *told* you not to play with those young cats. They're out for blood," Frank Chase chided him, turning a slab of ribs and shaking his head at Jeff's apparent stupidity. "But would he listen?" he asked an audience of frat brothers who were keeping him company while he commanded the grill. "No . . . not Jeff Conley. He still thinks he's the star athlete at Columbia."

"I'll tell you what, man, I never even got *beaned* in college. Never." Jeff smirked, his confidence unshaken. "Hey, but you gotta admit, I was holding my own until that last spike," he boasted, digging through his bag until he'd located his cell phone.

"Say, Jeff, look at Keith. He's about four years younger than you and he knows better than to play with my son and them," said Steven Watkins, a brother in his mid-forties.

Having found his phone, Jeff stood up and quickly examined Keith Meyers, a brother he'd met postcollege at one of these reunions. "Yeah, look at Keith, brother looks like he's about to drop a two-year-old baby. It ain't no mystery why he didn't join the game," Jeff shot back, good-naturedly.

A cacophony of "Oh, no"s and "Aw, snaps" reached Jeff's ears. Before breaking out into a grin at his own crack, Jeff glanced at Keith to make sure he hadn't taken any offense, and smiled puckishly when Keith laughed and responded, "You ain't right." Jeff moved farther away from his critics to a quieter space on the lawn to make his phone call. He ignored further male mockery, in the form of, "Uh-oh, he's whupped," "Who you calling?" and, "You gotta check in?" while punching in Ronni's cell-phone number. He touched the tender spot where the ball had connected with his head, hoping he wouldn't develop a knot before Ronni could see him.

"This is Ronni."

A sensation like an electrical current traveled through Jeff's body at the sound of her voice, his painful forehead immediately forgotten. "Where are you? I'm the only dude out here without a date or a family," Jeff shamelessly moaned into the phone, exaggerating his predicament. *And I can't wait to see you,* he thought, picking at the bark of a tree in Frank's yard.

Opening his mail a couple of days earlier, Jeff couldn't believe his luck. Frank Chase was throwing a family barbecue at his home in Evanston for their college chapter's twelfth anniversary. Jeff received an invitation like this every year—some brother or another organized an event for the frat to get together. Usually they planned something that didn't involve women, providing the married brothers with an excuse to get out of the house and enjoy a boys' night out. Sometimes Jeff went, but mostly he passed on the tedious gatherings. This year, with Ronni as his date, there was no way he was going to miss it. Of course, Jeff would have preferred to arrive together, but, as usual, Ronni had to do some more research on another presentation or paper or whatever for her class. He hadn't really been paying attention when she explained because he was so disappointed that she had opted to meet him there.

"I think I'm here, but half of the houses—I can't see their numbers, and they're so far back from the street, I don't know where I am," Ronni said, confusion evident in her voice. Satisfaction tugged up the corners of Jeff's lips. In the recesses of his mind, he knew it was chauvinistic, but he liked the tinge of helplessness in her voice. She needed him and he was ready to rise to the occasion, feeling born for the role of her boyfriend.

"I'm headed out front right now," Jeff said, hurrying out of the backyard to the consternation of his friends, who shouted more digs at him for running. At the front of the house, he spotted Ronni's silver car creeping along halfway down the block. Jeff waved his arm to get her attention. "You see me?"

"Okay," she said, relieved, waving her hand out the window in response. "Do you see a parking space?" Ronni asked, driving toward him and closing her cell phone when she pulled up next to Jeff.

"Hey, girl," Jeff said, leaning into the window and planting a kiss on Ronni's lips. He was captivated every time he saw her, as if meeting her for the first time. Jeff couldn't stop himself from looking past her face at the two small mounds of flesh barely visible at the top of her yellow sundress. His eyes took a leisurely trip over the unblemished skin on her cleavage, shoulders, and face, and wondered if her entire body was as photographic as the parts he was permitted to see. *It's even better,* his mind answered, filling in the missing pieces to her body puzzle. Jeff's Adam's apple bobbed down heavily when his eyes once again landed on her small face and he straightened up to peer far down the car-lined street. Thinking he spied an opening, Jeff leaned down to Ronni. "You park here, and I'll go find another space," he instructed, pointing a thumb at his Navigator, which was parked directly in front of the house.

Before she could object, Jeff had left her window, disengaged the alarm, and climbed into his towering black vehicle. Ronni drove her TT forward enough to let him out and backed into the recently vacated space. She turned off the engine, got out of the car, and looked toward a charming blue and white Victorian house she assumed was Frank's, since she could faintly hear festive sounds coming from the backyard.

Leaning against her car and rubbing her arms, Ronni couldn't suppress her uneasiness at the prospect of seeing some of the old crew from college. She had to remind herself that she wasn't the wallflower she was back then. Spotting Jeff running back to her from up the block, she felt a million miles removed from the woman who'd speculated with Cornell about Jeff's alleged treachery. Everything in his manner suggested that he was a man she could depend on. Even his choice of clothing contradicted Cornell's friend Randy's depiction of Jeff. He wore a pale pink, short-sleeved, button-down shirt with cream-colored khaki shorts and white gym shoes. *How could he have a split personality while literally running back to me and wearing pink?* she mused to herself while watching Jeff perform a quick sidestep to narrowly escape the fate of road-kill as a bunch of kids on bikes barreled toward him. Ronni noticed the way, even while running, Jeff maneuvered his body quite limberly.

At first, Ronni stroked her arms to calm her nerves, but the closer Jeff came, she felt the need to continue soothing her burning limbs to lessen her desire for the man in her sights. *Get a grip, girl,* she mentally instructed her lustier alter ego, who wanted nothing more than to wrap her arms around him and let her legs follow as they may. Amused, Ronni looked at her polished toes and shook her head to chase away the comical—yet more satisfying than she cared to admit—image of being ravaged by Jeff in broad daylight on this tree-lined residential street.

As if summoned, Jeff appeared in front of her. He placed his hands on the car's hood on both sides of Ronni's body and ducked his head to meet her eye to eye, just like he did on that pleasant night in front of his house when they agreed to be a couple. Heat radiated from his body as a result of his sprint down the street. Ronni briefly met his eyes, but found the unmistakable message they revealed more forthright than she could handle. Instead she focused on his luscious mouth. The pearly-white smile directed at her reminded Ronni that this dreamboat was actually *her boyfriend,* and though there would be no mid-day ravaging, she was free to do with him what she would. Emboldened, Ronni wrapped her arms around Jeff's waist, gently squeezing their bodies together at their chests, stomachs, and hips. She could feel his heart thudding behind his ribs, feel his stomach expand and contract and feel his heat on her torso.

"How you doing, sweetheart? You been having a good day?" Jeff asked, looking at her with the most adoring gaze he'd ever given anyone.

"It started out dull, but it's getting better by the minute," Ronni cooed with a smile to complement his. Jeff shifted his weight to close his arms around her and Ronni felt his heartbeat quicken against her breasts. She thought she'd better bring their scene back into a safer realm and recounted her morning apart from him. "I think I have the basics down. I picked up some brochures from a few neighborhood dealerships. You know, about how they attract and who they're targeting as customers." Ronni caught Jeff's smirk, and she knew what he was thinking. She let go of his waist and pushed at his chest. "All right. I see you laughing at me. I promise I won't bore anybody at the party with my boring dealership talk. Don't worry."

"What?" Jeff frowned, genuinely surprised. His brow cleared up when he realized what she was referring to. "Oh? Are you talking about this goofy grin?" he asked, pointing to his mouth. "It isn't about you, it's about me." He swayed their bodies almost imperceptibly. Holding her like this, Jeff was ready to forget the barbecue and take Ronni to a place where it would be just the two of them. "I was just thinking it doesn't make any sense for me to be so happy to see somebody. I missed you, baby girl. I couldn't wait to see you."

"The feeling's mutual," she responded pathetically. Ronni was aware that she still wasn't expressing her emotions as easily as Jeff. She liked him more than she'd ever liked anybody, but there was a block in her psyche that prevented her from letting go. As far as she was concerned, her issues of trust were off the table. After their discussion at his house, she had really let go of all her doubts, so she hoped her body language spoke more volumes than her words.

Fortunately, Jeff always challenged her walls. He cocked his head at her, speaking softly. "Is that all I get? The feeling's mutual?"

"I missed you, too," Ronni said, snuggling her reddening face into his chest to allow her to say more. "I could barely concentrate on my work for thinking about you."

Jeff could no longer resist her lips and leaned over to place his mouth on hers, tenderly tugging at her lips with his. Her back rested against the car and she allowed her mouth to express what her words couldn't.

Feeling her move against him, Jeff was inclined to protest, but he followed Ronni's lead and separated. Ronni's knees were shaky and she felt the need to fill the space with more meaningless words. She tugged at the fabric of his shirtsleeve.

"I can't believe you're wearing pink. If I'd gone with my first choice, we'd be one of those obnoxious matching couples," she teased. After considering a couple of outfits, Ronni had chosen a yellow cotton sundress with small, embroidered pink flowers and matching flat sandals.

"Haven't you heard? Pink is the new black," Jeff said,

rubbing his eye. He wished she *had* worn a pink dress. As crazy as it sounded, even to his own mind, Jeff thought he wouldn't mind being classified as one of those couples who openly displayed their bond through matching outfits. He, too, had once thought of them as nauseating, but with this woman, he was beginning to see life differently. Jeff's mind produced a rewarding image of himself and Ronni at a theme park or someplace, with a little boy and a girl, all wearing the same color T-shirts with blue jean shorts. He grinned at the fantasy.

"Yeah? Well, you have to be really confident in your manhood to pull off that look," she said, pretending to look unconvinced.

"Hey, if Russell Simmons can sport a pink hat, it's no longer taboo. Besides," Jeff said, stretching his neck in her direction, "I look good."

"You'd better watch it, or your big head's gonna float away." Ronni pushed him and twisted her lips at his bravado. She marveled at the power lurking behind his shirt where her fingers had shoved, and had to admit, pink or no, he came across as nothing but pure, grade-A, all-American male.

"Aw, you know I'm fine," Jeff joked. "Besides, I already defended attacks on my manhood from frat." He planted a kiss on her forehead, threw his arm around her shoulders, and led them across the street. "And when I show up with you, there'll be no doubt as to my sexual preference."

"Don't be so sure they'll be fooled. You could be on the down low," Ronni said, poking his stomach and making a mental note that it didn't give an inch. *I could've broken a nail.* Ronni's mind raced with images of what Jeff's toned naked body could look like.

"Are you challenging me to prove something to you?" Jeff smiled and something in his eyes signaled Ronni to make a run for it. She released his hand and dashed up the lawn and through the gate, the only available escape route. "Because I got your proof. If you want it," he shouted, a few steps behind her.

Jeff caught Ronni from behind, by the waist, and was duck-walking with her into the yard. When they turned the corner in view of the barbecue, Ronni was amazed at all the space in the back of Frank's house. There was no way to tell from the street that his lawn, though moderately wide, stretched yards away from his house, extending to the edge of a large and scenic pond. The neighbors' backyards didn't interfere with the private feel of his plot, thanks to a clever arrangement of trees, climbing flowers, shrubbery, and a stained cedar fence. Ronni observed a yard full of beautiful black people at various states of play, accompanied by the thumping beats from a CD player situated near the enclosed back porch. The gathering was definitely a family atmosphere, rife with adults, teenagers, little kids, and one or two toddlers. At a glance, Ronni thought she easily could count fifty people. Some people were playing cards, some men congregated at the grill, others stretched on lawn chairs, others were doing a line dance, and some were simply talking as they fixed their plates of food.

"Veronica Hampton." Frank Chase drew out her name and hung the tongs in his hand on the side of the grill. He wiped his hands on his apron, shaking his head disbelievingly as he extended his hand to her. "Still fine as ever. You actually dating this knucklehead?"

"Hey, Frank," Ronni said, placing her hand in his. Frank pulled her into him and gave her a hug and a kiss on the cheek.

"Get off my woman," Jeff warned Frank while Ronni accepted a round of kisses from the guys she knew and shook hands with the others, trying to retain their names.

"All right, Jeff, get ready to put on your fish," Frank instructed, nudging Ronni's arm when Jeff went over to his food. "You must have really put the mojo on him for him to try to pretend like he can cook."

Jeff heard him and sucked his teeth, looking over his shoulder at Frank. "Please." He pulled a large salmon fillet out of the cooler. "I can throw down on some food now."

"So he keeps telling me," Ronni said to no one in particular. She rubbed her hands together greedily after seeing the pink fish. "Mmm, salmon. My favorite."

A female voice piped in behind them. "Just because you can't boil an egg, Frank, doesn't mean Jeff can't cook." The snide comment came from a short woman with a cherubic face and chubby body to match. She came out of the back door and walked down the steps with a large plastic tray in her hands.

"Excuse me, Penny? Who's cooking all this meat and feeding these people?" Frank asked in his defense, waving his hand broadly to encompass the guests in his sight.

Penny bumped Jeff's arm with her elbow, stage whispering, "Once or twice a year, he sets a fire and watches the meat *I* marinated and *I* prepared. He never even puts his hands on a kitchen utensil on any other day of the year." She ended with her hand on her hip and the kind of neck roll only a Black woman can execute properly.

"You don't have to tell me, I know when somebody's full of it," Jeff said, rubbing Penny's back in solidarity.

"I'll guess you would, you do it enough." Frank cut his eyes at Jeff, then pointed at his wife. "Look, ain't nobody talking to you, woman. This is man's work, so get out of the way." He pretended he was going to hit his wife with the tongs.

She easily moved out of his way, laughing and then holding the tray out to Frank so he could transfer cooked slabs of ribs to it. Penny placed the tray on a small table next to the grill and assisted Jeff in finding a grilling basket for his fish.

"Go on with your stories. I was just leaving," Penny said once she made sure Jeff was squared away. She turned to meet Ronni. "How ya doing? I'm Penny, Frank's wife."

"Ronni. Nice to meet you," she answered, accepting the woman's warm hug and glad to have someone other than Jeff to talk with. "So, it's been like this all day, huh?" Walking with Penny, Ronni jerked her thumb at the men and their jibes.

"Yeah, girl. These men and all their boasting, and trying to one-up each other. But they've really only been arriving within the last thirty minutes or so. That's why Frank and I put eleven o'clock on the invitation. We knew these negroes wouldn't get here until one in the afternoon. Then watch, they'll have the nerve to stick around all night." Penny shrugged her shoulders, adding, "What can you do? But we're ready for them. You a Greek?"

"Yeah," she said mildly.

"Oh, good!" Penny said so excitedly that Ronni thought she was going to greet her as a soror and ask her what chapter she pledged. "Some of your sorors are here, too, along with some other sororities and whatnot." Penny gestured for Ronni to follow and started to lead her toward the back of the lawn.

"Hold up, Penny!" Jeff yelled from behind them. "Where are you taking my girl?"

"She don't want to hear all of y'all's lies and reminiscing about the college days. I'm taking her to the women . . . who can tell her what ya'll are really like, *at home,*" Penny yelled over her shoulder at Jeff, then returned her voice to a level only meant for Ronni. "I didn't pledge anything when I was in college. I never even thought about that stuff. I was too into the books, I guess. Do you know Frank?"

"I knew Frank at Columbia, but he probably doesn't recognize me. I looked different then," Ronni said, referring to her former glasses, twenty-five extra pounds, and longer hair.

"Ha! What about Frank? Doesn't he look different now? You'd think he carried our three kids himself, with that gut on him," she said, throwing her head back in her husband's direction. Penny then whispered honestly. "Not that I can talk. Look at my big butt. But hey . . . I don't have time to work out with three kids, and my baby is only three. That's her running over there. Carolyn." Penny pointed to a pretty little girl trying to keep up with a group of older kids.

"She's a cutie-pie. Oh, and I meant to tell you, you have a lovely home," Ronni said, marveling at the view of the pond again. A gaggle of geese had landed in the pond since the last time Ronni gazed at it. Penny was leading Ronni to a group of women reclining on lawn chairs, facing the water. They were talking and eating, but they took the time to look up to see the new arrival.

"Thank you, I'll show you around inside later." Penny touched her arm lightly and then raised her voice. "Ladies, this is Ronni. Show her to the food and stuff. I have to go back in the house and bring out some hot links and brats."

Penny was turning to go even before the sentence was fully out of her mouth. The other women smiled, spoke, and waved at Ronni, who stood there hesitantly.

"Hey, Ronni, come sit by me," one called out, waving from a reclining lawn chair. Ronni thought she was just being nice until she got closer. She squinted at the woman, realizing that she knew her. It was Leslie Mitchell, a member of another sorority she'd always talked to at joint events.

"Hey, Leslie." Ronni smiled and leaned over to hug the woman before sitting beside her in an awkwardly positioned lawn chair. "What are you doing here, girl? I thought you lived in Tampa."

"You have a good memory. I did." Leslie beamed at Ronni with open admiration. "Yep. I moved there right after school. Then a couple of years ago, I relocated to Chicago and married Skip Baker."

"Oh, you married Skip? You two make a great couple. He was always nice," Ronni said, nodding, thinking she should have thought to match them together. "And so were you."

"Well, thank you. You, too. You were one of the few girls in your sorority I could actually stand," Leslie said jokingly. Ronni laughed, accepting the comment for what it was, knowing that Leslie had had her run-ins with notoriously snobbish sorors like Stephanie. "Yeah, Skip and I always kept up with each other through e-mail, since we were both in microbiology, and then it just started to get more serious. He wrote the nicest letters. Ronni, I was hooked."

"That has to be love, to leave sunny Tampa," Ronni said, more to herself than Leslie. *Would I do that for Jeff?* She lay back on her chair, imagining Jeff sending her e-mails. She snickered and shook her head, because even though he was a romantic, she just couldn't picture him at his computer writing sweet letters. Ronni focused on the geese that were scrambling over each other to retrieve pieces of bread being tossed by children at the other side of the pond.

Leslie laughed, shaking her own head in reminiscence, then dropping her voice to a more cagey tone and grinning at Ronni. "But what about you? Was that you who came with Jeff Conley?"

"Yeah," Ronni said, briefly looking in the direction of the men by the grill. "Met him here, actually."

"Either way, with Jeff is with Jeff." Leslie turned in her seat to look at Jeff. He was talking loudly with his frat at the grill, the center of attention. Leslie muttered three short *mm*'s. "That man is fine. Looks better than I remember, and I remember him looking pretty good. When did you hook up with him?"

"A couple of weeks ago, I ran into him at my father's house." Ronni noticed a woman near the food canopy staring at her with a peculiar smile. The thin woman was best described with one word: beige. Her hair was a light brown, closer to blond. Her skin was honey-colored and she had hazel eyes. To top it off, she was wearing a taupe knit jogging suit with a white shell. Ronni smiled in return and nodded before quickly looking away.

"Girl"—Leslie stretched out the word like a drum roll—"you sound so casual about it. Don't you remember how we used to drool over him at the cafeteria? You were so nervous, you couldn't eat your food if he sat down with Stephanie. And speaking of Steph, she's going to freak out!"

"Stephanie?" Ronni stiffened at her name and her eyes darted around all the other women talking amongst themselves—except for the beige one, whose gawking made Ronni uncomfortable. "She's not here, is she? I thought she lived in Portland."

"I'm not sure it's Portland, but wherever she is when she hears the news, she is going to freak out." Leslie searched Ronni's face to see how she would take her next comment. "I know you were roommates and all, but did she work your nerves in school as much as she worked mine?"

"I know she was a bit conceited and not exactly the girlfriend type, but I kind of liked her in college. She was different."

"Oh, she certainly was different." Leslie smirked snidely. "You two were so different, I didn't even know how you roomed with her."

Ronni was about to explain when Leslie put her drink down on the grass. "I'll be right back, Ronni. I've been sitting up here sipping on these piña coladas and I've got to go to the bathroom, then I'm going to find Skip. See what he wants on his plate."

"Oh, sure." Ronni waved an unconcerned hand in the air and looked around at the beautiful scenery. Penny had a nice flower garden over on the right.

"Hi," the beige woman said. She had been circling nearby, and now that Leslie left, she seized the opportunity to approach Ronni. From a distance the woman looked attractive, but up close, she was strikingly beautiful. Her beauty fell into the model or actress class. She tentatively sat on Leslie's chair. "I know you from somewhere," she declared, balancing her plate in her lap and pointing at Ronni.

"Did you attend Columbia?" Ronni asked, thinking she also recognized her.

She shook her head. "I'm April Morgan, does that sound familiar?"

Concentrating, Ronni continued to search April's face. "Not really. Maybe we're sorors," she offered.

"No, I went to DeVry." April placed her chin on her fist. "But I'm a computer programmer for Ernst and Young. Maybe I was a consultant at your company?" she suggested.

Ronni shook her head. The words *idle rich* haunted Ronni too much to explain that she didn't work. Yet nothing about April was ringing a bell.

"Penny said your name's Ronni? What's your last name?" April tried another approach.

"It's Veronica, actually. Veronica Hampton." Ronni opened her hands, hoping her name provided more help.

Something clicked with April, and her face lit up in recognition. "Oh! I know some Hamptons." She scooted forward on the chair. "Are you related to Tamara Hampton?"

Ronni's expression changed as though a veil of indifference had suddenly fallen over it. "No," she snapped. Then, realizing how rude she'd been, she amended her answer to, "Yes."

April frowned, not sure what to make of Ronni's answers. "Um, I mean, her maiden name is Pritchard, it's her husband who's—"

"My father," Ronni said, finishing the sentence in a way the woman didn't expect.

"Oh." April blinked, not knowing where to rest her eyes. She ended up studying her plate of food. "Then I don't suppose I met you at the wedding," she mumbled, remembering that there weren't many people on the groom's side of the church.

On second thought, I don't think you look familiar anyway, Ronni deduced. At the mention of Tamara's name, Ronni had given up on trying to identify April. "I think I just have one of those familiar-looking faces," Ronni said and pushed herself out of her chair. "I'd better see what's taking Jeff so long with my food."

April had been hoping to make a new friend, but judging by Ronni's icy reaction, she supposed there was little chance of that. She decided she'd better seek out her own date and walked over to the garage where he was playing a boisterous game of Spades.

"Is it ready?" Ronni called to Jeff as she made her way across the grass. "Whoa—look out, sweetie," she said, touching the head of the toddler, Carolyn. The baby was screaming and holding on to Ronni's legs for dear life as she watched carefully to see if she'd escaped whoever was chasing her. When she considered that she did, she ran back into all the fun, giggling and screeching at the top of her lungs. It was a mild diversion that put Ronni in a more festive mood by the time she reached Jeff.

"Hey, I was just about to come get you," Jeff said, untying a faded green apron that informed viewers he was Master of the Grill. To bolster its claim, the apron showed an animated spatula, tongs, hamburgers, and chicken hovering over a grill with fire shaped like a crown. It was a ridiculous garment whose domesticity contrasted with Jeff's modern, bachelor stylishness.

Jeff beamed, delighted that Ronni joined him at the exact moment he was removing his masterpiece from the fire. Most of the fellas had left for other diversions and only one guy stood around, drinking a beer. "Grab the plates," Jeff said to Ronni as he took the fish from the grilling basket.

Jeff noticed that Ronni had a peculiar expression on her face. Though she was smiling, she gathered the tableware robotically. "What's wrong?" he asked as he divided the salmon onto the sturdy paper plates.

"Hmm?" Ronni didn't meet his eyes, watching his hands work carefully to keep the fillet halves from breaking apart. She smiled at how thorough he was about the presentation, like a bona-fide chef.

"You look funny," he said.

"Really?" Ronni asked, consciously clearing up her face. "I guess it's just . . ." Her eyes darted up to his and then to their food. She didn't want to burden him with her neuroses and tried to appear more cheerful. "I'm starving! Everyone's eating, and their food smells so good—I wanna eat!"

"Cool, then we're ready," Jeff said, reassured.

When Ronni saw the relieved look on his face, she knew she was right not to weigh him down with her catty problems. She could only imagine how Jeff would respond to her whining, "I don't like that girl. Her, over there in the beige." He would be within his rights to dump her depressing butt as fast as he could put it into words. So, she was determined to squash it and simply avoid April for the rest of the barbecue.

Handing Ronni a plate, Jeff led them to the canopy where the food was being served.

As they passed by an ear-piercing group of little kids at play, Ronni's heart went out to the youngest. "How does Carolyn know not to run down to that pond? I would be worried sick if I had a toddler and my backyard was so close to open water like that."

Jeff took a quick look at Ronni and followed her eyes to the little girl she was talking about. "Oh, Frank's daughter?" At the moment, the child was oblivious to the pond and fascinated by a spinning bubble machine. "That teenager there," Jeff said, pointing out a robust youth, "is her big brother Cody. He's keeping an eye on her."

Ronni looked doubtfully at Jeff because the boy he'd shown her was absorbed in conversation with other teens. Suddenly, as if to prove Jeff right, the toddler took off running to catch a bubble traveling on the wind. Ronni froze, ready to dash across the lawn and head off the girl, but Cody sprung into action. He caught Carolyn, scooped her up, swung her around, and tickled her before placing her back with the other kids.

"Believe it or not, we men can multitask, too." Jeff's mouth crept up in a knowing smile. Ronni cocked her head at him, impressed. He'd taken her question seriously, deciphered the precarious situation, and identified the solution within seconds. He would make a great father, she thought. Jeff loaded generous portions of the side dishes onto each of their plates and they sat down at a long table with a lively bunch of people.

If she had a belt, Ronni would've loosened it. It was a good thing her dress had an empire waist because, though no one else would have noticed, her tummy bulged. The salmon was marinated with lemon, pepper, and an herb Ronni couldn't identify. She thought it might be basil. Whatever Jeff used, the fish was delicious—even better than he'd hyped it to be. And the side dishes Penny made—potato salad, green salad, baked beans, macaroni and cheese and banana pudding—put her over the top. Ronni finished her entire plate. She decided that her next task would be to learn how to cook.

At the moment, it was time for a trip to the ladies' room. Ronni stood up and, leaning on Jeff's shoulder, kissed his forehead. "That was delicious, babe. You can cook for me anytime you like."

Jeff captured her hand and tugged her down, pursing his lips for a proper kiss. She obliged, briefly pressing her lips to his.

"See, you thought I was lying about cooking," he said.

"Guilty as charged. I'll never doubt you again." She squeezed his cheeks and rewarded him with another peck. "Now where's the bathroom?"

As stuffed as she felt, Ronni could barely lift her feet in the thick grass. She could use a nap. She passed by Carolyn, who seemed to be having the same problem. The small face looked up at Ronni in distress and she rubbed her eyes with the back of her hands.

"You sleepy?" Ronni asked, stopping to pick her up. Carolyn opened her mouth to answer, and produced a yawn that answered the question. She clung to Ronni's neck gratefully.

"She's tired. I'll take her in," Cody said, coming out of nowhere.

"No, I've got her. I'll give her to Penny. She's inside, right?" Ronni rubbed Carolyn's back and the baby laid her head on Ronni's shoulder.

"Okay, cool," Cody replied with typical teenage non-chalance and went back to his friends. This was the first time Ronni had held someone so young since Benji was this age. She wondered if it was her biological clock or the close proximity of suitable husband material that made her so fascinated with the little girl.

Once Ronni opened the door to the screened-in back porch, Penny jumped up from one of the wicker chairs on the back porch where she and Frank were entertaining another couple.

"Oh, thanks, Ronni, I should've known she'd want a nap," Penny said, reaching for Carolyn, who stretched out her arms to her mother. "Hey, honey, are you ready for a nap?"

"Did you survive Jeff's fish?" Frank teased.

Ronni twisted her lips. "I'll have you know my man is a very good cook."

"All right. You say that now, but wait until tonight, when you get the runs—"

"Shut up, Frank." Penny cut him off and jerked her head for Ronni to follow her into the house. "I swear, they never quit."

"Where's the washroom?" Ronni asked, following behind Penny.

"There's one right down that hall." She pointed. "But why don't you come with me and use the one upstairs? I'll put her down and then I'll show you the house."

It sounded like a plan to Ronni. She really liked Penny and made a mental note to include her and Frank amongst her and Jeff's married friends. Funny, one good meal and Ronni was already back into her fantasy life with Jeff.

April found Jeff relaxing on one of the chaises by the water. The crowd had shifted to more mixed groups all over the lawn. "Hey, Jeff," she said, touching his arm.

"What's up, April?" Jeff opened his eyes and reached for her hand, holding it in his until she settled down on the chair, next to his legs.

"I think I made an enemy out of your girlfriend," April whispered, shrugging her shoulders.

A crease crept into Jeff's forehead. "What happened?"

"I asked her if she was related to Tamara Hampton," April said with an embarrassed chuckle.

Jeff looked up into the sky. "Oh, man, that's not good."

"I could tell by her face. You should have seen how fast she got away from me. She apparently doesn't like her stepmom."

"Are you surprised? You know Tamara better than anybody," Jeff said, nudging her body with his knee.

"Yeah, that girl's dangerous. I'd hoped she'd change as an old married lady," she said.

Jeff nodded in agreement. "Crazy, I'll cop to. Dangerous might be going a bit far."

"Oh, please." April rolled her eyes. "Don't you remember some of the tricks she used to pull on men? Fake pregnancies, she can't make her rent, mickeys? The whole nine."

"Mickeys?" Jeff's eyes bucked and he looked sideways at April as though she were pulling his leg.

"Come on," April said emphatically. "You remember." She smacked his leg with the back of her hand. "Remember that night I caught her trying to slip one into your drink and I cussed her out?"

Serious concern wrinkled Jeff's face and he scratched his chin. "Naw, I'd definitely remember something like that." He shook his head. "You must have me confused with one of your other ex-boyfriends."

"No. It was *definitely* you. I was crazy about you. That's why I got so mad," she said, then looked over at the pond and searched her memory. "Well, maybe I didn't tell you about it. But, trust me, the girl is wicked. She's as evil as they come."

"And what exactly did she expect to gain by drugging me?" he asked, really annoyed at this point.

"She was going to take you home, of course," April said, rolling her neck like it was obvious. "Maybe when I went to the bathroom or something. Who knows how her mind works? She'd make it look like you really wanted to leave with her. I was going to jack that cow up, 'cause I was serious about my Jeff. I just knew we were going all the way." April paused meaningfully to observe his reaction. He watched her without comment and placed an arm behind his head. "Anyway, I remembered she said she'd pulled this crap on some guy before, but I thought she was kidding. I mean, who does something like that? That's when I stopped talking to her. I didn't speak to her for years after that. I only went to her wedding out of curiosity. I wanted to see what kind of man would marry Tamara, especially since I heard he's a millionaire." April shook her head and looked at her feet.

"Let me tell you," Jeff touched April's elbow for emphasis, "even if I woke up with that demon, it wouldn't have meant a damn thing. I'd have been out of there the next morning like a bat out of hell. So all her little efforts would have been in vain."

"Yeah, but a few months down the line, you would get your pregnancy scare," April sneered.

"Man, bump that." Jeff had heard about women like

this, from movies mostly. Even though he trusted April, he found it hard to believe a real person—a black woman, at that—could be so underhanded.

"Well, I'm sorry to hear that Ronni's father got involved with her."

Jeff shooed a mosquito from his arm. "You? How do you think she and her mother are taking it?"

"Ronni seems like a nice person. How many years has it been now?" April asked, referring to Tamara's marriage to Ben.

Jeff looked into the sky for the answer. "Seven, I think . . . because of Benji."

"Oh? So there actually was a pregnancy in this case?" April pushed Jeff's knee with her hand and let it rest there.

"Yeah, and he's handsome and real smart, too," Jeff said with so much pride, you'd think it was his own son.

"Didn't take after Tamara then," April surmised. "So what's with Ronni's dad? Is he—uh-oh, she's coming back. I'd better clear out, she doesn't like me." April grabbed Jeff's hand and squeezed it, then hurried across the lawn to find her boyfriend.

Ronni was indeed on her way back, and she had caught some of their cozy scene as she walked toward them. She tried to push the jealousy back in her mind as she stood over Jeff with two plates of food covered in aluminum foil. "You ready to go?" she asked.

"It's early, yet. Sit down." Jeff pulled her onto his lap. Instinctively, Ronni allowed herself to settle, there, but immediately started making moves to get up.

"I'll find my own seat, thank you," she said sulkily.

Jeff easily held her still with one arm around her waist. "Uh-uh, relax." He took the plates out of her hands and placed them on the chaise by his legs. He touched her protruding bottom lip with his index finger. "What's this?" he asked, one side of his mouth smirking.

"Who is she and how do you know her?" Ronni couldn't believe the words were coming out of her mouth, but there it was—her feelings laid bare.

"I thought you met her," Jeff said, nuzzling her neck.

She pulled away. "Meeting her is one thing, snuggling together is another."

"I didn't peg you for the jealous type."

"I'm not jealous," she lied. "I just want to know how you know a girl who knows Tamara." Ronni's eyes went to April. She was over in the canopy, preparing some plates under the direction of her boyfriend. Every now and then, April stole a quick look at Jeff and Ronni.

"April and I used to hang out," he answered, squeezing Ronni's waist gently. Jeff hadn't given up on the thought that this evening could still turn out very pleasant. Her perfume filled his nostrils, he stared at her exotically black eyes, and something stirred in his loins.

"*Hang out* hang out? Or hang out, meaning you two slept together?" she asked petulantly.

"We were a couple," Jeff responded with a mild shrug of his shoulders.

Is that shoulder thing supposed to be an explanation? "And I guess that means you slept with her?"

"I'm a couple with you and we haven't been intimate, have we?" he cocked his head, mildly amused. Her jealousy was a new thing for him. He was kind of flattered.

"No. And that still doesn't answer my question," she said, searching his eyes.

"Ronni, baby, what's this about? You know I had a past. I was walking around in the world before I met you."

"Yeah, but how many of your exes am I going to have to run into on a daily basis? And while you were hanging out, were you hanging out with Tamara?" she spat out.

The smile left Jeff's face and he shook his head, incredulous. "You have got to be kidding me."

"Well, did you?" Ronni pressed.

A muscle skipped underneath the skin in Jeff's jaw. "Excuse me? Did I *what?*"

"Did you sleep with Tamara?" Ronni saw Jeff's involuntary warning signal, but she couldn't stop herself. It was like she was watching herself make this mistake from far off in space. She wanted to call down to herself to just *stop it,* but the stupid mortal Ronni just kept on pushing him away.

"I'm going to pretend you didn't ask me that question," Jeff said quietly and she felt his hold on her waist loosen.

Ronni realized she had probably crossed over into the territory of one of those needy women who accused her man of looking somewhere else. She wasn't sure what made her behave this way. Was this what love felt like? Wasn't it supposed to be happy, carefree, sunshine, and roses? This kind of behavior didn't fit into the equation unless you'd been married for a couple of years and your man wasn't paying attention to you. Or, you found some floozy's phone number in his britches. Ronni hadn't had enough experience with love to be so jaded.

Jeff was staring out over the pond; his eyes were narrowed at the sudden turn of events that changed this discussion into something there was no way he could have anticipated or avoided. He watched the ripples being made by the wind blowing on the lake and wanted to attribute her line of questioning to the fact that Tamara's name was mentioned in the scenario.

While on the surface Ronni was going through the motions of accepting their relationship, deep down he felt she still didn't trust him. He recalled their conversation where she listed trust as an issue in her past. If he had a time machine, he would go back and beat down the dude who wounded her so emotionally that she couldn't let go in a healthy relationship. He would just have to strive to be better than that guy, by proving to her that he was true. *Even while I'm lying?*

Jeff nuzzled her neck, "Listen, I'll tell you." He kissed her neck softly, finding resistance, but ignoring it. "I was with April," he kissed her chin lightly, "and we were a couple." He kissed her right next to her mouth. "And yes, we were intimate and Tamara was April's girlfriend. She dated my buddy. But that's all in the past and doesn't have anything to do with us. How much plainer do I have to make it?" He held her eyes for a moment, then kissed her squarely on the mouth, pressing against her resistant lips and opening his mouth over hers. He slipped his tongue past her lips, sought out her tongue and explored its surface until she responded. Jeff's hands solidly measured the size of her waist, kneading her gently in her midsection. His hands slid up her back and pulled her body into his until her breasts were pressed firmly against his chest. He felt her relaxing as she glided her formerly inactive hands to his shoulders and pressed her seat down in his lap. That movement spurred Jeff to lift his head from the back of the chaise and open his mouth completely to her. He thought she tasted spicier and sweeter than even the most popular barbecue sauce. He wanted her, and his desire was progressing beyond his control. Realizing where he was, he reluctantly withdrew his mouth from hers and peppered her mouth with small, wet kisses. Jeff opened his eyes dreamily and watched hers until they opened. They stared at each other, searching each other's eyes for clues as to how they should proceed. She laid her head against his chest and spoke first.

"I'm sorry," she said quietly.

"It's all right, babe. As long as you're being open with me, I can handle whatever." He held her in his arms and felt her body quiver against him. Jeff had to get Ronni off his lap. He liked this too much for a daytime picnic.

"Hey, you two, stop kissing," Yusef Gray said, coming near the clinging couple. "We're about to form lines for a dance. You remember any steps, Jeff?"

"What do you think?" Jeff said smugly, remembering when he used to lead all the steps around the parties.

"All right, stop smooching and come on then. You, too, Ronni. Your sorors are trying to think of one they can do, too." Yusef started back over to the garage, where they'd cleared out the card tables and brought in the CD player to give it the real party feel. Ronni started laughing when she heard the familiar house music boom loudly from the speakers.

"I guess I'd better go help the sorors, or we'll end up doing National Step over and over again." She smiled and squeezed Jeff's neck, then pulled back, put one hand on his cheek, and looked into his eyes. "I'm so sorry. I'm blessed that you even put up with me," she whispered.

"Oh, course I do, I lov—" Jeff couldn't believe what he was about to say and edged to more sturdy terrain. "You're my lady. You're the only one I'm thinking about."

As she got up to join the sorors, Jeff hoped she hadn't caught his slip-up. He stood up and stretched, then watched Ronni cross the lawn.

She smiled to herself at what he'd almost said.

Chapter Nine

When she realized she was humming to herself, Ronni's hand stopped in midair. It was on its way to clipping a diamond earring on her right ear. She looked back at the happy face in the mirror and smiled, then started laughing like a woman who had recently escaped from Bellevue.

Like a clueless idiot, she had convinced herself that her life was going along fine and that she didn't have time for relationships. Weren't Jeff's exact words "That doesn't make any sense"? He was so completely and totally right. "You were lying to yourself," she said to the face in the mirror. She shrugged her shoulders innocently as if to say, "Who knew?" Who knew, indeed? Being uncontrollably attracted to the man who was pursuing her made all the difference in the world. Ronni hated to admit it, being the modern-day feminist that she was, but she felt more like a woman. Yes, she watched *Oprah,* and she knew that a man was not supposed to complete you, but didn't Oprah also say that you needed to be honest with yourself? And to be honest, she felt more alive around Jeff. She felt sexy.

The daring evening dress Ronni had chosen for this date was a testament to just that. She'd gone shopping for a new outfit that morning and just *had* to get the Donna Karan fitted black evening dress with a silver-plated cutout on the hip. It was new in Karan's fall line and took a big chunk out of her bank account, but she knew it would be worth it when she saw the admiring look on Jeff's face after he saw her in this dress.

She glanced at her watch. "Where is my mother?" Ronni muttered. She had called her more than two hours ago. Now it was only an hour before Jeff was going to arrive. Beverly was supposed to be bringing her a diamond necklace to go with her outfit. Ronni went to her bedroom and opened her jewelry box. She took out the diamond tennis bracelet she'd gotten for her sixteenth birthday and placed it on her wrist, then sat at her vanity to examine her makeup. The mirror here was unforgiving, so if there was something wrong with her application, she'd know right away. The girl at the MAC counter in Neiman Marcus had been attentive and helpful, but Ronni wasn't sure of her ability to reproduce the results.

As she raised her left hand to her eye, she noticed the bracelet and had a discomforting thought. Ronni remembered Stephanie had worn it all the time in college, especially if she was going out with Jeff. Her mind took her back to one of the times when she was sitting on her bed watching Stephanie get ready to meet Jeff.

". . . So, you've got to train them," Steph had said, applying another coat of lipstick.

"Train them?"

"Yes. I, for example, am high-maintenance."

Ronni had laughed, but Stephanie didn't bat an eye. So Ronni tried to look more serious.

"I am! And I'm not ashamed to say it. I wear my diamond jewelry so he'll know he has to support me in the lifestyle to which I am accustomed. When we get married, of course." Steph checked her hair and practiced throwing it and producing come-hither looks Ronni assumed she intended to later use on Jeff.

She remembered Stephanie labeling her "low-maintenance" somewhere during the conversation without a hint of irony. *Your jewelry? Don't you mean the lifestyle to which* I'm *accustomed?* Ronni thought, but she let it go.

Now, Ronni could see there were signs all along that corroborated Jeff's claim that Stephanie didn't have a high opinion of her. "But with age comes wisdom," Ronni said aloud as she removed the bracelet from her arm and tossed it back into the jewelry box. She didn't need any reminders of what a dupe she had been in college, and she certainly didn't want any associations with Stephanie to arise in Jeff's head.

She picked up the phone and dialed her mother's cell number. It rang twice and just when Ronni was afraid it was going to voice mail, her mother picked up.

"I'm parking at your building right now," Beverly said.

"Well, it's about time."

"All right, Miss. Just be ready to buzz me up."

"Okay."

Ronni left the door open a crack so that when her mother arrived, she could let herself in. She returned to the bathroom to put on some perfume.

"Where are you?" her mother called from the living room.

"In here!"

Beverly walked to the bathroom and stood in the doorway looking at Ronni with a big smile. "Oh, honey, you look incredible. Very sexy and yet very sophisticated."

"Thanks, Mom," Ronni said, looking at Beverly. She was wearing a straw hat, baby-blue velour sweats with sandals, and carrying quite a large tote bag. "Good heavens. What all did you bring?" Ronni gestured at the bag as she moved past her mother. Beverly followed her to the bedroom and started placing the contents on the bed.

"Well, I couldn't remember which necklace you'd

asked for, so I brought a few with me. Then I stopped by Walgreens to get you some control-top panty hose."

Ronni rolled her eyes. "I have panty hose. Actually, with this cutout, I have to wear stockings."

Beverly poked at Ronni's stomach. "What? No control top?"

"Mom!" Ronni crossed the floor to the full-length mirror and looked at herself critically, turning her body to the side to see if she saw a pudge. Since she was in her slippers, she had to stand on tiptoes to see how she would look. "Do you think I need it?"

Beverly removed her hat and joined her at the mirror, silently comparing the true and the reflected images of Ronni. "No, I guess not." She turned from the mirror and sat on Ronni's bed. "I guess I was thinking about the days when you were carrying a few extra pounds. These hose are probably not your size anyway. But aren't those stockings hard to keep up? You don't want to be constantly tugging on them during the gala."

"There are elastic bands on the top of them to keep them up."

"So, I guess you're not wearing any panties?" Beverly said, curling her mouth in a twist.

"Yes, Miss Nosy. For your information I'm wearing a high-cut thong."

"Thongs? What is it with you young women and those thongs?"

"What do you mean 'you young women'? This is the first time I've ever worn a thong . . . and I sure as hell didn't wear them when I had a fat ass."

"All right. I don't need all of that language," Beverly scolded, pursing her lips.

"What did I say? Geez." Now Ronni wished she had asked one of her girlfriends to borrow some jewelry, even if none of them had as great a selection as Beverly. Her mother was getting on her nerves.

In a matter of minutes, she'd already managed to make Ronni self-conscious about her dress, wonder whether she'd end up tugging at the stockings all night, and wouldn't let her talk and move around her own apartment the way she wanted. As Ronni opened the velvet cases and looked at the diamond necklaces Beverly had placed on the bed, her heart sank. "Mom, these are all too fancy. It's just at the DuSable. Half the people will be wearing African garb."

"And the other half will be dressed to the nines. Like you," Beverly said. Taking a cue from her daughter's disappointment, she chose one of the least ornate necklaces and placed it around Ronni's neck.

Ronni went to sit in front of the vanity mirror. "That's too much," she said under her breath.

"It looks elegant. It goes with the dress."

"Yeah, but you can dress this gown up or down. Couldn't you find the single diamond teardrop I wanted? On the thin silver chain?" she whined.

"I looked through my stuff and I don't know what you're talking about. Are you sure it was me you saw wearing it?"

Ronni unclamped the lace necklace with the large teardrop cluster. "Yes. At the—at the thing for breast cancer at the Park Hyatt. You wore that red dress."

"What . . . ?" Beverly was searching her brain for any images of the jewelry that fit this description. When it dawned on her, she waved a dismissive hand. "Oh. *That* necklace. Oh, honey, I got rid of that one years ago."

"Why? That one was cute and more contemporary."

"Yeah, not my style," she said, looking at Ronni with a raised eyebrow. When Ronni continued to look perplexed, Beverly elaborated. "I found it in your father's closet and *assumed* it was for me. I was going to surprise your father by wearing it that night. He was surprised, all right. Then I wore it to that gala out of spite." Beverly chuckled and returned the necklace Ronni didn't like back to its box.

Ronni frowned. It occurred to her that her mother had gone through a lot of pain before she and Benjamin finally separated, things Ronni hadn't even known about. She felt guilty for wishing she hadn't invited her mother over. This was the closest Beverly had been to preparing for a gala in years, which was probably the reason she brought so much stuff along to help Ronni get ready. Who was she to deny her mother that pleasure? She turned to her mother in a more understanding attitude.

"Well . . . let me try one of the other ones. It's getting late."

Beverly turned and looked at her with her hands on her hips. "You know, honey, that dress is pretty ornate in itself. Stand up."

Ronni did as she was told.

"Yeah, Ronni," Beverly said as she looked her over carefully. "With that thing on the hip and your earrings, it already looks very dressy. Wear your diamond bracelet and you're set. Keep it simple. Let me see your shoes."

"They're over there in that bag from Bloomie's. And I can't wear that bracelet—your jewelry isn't the only one with issues." She watched as Beverly found the shoes and examined them critically.

Beverly turned to her with a pronounced frown, realizing what Ronni had said. "What issues could that bracelet have? Your father and I gave that to you for your Sweet Sixteen."

"I'll tell you all about it next time. But look—you've got to clear out. Jeff will be here any minute."

"What's he wearing? With those dreadlocks, he'll

probably be wearing African garb." Beverly laughed to herself. "And a kufi." She laughed more loudly at her own joke.

"Ha, ha." Ronni rolled her eyes. "He doesn't wear dreads anymore, smarty-pants."

"These shoes are cute, but too plain. Plus, you don't want to break in new shoes tonight. I brought you some dressier ones."

Although Ronni was dubious, the silver ones her mother brought were better, and—though she hated to admit it—more comfortable. She fought off Beverly's attempts to saddle her with a shoulder wrap, stuck with her own choice of a small purse, and refused an umbrella (even though her mother heard it was going to rain) before finally shuffling Beverly out the door. And not a moment to soon. Jeff called to say he was in the lobby, probably at the same time Beverly was on her way down in the elevator.

Ronni looked around her apartment and had a moment of doubt about letting him up. She was frankly embarrassed that her place was so uninviting. She thought she could say she was coming down, but figured that would seem uncouth. *I should've asked Mom to bring some framed pictures. She would've wondered what the deal was, but at least I wouldn't look so . . . so lonely.* She examined the word in her mind. Lonely? Is that what she was?

Ronni's nerves were all in a bundle as she waited a few feet from the door until she heard Jeff's knock. This was it. This was a *real* date with the *real* man she'd wanted since forever. And now there was no obstacle to their dating except an apartment door. She thought the sound of her heels walking down the foyer and approaching the door would provide her with the grand entrance she was denied due to it being her place and took a deep breath before placing her hand on the doorknob, thinking, *Here goes.*

"Hey, you," Ronni said with a huge genuine grin.

Jeff had a matching smile on his face until he got a look at her. Then it dropped right away, he widened his eyes, and drew in a deep breath. "Oh, baby. You. Are. Stunning."

"You look mighty handsome yourself."

They stood looking each other over. Jeff was wearing a three-button midnight-blue suit with cuffs on the pants, a white shirt, a black silk tie embossed with a pattern, and a matching black handkerchief and black shoes. His hair was freshly cut and he had a small diamond stud in one ear. Ronni had never seen him wear an earring before and she liked it.

Ronni smiled, thinking they matched perfectly. She caught Jeff's eyes lingering on the skin exposed by the cutout in her dress, then noticed the bouquet of white roses dangling in his hand and snapped out of her daze.

"Are those for me? Oh—and come in."

"I don't think my legs will let me move." They both laughed. Jeff was joking, but felt kind of unsteady as he walked through the door. Once he was inside, he turned to watch her close the door as though he couldn't wait to get another look at her. He reflexively opened his arms and Ronni readily fell against his hard body. His head rested against her cheek and he gave her a passionate squeeze. She could feel his heart beating in his chest. She felt her nervousness evaporate and turn into something more urgent. As she inhaled his cologne and felt the heat of his hands at the small of her back, her legs betrayed her and she leaned more heavily against him. He kissed her cheek.

"Mmm . . . did I tell you you are beautiful?" he said quietly.

"You said stunning."

"That, too."

If she didn't break this hug soon, they weren't going to make it to the gala. Not that she was on solid ground in knowing what to do exactly, but the way her body was responding to his closeness, she felt pretty confident that her enthusiasm would make up for her lack of experience. "Here, let me put those flowers in a vase." Ronni took his hand and led him down the foyer into her living room. She took the flowers from him and he began to wander around the open space. "White roses again. Do you know what you're saying?" She wanted to know the answer to this question, but she also wanted to draw some attention away from his scrutiny of her apartment.

Jeff turned to offer a smile while he watch her go into the dining room. "I purely love your purity and I am innocent."

Ronni laughed. "Cute. But close enough," she said, finding a square-cut heavy glass vase to display her flowers. She decided they would be perfect on the dining room table. "Let me just get my purse and we'll be on our way."

Jeff stuffed his hands in his pockets and wandered around the communal areas. "I love your place."

Ronni called back from her bedroom. "Really? Thanks." She rushed around her bedroom quickly, trying to restore order to the chaos she and her mother had made. What if, later on tonight, he wanted to come back to her place? She snatched all the discarded hosiery packages, unwanted shoes, and extra clothing and threw them into the closet. She checked her makeup one more time, grabbed her purse, and returned to Jeff. She found him in the kitchen.

"When do I get the full tour?"

"There's not much left. It's nothing like your place."

"No, this is trendy," he said, looking at the huge Romare Bearden painting on her dining room wall. "Your apartment looks like something straight out of *Architectural Digest*. You must've thought my house was a cluttered mess."

"Actually, I liked yours better."

"Yeah, right," Jeff said, giving her a doubtful frown. "I can just see it. When we get married, you're going to throw out all my stuff."

Ronni stammered. How did she respond to that? Was it normal for men to just casually mention that they were thinking about getting married on the second date? Was it normal for Jeff? Maybe he was the reason why Stephanie had such vivid "Mrs. Jeff Conley" fantasies. Ronni looked at him sideways to see if he would hem and haw over a retraction. But Jeff was now checking out her steel and glass cabinets as if he hadn't said anything out of the ordinary. She decided she was overreacting. "Be honest. Which place would you rather have?"

"Yours."

"Which place would you rather *live* in?" Ronni tried again.

"Mine," he said. And just when she was about to claim victory, he added, "But move in all your stuff."

"Okay. I give up. I can see there's no arguing with you."

"That's one thing you'll discover about me. I don't like to argue."

"Says the lawyer. What's another thing?"

"Another what?"

"Another thing I'll discover about you?"

Jeff smiled devilishly and crossed the room to join her. "That, my dear, has yet to be discovered." He raised his eyebrows twice and leaned in for a kiss. Ronni pushed his shoulders.

"All right. Calm down, big boy. Let's go."

He sighed. "I guess we have to go to this thing."

"Yeah. I guess we do," Ronni's voice mirrored his resignation.

They didn't talk much on the way down in the elevator. They kept smiling and looking at one another like they couldn't believe they were actually in each other's company—as a couple.

When they got downstairs, Beverly's argument was vindicated since it was indeed raining. It was one of those nice summer showers that wasn't too heavy, came straight down, and made everything smell fresh. Jeff left Ronni in the lobby and went to bring the truck around. When he pulled up, Ronni indicated for him to stay in the truck and she could get the door for herself. However, he would not be deterred from his chivalrous duties. She noticed that he had removed his jacket to keep from exposing it to the elements.

Now that she was seated in the confines of his Navigator, her nervous tension started to return. When Jeff returned to the driver's seat, Ronni looked at him with a playful smirk as he pulled away. He fiddled with the CD player, scanning through various jazz artists, settling on Diana Krall when he noticed Ronni's eyes on him.

"What?" he asked.

"Do opposites attract?"

"Are we opposites?" He looked surprised at the assertion and glanced at her to see her nodding her head. "I thought we were alike. We attended the same college. We know the same people."

"But your place is a house. Mine an apartment. My car is a two-seater. Yours is a gas-guzzler."

"Ah . . . hold on. I take offense at that."

"Which? Gas-guzzler? It *is* a gas-guzzler."

"Yes. It happens to be. But that is an element of its design, not my preference. Your assertion is that we are opposites for the superficial choices we've made in big-ticket item purchases."

"Uh-oh. Why did I pick a fight with a lawyer?"

"No, hear me out." Jeff smiled because this was the real deal of relationships. Ronni being comfortable enough with him to share her opinions. "You've judged me as different from you because I chose a car I like, which fits my needs, as though it were a character flaw. I could pick on the design of your car, but I assumed it suits your needs. We—"

Ronni splayed her hands over her chest. "My car! What's wrong with my car?"

"I wasn't going to go there. My point is—"

"No." She pushed his arm. "Tell me—what's the complaint about my car? It's not damaging the environment or hogging the road. I can't even see the traffic around these SUVs."

Jeff cut his eyes at her and gave her a look that said, "Come on, you know." Ronni crossed her arms defensively and looked back. "What?"

"Yours is a vanity thing . . . more so than mine."

"No way!"

"Yes, it is. Can you drive more than one friend or family member in it at a time?"

Ronni opened her mouth to say something, but stopped, then looked out her side window. There was nothing to say. She didn't want to admit it, but she was sort of annoyed. What had started out as a friendly tease had once again turned on her to become an indictment of her solitude. With her face turned fully from him, her smile slipped away. She wasn't angry with Jeff. *Can't kill the messenger because you don't like the message,* she thought. It wasn't his fault that lately she was caught up in an endless loop of revelations that pointed out that her life was built around maintaining her isolation. She was right about their being opposites, except the distinction was that she was a recluse and he was outgoing. Ronni felt his large, warm hand touch her shoulder where it joined the neck. His thumb traced the line of her collarbone.

"Hey . . . where'd you go?"

Ronni looked over at him and tried to produce a smile, but it fell short.

"You're not mad, are you?" He stole frequent glances, trying to watch the road and her face at the same time. She shook her head, but didn't trust her voice enough yet to say anything. He wasn't sure what had just happened. "I wasn't saying you were vain. I wouldn't judge you by your car—other than you've got good taste. I was just saying it doesn't make us intrinsically different because we choose—"

"I know." Ronni cut him off, placing her hand over his and taking it down into her lap where she covered it with her other. Jeff intertwined his fingers with the hand on the bottom of the grasp. "I was just giving you a hard time. I actually did a presentation on this very same topic the night you came to my class."

"What? That people can't be judged by their cars?"

"Something like that, but more on the side of SUV owners. That they're not intent upon damaging the environment and they don't like paying high gas prices, but they like the luxury and utility of the big vehicles. And that it is our responsibility as auto dealers to put pressure on the automakers to give the people what they want—in a more environmentally friendly format."

He eyed her, impressed. "You're pretty serious about auto dealerships, huh, kiddo?"

"No. Not just any auto dealerships. Hampton's Auto Dealerships. I'm going to take our business to the next level. I've got to anticipate for the next century." She stuck out her chin proudly.

It just so happened that at that moment, Jeff needed to take his hand out of hers to make a left turn onto the property of the museum. But he was glad not to be holding her hand right then. He felt a pang of guilt in the pit of his stomach and he didn't know if that would have been transferred through their touch. Ronni noticed his sudden quietness and lack of response. She tried not to overthink it. After all, they had arrived at their destination.

"I'll drop you at the door and go ahead and park the car."

Ronni looked nervously at the people gathered around the entrance. "I wanted us to go in together. I won't melt."

"Out," he ordered, idling the car in front of the entrance. "Wait for me by the reception table."

"Yes, master," Ronni teased and got out of the car. She was immediately welcomed under the umbrella of her parents' friends, the Vincents, for the short walk to the door.

The affair turned out to be very well organized and the attendees could walk from room to room viewing the exhibits before sitting down to dinner. Jeff knew a lot about the artists and African-American history, and could explain most of what Ronni was viewing better than the placards prepared by curators. Ronni alternately spent time with Jeff and a group of women friends—most of them sorors—she would usually see at these events. In Jeff's company, she found it easier to be a carefree, social butterfly. It wasn't just his physical presence, it was also the notoriety of being there as his date. He often placed a hand at the small of her back while they were talking, and he certainly crossed the room to join her in conversation whenever she was speaking to a male in their age group. *Asserting his claim?* She smiled to herself and thought that if he were the jealous type, he should hang around when she was talking to the

older guys. Married or not, they were much more flirtatious and often bawdier than the young ones.

Several older women stopped Ronni to ask about her
parents, specifically her mother. Some were under the impression that Beverly was ill because they hadn't seen her
at any galas for years. She dispelled these rumors as best
she could but didn't even try to explain why Beverly was
never around anymore. She made a mental note to try to
get her mother to come to something in the near future.
Ronni used to urge her to go out frequently following the
divorce but gave up trying when she realized that accidentally bumping into Tamara might be too difficult for
her. Now Ronni was so involved in her classes that it hadn't
occurred to her to pester her mother lately.

Thankfully, Tamara had not attended this gala. According to some of her mother's friends, they hadn't
seen her or Ronni's father at anything either. This gave
Ronni pause because Tamara loved to show off her
clothes and newly acquired position in society. Ronni
didn't read much into that information but was pleased
to know that the coast was clear for Beverly's return.

At the end of the party, Ronni joined her sorors to do
the Electric Slide. She tried to pry Jeff out of his seat to
come to the dance floor with her, but he gave her a "no
way" look and enjoyed watching her dance before joining a group of young men outside for cigars. After the
live band started to play steppers' music, the women
raided the men's gathering on the tent-covered deck
and brought back their dance partners. Benjamin, who
was considered the prime choice of dance partner in his
day, had taught Ronni how to step when she was thir-
teen. She knew how to move her feet with the best of
them. Though Jeff was no Benjamin, he could hang and
surprised Ronni with a few creative moves. Renee Poplar
winked at her on the dance floor and Shelly Jones gave

her a furtive thumbs-up on her gorgeous companion. When the evening ended, Ronni had a good idea of what it would have been like to have been dating Jeff back at Columbia.

Except for one thing.

After the gala ended, Jeff drove Ronni to her building. When they pulled in front of her building, the rain had stopped. Their conversation about the evening's events tapered off and they sat looking at each other in a relaxed silence. Although she was nervous about the prospect of inviting him up, Ronni was a bit disappointed that he hadn't parked the car.

"Uh . . . why don't you park the car?" she asked, trying out Jeff's usual posture of emotional honesty.

"Oh, well . ." Jeff sighed and shifted the car into park. "I was afraid you might say that."

"Afraid?" Ronni laughed weakly, suddenly embarrassed. She looked at her hands. *I guess the evening didn't go as well as I thought.*

Jeff placed a hand on her forearm to draw her eyes back to him. "Yeah . . . because I really do want to come up."

"Then, why—"

He squeezed her arm gently to stop her. Jeff seemed to be having a hard time forming his words and Ronni feared the worst. He shook his head and laughed quietly. "I can't believe I'm even saying this." He placed both his hands on the steering wheel and looked out his side window.

"Just tell me," she said, barely audible, looking down.

He turned back to her, adjusting in his seat until his whole body was facing her, and turned down the radio. "Okay, look, I'm no angel . . ." He chewed on his lip, still searching for the right words. "You knew me in college . . . and you probably know I've been with a lot of women."

"A—a *lot?*" Ronni said cautiously. She had a vision of a ballroom full of beautiful women in all shapes, colors, and sizes standing around at some sort of horrifying Jeff's Former Lovers' Convention.

"That's not what I'm trying to say—I don't mean, like, hundreds or anything. I just mean that since you knew me, I've had my share of long-term and short-term relationships. Or, should I say, short-term and shorter-term relationships? As I'm sure you've had your share of yours."

Wanna bet?

Jeff looked intently at her. She nodded to let him know she was following him, although she wasn't sure she was. "But throughout them all there was always one constant. You."

Ronni had been looking at him mostly with her head and her body facing forward, to shield herself from possible rejection. But now she altered her posture to reflect his. "I—I'm not sure I understand—"

"After each breakup my mind always returned to you. Hell, sometimes *during* the relationship I found myself thinking about you. About how different a relationship might be if it were with you."

Ronni was quiet. Her face was burning and her breath was quickening. *Could Jeff actually be saying this?* She wanted to pinch herself. She thought she was the only one plagued by lingering fantasies about someone she'd never even dated. Never even talked to, really. And though her eyes wanted to be riveted to his—wanted to fully commit this moment to memory—the emotional power of the situation made her eyes once again return to the safety of her hands. She should've known Jeff wasn't going to let her off that easily. His hand caressed the side of her cheek before gently lifting her chin. He still didn't have her eyes.

"Ronni, look at me," he said softly.

She looked up and was met with the most affectionate gaze she'd ever seen from a man.

"And as much as I would love to come up . . . I've waited a long time for this—for *you*. I don't want ours to be another one of those relationships. I don't even want it to start the same as the relationships we've had in the past."

"No chance of that now, I guess," Ronni joked feebly, trying to deflect his intensity. To her relief, he did chuckle a little.

"No. I guess not." Jeff leaned on the armrest and rested his head on his hand. "I should stop being a chump and get upstairs."

"I don't know what all this fuss is about anyway. I was just inviting you up for cookies." Ronni shrugged naively and they both laughed. Jeff started picking at the crease in his slacks. "Besides, aren't you the one who's always giving me the—" Ronni raised her eyebrows twice to indicate his sexual teasing.

Jeff smiled and leaned in to raise his eyebrows at her right then. "Yeah—I'm good at that, huh?"

They both laughed. Ronni gently punched his arm on the shoulder and then opened her hand to soothe the area she'd struck. His biceps were rock-hard and his body threw off a sultry heat that the fine fabric of his shirt couldn't possibly contain.

Jeff's familiar, handsome face was extremely close to hers. She watched his deep brown eyes as they darted back and forth between both of hers. Her hand firmly gripped his shoulder and squeezed. She then slowly, smoothly slid her hand to the back of his neck. There, her fingers played with the line of his freshly cut hair while her thumb found the earring intriguing. Now there was nothing but pure desire behind Jeff's hooded eyes as he pressed his lips tightly together and swallowed hard. He closed his eyes, as though the absence of visual stimuli would stop the overpowering hunger he was feeling for the woman across from him.

With Jeff's eyes closed, Ronni found more confidence and her lips faintly connected with the small cleft in his goateed chin before sliding up to the corner of his mouth. She felt Jeff release a deep sigh from his nostrils, the breath brushing her cheek. Eyes or no, his hand deftly found her waist. He pulled her closer to him and his mouth skillfully took control of their kiss. First he kissed her lips full on, their mouths closed. Next, they peppered each other's lips with small, wet kisses. Then, all tension replaced by passion, they both explored each other's mouths with willful abandon, tongues pressed together and caressing. Soon he moved the armrest from between them and pushed their upper bodies together.

When Jeff realized that one of his hands had traveled the full length of Ronni's feminine form and was now gently squeezing a perfect palmful of breast, he abruptly unlocked his lips from hers. He moved the hand to cradle the back of her neck. As he pressed his forehead to hers and tried to catch his breath he noticed Ronni's hand on his thigh—mighty close to making him lose all resolve to take things slowly.

Ronni, who was watching his eyes intensely, followed them now to see her hand. She saw what he saw and slowly moved her hand away. During the kiss, she must have been trying to steady herself by leaning against him. But Ronni supposed she had let her hand slide up his thigh the more she pushed her mouth into his. Thinking how much she wanted to get inside his mouth, the nervous tickling feeling at the bottom of her stomach connected to a more hot-blooded one at the center of her womanhood, which confidently asserted that it wanted him inside of her.

Jeff looked at Ronni's stiff nipples, amplified by the

heaving of her chest. All he could do to stem his flow of longing for her was to close his eyes and fall back into his leather seat. He took in and let out a deep breath. Ronni slunk back in her chair, too, but he was facing the windshield and she was still facing him. She watched his chest expand with his breath and saw that muscle working in his jaw. She'd seen it before. It normally meant he was mad. It wasn't the case this time.

"Jeff . . . I didn't mean to—"

Without looking at her, he held up a hand. His voice was very husky and very quiet. "Could you give me a moment?"

"Oh . . . sure."

He rested his forehead in his left hand, then put his elbows on his thighs and supported his entire head on his hands, covering his eyes with the fingertips. Ronni watched his back move up and down with his breathing, and was just about to touch him when he looked up at her with a small smile.

"Now . . . what was I saying?"

She smiled uncertainly. "Huh?"

"Something about taking it slow, right?"

"Oh, yeah, that. You don't want to come up for cookies."

Jeff's eyes narrowed and reminded her of the previous moment they were pathetically trying to place behind them. "*Lord knows* I want to come up for cookies." He held his right hand out to her. It wasn't steady. "My hands are shaking, I want so much to go upstairs and taste your fine cookies."

Ronni grasped the extended hand and they both gave a small laugh. She held his hand while he continued his explanation. "But . . . whether it's solely my fantasy or not, I want our first time together to be special. So I have something planned for us next weekend. On Venetian Night."

Ronni's mind raced with the possibilities. "On a boat?"

"Of course, on a boat. What other way is there to do Venetian Night?"

"You own a boat?"

"It's a yacht. I time-share with a bunch of other people. You don't get seasick, do you?" He looked worried. He had been so busy planning their night that it hadn't occurred to him his plans could be out the window in one fell swoop.

"No. Not at all." She squeezed his hand. "I'm excited." Her smile was a testament to that.

"Great. Me, too." He carried her hand to his mouth and kissed it. Her face suddenly became cloudy.

"So wait—does that mean we won't see each other for a whole week?"

"What? Hell no. You think I'm going to wait a week to see my baby?" He smiled subtly at her and bumped his knee against hers. "You'll just have to resist the temptation to have sex with me."

"Oh. It's on *me*, is it?" she teased.

"Mm-hmm. I can control myself. You're the one who's pushing the envelope."

Ronni was going to joke back, but that was the easy way out. Something in his words struck her as too true to take lightly. Realizing that—for the first time—she truly desired a man and everything that assertion entailed, her voice came out rather quietly. "It *is* rather difficult . . . especially when I'm close to you . . . like I am now."

"I know," Jeff said, his face regaining its earnestness. "I thought about that, too."

"Then, what do we do?"

"No home dates. We go to neutral ground. Like the movies and dinner and stuff."

"Like the movies and dinner and stuff." Ronni vacantly repeated his words, like it was the dullest thing she'd ever heard. It wasn't that she had suddenly become Ms. Red-

Hot Mama. It was just that Jeff expressed an interest in having things start differently for them than either of their relationships had in the past. For him, that meant delaying sex. But for her it had already started differently. She wanted Jeff. She was ready to let her guard down and make love to a man for the first time in her life. Her mind nudged forward the scene of his hand on her breast, squeezing her nipple. She could feel the heat in her thighs just thinking about it.

Every other guy she had ever dated had been a dinner, a movie, and stuff.

"It's only for a week," Jeff said, watching as her face registered a setback.

He knew she was a virgin in college, but now he was sure that this was a sexually assertive woman who was used to getting what she wanted, when she wanted, and from whom she wanted. *Just look at her. She's gorgeous. She's wondering what kind of potato-headed chump did I go out with who can't even come upstairs and satisfy me right now?*

He looked at her; she was staring wistfully out the front window with those onyx eyes. The rain was starting again. The shadows made patterns on her skin that drew attention to its flawlessness. *Fuck it,* he thought and started to shift the car into drive to go and park, but just then Ronni said something he didn't catch.

"Sorry?" he asked.

"You'd said it might be only your fantasy that our first night be special. And I was just saying it's mine, too—my fantasy, too."

"So you'll wait?"

"I've waited twenty-seven years. One more week isn't going to kill me, especially if I get to see you during it." She leaned over and kissed his cheek, then gathered up her purse. "There is a new Denzel Washington movie opening this Wednesday."

"Oh, yeah. I want to see that, too. So that's a plan."

Ronni opened the door and got out. The car pinged maddeningly until she shut the door. Jeff rolled down the window and Ronni leaned in. "But if I get hit by a bus or something before Venetian Night, I'm going to come back and haunt you for denying me my chance to experience carnal pleasure." She smiled, pointing an accusing finger at him, before turning it into a wiggling wave and heading through the doors of her building.

As he watched Ronni waiting for her elevator, it all suddenly registered with Jeff. His eyes widened and his head jerked to look out the front windshield as if trying to remember something. *Twenty-seven years?* He quickly tried to run all their conversations through his mind to see if there was another clue. Something about trust being an issue, something about no time for relationships, but nothing really telling. *She couldn't be! No way . . . Ronni is still a virgin!*

Jeff looked back through the glass to where she was waiting for the elevator, but Ronni was gone. He put the car in drive and pulled off. He didn't know what to think about her possible virginity. It definitely made him more apprehensive about their upcoming night together, but he was also flattered that she had decided to share her first experience with him. *She was ready to do it tonight. She was more than ready.* But then again, being a virgin, she would have nothing to compare to his sexual prowess, right?

He felt like a cad, but it was important to him that she knew he had skills. Legitimate skills. Jeff had envisioned a night of passion where he pulled out his most reliable tricks, the ones he was not inclined to perform on just anyone. They were guaranteed to bring a woman multiple orgasmic pleasures. If his suspicions about Ronni were correct, he would have to revise his technique to accommodate her comfort and inexperience. *But she didn't touch me like she didn't know her way around a man.* Maybe she was one of those virgins who did everything in the Kama Sutra except actual intercourse. Jeff doubted it. As fine as she was, if she had a reputation, he would definitely know. All the fellas in their circle would know. He recalled that at the gala earlier, quite a few guys asked him how they had met. Guys never cared about how-we-met stories—unless your woman was really fine or unattainable or, as in Ronni's case, both.

As he pulled into his driveway, he wasn't sure she had said anything to lead his mind down this virgin path in the first place. He would have to talk to her later this week and see if anything like that came up.

After all the dancing, wining, and dining, Ronni knew she really should take a shower or a bath, but she peeled off her clothes, wiped off her makeup, and only brushed her teeth before retiring to bed. She wanted to fall asleep with the smell of Jeff on her body. She wanted his cologne to scent her sheets so that her memory of the way his mouth joined with hers and the way his large hands outlined her body was made all the more vivid in her dreams. After she climbed under the covers, she lay smiling to herself, recalling each second of the wonderful evening with Jeff. She pressed her face into the pillow and screamed as loud as she could. That was little relief. Ronni would have to wait a week to discover the mysterious release her body yearned for, but she'd have fun getting to know Jeff better in the process.

Suddenly, Ronni jumped up, ran to her closet, turned on the light, and searched the top shelves until she found what she was looking for. Last year, she had sprained her knee and relied on a full-body pillow to prop her injured leg against while she slept. Now, she brought the pillow out of the closet and threw it in the bed. It would have to momentarily stand in for snuggling with Jeff.

Chapter Ten

In her dream, she and Jeff were on a picnic in the park by the lake and Ronni was wearing a Vera Wang wedding dress. It was a cute empire-waist slip dress with intricate beading around the top. He was dressed casually in a short-sleeved African-inspired top that was black with a Kente design on the deep V-neck collar and edge of the sleeves, along with blue-jean shorts and sandals. Jeff commented that the food she'd prepared was good and smiled at her. She smiled back and said, "Jeff . . . I love you." He stopped smiling and looked out over the water. Her face fell. *Did he hear her?* She moved in closer to snuggle with him and placed his arm around her shoulders. She tried again. "Jeff. I love you." He stood up, stony-faced, and turned his body away from her. She stood up and started screaming at him. "I love you! Why won't you say anything!" Now she was crying. He ran away and she was about to run after him when Tyler came from behind a tree and grabbed her by the waist. He said, "Let him go. You know he doesn't love you." Ronni was trying to pry Tyler's arms from around her.

The phone blared again. Ronni was disoriented as she finally settled her eyes on the clock by the bed. It was seven o'clock in the morning. She rubbed her eyes, sat up, and stretched. Her throat felt raw and her feelings were still hurt from the bad dream. Ronni looked toward the phone, which was now ringing again. *Who in the hell?* She felt both annoyed and worried about who would be calling her so early. It could be her family with some sort of emergency. After all, her parents weren't getting any younger. She looked at the caller ID and saw that the phone number indicated someone was in the lobby. She trudged to the living room to turn on the television, still rubbing her eyes. She saw some sort of newspaper article being held to the camera downstairs, obscuring the face of her visitor, and answered the phone. "Hello?"

"Open the door, heifer." She could tell by the voice that it was Cornell. He took down the paper and looked into the monitor. Ronni cursed under her breath and pushed the phone buttons to open the door downstairs. She opened her own door a crack and went back to her bedroom to get her robe. She shook her head because she knew she was in for a tongue-lashing. She didn't feel up to it. It was like all her energy had been sapped out by her dream argument with Jeff. Sure enough, she could hear Cornell from her bedroom once he entered the front door.

"So, you don't return my calls for weeks after you bent my ear about your lame-ass problems. *You* asked for *my* advice. I called Aunt Bev to see if you were still alive. I know she called you. Yet you *still* didn't call me!" he bellowed, now standing in the doorway to Ronni's bedroom. "Then I see your picture in the *Tribune* magazine. On the social pages of all places! With Jeff Conley!" He threw the paper on the bed, just missing Ronni's head, where she was kneeling, trying to find her other house shoe.

She glared at Cornell for throwing the paper so close to her head. She picked it up and saw a nice black and white photo of her and Jeff at the gala for the DuSable museum. Others were pictured at the same gala, but

Ronni and Jeff's was the most prominent photograph in the layout. In this photo, they made quite a striking couple. Ronni smiled, recalling that night. "We look good, don't we?"

Cornell cut his eyes at her and twisted his lips as though he couldn't stand her.

"Anyway. That was more than a week ago." Ronni went back to looking under the bed.

"No, she didn't just make a reference to the fact that it was more than a week ago!" Cornell shook his head as if Ronni was hopeless. Tired of the view of her robe-clad butt sticking up in the air, he looked under the bed, found her house shoe, and handed it to her.

"Thanks," Ronni said. He plopped down on the bed and pouted. She placed the shoe on her foot and headed out of the bedroom and into the kitchen. She needed coffee if she was going to have to deal with Cornell so early in the morning. The best way to neutralize one of his attacks was to shake things up. Not respond in the way he was anticipating. He would have to regroup or try another strategy to continue to follow her into the kitchen, but she was ready for him.

The truth was that she did miss Cornell, and she didn't like having to play these games with him. But she wasn't ready to admit she had done anything wrong. She wasn't ready to apologize. Ronni didn't want to come clean about that first evening with Jeff at his house and the promises he'd made. She didn't want to dissect Jeff's every action after the gala that night. And she didn't want to share his most private words to her. She covetously wanted to keep Jeff Conley all to herself.

Cornell came into the kitchen and sat on one of the stools at the counter. Ronni was wrong—he decided to follow her with the same exaggerated pout. "You want some coffee?" she asked.

"Yes. Starbucks wasn't even open when I passed by and there's no way I'm going to go into the office without my coffee fix." Cornell couldn't keep up the sulky act much longer. He wasn't used to it in the presence of this cousin. They were both the same age and were both only children, well until Benji came along, but Benji as a brother didn't really count. More or less, they were like siblings. That's why Ronni's snub of him now—when he could see she was experiencing something real for the first time in her life—hurt him so badly.

She gave him the first cup before pouring her own, then leaned across the counter and watched him as he sipped his coffee quietly and kept glancing at her. Ronni smiled, showing all the pearly-white teeth her lips would allow. Cornell lowered his coffee cup and smiled the same way, then they both started laughing. It was a deep belly laugh they couldn't explain. But when it tapered off, they would look at each other and then start up again.

"So, are you in love?" Cornell said after Ronni prepared her cup of coffee and settled down.

She smiled into her cup. "Oh, Cornell . . . I don't know. I'm definitely in *something*."

Cornell squinted at her and thought he saw something different in her face. "I never thought I'd see the day. You slept with him, didn't you!" His mouth was open in a wide gape.

Ronni shook her head. "No! No, I haven't."

"You wouldn't lie to me, would you?" The way she was glowing and looking so happy and relaxed, he was sure he had guessed right. She shook her head again and eyed Cornell critically, trying to consider whether to share her secret with him.

She pointed a warning finger at him. "This is nobody's business but our own Cornell."

"I wouldn't gossip about you to other people. You know that." Cornell waved a dismissive hand and looked offended. He sipped his coffee again and maintained a serious face.

Ronni looked at him for a moment. The truth was she did not know that. In high school, he had hurt her pretty badly by telling Ronni's friends' secrets to some popular girls he wanted to get in good with. It had worked to boost Cornell into the in-crowd, but it had hurt Ronni's relationship with her cousin for years afterward. Over the years he had apologized profusely, claiming that adolescence was brutal—especially if you were a young, gay, black man. Ronni had countered that it wasn't any better for a painfully shy, pretty girl, but he had made it worse. She never knew of another incident where he'd betrayed her trust. But then again, she hadn't really had any secrets worth guarding lately. She had run down every disastrous date she'd experienced in the past with no reservations. But this was different.

Cornell could imagine what she was thinking as she eyed him. "Will I ever be forgiven for high school?" he asked quietly.

"I've forgiven you. I just haven't forgotten," Ronni snapped back.

"To paraphrase our grandma: what good is burying the hatchet if you insist on marking the grave?" Cornell pointed to his chest. "You take me out to that grave site every couple of years, Ronni. And trust me, I mourn. *God knows,* I mourn."

Now Ronni felt bad. She looked into the creamy coffee. Cornell had never put it to her that way before. If she considered herself a forgiving person, she had to let go of the past. Holding on to it was only holding on to that insecure, shy girl who had little to do with the woman she now was. It also held Cornell to an image of himself he would rather let go. She touched Cornell's hand. His eyes looked awfully watery. "You're right. I'm sorry. I didn't even realize what I'd been doing. I guess it allowed me to be a smug bitch about the whole thing."

"It was the first thing my mind went to when I didn't hear from you. I thought . . ." His voice was low. "I thought . . . she still doesn't trust me."

"I know and I'm sorry." Ronni looked around the kitchen.

Cornell stood up to refresh his cup of coffee and checked his watch. "I've got to go to work soon. I'm assisting with a surgery this morning. You better tell me your news."

"Cornell! Good for you! Are you going to be able to do anything during the operation?" Ronni beamed at him.

"Surgery. Get your terminology straight. Plastic surgery is surgery," he scolded, but he was obviously proud. He was a resident at the University of Chicago Hospitals, specializing in reconstructive and cosmetic surgery.

"Operation. Surgery. Whatever. Are you going to get to work on the patient?"

"I'm sure Dr. Veena will probably let me do some of the closing. I'm just finally glad to be assisting in the OR."

"You know I'm proud of you." Ronni smiled. She knew that Dr. Saraj Veena was an expert in her field and she'd told Cornell he was the brightest resident she had seen in years. Cornell waved the sentiment off.

"Enough about me. What's up with you two?"

She sighed and shrugged her shoulders. "Well . . . tonight's the night. I'm finally going to do it." You couldn't wipe the huge smile off her face.

"Do it? *It* it?" Cornell sat back down. This was worth

taking a few minutes out for. The surgery wasn't until ten, but he usually liked to be in early so he could go over the procedure in his head before viewing it.

She nodded triumphantly. "Jeff and I on his boat for Venetian Night."

"What! Last time I talked to you, we weren't sure if he was a shyster. What happened?"

Ronni quickly filled Cornell in on the events that had occurred in her life, but not in too much detail because she knew he had to go. She started with the night she went over to Jeff's house, through their date at the museum, their seeing Denzel's new movie, and the dinner they'd had last night at Tru.

"I swear, the more I see him, the more I am falling for that man. Cornell, he is beautiful. Beyond my wildest dreams."

"Beyond *our* wildest dreams," Cornell teased. Then he looked critically at his happy cousin. This was her first real love affair. He didn't relish being the voice of reason, but she was so on cloud nine that he had to speak up. "So . . . you're happy with his explanation of what was going on with Uncle Benjamin? You're not worried about his character anymore?"

"Like I told you. He said he's not representing Daddy anymore, and if you just knew him . . . the way he is. There's no way Jeff could be a snake."

"What did he say about what happened with Randy Marshall's father?"

Ronni looked into her coffee. This was probably the real reason she had been avoiding Cornell. It wasn't so much his penchant for gossip. It was that she didn't want to face these questions. She had put that doubt out of her mind. "I didn't get into all that." She waved her hand in the air as if to flick off that thought. But her mind returned to the disturbing dream.

"Mm-hmm." Cornell was quiet, considering whether to press further. He looked at his watch. "Well . . . I'm happy for you. He sounds terrific. And he has a boat?"

"It's a time-share thingy."

"Time-share or not, we don't have any claim on a boat. Is it a yacht or what? How many feet?"

"I don't know."

Cornell rinsed out his coffee cup and placed it in the dishwasher. "Oh? You know every little thing about cars down to the horsepower and how much cabin room they have and other boring stuff, but you're a dumb blonde when it comes to boats?"

"Shut up." Ronni stood up, stretched, and tightened her robe around her body. She had a lot to do to get ready for tonight. Cornell held out his arms for a hug and Ronni eagerly obliged.

Cornell kissed her forehead. "Well, sweetie pie. I hope Jeff is the right man for you and you relax and have fun tonight."

"I will, but I can't promise you I will call with all the details." They held each other's hands as she walked him to the door.

"Understandable," Cornell said. Ronni noticed he was being very reserved and figured something was on his mind. He turned to her when they got to the door. "But I will kick his ass if he does anything to break your heart."

She rubbed his arm. "He won't." Cornell almost made it to the elevator before Ronni yelled to him. "And Cornell—he's pretty tough."

Cornell turned on his heels and put his hands on his hips. "That's why, if he hurts you, I'll sneak up behind him and hit him with a two-by-four." They both laughed. Ronni closed the door, shaking her head about that nut.

Chapter Eleven

Apparently Cornell wasn't the only one who had been alerted to the fact that Ronni and Jeff were dating from their photograph in the *Chicago Tribune*. Jeff's mother caught him at his downtown office and raved about their picture. She also had high praises for Ronni's family and made him promise to bring her over for dinner soon. It was two o'clock and he was smiling to himself as he locked up the office. He was thinking about the last-minute things he needed to do before Ronni arrived on the yacht. He was also thinking about his frat brother Lonnie Cook, whom he hadn't seen or spoken to since college. Lonnie's unexpected call earlier that day pleasantly surprised Jeff. The first thing out of his mouth was "*B.M.O.C.!*"

"Naw, brother," Jeff had responded, falling into his college banter. "You're the big man on campus."

"Aw, don't give me that bull—Veronica Hampton!"

"Oh . . . is that what this is about?"

"She's still fine. Finer even—if that's possible."

Jeff shook his head, recalling how the guy had begged for him to "just give a brother some details. Is she everything we imagined she would be?" Jeff had to remember that he was a grown-up now, and though he was happy to experience a little of what his campus reputation would have been if he had been dating Ronni back then, he responded, "A gentleman doesn't tell."

Lonnie didn't like his answer. "Oh? It's like that, huh?"

But Jeff told him the truth. "This is different, man. She could be the one."

Jeff turned to go to the elevator and was startled by the woman standing at the end of the hallway. Tamara Hampton was positioned between him and the elevator. Jeff composed himself. He couldn't imagine what this was going to be about, but whatever it was, it couldn't be good.

"Hello, Mrs. Hampton," he said, approaching her and taking her arm to lead her back in the direction he was going to the elevator. The reminder that she was another man's wife tripped-up her self-assured pose.

She looked over her shoulder at his office door. "Hi, Jeff. I, uh, needed to talk to you."

Jeff pressed the DOWN button. "So I gather."

"You're leaving so soon? I was hoping to catch you at your office." Tamara tugged at the hem of another of her tummy-baring shirts. Today she was wearing a thin floral peasant-styled blouse with tight white slacks. She had on three-inch white heels that still only brought her height to Jeff's shoulder.

The elevator couldn't come fast enough for him. "What can I do for you?"

"Oh. It's about . . . well . . ."

Jeff eyed her guardedly, waiting. Whatever she had to say, he wished she would just spit it out.

"Can we talk in your office?"

"I'm gone for the day. You can talk to me on the way to my car."

Tamara was confused. This wasn't going according to her plan and she was working with too little brainpower to recover so quickly. Her usual weapon of choice was sex appeal, but it didn't seem to be working on Jeff. The elevator arrived and Tamara was dismayed to see so many other people on it. Jeff pressed the LOBBY button and turned to her expectantly. She shook her head, indicating that she would talk to him when they got off.

In the lobby, she turned to him to talk, but he pointed toward the exit.

"The parking garage is this way," he said.

She refused to budge. "Jeff . . . look."

That was fine with him. She could have her say and then they could go their separate ways. He knew he was being short with her, but he didn't have any business dealings with Tamara. His business was with Benjamin. And, more importantly, Ronni.

"Benjamin and I saw your picture in the paper and we're not comfortable with you dating his daughter." She slung her hair out of her face for effect.

Of all the things Jeff expected she might say, this was definitely the last thing he ever thought would come out of her mouth. He crossed his arms in front of his chest and just stared at Tamara. She, of course, didn't expect this reaction and wasn't sure how to proceed.

"So . . . uh . . . we would appreciate it if you just kept your relationship with our family on the professional level." She placed her hand on her hip and stared at him as though she had some authority.

He'd heard enough. Jeff turned to go to his car. He needed to stop at the florist, check with the staff on the yacht, and do a million other things before picking up Ronni. He could hear Tamara's heels clicking on the floor behind him as she ran to catch up. He didn't stop his progress until she grabbed his arm.

"Did you hear what I said?"

Jeff turned sharply to face her. The only evidence that he was furious was the telltale twitch in his jaw and the narrowing of his eyes. His deep voice was a study in control.

"It should have occurred to you at some point during this little diatribe of yours that you are talking to a grown man. Moreover, I've been meaning to tell you that my 'relationship with your family,' as you say, is between your husband and me. And my relationship with Ronni is none of your business. It just so happens that I discussed the fact that I'm seeing Ronni with Benjamin and he had no objections. If he's changed his mind, he knows where to find me and he can talk to me about it man to man. But if this is some crazy scheme you've cooked up in your head, for Lord knows what purpose, I'd advise you to let it go. As far as I'm concerned, this should be the last time I ever see you without your husband."

Tamara's eyes were as big as saucers and she didn't realize that her head had shrunk back into her shoulders from his scolding.

"Is there anything else?" he asked. She could barely shake her head no in response. "All right, Mrs. Hampton. You have a good day."

Tamara stood frozen in place as she watched Jeff go through the doors and into the street. She had set her sights on him ever since he started coming to their house, thinking she might trade up for a newer model the way Benjamin allowed her to do with her cars. But she had greatly misjudged Jeff. After this confrontation, she realized she had played her previous games on old men past their prime—pathetic chumps. Jeff was way out of her league and not to be acquired through Mickey Mouse games.

She dug her sunglasses out of her purse and put them on her face before leaving the lobby. Tamara just hoped she hadn't parked in the same garage as Jeff so she wouldn't have to run into him again.

* * *

Venetian Night was the oldest festival in a city that loves its summer festivals. For nearly fifty years, crowds had lined the shore to watch the parade of boats decorated gaily with lights and paint in accordance with the annual theme. This year's event was titled "Tales from the Sea" and the boats traveled slowly up the Lake Michigan shoreline from the museum campus to Monroe Harbor, reflecting images relating to sea stories, captains, and their crews. Starting at nightfall, Grant Park and Navy Pier were packed with more than seven hundred thousand people enjoying a flurry of activities, including music, food, and nautical exhibitions.

Those lucky enough to own a boat secured the best view from the water where the fireworks would burst overhead at nine-thirty and shower the sultry evening with enchantment. This was exactly the reason Jeff chose this night for his first intimate encounter with Ronni. He had moved mountains and molehills to secure an evening alone on the yacht. Venetian Night was the time when everyone in the timeshare wanted to use the boat. The last holdouts were an older couple that wanted to celebrate their fortieth wedding anniversary. Jeff finally got their consent by buying them an expensive weekend package for a luxury suite at the Ritz-Carlton.

After the crew took Ronni and Jeff out to a prime viewing spot on the lake and their chef concluded his preparation of a sumptuous seafood feast, Jeff dismissed them for the evening.

"Alone at last," Jeff said as he hurried up the stairs to where Ronni was waiting for him on the upper deck railing. He placed his hand on the rail on the opposite side of her waist to encircle her as they watched the staff return to shore in a small speedboat.

"Yes, finally. And everything is so beautiful." Ronni looked out on the lake and then followed her impulse to wave at the crowd gathered along the shore, even though they were probably too far away for anyone to see her. Jeff's eyes were captivated by another sight—the striking woman beside him.

She was wearing a chocolate sleeveless blouse with a plunging neckline. Her top was fitted and the back was a column of four string-bikini-type ties. She wore this with a short white linen skirt that stopped midthigh and chocolate sandals with a short heel. He could see a toe ring on one of her toes, which were accented by peach nail polish. Her muscular thighs and calves and the exposed skin on her back captured his concentration as frequently as her face and hair. He didn't think two eyes were enough to take in the splendor of Veronica Hampton.

"You're beautiful," he said, no longer able to resist the temptation to kiss some part of her body. He chose the smooth bare shoulder nearest to him. While he bent close to her, Ronni kissed the top of his head. It was easy for him to raise his head and place his soft lips to hers. She turned in the little space within his arms to face him and they unreservedly opened their mouths to each other for a deep, soul-baring kiss. Jeff's hands left the railing and firmly circled her waist before traveling slowly up her back. His hands explored the strings, noting for later that they would be easy to pull free. He squeezed her tightly, unable to believe she was really here.

But they had an entire evening ahead of them, so when their kiss tapered into hungry, wet lip samplings, he pressed his forehead to hers. "Mmm . . . okay . . . I've been waiting for that all day." He kissed her forehead and let his mouth rest there.

Ronni wanted to say "Me, too," but she could only manage a deep exhale in response. Her whole body told her this was where she should've been years ago. Right there in his arms. Kissing had never felt so right to her before she met Jeff. With the other men it felt nice but never this *true*. She was sure now that Jeff had captured her heart and she was in love. Her heart was pounding furiously.

Jeff looked into her seductive eyes and decided to ignore the burning messages they were sending him. At least for a little while longer, anyway.

"I think we'd better eat," he said. He grasped her hand and pulled her toward the elegantly decorated buffet table a few feet away from where they were standing. "We have lobster, crab legs, shrimp, three different kinds of pasta salads, roasted veggies . . . what else do we have here?"

Jeff started to lift the lids on some of the heated serving platters. Ronni glanced at the food, but she was more interested in looking at the rear view of Jeff. She let her eyes slowly drift over his exceedingly male body. He was wearing a short-sleeved white rayon and cotton blend shirt, a brown belt, beige shorts, and thick brown sandals. She loved his hairy legs and was caught appreciating his athletic calves when Jeff turned to see why she hadn't responded to something he'd asked.

"Are you even listening to me, baby girl?"

"Honestly . . . no." She gave a mischievous grin. He rewarded her distraction by placing a palm to the back of her neck and affectionately pulling her forehead to his lips. Jeff turned back to the table and picked up a fine china plate.

He looked back at her expectantly, ready to fix her plate. "What do you want?"

"You." Another honest answer. Ronni gave herself a mental pat on the back for effectively letting her emotional guard down.

Jeff sighed in mock exasperation. He picked up a fork

and shook it at her. "You keep talking like that, and looking at me like that, and we won't make it through dinner."

"Is that set in stone?" Ronni said, moving closer to him and rubbing his back.

"What?"

"That we make it through dinner?"

To his astonishment, Ronni took the plate and fork from his hands and set them back down on the table. She didn't want to be sated with food. Truth be told, she was too nervous to eat. An anticipatory nervousness, but nervousness nonetheless. Besides, she couldn't imagine doing what they were about to do on a full stomach. She began to replace the covers on the serving platters. "Because if you're hungry, I'm sure we can—"

"No," Jeff said, recovering from his stunned amazement. "No. We can raid this buffet later."

"That's what I was thinking," she said faintly. Now that she'd declared her intentions, Ronni took a fleeting look out over the lake. She'd gone as far in kicking things off as she knew how, and was ready to relinquish the reins to Jeff. She had been so forthright that it took Jeff a moment to realize that completion of the evening's feature attraction was up to him.

He reached his hands out to her. When she placed her palms in his, he could feel their shakiness, but his almost certainly conveyed the same. He pulled her into his body, intending just to hold her. But at that moment a boat of revelers approached and they could hear the old-school music blasting from it. As "Sparkle" played, Ronni and Jeff automatically swayed together in a slow dance. He pressed his cheek to hers.

"Like the stars at night, high in the sky, how I wished . . ." Jeff whispered the song into her ear. Ronni's scent was intoxicating. He simply had to taste her. His lips dragged slowly over her neck, leaving a wet trail with the tip of his tongue. Ronni closed her eyes and leaned heavily against him. She let her head fall aside so he could have as much access to her neck as he wanted. Oh, he wanted. Jeff kissed her ear and sucked in her little amber earrings and small earlobe. His hands burned into the velvety skin of her back. As she wrapped her arms around his neck, she experienced his body as a rock-solid mass of pulsing muscle and heat.

When Ronni could stand the teasing kisses no longer, their mouths connected hungrily. Their tongues mingled together like old friends sharing a secret language. Their embrace was so tight that they could barely breathe but were desperate to get even closer. A great amount of heat and rigid pressure was announcing its presence against Ronni's torso. There was only one way to achieve the closeness they most wanted. Jeff lifted Ronni off the floor in his final embrace before letting her go. He stared into her eyes and she into his. The conversation their eyes transmitted to each other convinced Jeff to take Ronni's hand and lead her to the lower deck.

Entering the opulent mahogany bedroom quarters, Ronni was struck by the number of vases filled with dozens of white roses with one red flower in the center of each. The room was bathed in subdued lighting from a few lit candles on the shelf of the headboard. Jeff, who was still holding her hand, sat on the large bed and pulled her toward him as he lay back. Ronni resisted his gentle tug and stood frozen between his legs. Her eyes meant to drop to the floor, but they became transfixed on the prominent swelling in Jeff's shorts. As usual, her nerves wanted to take control.

Jeff released her hand and sat upright. He held her around her legs and kissed her stomach through the blouse. During the week, Jeff hadn't found a moment where he felt the time was right to ask Ronni about her experience—or lack thereof—with men. As this day neared and he hadn't broached the subject, he decided that when the time was right, he would just fly by the seat of his pants, no pun intended.

Ronni placed her hands on his shoulders. He stroked the back of her smooth legs. Her body was having an equally excited but different response to his caresses. She felt herself becoming more supple and physically desirous of what he had to offer. But that still didn't eliminate her apprehension. "Um, Jeff . . ." she started, but he interrupted.

"You remember when you asked me if I knew the meaning of flowers?" His voice was a mere whisper as he looked up into her face. Ronni nodded. He took a moment to clear his throat. "Well, when I first presented a white rose to you, I did have an idea of what I was trying to say." He winked. "I talked to the florist."

Ronni smiled, some of her tension abating.

"I gave you the roses as sort of a tease about the way you were such a baby in college. But then, as I spent more time with you, I realized the joke was on me." He placed his head against her stomach. "Because I purely . . . innocently . . . fell in love with you."

Ronni hugged his head and cradled the back of his neck in her hands. Her heartbeats were coming more quickly now. Her eyes found his again when she felt his neck turning up to see her.

"Then something you said after our first date told me that these . . ." he reached next to the bed and plucked one of the white roses from its vase; he placed it in her hand, ". . . that these also held a another, more personal meaning for you." His eyes bore into hers. Ronni blinked and swallowed.

"Am I right?"

"Yes," she whispered, nodding slowly. "I know it's ridiculous, but—"

"No. It's not, it's—" he started, but Ronni put a finger to his lips.

"It's just that it never felt . . . *I* never felt . . . the way I feel with you."

Jeff kissed her stomach. "Which is?"

"You know. . . ." She wanted to say it and his eyes told her that he needed to hear it, but years of defenses told her she had better not open herself up to heartbreak in the unforeseeable future.

Jeff couldn't accept that answer. Just because he was feeling the most intense emotions he had ever known in his adult life didn't mean Ronni reciprocated them. For all he knew, she could be here because she felt safe with him, or because she fantasized about sleeping with him back in college, or because she was tired of being a virgin. There were a myriad of possible reasons she was letting her guard down and opening up to him.

"I need to hear you say it," he said softly. Ronni wanted his beautiful brown eyes connected back to hers and knew she couldn't allow her foolish defenses to govern her life.

She finally came out with it. "I . . . love you, of course."

He continued stroking her legs. "It wasn't a given."

"Yes, it was. Or else I wouldn't be here."

"Listen, sweetheart, are you sure this is what you want?"

"What do you mean? You?"

"No, I mean tonight. I'll tell it to you straight: I want you. You can see that. But I'm in it for the long haul. So we can take this relationship as fast or as slow as you're comfortable with."

She rubbed his shoulders. "I want this. I'm just . . . a little nervous."

"You've got no reason to be," Jeff said hoarsely, then pressed his lips together tightly. His uncontainable arousal made him single-minded. He couldn't resist her feminine form any longer. His hands, already exploring the backs of her thighs, traveled the short distance up under her skirt to encircle her firm buttocks. He touched lacy and delicate panties. His fingers crawled under the edge of them to feel flesh as velvety smooth as that on every other part of her body. Ronni's hands dug deeply into his shoulders, barely able to stand on her shaky legs. Jeff found gratifying visual stimulation in her heavily rising and falling breasts. With her back-out top, she couldn't wear a bra, and her erect brown nipples were slightly visible under the lightweight fabric. He squeezed her bottom and slowly pulled her down on top of him as he lay back on the bed. They kissed deeply, reestablishing their long suppressed hunger for each other.

With her body weight resting against him, Ronni became fully aware of the immensity of his manhood and had misgivings as to whether she was about to experience pleasure or pain. As they kissed, Jeff's fingers worked their magic under her skirt, testing her body to see if she was ready. She was very ready. His kiss intensified and he turned them over so that he was on top. Ronni kicked off her shoes and scooted back to be more fully situated on the bed. Her eyes needed his and she was reassured to see that he never broke his gaze, even as his hands rubbed over her breasts, enjoying a sensation like stony pebbles rubbing back against his palms. Ronni unbuttoned his shirt and her eyes widened at the solid expanse of his chest. His chest was covered lightly with hair that increased its density on the bottom of his six-pack stomach. At the top of his shorts she could see a sexy distinctiveness at his hip joint, where his legs met his torso, that was enough to make her breath catch in her throat. This man was beyond her most X-rated fantasies.

"Jeff," she called quietly, her own desire choking back her words.

"Mm-hmm?" He didn't think he could manage language.

"What if I'm . . . You've been with lots of women . . . and . . . what if I'm not—"

"You will be," he said huskily. His face was so serious. Ronni chuckled nervously.

"How do you know?"

"Because . . ." His hands went underneath her blouse and squeezed the fleshy mounds. He cleared his throat, but he was still barely audible. "No one has ever touched me the way you touch me. You handle me like a woman who knows what she wants."

Ronni looked pleased with this assessment but unconvinced. Jeff, wanting their bodies to communicate all that needed to pass between them, managed to say more.

"Just follow your instincts . . . don't be timid . . . touch what you feel like touching . . . say what you feel like saying . . . relax . . . and don't hold back on me."

With that recommendation, Ronni unbuckled Jeff's belt. Her hands shook as she moved it through the belt loops of his pants and tossed it aside. Her fingers were now poised on the top button. She felt his soft hair on the back of her hands as she released the button and slowly drew down his zipper. Her eyes widened at the protrusion in his silk boxers, but she'd gone too far to stop now. Watching her face, Jeff kneaded her plump breasts, his thumbs teasing each nipple. He shifted his weight over her body to give her more room to remove his pants. Ronni slipped her hand under the band of his boxers and pushed both the underwear and the shorts below his buttocks.

Eyes drugged with desire and breathing hard, Jeff stood and stepped out of his clothes, nearly tearing his shirt off. This should've been the moment Ronni removed her clothing, too, but she was mesmerized by Jeff's nude body. She gulped self-consciously, taking in all his beautifully defined form, but her eyes kept returning to his center. She had never seen a fully aroused man before and Jeff seemed more endowed than she was capable of handling.

Jeff saw her uneasiness and put a knee on the bed between her legs. He grasped her back and guided her body on the bed until her head was on the pillows. He felt her tensing up as he leaned over her and blew out the candles on the headboard. Now, only the faint, recessed lighting in the walls illuminated the small room. He kissed her chin and the column of her neck, then his hands slid under her back and pulled the strings to her blouse. Encouraged, she pulled her top from the front of her body and scooted out of her skirt. Jeff did the honors of removing her black lace panties as Ronni rubbed his tightly muscled arms. His Adam's apple bobbed up and down as he looked her over, pressing his lips tightly together to stem his desire. He'd seen naked women in his time, but he was enthralled with Ronni's completely flawless skin, the way her feminine hips melded into her small waist and the definition in her flat stomach. Her body practically shimmered in the dark.

Jeff wrapped his arms around her. They were breathing into each other's mouths urgently as they pressed their burning bodies together. Their moist tongues connected unhurriedly and expressively. Jeff was more than ready for her, but he wanted to make sure she was as relaxed as possible. He kissed her neck and allowed his tongue to trail down to her shoulders, then her breasts. Ronni held the back of his head, panting heavily. Jeff's hands stayed with her breasts as he continued to kiss his way down her body. When he reached her stomach, Ronni tensed again and pushed at his shoulders.

Undaunted Jeff allowed his head to lead the way. Her stomach fluttered and she relaxed as his tongue expertly took her desire to the next level. Her breathing became heavy and she yelled out. She didn't know what she'd said and didn't care. She gripped his shoulders and instead of pushing him, she held him in place until she was drunk with desire for something she no longer feared but had to have. As her second volley of screams reached Jeff's ears, he realized he was well past the stage for foreplay and positioned himself above her. Ronni gripped his back and opened herself to him as they kissed deeply. He felt her slickness before reaching under the pillow for a condom. Wanting her to do the honors, he guided her hand to his manhood. She touched him and the heat she felt made her immediately let go. Jeff watched her intently with passion-filled eyes and gently guided her hand back to him. Ronni more confidently placed the condom and steered him to the only place he could ease her longing. She drew in a breath upon his cautious entry and gripped his bulky shoulders, squeezing his hard muscles. She chewed her bottom lip and held her breath. It was painful, but it was also so pleasurable. As Jeff worked his hips slowly, slowly, she released her breath and hugged his shoulders, pulling him to her. Ronni closed her eyes and fell into his rhythm.

True to their word, they raided the buffet after they made love and brought a bounty of overstuffed plates back to their bed. They each took a bottle of champagne as their drink. "We're making a mess," Ronni said, trying to corral some raspberry cheesecake off the bedspread and back onto the dessert plate.

"Another mess," Jeff said and was promptly given a punch in the arm.

"Throw that towel on the floor. Then our eating area will be neat and clean," Ronni ordered.

Jeff tossed the soiled towel onto the floor. Ronni licked some cheesecake off her thumb and was going to do it to her other fingers when Jeff caught her hand.

"Here, let me do that." He sucked the sticky cake off her fingers.

She teasingly shook her head at him. "Ah-ah-ah. You have to have dinner before dessert."

Jeff gave her a roguish grin. "We already broke that rule, darlin'. Don't try to get prim and proper on me now." Cake consumed, he kissed her hand before letting it go.

"Fine. Be a brute. Break all the rules." She smiled to herself as she bit into a jumbo shrimp. Jeff looked at her and fell silent. She was situating a napkin on her lap, oblivious to his eyes on her.

"Ronni . . ." They were both wearing loosely tied satin robes. He rested his hand on her naked thigh to get her attention.

She looked up cheerfully. "Yeah?"

"Was I . . . a brute?" It just crossed his mind that although he had been attentive, his own strong hunger for her had driven his passionate lovemaking. They'd started slowly, with his talented mouth giving her another first-time pleasure. Then, after he'd gotten her past the initial shock and momentary pain of his slow entry, the sensations he was experiencing hijacked his body. Once she started emitting ecstatic moans, he'd remembered making love to her as his sexual equal.

Ronni touched his face and leaned over their food to

kiss his lips. "You were perfect, sweetie. It was beyond anything I could have ever imagined."

Jeff smiled, but looked kind of doubtful.

"Couldn't you tell? I was pretty vocal."

"Oh, yeah," Jeff said, plucking a shrimp off Ronni's plate. "You're definitely a screamer."

"That was something I didn't know about myself." She cocked her head, thinking back on her actions. Then impulsively, she raised her arms into the air and triumphantly yelled. "I'm a screamer! I'm a screamer!" Jeff was surprised by her outburst and grinned at the proud declaration.

She stopped yelling and looked at Jeff. "Is that good or bad?" she whispered, mock serious.

"A screamer is good. A nutcase is bad. And unfortunately, baby, you're also a nutcase."

"I'm a nutcase!" Ronni yelled thrusting one arm in the air. She laughed and picked some pasta salad off Jeff's plate and ate it with her fingers.

Jeff laughed, too. "Oh, Lord . . . what have I gotten myself into?"

"You've gotten yourself into me, baby . . . and I loved it." She fell into a giggle fit.

"Now, now, don't be vulgar," Jeff scolded gently, eating some lobster.

As she ate her food, Ronni thought about his skilled touches, the heat that emanated from his sex, his virility, and the way he intensely watched her face. Her whole body began to feel warm just thinking about it. She started singing, "Tonight is the night that you make me a woman. . . ."

Jeff laughed, raised an eyebrow at her, and asked. "You are giddy, aren't you?"

She shook her head and looked honestly at him. "No, Jeff, I am *absolutely* happy." She leaned over and laced her hands behind his neck. "I am with you, and I love you and I am *completely* and *totally* happy." Ronni ended her little speech by pressing her lips to his. He put his hands on her waist and opened his mouth to hers. They pushed their foreheads together, then snuggled each other's cheeks.

"I love *you*, Veronica Hampton. You're the woman of my dreams." He sat back and fed her some roasted eggplant before sampling some himself.

She returned to her happy declarations. "I want us to be like this forever!"

Jeff smiled, enjoying her merriment. "God willing, we will be."

"Can we live here and just sail around and be happy together forever? We can wave at people and throw things from our yacht. We'll be that happy, crazy boat couple from Chicago." They both laughed together.

Ronni's amusing mention of staying on the boat forever made Jeff think about his reluctance to face the real world. Real life—where he was still representing Benjamin and she didn't know about it. Worse yet, he was about to force Benjamin to do something he wouldn't want to do. Jeff experienced a deep pang of remorse and the smile left his face. He glanced at Ronni and thought she was radiant in her happiness. If he lost her, he wouldn't know what to do. But he convinced himself that what he was doing was going to make her happy in the long run and she would forgive him for lying to her. She saw him staring at her so solemnly and smiled at him.

Pow! Pop! Pop! Bang!

"Oh! It's the fireworks!" Ronni said. She pushed the food aside and grasped his hand. "Let's go."

They started to run up and Jeff pulled her back. "Let's not forget our drinks."

"Oh, right." They ran back and grabbed their champagne bottles before dashing upstairs.

They sat on a rug on the upper-deck floor and held each other as they drank their champagne. It was their own little picnic under the stars. With fireworks bursting over the Chicago skyline, Ronni thought that she liked this womanhood thing and felt more confident in trying some things with Jeff she was curious about. Turning to him, she offered Jeff a wicked smile as she pushed him back and crawled on top of his body.

Chapter Twelve

Despite Ronni's proclamation that she wasn't going to share the details, she couldn't wait to meet with Cornell to shop several days later. They decided to go to the Oakbrook Center because it was such a beautiful day and this was one of the last outdoor malls in the Chicago area. After a couple of hours, Cornell grabbed Ronni's shoulders just before she led him into yet another lingerie shop.

"Look, despite popular TV shows, not all gay men love to shop till they drop. And, baby, I'm about to drop. If I have to go into one more Victoria's Secret with you, I'm going to jack you up."

Ronni looked surprised. She looked at her watch. It was past two o'clock and she hadn't even considered food. "Oops. Sorry."

"Sorry is right. You fall in love and all the world can just go to hell for all you're concerned."

"That's true. You got me." She laughed. "Where do you want to eat?"

"Cheesecake Factory is out here. I want to get some of those Southwestern egg rolls."

"That's cool with me. Plus they have great drinks," Ronni added.

"Didn't you drink enough on Venetian Night?"

"Yes. Yes, I did." She smiled and hummed to herself thinking about Jeff again.

Once they were seated at the restaurant, Cornell filled her in on how his first surgical assist had gone. Ronni was interested but she only heard half of what he said about Dr. Veena allowing him to do the eyes and the chin. This was a big achievement for Cornell and she wished she could be as great a listener and booster as he always was for her, but her attentions were constantly drawn back to her time spent with Jeff.

So this was the great secret that couples shared. The intimate knowledge of each other's bodies. Which things really drive them wild in bed. How they look in the afterglow of lovemaking. What they think about the politics, news, and . . . everything. *And you're interested in it all.* She thought Jeff was like a totally different person when he was with her. His public persona was so gregarious, cool, and in control, but when he was alone with her he was a vulnerable, down-to-earth sweetie pie.

Since Venetian Night, she and Jeff spent as much time together as they could. Sometimes he would ask her to take the train into downtown for her class so he could pick her up afterward. That was another thing—he altered his schedule to be at his downtown office and meet up with her on class nights. She could tell on those nights that he was tired, but he would shake it off to take her out to dinner or a movie. And relaxing around his house? That was one of their favorite things to do. Sometimes they could barely get through the door and feed Hannibal before they'd run upstairs and spend some quality time together in the bedroom. But just as commonly, Ronni could be preparing her reports for class on his computer while Jeff pored over his legal papers.

All she knew is that if this was love, she should have let herself fall into it years ago.

Cornell could tell by the wan look on Ronni's face that he had lost her somewhere within his description of the surgical procedure. He stopped talking midsentence and she didn't even notice. He gave a small laugh and shook his head as if she was hopeless. Ronni looked up and asked a question she thought was related to his tale, but it was too late. She was busted.

"Cornell . . . I'm sorry. I swear I was listening . . . and then my mind—"

"Don't worry about it." He waved a hand. "This is your first love and that trumps a first-surgery story any day."

They ate for a while in silence. Although he'd brought it with him and left it in the car, Cornell changed his mind about showing Ronni the article in the *Defender* about Mrs. Cathleen Winters. The story was about her selling off the cosmetics arm of her business to a multi-national corporation and concentrating on the smaller beauty-supply line. In the article, Jeff's name was mentioned as her counselor. Cornell decided he would never show her the article and it wasn't his job to point out the cracks in the mirror. All she saw reflected in it was she and Jeff and possible babies and everlasting love. And if Ronni was destined to experience sorrow, then at least let her have this time of pure unadulterated happiness.

Chapter Thirteen

Benjamin slumped down in the chair next to Jeff and looked desperately around his office as though the answer would come from something in the room. "But . . . isn't there any other way?"

"Ben, I've looked at this from every angle. That's your only option." Jeff's voice was measured as he delivered the news. He didn't like scenes and he could see from Benjamin's wild eyes that a scene was imminent.

Benjamin turned to face Jeff and gestured with his hands. "Look . . . you have money . . ."

Jeff shook his head and stood up. "Benjamin, don't go there." This was the part he dreaded.

"Look, man. Hear me out!" Benjamin wasn't aware he was shouting until he saw the stunned look on Jeff's face. Behind Jeff, he saw Tamara passing in the hallway and gestured for Jeff to close the door. Jeff did as he was instructed but was disinclined to turn around and return to the conversation.

"Just listen to me." Benjamin got his voice under control. "If you're confident that your assistance is going to make everything right, loan me the money and I'll pay you back when—"

"Sorry. The answer is no. You know I can't do that." Jeff sat against Benjamin's desk with his hands interlaced on his lap. Benjamin looked up at Jeff and suddenly became irritated at his cool attitude. He stood up and pointed a finger at Jeff's face.

"You should show some respect! Do you know who I am? I was creating dealerships while you were still in diapers!" Benjamin watched Jeff's stony face. He turned his back to Jeff and smacked his fist in his hand. "I knew your father! Aaron Conley—now there was an honorable man. There was a man with some principles! If you were half the—"

Jeff, furious, slammed his hand against a stack of papers on Benjamin's desk and rose to his feet. Benjamin whipped around, startled at the thunderous noise. He was taken aback by the rage he saw burning in Jeff's eyes. "I know you knew my father, you son of a bitch! That's why I'm in this mess with you in the first damn place!" Jeff knocked over one of the office chairs. "My father! Senator Aaron Conley!" Jeff sneered. "You think he could have saved you? From this?"

Jeff approached Benjamin and jabbed a finger at his chest. Benjamin shrunk back. Jeff stopped shouting and resumed the cold-as-ice persona he was famous for in the courtroom. "I've already loaned you money . . . because you knew my father . . . because I like you. But no more. Understand? No more."

Benjamin put his hands up and shook them to back Jeff off. "All right. All right. Calm down. Calm down, Jeff." He tentatively reached a hand toward Jeff's arm until Jeff's face looked calm enough for him to touch him. "You're right. I'm sorry. Tell me again what you want me to do," Benjamin said.

Jeff turned from Benjamin and picked up the chair he'd knocked over. He couldn't believe he had let himself lose control like that. He supposed it was Benjamin's throwing his father's name in his face. It could also be that every moment with Benjamin was now a boldface lie to Ronni. He sat down heavily in the chair he'd picked up and buried his face in his hands.

He only looked up when he felt Benjamin settle beside him. Jeff leaned on his knees and placed his chin on his clasped fists. He looked sideways at Benjamin. The old man looked tired. Jeff was thinking that despite Benjamin's reluctance to do as he asked, he would probably be relieved to have it all over and done with—public humiliation or not. For Ronni's sake, Jeff was determined to see that Benjamin got out of this with his dignity and reputation intact.

"You've got to sell off your location in Algonquin." He saw Benjamin's mouth start to open. He put a hand up to stop him. "And before you even ask me—no, you can't assign the employees to other dealerships. They have to be terminated and the inventory has to be liquidated."

"What about severance packages?"

Jeff looked confused. "You can offer it to the employees with fifteen years or more. But that's a new location, isn't it? Nobody there has that kind of time."

"I have a guy, Chuck Miller . . ."

Jeff sat back in the chair and pondered this wrinkle. "Oh, right. I forgot about Chuck Miller."

"Yeah. He's been with me for twenty-three years. He started at the original site and transferred up there to manage Algonquin." Benjamin thought about this predicament, too. "Maybe I can transfer him back to Matteson and bump out Leon Daniels."

"No. That won't do. That would start rumors of a systemwide shake up. Let's keep it isolated to the one facility." Jeff looked at his watch. He needed to think this thing through clearly—and quickly. He wanted to pick up a gift for the love of his life before his jeweler closed.

"But I can tell the guys that the Algonquin office failed. We expanded too fast. And they would have to understand me keeping a long-term guy like Miller around. He's got a family, you know. Two kids in college. Plus a wealth of experience."

"I'm sorry, I still have to say no on Miller."

Benjamin looked at Jeff as though he might be the most heartless guy he had ever met in his life. "But why?"

"Miller was the manager at Algonquin, so first thing he does when he gets to Matteson is start to shoot off at the mouth about how he just can't understand it. Benjamin says that location was doing poorly, but he can tell you everything looked fine." Jeff tilted his head and cocked an eyebrow at Benjamin. The older man nodded slowly and looked away. This is why Jeff made the big bucks. He was good. He thought of every angle.

"Since Miller is the only one with the time for a severance package from Algonquin, you give him a *very generous* deal. Tell him to take an early retirement, that there're some past bonuses and stuff in there you owed him. As far as the two college kids, give them both applications for the Aaron Conley Educational Scholarship Fund, and I will personally see to it that they don't even notice that their dad is laid-off."

"All right. I hate to see the other guys lose their jobs, but—" Benjamin didn't need to be cut off then. He stopped himself from pretending he was the victim and Jeff was the hatchet man.

"But you only have yourself to blame. The first step is acceptance." Jeff stood and pointed to him. "So am I going to see you Wednesday?"

"Mommy, will you read me this book?"

Tamara jumped. She was trying to listen to Benjamin's and Jeff's conversation when Benji startled her. She was in a seldom-used library that adjoined Benjamin's office. The door connecting the two rooms was cleverly disguised as a bookcase on both sides. But right between them was a very narrow between-wall space. She had left the library-side bookshelf cracked and that was how Benji saw her. She had been listening because she was worried Jeff would mention her visit to his office and the lie she told. Now she stepped out of the wall space and looked at her son.

"Benji," she whispered, turning to him, "you can read it yourself. Stop bothering me."

"Why are you whispering?" he asked.

Tamara cringed. He wasn't loud, but he wasn't quiet either. "Because I'm playing the library whispering game and I want you to whisper, too."

"Okay," he whispered back. "Are you going to read it to me?"

"No. Go read your book. You can read."

"But it's more fun when you do it. It's funny when you do the voices." He laughed just thinking about the funny voices Tamara made when she read. Tamara cringed again and shushed him. He put his hand over his mouth. "Oh, right. I forgot."

"You go upstairs to your room and you do it lickety-split. Mommy will come and read the story and make funny faces along with the funny voices, okay?"

"Okay!" He turned on his heels, but before he bounded out of the room, Tamara grabbed his arm and loudly whispered at him.

"Walk, don't run! And I'll be up in a minute." After she watched him leave, she ran and locked the door he'd come through before returning to the small wall space. They were shouting before; now she could hear them talking more calmly.

". . . yourself to blame. The first step is acceptance. So am I going to see you Wednesday?"

"Probably so. It would do me some good."

"Meet some new faces."

"Yeah, that part's always nice. So how are things with you and my daughter?"

Jeff must've done something funny because Benjamin was laughing and saying, "Ah, cut it out."

"I'm serious. I have to kiss the hand of the man who created such a heavenly creature."

"This better be real—or you can kiss the ass of the man who created her."

"Oh, it's real. As a matter of fact I'm headed to the jeweler's to get something for her right now."

"Bought her something nice, did you?"

"No. I had a bracelet that belonged to my grand-mother repaired so I could give it to Ronni."

"Well, all right."

Tamara figured they were shaking hands. It sounded like hands smacked together. "You're really serious about my girl, huh?"

"Never been more serious about anything or anyone in my life. I have to tell you . . . I love her."

"Well. I'm glad. Her mother and I tried to push her to-ward Tyler, but she never really was interested in him. She was right to wait until her heart led her to you. She doesn't talk to me much anymore after my . . . well . . . but I know she really likes you if she's been with you this long. Ronni lets guys go if they don't cut the mustard. I'm sorry I tried to discourage her from dating you in the beginning. It's just . . ."

"Forget it. We're together now and I realize I'm a lucky man. Look, Ben . . ."

"Yeah?"

"Do you talk to your wife about what we discuss together?"

"No. You know . . . she knows you're helping me. I don't tell her anything specific."

"And about Ronni? Does she know I don't want Ronni to know about our relationship?"

"No. There was no need for that. She never talks to Ronni and vice versa. Why?"

"Cool. Let's just keep it that way. All right, man, I have to run. I'll get back with you on those plans to close Algonquin and the severance package for Miller."

"Great. Soon I'll . . ." Benjamin's voice faded away.

Tamara figured they must have gone through the office door that led to the foyer. She stepped back into the library and closed the bookcase door, then ran out of the library and up the back stairs to read to Benji just in case Benjamin came looking for her.

After she read Benji's book and made the funny voices with the faces, he wanted to try it himself. As she watched him, her mind was racing with how she could best utilize the information she'd heard. She didn't have much to work with, but the one part that set her blood to boil was that Jeff claimed he was in love with Ronni.

Tamara hated Ronni and Beverly. She thought they were a pair of pampered, frigid snobs who wouldn't know how to keep a man if he were locked in a cage. Ronni had some nerve holding herself above Tyler Washington like she was too good for him. Who did she think she was with her fat ass? Well, formerly fat ass, but whatever. Tamara grudgingly assessed Ronni as not that ugly. She convinced herself that if Ronni weren't rich, she'd be a plain, unfeminine, manless nothing.

Tyler was good-looking and rich, and a gentleman and probably a tiger in bed. When she first became Beverly's assistant, Tamara had her sights set on Tyler. But it quickly became apparent that he would never accept a girl from the wrong side of the tracks, educated or not. She'd known three of her similarly inclined girlfriends who'd tried to capture Tyler's attentions with all sorts of wild sexual promises and naughty propositions. Everyone, even Tamara, who'd put on her best trustworthy-girl act, found out he was a no-go. If your family didn't have a name that made the papers, you could forget catching Tyler's heart.

It was so much easier to get Benjamin away from that pretentious old bat Beverly. Now, the real trick was keeping him from going back.

Tamara used to serve Benjamin a nightcap with a small dash of rohypnol, also known as GHB. Not enough to knock him out, but enough to make him less aware of what he did in the hours he had stayed up a little later than his wife. If he found himself laid out on the couch next to sexy, breast-augmented Tamara with her hand lazily stroking in his lap and telling him how great he was, who was he not to think they were having a torrid love affair? It's too bad he couldn't remember it. Ha! Benjamin would elicit promises from Tamara not to mention this to anyone and guiltily run upstairs to Beverly's bed. He looked so pained when it happened again and again. He didn't understand. What did the old Hamptons know about Roofies?

But hey, she was on a mission. To ensure the notion of their affair, Tamara began to flirt with Benjamin during the day, throwing knowing glances at him behind Beverly's back. Tamara was getting older and she'd be damned if she was going to take care of herself for the rest of her life. She thought he would be happy to dump the old woman once he found that he was sleeping with a young one—but she was wrong. She began to mount him more frequently during his drugged stupors. She needed something that was money in the bank, and her hard work was rewarded when she became pregnant with Benji. Those Hamptons thought they were so high and mighty, yet when they found out about the pregnancy their family crumbled with as much momentum as hers had when her father ditched her mother.

When Tamara was single, she prided herself on keeping up her music-video-worthy good looks and only dated the hottest guys. They didn't have any money but they were fun and frisky playmates. Now, crawling into bed with Benjamin's old butt was distasteful at best. He looked good for his age, but he didn't look good for hers.

She couldn't believe Ronni was fortunate enough to capture someone as rich, young, successful, handsome, and sexy as Jeff Conley. Jeff didn't even come across the snobbish, credential-checking way Tyler did. That wasn't his style. Jeff was always an easygoing guy. Tamara could remember years ago, when she was seeing a friend of his and he was screwing a friend of hers, April, who worked retail at Barneys. Even though they were dating each other's buds, Tamara had her eye on Jeff and would flirt with him something fierce. He never bit. But he was never as dismissive of Tamara as he was that day she saw him at his office. That day was surreal. He was downright nasty. Yet, she had to remember—she was running a game and Jeff was too smart for that kind of nonsense.

If Ronni married Jeff, then she would have trumped Tamara. Ronni's husband would be richer than hers, and younger. Being beaten in the game of life by the pathetic Ronni Hampton, who was only valuable because of the circumstances of her birth, was annoying, but worse were the implications that the "Jeff and Ronni" union could have on the sanctity of her own marriage. A wedding would guarantee that Benjamin and Beverly came into frequent contact with each other. Tamara was barely keeping them apart as it was. Obviously, the old fool still loved his ex-wife. At least Benji would be taken care of, she reasoned, because Ronni liked him. Nevertheless, Ronni would be the queen of the world and Tamara would be screwed.

She had *not* gone through all her planning to catch Benjamin simply to see it all go down the drain on the back of a couple of "I do"s. To protect her interests, it was mandatory to break up Ronni and Jeff. Tamara knew she wasn't the brightest cookie in the bunch, but she did know a lot about men and women. She was on more solid ground sharpening her claws against Ronni because the girl was smart, but she didn't know the first thing about handling a man. Schemes she might not be able to put past Jeff might just do the trick with that sheltered cow. Now all she needed was to figure out how best to put the pieces in this puzzle together. Tamara had to think about what she overheard and manipulate it—in a relationship-ending way.

"Didn't I read it funny?" Benji said proudly. "I'm really good, aren't I?"

"Yes, honey. That was good. Do it one more time."

Tamara needed time to think.

Chapter Fourteen

"So could you do that for me, girl?" Ronni said into the cell phone.

"Of course! I would cut class too if I had such a handsome playmate to spend the day with. Is he with you now?" Theresa whispered the question conspiratorially. Her enthusiasm for details about Ronni's relationship had been irrepressible ever since she saw Jeff at the classroom door.

"Yeah." Ronni smiled and looked over at Jeff. He was a few yards away, buying their lunch at a hot dog stand.

"Wooo . . . bring him by my lot before I get off work," she said excitedly.

"What! No way. We're at Navy Pier. We're not coming all the way out south just to pretend to be customers for you."

"Aw, come on," she prodded.

"No way." Ronni chuckled.

Theresa sucked her teeth. "Well, I understand. I wouldn't want to come by no boring dealership if I was with him either. But don't worry about the class, I'll hand in your paper and tell you everything Lance says. But you know, with the boys, I've missed plenty of classes. You can hand it in next time."

"I know, but I want it to be on time. Get his comments on it. I sent it to you this morning." Jeff came back and handed Ronni her hot dog. "Thanks," she said quickly.

"That's your problem—you always got to do things right. I'm glad you met him so he can loosen you up," Tee teased. Ronni laughed. "I'll check my e-mail and print it out. You go ahead and have fun."

"Thanks, Tee."

"No problem."

That settled, Ronni put the phone in her purse and sat on the bench next to Jeff.

"All squared away?" Jeff asked, biting into his food.

"Yep. I'm yours for the day." Ronni took a bite of hers. "Tee wanted me to bring you by her dealership."

"What? I need a new car?"

"She's got a crush on you. She says you're good for me because you can loosen me up."

"I like this Tee. She sounds like she's got a good head on her shoulders," he joked, nudging her knee with his own. "You were sooo worried about cutting a class."

"Shut up." She looked at him affectionately over her hot dog. "So now we're free to frolic."

He watched as Ronni repositioned her napkin over her knees.

"Did you ever miss any classes in college?"

Ronni gave him an insulted look. "Of course."

He raised a doubtful eyebrow at her. "When you *weren't* sick?"

"Well . . . no." She smiled and considered his question, eating a couple of his fries. "Did you?"

"Hell, yeah." He gave a short laugh. The more he discovered about Ronni, the more he realized how lucky he was to be her man. From outward appearances, Ronni seemed so by-the-book that most *would* consider her a natural match for Tyler Washington. But there was an unguarded, fun-loving, nutty side to her that most people weren't allowed to get close to. Jeff appreciated the fact that once she'd committed to their relationship, she dropped her defenses and was herself with him.

"In high school, too?" Ronni asked prudishly.

"No. No, I was a choirboy until college." He thought back on his school days and became rather somber. Undeniably, college was where his life took a turn for the worst. Although he'd put most of that behind him, he only considered now—this phase with Ronni—the time when his life was getting back on track.

"How much of a bad boy were you at Columbia?"

"I was . . . pretty bad, darlin'. In ways you don't even want to know." Jeff polished off his hot dog and crumpled the paper wrapping. He stretched out his legs and crossed them at the ankles.

"Oh? Now I'm intrigued." Ronni caught the brief cloud on his face. "I *definitely* want to know."

Jeff shook his head, indicating that he wouldn't talk about it, but his face was pleasant. He placed an arm on the bench behind Ronni's back and gazed at her. He wondered why he was being so honest. Did he have a desire to open up? Tell her everything?

"You mean with women?" Ronni probed playfully.

He gave a small shrug and smiled. "That, too."

"What else? Drugs?" she asked apprehensively.

"No." He chuckled. "Now you're barking up the wrong tree. I was an athlete."

"Hey, it's been known to happen with athletes." She thought more. "Drinking?"

"Oh, I definitely did my share of that." They both laughed.

"I've got it! Cheating on tests and stuff." She jabbed his leg, hoping she was wrong. Now Jeff was the one to give her an offended look.

"Give me some credit here. The brains come naturally."

"I certainly hope so," she said, finishing her hot dog

and wiping her hands with a napkin. "Well, I can't think of what you could be talking about. I was too much of a bookworm to guess anything else. You'll just have to tell me."

"Let's just say that . . ." Jeff trailed off as he gathered their trash, ". . . all of it together made Jeff a very bad boy."

"That's not so bad, that's just college. You like to—" Ronni looked up and someone was closing in on them *fast* with her eyes fixed on Jeff. She was an older woman, wearing a floppy hat, sunglasses, and a bright purple nylon sweat suit. Jeff turned to see what Ronni was looking at. When he saw her, he sat up straight.

"Cathleen," he said, rising to his feet. It was only then that Ronni could see that it was indeed Cathleen Winters. Ronni had never seen her looking so untailored. Then again, she only saw her at dinners and formal social events. Jeff had apparently seen her like this, or he wouldn't have known who she was so quickly.

Cathleen clasped Jeff's arm and was talking in a rush.

"Hi, Jeff. I'm out here with my grandbaby. He's at the children's museum with his mother. I just came out to get him a hot dog, but I'm glad I ran into you. I've been trying to call your office all day. I don't know if what you told me—" Something in Jeff's face made Cathleen aware that there was someone else with him. She looked at Ronni over the top of her sunglasses. "Hi, Ronni, how're you doing?"

"Hi, Mrs. Winters."

"How's your mother?" Cathleen asked, taking time for pleasantries.

"She's fine," Ronni answered hesitantly, wondering about the urgency in Cathleen's behavior. Jeff turned to the bench and picked up their garbage.

"Walk with me," Jeff said briefly, taking Cathleen's elbow.

"That's good. Tell her I said hi, hear?" she called almost over her shoulder as she followed Jeff to the garbage bin. Ronni noticed that he threw the trash in a basket quite a distance away from where she was sitting, even though there was one closer.

Observing their posture, Ronni saw Cathleen place one hand on her hip. She was gesturing with the other and Jeff's arms were crossed over his chest. He did a lot of nodding, and she did a lot of talking. She soon gestured with both her hands and Jeff put his hands on his hips, still nodding. He said something and Cathleen was momentarily loud enough for Ronni to hear "That's the thing . . ." before she was too low for her to hear again.

Ronni was torn between staying on the bench and going over to the animated pair. But what excuse would she use for intruding on their conversation? Jeff placed both his hands on both Cathleen's shoulders and talked right in her face, the way adults talk to children when they're really trying to get them to understand something important. Ronni was now certain that she should keep her seat.

It made her think about something she saw in the *Defender* Cornell had accidentally left in her car. Cathleen Winters was doing something with her business. Ronni had only glanced at the various headlines while leafing through the periodical but hadn't really read any of the articles. Now, she was hoping she hadn't thrown it out. When she got home, she was going to find that paper.

Finally, they were stepping away from each other and Ronni was relieved to see that they were both amused about something and smiling. Jeff touched Cathleen's arm one more time before saying good-bye and walking toward Ronni. Cathleen waved to Ronni and went to the hot-dog stand. Ronni waved back.

Jeff returned, standing over Ronni with a big smile.

"Okay. Sorry about that. Where shall we take our frolicking next?"

"What was that all about?" Ronni asked, hoping her face looked pleasant.

He waved off Cathleen with a quick backward glance. "Ah . . . the life of a lawyer. Your clients think you're on call twenty-four seven."

"So she's your client?"

"Mm-hmm." Jeff held out his hands. Ronni grasped them and he pulled her to her feet. "Let's go to the OmniMax theater. They're showing *The Matrix* on the big screen," he said, placing his arm around her waist.

Ronni could feel her defenses slowly regrouping. "What was the emergency?"

Jeff was leading them to down the boardwalk. "No emergency." He hoped it was just his imagination, but he felt tension coming from Ronni. She felt stiffer in his arms than she did before.

"She said she'd been trying to call you all day."

"With Cathleen, everything is an emergency. It was nothing, really." Jeff glanced at her. He could see she wasn't exactly pleased about something. "Is there a problem?"

"No. I . . . she just looked upset. I hope you're not neglecting her just to spend time with me."

"Ronni, she wasn't upset." As they walked, he wrapped his arms around her shoulders and kissed her forehead. "She just gets nervous about every little thing." He looked into Ronni's face to see how she was processing this information. Her brow was slightly furrowed.

"You don't have objections to my being her lawyer, *too*?"

Chastened, Ronni felt silly. *Am I going to have this reaction every time I see Jeff talking with a client? Of course they went off and talked. Lawyers never discuss private legal matters with their clients in front of other people. Didn't Cornell tell me that if I buried the hatchet, not to mark the grave?* She gave a small laugh and relaxed in Jeff's arms.

"No. I guess I feel guilty that we're taking the day off and leaving the world behind."

"That's the thing about playing hooky. If you decide to do it, don't even think about the place you're supposed to be, or it'll ruin your day."

"Is that how it's done?"

He nodded. "We were just unfortunate that the real world intruded upon us." Jeff hugged her. "You're just a neophyte. I'm an old pro at this, baby. You do what you gotta do and don't look back."

As Ronni sat in the darkened theater watching the on-screen action, a thought occurred to her. What if Cornell didn't leave that *Defender* in her car by accident? What if he wanted to show her the article? He must have—the paper was turned to the page with the article on Cathleen. Why else would he have brought it with him? When she got home she would have to find that newspaper.

Chapter Fifteen

"I really wish you would come with me," Jeff said softly, looking deep into Ronni's eyes and wrapping his long arms around her, his hands lightly tapping her bottom. They were oblivious to all the other people at the boarding gate.

She kissed him and touched his neck. "We've been down this road already. As much as I would love to come with you, I've missed enough classes already."

He twisted his lips. "What? One?"

She smoothed his collar. "Two. That time we went to Navy Pier and then again yesterday."

"Yesterday—last night—was necessary because I won't see my baby for three days." Jeff punctuated those words by letting his soft mouth linger on her neck. He could feel her flush with his mouth and, though they had just completed a marathon lovemaking session, his body stirred with renewed desire for her.

"Three whole days?" Ronni moaned miserably, leaning into him. Her whole body felt tingly from the touch.

"I know." Jeff looked over her head. The flight attendant was calling passengers in the final rows. He watched unhappily as the line of people dwindled and he squeezed Ronni tightly. They had called first-class ages ago, but he was in no hurry to get to San Francisco without her.

"Well, somebody's got to feed Hannibal and give him

his medication." Ronni tried to lighten their separation with logical duties.

"Mr. Walker across the street would do that if you came with me. All I'd have to do is call. He's probably over there now," Jeff kidded, still hoping she'd change her mind. He would never give up until the plane left the ground. It would be a simple thing to buy another seat.

"Hannibal would like that. He likes him better than me."

"What? My dog doesn't like my baby?" His voice was syrupy sympathetic. "Then he's outta here."

Ronni laughed and pushed at his chest. "No—no. I was only kidding."

"To the pound, buddy. Pack your bags." Jeff jerked his thumb in the direction Hannibal could leave. They laughed and their hips swayed together instinctively like a slow dance.

Ronni looked behind her at the line. "Aw . . . it's almost time for you to go."

He kissed her forehead and stroked her hair. Jeff was still in awe that she was with him. He had a crazy idea to look around while he was in San Francisco to see if he could find a T-shirt that said "She's With Me" so he could announce his possession proudly to the whole world. For a moment he had an inclination to yell "I love this woman!" to the entire room, the way he had seen some lovesick sap yelling on a commercial in the middle of a piazza in Venice. But that guy had a ring.

"Okay. Let's synchronize our watches."

"What?" Ronni gave a small laugh and frowned. Jeff picked up her arm and looked at her watch. He held his next to hers, then looked at the clock on the wall.

Jeff began to fix them. "Yours is a little slow and mine is a little fast."

"Excuse me, MacGyver, why are you doing this?"

"You're going to go over and give Hannibal his pills, right?"

"Mm-hmm." Ronni watched, amused as his muscular hands set her timepiece.

"I'm going to call you at the crib at two-thirty. On the nose." He kissed her lips lightly. "Tell you how much I'm missing you."

"Oh, really?" She wrapped her arms around him and rubbed his back. "How do you know you'll miss me?"

"'Cause I miss you now. I want to wrap you up and stick you in the overhead luggage bin."

"Can't I ride in first class?"

"Too late for that. Now you've got to stow away. You'll be in first class—just overhead." They smiled at each other and stared, captivated. The final boarding call was announced. "I'm going to bring you back something nice from San Francisco."

"Rice-A-Roni?"

"I was thinking something nicer, more like something to go with Grandma's, I mean *your* bracelet."

"Like . . . a ring?" Ronni raised her eyebrows.

Jeff hadn't meant that. Even though, lately, getting engaged to Ronni had been foremost in his thoughts, proposing was so important that he would never have referred to it casually at an airport gate. She should know after his considerable plans for their first intimate evening together that he was a big-production kind of guy. His proposal would be done very romantically and on the down low. But now that she mentioned it, he wanted to see how she would respond.

"Would you like that?" he asked.

"Oh, no, mister. You can't hedge your bets, try to get hints as to how I would answer." She poked a finger at his chest. "You just have to plunge in there and take a leap."

"A leap? I've already fallen."

"Then you've got nothing to worry about. You should know the answer."

"True. I'm pretty confident," he said, narrowing his eyes. "But you never know."

"Okay, I'll give you a little hint." She wrapped her arms around his neck and was torn between staring into his deep brown eyes and actually giving him the hint that would result in more of a cheat sheet. She pushed her body forward, connecting her most relevant parts, those that separated a man from a woman, with his. Her lips seized his bottom lip and sucked it softly into the heat of her mouth. As Jeff felt the sultry curvaceous hips and her firm breasts push into his body, his mind told him he needed to back up.

A full night followed by an early morning of lovemaking in no way diminished his desire for her. Could he be arrested for boarding a plane harboring a barely concealed weapon? He was lost in the world of their embrace and closed his lips over her teasing ones. Her wispy, vanilla musk smell filled his nostrils and his hands staked his claim on her womanly rear, squeezing gently. From the pull in the pit of his stomach and the heat burning in his thighs, Jeff knew he had to let this woman go to make his flight—especially to make his flight in a family-friendly condition. His lips trailed to her cheek and his hands rose reluctantly to the safety of her back.

Ronni's intentions were to provide Jeff with a burning reminder of why he should return from San Francisco as soon as possible. Instead she was slowly convincing herself that she ought to go with him. Now, she fully appreciated why three days would feel like an eternity. Ronni's eyes were still closed and her skin was flush as Jeff gazed at her. He wanted to make contact with those exotic eyes, but he enjoyed this look—what he considered her bedroom look—as well.

"After that hint," he sighed deeply, "my odds are looking better and better."

"But mine are looking worse. Who buys the cow when they can have all the milk they want?" She placed her head on his chest. Jeff raised a hand in front of her face and spoke softly to her.

"I'm sold. I would like to buy the cow, the milk, the stable, the nutritious hay she needs . . . and could you throw in anything extra?"

"Depending on how romantic your offer is, I'm sure I could come up with a few other perks."

"Ooh, babe. If you've got something you've been holding back on me, I'll be back *tonight*."

"Is that a promise?" Ronni squeezed him tightly. She really didn't want to let him go. This was another thing she always thought was corny when she witnessed it while waiting for flights—kissy, mopey couples acting as though they just couldn't let go. Now she was one of them and she could tell the skeptics: what they're feeling is real. Shakespeare was right. Parting *is* such sweet sorrow.

"I wish it were, babe. I wish it were." Jeff reluctantly withdrew from her. "Man! I wish you were coming with me." He rubbed his face and took a deep breath. Ronni smiled tenderly and gave him more space. "Okay, sweetheart. I guess this is it."

"Yeah."

Jeff picked up his bag and reached for her hand. She accompanied him to the ticket-taker and gave him a final kiss before watching him walk through the tunnel. He blew her a kiss before he disappeared; she returned it and turned away, completely satisfied with her life.

As Jeff settled in his seat, Ronni dominated his thoughts. She was definitely the woman he had been waiting for. Jeff looked at his parents' long-term marriage and knew that that was what he wanted—even as an undergraduate. But his experiences with women had made him almost give up on that dream. He smiled to himself at the thought of all of the women he'd dated who thought he had commitment issues. He had heard that so many times that he was beginning to wonder if what they said was true. And then he ran into Veronica Hampton. All his doubts about whether he could be a husband and a father went right out the window. From the moment he kissed her at his house, he wanted Ronni to stand beside him at the altar.

He knew this trip to California could be a turning point for them. He'd simply told Ronni that he was going to San Francisco to see if he could land a new client. What he hadn't told her was that he was working on their future together. When he returned to Chicago, he *would* be ready to plan his proposal to her. And he wanted to completely put the past behind him. This client could mean a brand-new start.

He'd seen the skeptical look on Ronni's face while he talked to Cathleen Winters. It was as though she knew there was something deeper in his dealings with Cathleen, and he couldn't tell her what she needed to know to ease her mind. But if everything went okay and he could change the focus of his law practice, he would be free to fill her in on his past. Plus, he was constantly guilty about lying to Ronni about Benjamin. He was getting out of the business of saving his father's friends and was going to be more hands-off with clients in the future. Pretty soon, he'd wrap up his business with Benjamin and there wouldn't have to be any more lies between them.

Was this providence or what? Tamara pulled her cream-colored Cadillac into an empty space far down the street and turned off the radio. She pulled out her cell phone.

"Why did we stop?" Benji called from the backseat. He looked up from his Game Boy and tried to see what his mother was doing. "Are we going back to see Ronni?"

Tamara had just picked Benji up from his peewee-league baseball game and they were passing through a neighborhood close to the ballpark when Benji alerted her to something she'd almost missed.

"Ronni! There's Ronni, Mommy!" he had yelled, excitedly pointing.

Tamara looked around frantically. "Where?"

"Right there! Stop. Go back!"

She hadn't stopped, but she slowed down in time to see Ronni going into a house. She went around the block and came around again. Ronni was gone now, but her car was in the gate. She knew Ronni didn't live around here, so that must be Jeff's house. Tamara had never been to his home, but she knew he lived in this area. This situation would suit her needs perfectly. She turned to answer Benji.

"No. I'm calling a friend, sweetheart. I want you to be real quiet until I finish my call, okay?"

"Okay." Benji went back to his game.

Tamara became aggravated. That *beeping* and *blipping* noise would not work in the background of her telephone call. Plus, she couldn't count on Benji not to talk whenever the mood struck him, especially when he heard the name Jeff. He liked Jeff and, sweet boy that he was, would no doubt ask if he could say hi.

She looked at him in the rearview mirror. "Benji, honey, I need you to get out of the car."

"Why? What for?"

"Just get out of the car so Mommy can make a phone call."

He looked back at her through the rearview mirror. "You can make a call while I'm in the car." Tamara rubbed her forehead. Benjamin Jr. *was* a Hampton and Hamptons could be a real pain in the ass. They were always thinking and questioning. She looked around her seat and gave him her meanest look.

"Look, mister, I don't want to hear your mouth. You do what I say."

"All right, all right." He unbuckled himself and started to get out.

"No. Get out on the other side—by the curb." She watched him cross the seats and open the door. "And take your Game Boy with you. You can lean on the car and play it while I make my call. I'll tell you when to come back in."

Benji sighed heavily and reached back for his game before closing the door behind him and leaning against the car door. *Good.* Tamara looked at her phone. She knew that Jeff was out of town and Ronni must be going by his house to water his plants, feed the dogs, pick up the mail, or whatever clueless, doting girlfriends like her did.

Fortunately, back when she thought there was a chance that she could exchange Benjamin for Jeff, she'd programmed his home phone number into her cell phone. Now she just prayed that Jeff used an answering machine instead of voice mail or else she'd have to think of a Plan B. She cleared her throat, readying herself for her performance.

Ronni was petting Hannibal while he devoured his food when the phone rang. She got up and went to it, smiling. She looked at her watch. *Not quite two-thirty.* His watch still must've been running a little fast, she figured. Ronni listened to the juvenile outgoing message, think-

ing she would tell him she didn't pick up right away because she wanted two chances to hear his voice.

"This is Jeff. I ain't home. Leave a message."

"Hi, Jeff. It's Tamara. Pick up, please."

Ronni's blood ran cold.

"Jeff? Pick up. Okay, so, I guess you're not home. But
this is important. I'm a little worried about Benjamin. You
know how he gets. I know you constantly tell me he's old
and I have to bear with him, but he's really working my
nerves. He's freaking out about having to close the Algonquin location. He keeps saying, 'Jeff is forcing my hand,'
and . . . well . . . I really think you should talk to him. Tell
him again that it's the right thing to do. That's all. Call me
when you get a chance. Bye-bye."

Ronni, who was listening with her back against the
wall, slid to the floor. She was too stunned to do anything
but stare blankly into the room. Her throat felt raw. She
recovered from her daze enough to cover her face with
her hands. She pulled her hands down her face and
started to cry in body-wracking sobs. As she listened, she
hugged her knees, rocking and crying.

The phone rang again.

"This is Jeff. I ain't home. Leave a message."

"Hey, baby, you there? Ronni? Ronn-nee. . . . Well. I
don't know where you could be. Didn't we synchronize
our watches?" Jeff gave a small laugh. "Anyway, maybe
you got caught up in traffic or something, but I love you,
and I miss you already. Can't wait to wrap this up and get
back to my baby-boo." He offered smooching sounds
and then another small laugh. "Love you, sweetheart.
Call me on my cell."

Touchdown! This time when Tamara came around
the block, she sat in a space far down the street where

she could face Jeff's house. At first she was wondering if her little impromptu plan had worked because she didn't see any movement for the longest. Benji played his little game, oblivious to the fact that they had been on this block forever. Finally, her patience was rewarded. Ronni came storming out of the house and—Tamara was thrilled to see— *wiping her eyes!* Ronni dropped the keys trying to get in the car. But she sat inside her car for a while before peeling off so fast her tires screeched. *What the heck was she doing?*

Tamara laughed out loud and hit the steering wheel, accidentally honking the horn. Benji looked up but decided not to say anything since he'd been banished before for not being quiet. Now if she could just get the tape back from Jeff's machine. She would have to think about how she could do that before he got back in town. But she figured she'd have to admit defeat on that one. It would probably come back to bite her in the ass. *Whatever.* Right now, she was on cloud nine.

Tears filling her eyes, Ronni couldn't find the right key. *Jeff's a liar! And a snake! And he's trying to loot our business!* She dropped the keys and stomped her foot before finding them again and, mercifully, placed the right key in the door and slid into her car. *He's a lying, swindling . . .* She started to cry again and leaned over the steering wheel. *He talks to Tamara . . . about Daddy. And what else?* She picked up her cell phone and called her father's office.

"Hello."

She sniffed, trying to get her voice somewhat under control. "D—daddy?"

Benjamin's voice immediately became worried. "Ronni. Sweetheart, what's wrong?"

She cleared her throat. "Daddy . . . tell me the truth.

Are you . . ." She held the phone away and cried hard before wiping her eyes and finding the strength to go on. She took a few gasping breaths, trying to regain her composure. When she put the phone back to her ear, Benjamin was in a frantic state.

"Honey, where are you? What's going on?" he shouted into the phone.

A stony numbness came over Ronni so that she could ask him. "Daddy, are you closing the Algonquin location?" *Please let that cow be lying. Please. Please.*

Benjamin was silent. "Honey . . . what's this all about?" he said, still worried.

Her face crumpled. "Are you closing the Algonquin site? Just answer me!" she yelled.

"Yes . . . yes, sweetheart." Benjamin was confused. "But what's—"

Ronni turned off the phone and threw it against her windshield. A chip flew off the phone and she didn't give a damn. Right now, she couldn't think of her father as a victim. He was business-savvy enough to hide his relationship with Jeff from her, but now *he* was a liar, too. She gave into one last wave of tears before putting her car into gear and pulling off Jeff's property. *Screw his gate! His place can get robbed for all I care,* she thought.

Chapter Sixteen

Finally alone in a cab, Jeff sat back and rubbed his eyes.

The dude he'd gone to San Francisco to see was definitely crazy, but Jeff thought he might have landed his first sports client. Tony Maldonado was a rookie shortstop with the Oakland As and he looked promising—if he could keep his nose clean. As screwy as he was, Jeff could envision getting a call in the middle of the night asking him to come bail his client out of jail.

Crazy clients or not, Jeff was trying to make a new start for himself as an entertainment and sports lawyer. Pete Colón, Jeff's former college teammate, had hooked him up. He was in management for the Oakland As and he'd been very receptive to Jeff's call asking for client leads. After several weeks of waiting, Pete called back and told Jeff he needed to meet this young guy. Pete said he was looking for a lawyer he could trust; Tony was sure his last lawyer screwed him on the contract negotiations—he thought he could've gotten a better deal. Before leaving Chicago, Jeff had studied Tony's contract and found a few inconsistencies and loopholes he would present when he met him. Jeff might have intended to get right down to business, but the player had other ideas. He apparently wanted to test his compatibility with Jeff. Tony took Jeff with him everywhere—from location to location—chattering wildly all day.

Whenever Jeff tried to talk about the points he wanted to present regarding Tony's contract, the guy implausibly changed the subject and talked about the weather, the difference between California girls and girls in other parts of the country, playing ball in college, who were the best designers of men's clothes, a dog he used to have as a kid—*man, he missed that dog*—buying a house, his relationship with his parents and siblings, he'd visited Chicago twice and didn't like the pizza, his relationship with his current girlfriend, and on and on. Jeff had been shopping with Tony, taken to his house, driven around the city, then taken back to the house for Tony to change clothes before they went partying.

After they arrived at their third nightclub, Tony was finally ready to talk about business and listen to Jeff's ideas. Jeff was so loaded at that point, he wasn't even sure he got in all his impressive details. But something he said must have satisfied the young athlete because during the night he clasped Jeff on the shoulder and said he really liked him and thought he would give him a shot. Jeff had to meet him for breakfast the next morning and they would talk again. *The things you do for money . . . and for love,* Jeff thought.

As he sagged in the seat and felt the effects of the alcohol spread through his body, he reached into his rumpled suit jacket and pulled out his cell phone. He hadn't heard from Ronni all day. True, most of the time his phone was off—he had to pretend interest in what the nutcase was saying—but whenever he had a moment, he would leaf through the caller ID. She hadn't called. Now he looked at it again. Still no call from Ronni, but Benjamin had called four times.

The thought that occurred to him had a sobering effect

on his body that combated the liquor. He instantly sat up straighter. *No calls from Ronni and four calls from Ben.* Jeff's heart began to race at the implications. *Please let her be okay.* He looked at his watch and retrieved the voice mail. In all his calls, Benjamin had only left one message, saying, "Jeff, call me as soon as you get this. It's very important." If it was about three-fifteen in California, it was five-fifteen a.m. in Chicago. Benjamin might not be up, but Jeff couldn't wait. The phone rang twice before Tamara answered, sounding sleepy but angry with the early caller.

"Hello?"

"Let me speak to Benjamin."

Jeff heard a lot of movement, then, "It's for you!"

Benjamin, obviously in another room, said, "I got it," and Tamara hung up. "Hello?"

"Hey, Ben, it's Jeff."

"Jeff, thank God. It's about Ronni."

Jeff's heart sank. *God, I don't know if I can handle this.* He couldn't find his voice. He leaned over his knees and pressed the phone to his ear, waiting.

"Did you tell her about our plans for Algonquin?"

Jeff hadn't realized he was holding his breath until he shakily released lungs full of air. Whatever this was, at least it wasn't what he thought. "You know I can't talk to her about that," he said wearily and rubbed his forehead.

"Well, she asked me about it yesterday. She was pretty upset. I can't get in touch with her. I've been up all night." Benjamin sounded miserable.

"What did she say exactly, Ben?"

"Just . . . she demanded to know if I was closing Algonquin . . . and . . . she hung up on me."

Jeff tried to consider what might be going through Ronni's mind.

"She was crying, Jeff. I don't know. . . ."

"When was this?" He knew that somewhere in Ronni's

thinking, she connected this unhappy discovery to him—
or else he would have heard from her. Yet he couldn't bear
the thought of her being upset and hurt somewhere and
his not being able to comfort her, to explain.

Benjamin sighed. "Yesterday afternoon."

Jeff wasn't aware that he was at his hotel until the cab
driver told him the fare. He dug into his wallet, paid the
man, and got out of the car.

"Have you talked to her mother?"

"No. I don't want to upset Beverly. I'm sure if Ronni
talks to her, she'll call me."

"She couldn't have heard about it from Tamara—or
Tyler?"

"You know we haven't finished drawing up everything
yet. Besides, I wouldn't tell them. Nobody knows but us."

Standing on the sidewalk in front of his hotel, Jeff
looked sullenly at the sparse early morning traffic. He
rubbed his hand over his closely shaven head, a habit
of gathering his hair that he'd developed when he wore
dreads. "I'll be back tomorrow . . . today . . . on the first
flight I can get out of here. In the meantime, I'll try
to reach her."

Benjamin was relieved to have someone to share his
misery. "All right."

"Okay." Jeff, chewing his lip, looked into the lobby of
his hotel. His thoughts were racing through a thousand
things. He would have to call Tony from the airplane so
he'd have an excuse to get off the phone. *What are you
thinking about, Ronni Hampton?*

As a medical resident, Cornell was usually so exhausted when he arrived home from work that it was all
he could do to get through the door and collapse on the
bed. Tonight, as he turned his key in the door of his

apartment, he was fully alert. Ronni had called him at
the hospital and said she would be crashing at his apartment for a while. She didn't—and given her voice, he
guessed she *couldn't*—go into detail about her reasons
for being so distraught, but he speculated it was probably due to a painful breakup with Jeff.

The small living room was dark except for the glow
of the television and he could see that the poor thing
had fallen asleep on the couch; the rug was littered with
tissues. It was a few minutes past midnight. Cornell was
taking the throw blanket off a chair to place over Ronni
when he saw her blinking and realized she was still
awake. She was wearing her pajamas. He dropped the
cloth over her lower body and sat on the couch.

"You had anything to eat?" Cornell consolingly
rubbed her hip. She shook her head. "Let me get you
something." He stood to go to the kitchen.

She gave a sniff and shook her head again. "Cornell,
no."

"You've got to eat something," he said weakly and sank
back down beside her. He watched her for a minute and
she didn't move a muscle. "So . . . you want to tell me
about it?"

Ronni watched indifferently as cheery commercials
flickered across the screen. She sniffed again. Cornell
was about to give up on persuading her to talk when she
said, "We were talking about marriage." Her small face
crumpled briefly before she willed her mind not to take
her down that path.

He waited. She would tell this tale in her own way.

Ronni sat up and wrapped the throw around the front
of her body. "We were right. He's a big fat liar."

"What happened?" Cornell asked quietly. His hand
found her knee underneath the cloth. With intermittent

stops, tears, and restarts, Ronni told Cornell how she found out the truth about Jeff.

"And I did have my doubts, Cornell, but I pushed all that aside. Y'know, I wanted to get outside of my head. I wanted to believe in . . ." She stopped and tears slowly made their way down her face. "I know you tried to give me hints, with the paper and all, but . . ."

Cornell's hand froze on her back. *The paper!* He hadn't meant to leave the paper in her car.

"I saw him with Mrs. Winters and it all seemed so innocent. He seemed . . . they seemed . . . okay." Her entire tale was told with a quiet resignation. Like she didn't have much more energy to expend on speech. She wiped at her eyes with a new tissue and returned her hand under the safety of the throw. "They were *laughing.*"

"But what about Uncle Benjamin? What did he say was going on?"

"I told you—I haven't talked to him. I don't want to talk to either of them."

"You say Tamara said Jeff was forcing his hand?"

Ronni nodded. Cornell watched the television, not really seeing the show. He glanced at Ronni. She looked terrible. Her eyes were raw and puffy and her normally cute hair was in total disarray. He'd have to get her to talk to her father or he'd talk to him himself. But right now, he could see she needed sleep. "You've got to go to bed."

"I know, but I can't seem to go to sleep."

"Go to the bed, it's much more comfortable. I'll crash here." When he saw her starting to protest, he insisted. "Please, I'm a doctor. I'm use to crashing around the hospital wherever I can. I'll be fine right here."

He reached over and turned on the light and it had the effect on Ronni he expected. She shrank from its brightness and rose to her feet. Another, darker room would be much more welcome. Cornell rose, too. "At least get some juice or cocoa or something while I change the sheets."

"You've got a king. We can share the bed," she offered weakly, worn out.

"Oh, no! Been there, done that. You thrash around like a wild woman. I need my sleep. I *love* sleep! I'd marry sleep if it weren't seeing so many other people." Cornell couldn't suppress his naturally effervescent nature any longer.

Ronni tried a smile and waved a dismissive hand at him. It was years ago when she slept like that. They hadn't shared a bed since they were teenagers—finishing their homework and staying up all night talking about their high school crushes. But she didn't argue as she headed to the kitchen to find something to put in her mouth.

Chapter Seventeen

Once Jeff landed in Chicago, he called Ronni as frequently as he could without coming off like a crazed stalker. He'd left only a couple of vague messages. There was no reason to get into what Benjamin told him until he actually talked to her and found out what had upset her so much about Ben's closing the site. He tried both her cell and her home phone with no luck. Once he arrived at his house, he threw his keys on the hall table, removed his suit jacket, and saw Mr. Walker coming up the hall, limping. Hannibal, wagging his tail, followed along behind his mature friend. The two made quite a pair with their bad hips.

"Hey there, Jeffrey!" Mr. Walker said brightly. He always called him this, even though Jeff's name was not a diminutive. But Jeff never corrected him from the beginning and it was too late to be touchy about it now.

"Hey, man." Jeff squinted at him. "You taking care of my dog?"

"Yeah, your girl called me yesterday and told me I need to get over here." He noticed Jeff's unwavering frown. "We were going to go down to the park—uh, if that's okay."

"That's fine. Fine." He tried to clear his face. "What time did she call?"

"Last night. Said she couldn't get here—got caught up

with something." The man smiled. "I had to come over last night and close your gate. You know women, they claim they're smarter than us, but they're always forgetting things." For some reason, Mr. Walker thought this was truly funny. He determined that it wasn't so amusing when Jeff's brow knitted again and he busied himself by leafing through his mail. Deciding he'd better shut up, Mr. Walker found the leash and clipped it to Hannibal's collar. "Well, we're off."

Jeff had the presence of mind to look up and nod before they went out the door. *So, she was here.* He wanted to get a quick shower and change out of yesterday's rumpled suit before heading over to Ronni's apartment. He scratched his stubbly beard. He needed a shave. Instead of sleeping this morning, he had worked the phones trying to change his ticket and get a plane back to Chicago. After he got to the airport, he discovered his flight had a two-hour rain delay. He managed to shut his eyes on the airplane but couldn't really fall asleep.

Maybe she did call me. He pushed the button on his answering machine, removed his cuff links, and collapsed in a chair, rubbing his eye.

Most of it was the usual stuff—his buddies, his mother.

When Jeff heard Tamara's voice, his hand halted in the process of rubbing his eye and slowly fell to grip the arm of his chair. His eyes narrowed and his jaw was clamped so tightly he was in danger of cracking his teeth. He chest rose and fell under ragged breaths. Jeff went over to the machine to repeat the message so he could hear the time tag on it again. It came it at two twenty-seven, a mere three minutes before he called Ronni. She was definitely here and she had heard the entire message—as it was being delivered.

Jeff got a sick feeling in the pit of his stomach. Now he understood the full extent of Ronni's torment and why she demanded an answer from Ben. In that instant, he also understood how cruelly malicious Tamara could be. This was his private number. Anyone who wanted to call him about business either reached him on his cell or left a message on the office machine upstairs, with the exception of Ben. To leave the message here with a sugary-sweet voice and imply that they always characterized Benjamin as a doddering old fool was beyond even the worst things he could've attributed to Tamara. It became apparent to him that Ronni felt seriously hurt and betrayed. At this point a phone call wouldn't ease her pain and she would never answer it anyway. Jeff had to go see her in person. He had to explain everything—from the beginning. But first he would have to go see Benjamin . . . and his wife.

It appeared Tamara had the foresight to make herself scarce when Jeff, dressed comfortably in blue-jean shorts, loose gray T-shirt, and sandals, arrived at the Hamptons' house that afternoon. A restless Benjamin greeted him at the door.

"Is Tamara here?" Jeff asked as Benjamin led him to the substantial peaches-and-cream living room, instead of the office where they usually met.

"No. She went to Benji's game. Have you talked to Ronni?"

With the white furniture, delicate knickknacks, and pale peach carpeting, Jeff couldn't imagine that this room was a welcome area for a seven-year-old. Benjamin indicated a seat, but Jeff stood by the fireplace mantel, looking at the large photo of the family. He contemplated the evil shrew with her arm around her son, smiling in front of her husband. In one fell swoop, she had put everything together in the most damaging way.

How did she know Ronni would be there to hear that message? It obviously wasn't meant for Jeff. How did she know exactly where to hit him where it hurt the most?

"Ronni found out about our plans from Tamara," Jeff said suddenly, turning from the picture to witness Benjamin's reaction.

"What?" Benjamin said, baffled and shaking his head, his brow wrinkling. "What . . . that's not possible."

Jeff sat in a chair. "It's possible. Because she did." The fingers on his right hand rubbed his forehead and he closed his eyes. Images of the previous morning with Ronni plagued his thoughts. His mind offered body-stirring visions of their tender early morning lovemaking before their trip to the airport. He recalled Ronni's flush, moist skin; her radiant eyes expressing bliss, love, contentment, and *trust*. He had been the happiest man on the face of the earth. What a difference a day makes.

Benjamin looked at Jeff, confused. "They never talk."

"And you never talked to her about your business plans?" Jeff eyed him levelly. He wasn't ready to reveal the full manner in which Tamara's knife had penetrated his heart. He identified with Ronni's emotional detachment from her father. How could a nice guy like Benjamin wind up with such a conniving woman?

"No." Benjamin stood and paced the room. "Never."

"She must've been listening in on our conversations," Jeff said, satisfied by the look on his face that Benjamin was telling the truth. But he needed to know something else to put all the pieces together. "Did she know I was out of town?"

"I might have mentioned it." Benjamin saw a pattern in Jeff's questioning. "Did she approach Ronni when you left yesterday?" Before Jeff could answer, he had come to his own conclusion. "I can't believe Ronni would entertain any one-on-one conversation with Tamara."

"She wouldn't, and Tamara knew that. That's why she left it on my machine," Jeff said, shaking his head. "Your wife called me—I don't even know how she knew Ronni would be there—and she left me a message saying that you were upset about closing Algonquin and I needed to talk to you. Not before she said you were an old goat who couldn't understand a simple business deal."

Benjamin sat down heavily, not wanting to believe his ears. He knew there were reasons a lot of people didn't like his wife, and he thought Beverly's friends were the reason she wasn't really accepted socially. But it never occurred to him that it might be her own fault she was so unpopular.

"You have to talk to Ronni, Ben. Tell her everything . . . from the beginning."

Even as Jeff was saying this, Benjamin was shaking his head.

Jeff, who thought he'd contained his anger on the way over, could feel his face getting hot. "What do you mean, no? You've got to tell her." He leaned forward in his seat and methodically wrung his hands.

"No, no. Let's stick with our plan and when everything gets back on track, we can tell—"

"That won't do. Whatever personal embarrassment you'll face—"

"I can't—I can't see the look. I've already damaged my relationship with her, and—"

"What about *my* relationship with Ronni?" Jeff pressed his fingertips to his eyes, trying to calm himself. He looked at Ben coolly, who stared back defiantly. "Now *your* mess is ruining *my* relationship with Ronni."

"Look, Jeff," Benjamin continued carefully, not wanting to raise the ire in Jeff, but desperate not to have to do what he was proposing, "I want her to see me the way she used to. It's the only thing I have. . . ."

"*She's* the only thing I have." Jeff stood, pointing a shaky hand at himself. He was through talking to Benjamin if he wouldn't be reasonable. "She's the only thing that matters to me. And that includes your personal concerns. As a matter of fact, I was wrong—*your* mess isn't ruining my relationship with Ronni, I'm doing that myself with secrets and lies. I don't care what you're going to do. I'm going to talk to her." Jeff cut the air with his hand as if that were the last word on the matter.

Benjamin jumped up quickly to grab Jeff's arm. "Jeff!" The frustrated look in the younger man's eyes made him waver, but he persisted. "Just give me a week. We were almost through fixing my financial stuff. I'll tell her then."

Now that he'd placed the blame on himself, Jeff wasn't as upset with Benjamin. His voice was controlled, but decisive. "A week? Do you understand that she is probably home right now feeling hurt and betrayed? By me? I can't let her go on for another minute thinking I was involved in pressuring you to do something you didn't want to do. That I've been talking with Tamara like we're old friends." Jeff swallowed at the thought of Ronni rebuilding those defensive walls that had taken him so long to break down.

Benjamin glanced away. He knew there was no stopping Jeff once he'd set his mind to something. He also had to factor in Jeff's feelings for Ronni. The man evidently was head over heels in love. He admired that and he couldn't ask for a better man for his daughter, but Benjamin had to protect his own relationship with Ronni, too. He had one trump card in his control. He looked up tensely, wondering if he should use it.

He took his chance. "Lawyer-client confidentiality, Jeff. I don't want you to tell her."

Jeff's sympathetic eyes turned icy. "You sure you want to go there?"

"If I have to," Benjamin said. The truth was, he wasn't sure, and now that he had roused Jeff, he was pretty certain he didn't want to go there, wherever that was. Benjamin's resolve was fading under Jeff's silent, steely gaze. Yet their eyes challenged each other quite a while before Jeff spoke, leaning into Benjamin, gesticulating with his hand.

"Ben . . . I'm *going* to talk to her. I'm going to tell her about my relationship with you and Cathleen and George—and about *me*. So, you do what you gotta do. You want me disbarred?" Jeff gave a flippant shrug. "That's on you. You know I've scraped myself off the ground after worse situations than this. I'll find another career. All I care about now is salvaging my relationship with Ronni."

Jeff walked across the room and stopped at the doorway. He dug into the pocket of his shorts and pulled out something small. "Oh, and if you want to know what kind of woman you destroyed your family for . . . you'll need this." Jeff tossed the tape from his answering machine to Benjamin, who was surprised, but caught it.

Benjamin looked at the miniature tape in his hand as he heard the front door slam and Jeff's car starting. He wilted onto a nearby couch. He had no intention of having Jeff disbarred. He knew he was being ridiculous. He would just have to be a man about the whole situation and face the shame. He could just tell Ronni and Beverly the trouble he'd gotten himself into since he married Tamara and how his world had been crumbling around him until Jeff stepped in.

Ever since Ronni was a little girl, he had always been a hero in her eyes—until Beverly divorced him. He never wanted to see that kind of hurt and disappointment in her beautiful black eyes again. After seven years, they were tentatively reestablishing their connection. The only thing that really held their current relationship together was that Ronni was preparing to take over the family business. And with her taking the NADA classes, they were becoming closer; he almost had his little girl back. If she knew his problems with self-control were threatening the once-solid business he was to pass on to her, he might never get her back.

But Jeff was going to tell her the truth and that was that. He examined the tape again. He had voice mail, so he would have to go out and buy a minicassette player to hear what had been recorded. He was very interested in knowing the true nature of this treacherous witch he was living with.

Chapter Eighteen

Ronni was doing her best to concentrate on Lance's lecture when Theresa pulled her arm.

"That's your man at the door," Theresa whispered excitedly, giving Ronni's arm another tug. Ronni had seen him there, but chose to ignore his presence. Her feelings were too raw to tell Theresa that she was through with Jeff.

"I see him," she said so coolly that Theresa uncharacteristically dropped the matter and Ronni's arm without further objection.

This class was Ronni's first outing since she had heard Tamara's message the day before. Cornell had gone to her apartment and brought back more of her clothes. She also asked him to check her home and cell phones and clear out any messages from Jeff or her father. Her cousin, who was vocally opposed to her shutting the two men out of her life without answers, announced, "He called ten times. There were only two messages, though." Ronni told him she didn't want to hear them.

She didn't know what else to do but continue to go through with her classes. She and Cornell had agreed that whether or not she ended up in a fierce legal battle with Jeff for the dealerships, it would be better for her lawsuit to receive her certificate of completion from NADA.

She couldn't believe Jeff was back in town. At least he

had the sense not to knock on the classroom window or something, she thought. Ronni was thankful that Lance told everyone at the beginning of the class that there wouldn't be a break tonight because he had a lot of work to present to them before their preliminary exam next Friday. The class could take bathroom breaks individually, but Ronni didn't want any part of a scene in the hallway, so she drank very little coffee.

Thankfully, when she got out of class three hours later, Jeff wasn't there. Theresa walked with her to the garage and they talked about how well they thought they would be prepared for the test and agreed to meet for a study session. Finally, Theresa broached the subject Ronni had been steering clear of.

"Okay. I've held my tongue long enough—what's going on with you and my cutie pie?"

Ronni pushed at her glasses and fell silent, watching the ground as they walked.

"Ya'll have a fight or something?" Theresa asked as she nudged Ronni's arm. "Well, obviously you had a fight, but I mean, what happen—"

Ronni looked up at Theresa and then followed her amused stare to Jeff. He was leaning with his back against his car, parked not too far from hers. Ronni cursed under her breath. That damn TT of hers was so conspicuous that you could pick it out in a parking garage as large as Grant Park. All Jeff had to do was know which garage she usually parked in—which he did—and drive around all the levels until he saw it. *He waited three hours?*

"Well, call me later, girl." Before Ronni could stop her, Theresa veered off toward her own car.

Ronni tucked her head down and tried to pass Jeff. He touched her arm, but she continued to her car. He followed her. "Ronni. I know what happened . . . with Tamara's message . . . and—"

Ronni threw a cold stare in his direction. "Don't mention her name to me."

"Let me explain. She's lying. She tried to—"

"Is she lying about you representing my father?" She was at her car door. Jeff stood near the back of her car.

"No, but I can explain that—"

"Is she lying about closing the Algonquin site?"

Jeff shook his head and glanced briefly at the ground. Ronni could be fierce when she was angry. And right now, she was angrier than he had ever seen her. Her nose was turning red, right on the edges where it flared furiously.

"But—"

"But let me guess: she's lying about everything else, right?" She glared at him. It broke his heart to see her look at him like this. It was worse than he thought it would be. His breath caught in his chest. "So do you talk to her about what a fool I am, too?"

"What?" he choked out, his face showing irrepressible hurt.

"Stupid little virgin, maybe? Me and my stupid old father? We can't keep up with cunning geniuses like you and Tam—" Ronni's voice broke. She wanted to fall to the floor and cry, but she held it together long enough to turn the key in the car door. She struggled with the door, breaking a nail trying to get it open. Jeff put his hand on the door to keep it closed.

He couldn't believe she was saying this. "Baby, you know how Tamara is. She's a—"

"No. No. Don't call me that. Don't call me baby." Ronni waved a hand at him as though she didn't want to hear anymore and shook her head at the ground. She swallowed hard. "I know how *you* are."

Jeff was staggered. The Ronni he imagined apologizing

to wasn't available to him anymore. He now faced her tougher, shielded, more public persona.

"I was so . . . stupid." She berated herself under her breath. She snatched off her glasses and wiped her eyes. The glasses were fogging up from her tears and the heat in her face.

"Ronni." Jeff couldn't stand it any longer and reached out and draped his arms around her shoulders. She pushed him off with two stiff arms. Tears were flowing freely from her eyes, but she would not break down.

"Don't touch me!" she yelled. Jeff let go immediately and backed off. He stuffed his hands in his pockets to keep from touching her, comforting her, holding her.

"Why are you being like this?" His voice was very small. As strong as he could be in any other situation, he had no defenses when it came to her. Jeff couldn't believe this was the same woman he'd held in his arms just twenty-four hours ago. "Bab—Ronni—talk to me. We can grab a coffee or something."

"I'm not going anywhere with you."

"Well, at least sit in my car—or let me sit in your car—so I can explain."

"Explain what, Jeff?" She opened the door and tossed in her briefcase, then turned to him. She was regaining some of her composure by replacing her heartache with anger.

The garage security was keen at this time of night, especially when it came to women alone. A voice came over the loudspeaker. "Ma'am, are you all right?" Ronni waved an unconcerned hand at the air. Jeff took another step back, glancing at the ceiling. His eyes fell to the floor. She crossed her arms over her chest and eyed him steadily.

"Do you want to explain how you're a liar? Explain how you're a cheat? Or are you going to tell me exactly how you go about looting people's hard-earned family businesses?"

His ears had to be deceiving him. What was she *saying?* He had been looking at his shoes; now he turned a distinctly confused face up to hers. He gave a voice to his thoughts. "What are you implying?"

"I'm not *implying* anything. I'm coming out and saying it. Cornell told me you were a snake, but I wanted to believe that you—" She stopped herself from going down that path. She was going to say "loved me and wouldn't hurt me," but that was too painful to utter. She attacked instead. "What happened with Randy's father?"

"What? Who's Randy?" Jeff said, breathless. He rubbed at nonexistent dreadlocks, frowning.

"A carpeting business you looted a few years back, or are they all too trivial to keep up with?"

Where is this coming from? Jeff realized she had to be talking about George Marshall, his second big mistake. As a matter of fact, George was one of the people Jeff was going to tell her about, but he didn't like this negative characterization of him she seemed so readily to accept. He felt his stomach turn over.

"Is that what you think about me?" he asked in a barely audible voice.

Ronni tilted her head at him. "No. It's not what I *think.* It's what I *know.*"

He wasn't expecting this. This was so out of the blue. What was she talking about? Looting businesses? After all the time she'd spent with him, how could she believe this about him? "Then why did you go out with me?"

Ronni saw the muscle working in his jaw. A security vehicle pulled up beside them.

"Ma'am, is this gentleman bothering you?" the driver asked.

Ronni gave Jeff one long look before turning her attention to the guard.

"Yes. As a matter of fact, he is."

Jeff watched Ronni with a mixture of detachment and raw pain. The security guard stepped out of his vehicle. "Sir, can I see some ID, please?"

Ronni slid into the seat of her car and shut the door. When she started the car and rolled down the window, she saw Jeff reach into his back pocket for his wallet. "Can I go, please?" Ronni asked the guard, leaning her head out the window.

"Oh, yes, ma'am. Sorry." The man, who had Jeff's driver's license, told him to wait and proceeded to move his vehicle out of Ronni's way. The guard waved at her to get her attention. "Did this man assault you?"

"No." Ronni looked at Jeff. He stared back unemotionally. "I'd call him more of a nuisance."

As she drove away, she looked into her rearview mirror and could see that Jeff was still watching her.

Thank God the nightmare of a day was coming to a close. Jeff plopped down on the side of his bed and removed his watch. His muscles ached and his head was spinning. Usually he had the leisure to sleep off a bender. With the exception of his cousin's bachelor party, he hadn't drunk that much since college. Today, he fought drowsiness with vast amounts of coffee as he drove all over town trying to catch up with Ronni. *Ronni.* Jeff pressed his hands against his eyes. He felt a headache coming on, but hadn't stopped in the bathroom to get an aspirin. He was too worn out to get up now and go to the medicine cabinet. He peeled off his shirt and shorts and threw them carelessly on the floor.

The time with the guard had been nothing. He'd taken

Jeff to the security office, then asked a few questions about what he was doing there. He ran his name and his license plate. When Jeff came up clean and the man found out he was a lawyer, he quickly determined Jeff to be harmless and even gave him a ride back to his car.

Jeff placed his legs under the covers. Once his head hit the pillow, the room started to spin. As far as he was concerned, that was great. Maybe this day had been one long, horribly vivid hallucination. Maybe when he slept this off, he would be in a hotel room in California and the woman he loved would still love him. What had she said? Did she know what she was saying? Ronni—*his Ronni*—couldn't have been that coldhearted, that hurtful.

He turned on his side and burrowed his face deeper into the pillow. He could smell traces of her perfume. The last time he was here, in this bed, he was half of a couple. His chest hurt as though he needed to eliminate some phlegm; he coughed into his hand and couldn't stop. Jeff quit deluding himself that he was coughing and let the wave of emotion wash over his body and release his pent-up sorrow. Every scene his mind presented involving Ronni, whether happy or sad, only increased his crying. The only two words he could mutter repeatedly through his inconsolable sobs were "Oh, God."

Hannibal, who had been alerted to Jeff's misery, went to the bed to comfort him. Being a pug, his legs were too short and he was too old to jump onto the bed, so he snuggled next to his owner's leg instead. Jeff was exhausted, his muscles were aching, his head was pounding, and the room was revolving, but he didn't restrain his emotions. He was man enough to admit that this was significant— he'd just lost the love of his life.

Chapter Nineteen

After four days of hiding out at Cornell's small apartment, Ronni was glad to be going back to her own place. Because of his schedule at the hospital, he was barely home anyway, but she was sure Cornell was glad she was leaving, too. He was more of a social creature, and overhearing a few of his softly spoken phone conversations with his friends, Ronni was certain that on a couple of his off nights he'd opted to stay home, baby-sitting her instead of going out.

The only person she had seen outside her family was Theresa. Ronni hadn't been good company, but they'd met earlier that day at a university library and covered a lot of material for the upcoming exam. Ronni could tell Theresa was dying to know what was going on with her and Jeff, but she only asked once if they were still mad at each other and offered her advice. "As much in love as you two are—I've seen it with my own eyes, girl—you shouldn't throw that away." Ronni had given her an evil look and she shut up, promised that she wouldn't bring it up again, but insisting she just had to say that.

Ronni drove down the street with all the windows open and the radio tuned to National Public Radio. At least on that station they talked all day and she didn't have to listen to any evocative love songs. It was all she could do not to think about Jeff. She didn't need that kind of stimulus. She was already confused about her feelings for him. Of course he was a liar, but everything she recalled about their time together filled her with longing for him . . . his kiss . . . his touch.

She'd heard about this condition on a radio program, on NPR, as a matter of fact. That the reason a lot of couples get back together even though they're not right for each other—like women whose spouses are abusing them—is that they mourn for the relationship more than the person. In scientific terms, they explained that each couple creates a chemical odor that triggers something in each other's brains and bonds them together. So when they break up, they have a physical reaction, similar to withdrawal, from one another. Ronni seized on this plausible explanation as though it were the Gospel. It was how her brain operated. To stay out of emotional territory, she needed a logical explanation for everything.

Before going home, Ronni needed to stop at the dry cleaner's to pick up some of her clothes Cornell had dropped off, along with a few of his. She pulled into the space and dug in her purse for the claim ticket. Cynically, she shook her head. Cornell was a dry-cleaning freak. He must have trolled through her apartment looking for something to put in the cleaner's for her. Someone knocking on the roof of her car made her nearly jump out of her skin. She looked up to see the face of Jeff and her heart leaped. After staring at the face filling her window, she was chastened to see it wasn't Jeff at all. *Wait a minute—it's only Tyler. What's wrong with me?*

Tyler had a huge smile. "Hello, there." *He must've heard about the breakup.* "I'm sorry if I scared you."

"Hi, Tyler." Ronni found the ticket and got out of the car. "I guess I was preoccupied."

"So we use the same dry cleaner," he said, falling in step beside her.

"Yes, I guess so," she said. There was no point in telling him this was really Cornell's favorite place. For some reason, Tyler's dull conversation wasn't as annoying as it usually was. "So what are you up to today?"

"As you can see, I'm running errands," Tyler said, opening the door for Ronni and following her into the building. She handed her ticket to the smiling clerk and reached in her purse when she heard the price.

Tyler had his wallet out before Ronni could stop him. "Here, let me get that."

"No, Tyler, it's mostly—"

"I insist." He handed a couple of twenties to the lady, not getting much change in return. Tyler openly appraised Ronni. "You look terrific, as usual. Where are you headed?"

"Home. I've been downtown studying for an exam," Ronni said, not looking at him. She was pretty sure she looked like a bum, wearing no makeup, blue jeans, a white cotton shirt, and sandals, but Tyler was always full of compliments. The lady came back with an armful of clothing.

"Oh, these are Cornell's clothes? We know Cornell clothes," the woman said, handing the bundle to Ronni. Ronni thanked the lady and looked sympathetically at Tyler as they headed out the door.

"Sorry, I tried to warn you. Cornell uses the dry cleaner as a washer and dryer."

"Well, that's all right," Tyler said, shrugging. "If it's something you have to do, I'd just as soon do it for you."

Ronni peered at Tyler. This was the closest he had come to saying anything remotely flirtatious in ages. It might not sound like it, but this was flirtatious *for Tyler.* Now she was sure he'd heard about her breakup with Jeff. "Thanks, Tyler." She turned to open her car.

Tyler cleared his throat. "Um . . . Ronni," he began.

Ronni put the clothes on the passenger's seat and

turned to him. She didn't respond, just looked at him pleasantly and waited.

"Well . . . I heard about your disentanglement with Conley, and I want you to know I'm here for you." Tyler couldn't hold her eyes. Ronni thought this sentiment was difficult for him, but he was trying to be sweet.

"Thanks, Tyler. I appreciate that." *Disentanglement.* His overly proper speech made her want to retch.

"Also, I don't want to present myself as opportunistic, but would you like to accompany me to the Metropolitan Chamber of Commerce's gala?" Tyler took a chance and punctuated his question with a light touch at Ronni's elbow. "Your father's going to be honored, and I thought—"

You have got to be kidding me. "Tyler, I'm not ready for—"

"You don't need to say another word. I completely understand. I'm sorry." Tyler waved his hand apologetically and looked at the ground. "But don't let my *faux pas* detract from my heartfelt sentiment."

"I won't. Um, thanks for asking," Ronni said, not knowing how to get out of this awkward exchange. She got in the car and Tyler closed the door for her.

"Well, have a good day," Tyler said.

Ronni smiled and waved. When he turned to his car, she exhaled, relieved to see him go. She hurriedly put her car in gear and drove away.

As she left, thinking about Tyler's clumsy proposition, something became apparent to her. She had waited years for the right man to come along. She had tried the love route and failed miserably. Her mother had tried the love route and also ended up with a broken heart. Ronni considered the chemical thing the scientists were talking about and wondered if a woman could be wired to be attracted to the wrong kind of man. Maybe a lot of women were. That's why they always fell for the bad boys and weren't attracted to nice guys.

Tyler was handsome, respectful, successful, and nice, and from everything she knew about him, he was honest. She wasn't physically attracted to him. More like repulsed. But she could work on that. Maybe what repelled her was his discomfort with her and his overly solicitous attitude toward her father. Maybe he would be more interesting when she got to know him. Maybe if she took the lead and stopped his boring conversations with a kiss, they might have some chemistry. Maybe he could relax in the comfort of a relationship, the way she did. In Tee's words, *I could loosen him up.*

If Ronni was going to change her life and break out of her Pollyanna cycle, she would have to start doing a few things differently—go against her instincts. They weren't working for her anyway. She decided that the next time Tyler called or asked her out, he would be in for the surprise of his life. She would be ready to take the relationship as far as he wanted. If that meant all the way to the altar—fine. And if, later in marriage, he lied to her or cheated on her, she wouldn't care. With his brains and skills combined with hers, they could be a power couple, like Bill and Hillary Clinton. They could have bright and talented kids. *In our loveless marriage,* she thought sarcastically. No, she wouldn't listen to that emotional side of her brain. Who's to say they couldn't fall in love? A pang gripped her stomach when her mind went to the next thought—*like me and Jeff.*

That did it. She couldn't allow any more dissent from the love-struck, naive side of her mind. She had to be strong and lock-in her new resolve. She pulled out her cell phone and dialed Tyler's number.

"This is Tyler Washington."

"Hey, Tyler. It's Ronni."

"Hello. I was just thinking about you," Tyler joked.

Ronni had to remember: new plan. Be nice.

"Good, because I was thinking about you, too." She could hear Tyler give the phone more attention. Although she felt tired and numb, she aimed for a more cheery tone with him. "Tyler, I would love to accompany you to this chamber of commerce gala thing."

"Wonderful." He sounded more excited than she'd expected. "Wonderful. I'll call you later to solidify our plans."

"That'd be great. Talk to you later."

Jeff and Tamara weren't the only ones who could achieve their goals by any means necessary. *Do what you gotta do and don't look back.* Her new, more-in-charge life started right now.

Chapter Twenty

"All right, you should be okay," Jeff said, turning from his computer and pulling his robe tighter around his body. He picked up one of the documents on his desk and handed it to Benjamin. "This one is Miller's package. You'll just have to cut him a check and add that to it. Did you give anybody the heads-up?"

"I had a meeting with the Algonquin staff last week. I warned them that some changes were coming down the pipe and the situation didn't look good," Benjamin said. His eyes were drawn to a trophy display case in Jeff's home office. He had a lot of sports awards and plaques, mostly topped with baseball players, but some featured little golden swimmers and tennis players. Equally impressive was the number of plaques from debate teams, prize-winning essays, and academic achievement.

Of course they had buried the hatchet between them. Benjamin never even thought about calling the bar about Jeff's indiscretions and didn't ask him about his disclosures to Ronni. He genuinely liked the younger man. Jeff was a man's man. Benjamin had heard a lot about him being a ladies' man, too, and he could see why. He was wealthy, athletic, good-looking—and nice. Not to mention the fact that his gut feeling told him Jeff had been totally devoted and faithful to Ronni.

Benjamin watched Jeff rub his eyes. The younger man

had surprised him when he answered the door earlier wearing pajamas and a robe. Benjamin had listened to the tape from his underhanded wife. He felt guilty for his role in Jeff and Ronni's obvious breakup. Now he knew better than to have Jeff come over to his house.

"So what have you got? The flu?" Ben asked.

"I hope not. It's probably just a bad cold. But I feel really exhausted." Jeff sniffed. He put his hand on more documents and leaned over to explain them to Benjamin. "These are to settle with the creditors. You sign here. This is your agreement on the value of the inventory. You satisfied with that amount?"

Benjamin eyed the figure Jeff was pointing to and nodded his head. "That's why I got you. You're the best. That's almost what I paid for everything."

"Cool," Jeff said mildly and grabbed some paperwork off the printer. "Now, this is the plan I've outlined for you to make payments back to your company and keep you out of jail. This is your copy. I'll present it in court. You don't have to appear."

Benjamin looked over the plan. "That's good. Good. I can do this."

"And . . ." Jeff stretched and scratched the back of his head, "I think that's it. I've already given you everything else."

"Thank you, son. You've done a great job," Benjamin said, smiling at the documents in his hand.

Jeff smirked at the word *son*. *Yep, that's what I was determined to be, officially.*

Benjamin noticed the apathetic mood and cheerless look on Jeff's face. This was a good time to bring something else up. "You don't do divorces, do you?"

Jeff looked up, mildly interested, but not at all shocked. He leisurely shook his head and managed a small smile. "Making a clean break from *all* your problems?"

"Yeah." Benjamin's eyes fell back to the documents in his hands. "I've got to get back to being the me I knew."

"Yeah, I hear you."

"I finally moved out of the bedroom, for good. The same day I heard that damn tape. Not that Tamara noticed—or cared, for that matter. I'd been sleeping apart from her on and off anyway." He assessed whether Jeff would be interested to hear more and decided he looked relaxed enough. "I haven't confronted her. I don't want to give her an advantage until I consult somebody about custody of Benji."

Jeff nodded.

"Do you like my chances?"

"For what? Full custody?" Jeff said. Seeing Benjamin's nod, he continued. "I don't know . . . it's not my field. But I think your age would be a factor."

"That's what I was thinking, too," he said. "But grandparents raise kids all the time. I know I'm pretty healthy, and if I build a home for him. . . ."

"But you'd have to prove the same thing those grandparents do, that she's an unfit mother and incapable of providing a safe home environment for Benji. I know she sucks, but can you say that?"

"I don't know. But I'm thinking I'll have a two-parent home and she'll be a single mother."

Jeff raised an eyebrow. "Two-parent?"

Benjamin smiled sheepishly. "If she'll have me back. I've found myself talking to Bev more and more. We even met for dinner last week. I told her . . . a lot of what I've been going through. You know, I never stopped loving her."

Jeff's brow creased irritably. He tilted his head and sat back in his chair, trying to figure out the man before him. "Then, Ben, *why in the hell* did you get involved with that manipulative, evil female? I've known of her for years, and she's bad news."

"I don't know, really. I've thought back on it all these years and I don't really remember making a conscious decision to start fooling around with her."

"So it was a sex thing?" Jeff said, deadpan. This was really more information than he wanted to know, but since he liked Benjamin and thought him to be honorable, he was trying comprehend how he could do something so out of character, so vile in Jeff's mind. You didn't leave your wife and child for sex, no matter how good it was.

"Honestly, I don't know, Jeff. I'd have to say, not really. Bev and I had a healthy sex life until she entered the picture. I know you think I'm crazy or lying, but I can't even remember seeing Tamara as a sexually appealing person. I just wound up having sex with her."

Jeff shook his head, disgusted. "Whatever. I think you need to accept responsibility for your actions. You destroyed your marriage, for Pete's sake."

"I *would*." His eyes pleaded with Jeff to believe what he was about to say. "You *know* I would if I had pursued her . . . had wanted her. But that's the thing—I didn't want her. Do you think I could've been drugged or hypnotized or something?"

Jeff snickered. "By her womanly wiles?"

Benjamin disconsolately shook his head and looked at his hands. "I'm serious, Jeff. You don't know how I've agonized about this over the years, even before you gave me the tape. I look at Benji and I love him with all my heart. But I look at his mother and wonder—where did she come from? How did I wreck my family and wind up with her?" He glanced at Jeff. "I have needs . . . in our marriage . . . but even—even that doesn't feel like anything but a physical release. I don't want *her.* I ended up with her."

Something about Benjamin's bewilderment did strike a chord with Jeff, but he couldn't put his finger on it.

The man obviously had no one else he felt he could discuss this with, so he was trying to take it seriously, but what he was suggesting seemed so implausible. "Would you admit it if you had pursued her? You didn't seem too ready to admit your problems to Ronni and her mother."

"No, that's different. I didn't want to *tell* them. But, as you know, I acknowledged that I did it. I accepted responsibility for the mess I made. I just didn't want to reveal it. I've got no reason to lie to you about Tamara. About my pursuing her."

That's true, Jeff thought. He really didn't feel like he had the energy to delve into this. He didn't want to be both Benjamin's attorney and his psychoanalyst. Besides, he had his own problems. But since Benjamin was the only person he was scheduled to see today, he gave him a little more of his time.

Jeff spread his hands over his knees. "Okay, so how did it start?"

"What do you mean?"

"With you and her? More to the point, how did you start sleeping with her?"

"I can't really remember. She worked for Bev. She would stay over late, finishing stuff. I was up late, too. I'd wind up screwing her." Benjamin felt there was no need for delicacy. They were both grown men and he was sure that, as a guy and a former athlete, Jeff had heard worse language and licentious tales.

"I know you said that, but I need you to be specific, Ben. What did you say to her and she say to you to have sex?" Jeff spoke slowly as though Benjamin were too thick in the head to understand. Benjamin caught it and he didn't mind. He was happy to tell him everything. He was glad to have someone who was actually taking an interest in helping him with this thing that had been weighing on his mind for years.

"That's what I'm trying to tell you. I'd be up late . . . she'd come into my office . . . or if I was watching television, she'd come in there and make conversation. She'd ask if I needed anything, or freshen up my drink, or see if she could get me a snack. I'd barely notice her and her pointless chatter—and we'd wind up having sex." Ben punctuated his words by giving an explicit shrug.

Jeff stared at the man unbelievingly for a second, frowning. Then his face cleared and he stood up. *Oh, my God.* He rubbed the top of his head with both hands and looked at the ceiling, then walked over to the other side of the room and rubbed his chin. He came back to Benjamin and leaned toward him, supporting his rear on the edge of the desk. "You say . . . she'd freshen your drink?"

"Yeah." Ben nodded vigorously. "Do you think that's when I was drugged? I thought that, but then I wouldn't be able to function, right?"

Jeff quickly shook his head. "Not necessarily. Depending on what she was using, you could perform sexually but not have full control of your faculties. But let's not get ahead of ourselves here. Do you remember her preparing you a drink every time you wound up with her?"

Benjamin searched his mind. "I think so—I can't say for sure. It didn't happen every night. But I don't mean just alcohol. I mean, sometimes I would have a Scotch, but, you know, hot cocoa or soda or whatever."

"That's okay. If it's what I'm thinking, it'll work in anything." Fire burned in Jeff's eyes. This woman was *unreal.* But he wouldn't put it past her, now remembering his conservation with April at the barbecue. And he'd already seen that she would go to any lengths to obtain what she wanted. Though she found him categorically unattainable, she'd spitefully ruined his relationship with Ronni anyway. "You remember the sex?"

Benjamin shook his head sadly. "Like a haze. Like a dream fading in and out."

"Until you got married?"

"Right. Only then was the nightmare vivid," he said with a shudder.

Jeff clasped his hands together and then placed his palms against his forehead. He pulled his hands down his face and covered his mouth. "Oh, my, God. Oh, my, God, Ben." He looked back at the man, thoroughly sympathetic. "You've been living a lie. Your marriage is a complete and total lie!"

"I know!" Ben stood up and went to the other side of the room. He felt his anger rising. He turned back to Jeff. "So you believe me?"

"With that witch, I could believe anything. Besides, a friend of hers told me that she pulled tricks like this on guys in the past." He sat in the chair Benjamin had vacated. "If what we suspect is true, you'd have excellent grounds for full custody and invalidation of the prenuptial agreement." Then Jeff's face grew somber. "But you can't prove it. That was seven years ago. Any trace of the drug is long gone from your system and I'll bet she had the sense to get rid of the evidence."

Benjamin sat opposite Jeff on the chair at the desk. He leaned forward and intertwined his fingers together. "Maybe I can trick her into using it on me again."

Jeff leaned back in his chair and stretched his feet to the desk. "I don't like the sound of that. If it's what I'm thinking—Roofies—that stuff can be pretty harmful."

"But if I knew she had it, I could say she used it on me when we got married?"

"I don't think so. I'm not a divorce lawyer, but if I were on the other side, I would attack you as very creatively trying to get out of your prenup."

"What if I told her I wanted a divorce? Then she would

probably use it on me again, to make me sign something, or so she could get pregnant again." Benjamin became excited with his planned trap.

"Or kill you," Jeff said dryly, but his face told Benjamin he was quite serious. Benjamin was visibly stunned and sat back in his chair. Jeff continued. "You don't want to start messing with her on her territory. I've heard that kind of trickery and game-playing is totally her world. You're a novice. Figure out what you can do to fight her above-board."

"You're right. I guess in my anger at being made such a fool, I got carried away," he agreed quietly.

"Look," Jeff said, removing his feet from the desk and leaning over his knees. "I didn't want to mention this as long as I thought you were going to hang in there, but I think you should be able to find more solid ground in . . . in her having adulterous relationships."

"What? You know about—"

"No. I don't know for sure about any guys. But it was no accident that she pulled that bull with Ronni and me. I don't think the target was Ronni as much as it was *me*." Jeff held the older man's eyes. Understanding came across Benjamin's face as Jeff continued. "Ever since I started coming to see you, she's been coming on strong. I shot her down, but it makes me wonder—"

"If someone else took her up on it?" Ben finished, looking numb. "I've been such a stupid fool."

Jeff touched his forearm and let his hand stay there. "No. Don't beat up on yourself. Don't even give it another thought. You were married for years. It's been a long time since you've been out there, and back then you weren't well off. You've never had to face these kinds of scheming, winner-takes-all females."

Benjamin rubbed a hand over his eyes, breaking his contact with Jeff and wilting in the chair. "What have I

done? What have I done to my Beverly? My Ronni?" He
looked at Jeff. "You and Ronni?"

Jeff spoke consolingly to him. "What did I just say?
Don't blame yourself."

His face was red with anguish and rage. "But I'm the
one! I *am* the doddering old fool!"

"Benjamin," Jeff called his name to calm him down.
Being a man, he understood why Benjamin was angrier
at possibly being a cuckold than he was about the drugging. It was one thing to be made a fool of privately, but
an entirely other matter to imagine being mocked by another man who was sleeping with your wife.

"No! Why didn't I tell Beverly about it the first time it
happened and have her fire that bitch?"

"You felt guilty and ashamed," Jeff offered.

"Flattered, no doubt!" He stood up and tugged up the
belt of his pants, a nervous habit.

"That might have been a little of it, but you didn't
want her. Remember that." He watched Benjamin pace
to the window.

"Oh, I remember. How could I forget? I have to look at
my repugnant wife every damn day of my damn life!" He
looked back at Jeff, calming a little, desperate. "How can I
live with her without killing her? How do I go back, after
what we've uncovered, and look in that wicked face?"

"You'll have to calm down." Jeff stood and went to
Benjamin. He put his hand on his back and led him over
to the leather couch. They sat down together. "Hire a
private investigator. Tell Tamara you want to take Benji
with you on a trip. Make it a week. Somewhere where
you are totally responsible for his care. You can't take
Beverly or else you'll be culpable."

Benjamin glanced admiringly at the younger man,
who he considered really brilliant. Jeff knew exactly how
Benjamin's mind worked. He had, indeed, immediately

envisioned a relaxing trip with Benji *and Beverly*. It would have been a chance for both him and Benji to get closer to Beverly.

"While you're out of town, I can almost guarantee you that Tamara won't be able to just sit around and look after the house. With your detective on her, you should have some strong evidence for court to prove that she was having an affair, or even multiple partners . . . depending on how she meets the man on film. Does your prenup cover adultery?"

Benjamin was beginning to feel better. "Oh, definitely. At least I wasn't that much of a fool."

"Good. Who handled your last divorce?"

"Tyler. But that one was pretty amiable. Beverly initiated it and I didn't want to give her any problems."

"Well, in this case, you'll need someone who specializes in this sort of thing." Jeff went to get his BlackBerry. "I've got just the person for you. A buddy of mine." He scrolled through the device. "Here it is, Frank Chase. The boy is good. And it doesn't hurt that he thinks your daughter is the best thing since sliced bread. He'd do anything to see that you get what you want out of your split. As a matter of fact, call him before you hire the private eye. He'll recommend someone." He wrote Frank's information down on a piece of paper and handed it to Benjamin.

"Thanks, Jeff. You are a lifesaver. I owe so much to you."

"No problem. Now, just play it cool until you get what you want. You were ready to try an ill-advised covert plan on her before. Let this be your plan. Play it cool and avoid her around the house as much as possible." He tilted his head and looked at Benjamin doubtfully. "Think you can do that?"

"To get rid of her? I can be as cool as the iceberg that hit the Titanic."

They both smiled. "Good analogy. She'll be blindsided."

Chapter Twenty-One

Uh-oh. Cornell saw him first, but there was no way to divert their course. He and Ronni were leaving the tennis club's dining area. Cornell had finally managed to get his cousin to laugh at one of his outrageous stories after weeks of moping . . . and *now this*. Jeff was heading right for them—with a woman. He and the woman were laughing together and hadn't seen them yet. Cornell looked at Ronni. From the sudden horrified expression on her face and the hesitancy in her step, he knew she now saw them, too. "Come on, baby. Keep walking," he whispered out of the side of his mouth. "And keep smiling."

Ronni attempted to look jovial, but the false smile died on its way to her lips. The girl was really young and very pretty. She had beautiful brown skin, shoulder-length crinkly hair, and a perfectly voluptuous figure. Most depressingly of all, the woman was wearing a cute tennis outfit. Ronni's eyes fell to the floor. Unfortunately, that only gave her an unwanted view of her oversize T-shirt and ugly blue sweat shorts. *Why? Why did I wear this? Didn't I even consider the possibility of running into him?*

The answer was no. It had been several weeks since her breakup with Jeff and even though earlier she dreaded the likelihood of seeing him, she hadn't yet encountered him. Even though they first met here, they never came to this club while they were officially dating, so she hadn't put this on her mental list of places to avoid. She thought it was a safe place to make a public show that she was still alive—not hiding in the house like her mother. Now, it seemed her efforts backfired.

Rule number one of a breakup was you've got to look fantastic the first time you see your ex. Let him know what he's missing out on. She'd already failed that assignment. And she was about to fail rule number two: look like you're having the time of your life. Ronni glanced quickly from left to right. There was no quick exit to dash into. She would have to meet him head-on.

As Jeff crossed the lounge, he looked up and almost tripped over his own feet. Ronni and her cousin were walking along the same path as he and Lizbeth. There was only one big aisle patrons could travel without snaking through countless dining tables. Jeff recovered from his near-stumble by hanging back and pretending he was waiting for Liz to catch up. She was a step or two behind him. When Liz drew even with him, Jeff slung an arm around her shoulders. Liz, who'd seen him lose his footing, assumed he'd wrapped his arm around her to prevent himself from falling. She made a crack about it. She frowned, though, when Jeff laughed too hard at her small joke.

Jeff's eyes never left Ronni. It was the first time he'd seen her since their breakup. Impossibly, she was more beautiful now than he had ever seen her. Her casual appearance pulled heavily at his heart. He thought she looked identical to the way she did when they used to relax around his house or at her apartment. As far as he was concerned, this was her private look. She would wear one of his T-shirts and he'd lustily watch her pad around the house in her little socks as he tried to concentrate on his paperwork. Even if they just left the bed, watching her would make him want her again. Now, so many days from that happy time, he steeled himself for the cold shoulder. He didn't know if he could stand it if she didn't speak at all so he took the lead when they reached each other.

"Hi," he said, grinning like a damn fool. Was it his imagination or did he say it too loud?

"Hey," Cornell responded dryly. He tried to walk around Jeff and Lizbeth, but he had to stop when he saw Ronni frozen in place. Cornell wanted to rescue her, but there was no way to pull her away without Jeff knowing how miserable he'd left her.

"Hi," Ronni thought she said, but it came out as "Ha" because the word got caught in her throat. She didn't intend to, but her eyes darted around Jeff's face as though she was only allowed so much time to memorize his features. He was so heartbreakingly handsome and desirable that she thought she would cry. And even if he was a liar, the look in his eyes was the same adoring one she remembered.

"So, you guys came here to hit?" Jeff would've said or done anything to keep those deep black eyes on his. He swallowed hard, his heart pounding. He was gripped by an overpowering impulse to pull Ronni to him and kiss her.

"Um, yeah." Ronni found the meager words difficult to utter but she tried for more. She wanted to appear composed and over him. "It was . . . Cornell was . . ." She couldn't do it. She looked at her shoes.

"Hi," Liz said. She waved and looked from Cornell to Ronni to Jeff with a pleasant smile that nobody returned.

It was the first time Ronni remembered the girl was there. She now looked at her and blinked blankly before she felt Cornell tugging her arm.

"We were just leaving," Cornell said and gently pulled Ronni away. "Let's go."

"Okay. Have a good day," Jeff said, turning his body to

watch them disappear into the club. He only realized that his hand was waving idiotically in the air after Liz pulled his arm down.

After they passed through the dining room doors and out of Jeff's sight, Cornell immediately led Ronni around a secluded corner and allowed her to collapse against him. To the casual viewer it appeared that Cornell slipped his arm around her shoulders when they left the presence of Jeff. In actuality, he was supporting Ronni's body and coaxing her to "walk" and "hold it together" the entire time. It was all Cornell could do to keep his own eyes from watering as he comforted his cousin, who was dampening his chest with body-wracking silent sobs. He blamed himself for bringing her to the club. He should've kept his promise to hit Jeff over the head with a two-by-four when he broke Ronni's heart. That jerk. He was supposedly so in love with Ronni and here he was already dating someone else.

Ronni wiped her nose on Cornell's shirt and he didn't object. He was drawing a blank, trying to think of something to do to make her feel better. He knew what wouldn't work, and he thought he heard Ronni trying to suggest in a small voice another bad idea.

"No. Let's go," he said, trying to steer her to the door.

"No—no. I just want to . . . to go upstairs . . . and watch them. I—I . . . *have* to see them together."

"No, you don't. Let's go." She was struggling against him to go upstairs and watch Jeff and his date from the big windows, but she didn't have enough energy to effectively fight. Cornell offered a compromise. "Here. Put my sunglasses on. You can glance over at them as we go to the car. But we *are* leaving."

Ronni slipped on Cornell's sunglasses. She had always heard people say that it was hard seeing your ex for the first time if you were in love, but she didn't think it would be that bad for her. After all, she was angry with him, right? And she was supposed to be the tough, new Ronni who'd decided to move on. But actually seeing him was a whole other animal than imagining running into him. When she saw him, she realized that no matter how she tried to delude herself, she still loved him.

She glanced over at the courts before Cornell shuffled her into his car. She hadn't really seen anything telling. From what she could see, without obviously staring, Jeff and the girl set their stuff down and went out on the court. As they left the club, Ronni kept Cornell's sunglasses on as she cried freely. Why should she be so affected by his dating again? That was his nature, wasn't it?

Lizbeth collapsed on the chair adjacent to the tennis court. She was done in and breathing hard. Jeff had played that round of tennis as though it were a blood sport. Liz could barely keep up with him as he aggressively hurled slams and aces at her. Drinking her water, she glowered over at him. Jeff placed a towel on his head and leaned over his knees.

"You want to tell me what that was all about?" she asked, nudging his foot with hers.

Jeff lifted his head and removed the towel. "Hmm?" he said, clueless. When he saw Liz's mean look, he realized he might have been a bit harsh on the court. "I'm sorry. I guess I played too hard."

"You think?" She cocked her head sarcastically, cutting her eyes at him as she rubbed her leg. "So, who is she?"

"Who's who?" Jeff busied himself furiously untying and retying his shoe.

"Jeff, come on. Your whole mood changed when you saw her."

Jeff moved on to the other shoe, still not making eye

contact with Liz. His jaws were tight. But Liz wasn't the type to back down from a fight, or else she would never have gone into law.

"You didn't introduce me—and we were awfully *chummy* all of a sudden." She watched him calmly, even as his eyes told her to drop it. Liz hugged one of her knees. "So what's up?"

"Are we gonna play tennis, Oprah?"

"Not if you're going to try to kill me out there." She surveyed his face. Jeff sat back in his chair, grabbing a sports drink. "Plus, it's interesting that you called me Oprah. You should've called me Dr. Phil, because it seems that *someone* needs to get in touch with his feelings."

Jeff cut his eyes at her.

"Let me tell you, Jeff. It hasn't exactly been a pleasure working with you lately. You've been snappish and impatient. I can't seem to do anything right. You're even short with the clients."

"We—we just have a pretty full workload . . . and with Mr. Yates's contract coming up, I've been a little on edge." He looked at her sympathetically. "It's not you. You're doing a good job."

"Oh, I know it's not me. I had my doubts there for a minute, but now I'm sure it's her." She gestured toward the clubhouse with her head. Jeff stole a quick glance in the direction she was indicating and started to chew his bottom lip. "That's Ronni, isn't it? The reason I used to have some blessedly short workdays?"

He leaned over his knees and rubbed his face. Why did he have to hire such an intelligent smart-ass? "Just drop it." He emphasized that instruction with a chop of the hand and returned to rubbing his chin.

"All right, but as Dr. Phil would say, how's that workin' for ya?" She did her best Phil McGraw voice and smiled at Jeff.

He didn't smile back.

Chapter Twenty-Two

Catching up with mother had been noticeably difficult lately. With her NADA classes and dating, Ronni knew she had neglected to spend time with her. She took into account that her mother might be pulling an attitude, to prove that now *she* was too busy for *her.* Beverly hadn't attended any social events that Ronni knew of, but if she at least had resumed her relationship with her girlfriends, that was some improvement.

That's why Ronni, who had been kind of depressed and lonely lately, seized her opportunity for quality time by attending church with her mother. Although a lot of Beverly's friends preferred the more staid atmosphere of the Episcopalian church, she favored the soul-stirring, animated sermons and spirited, room-rocking songs at her century-old Baptist church. As Ronni listened to the sermon, she thought she had made a great choice for what otherwise would have been an uneventful Sunday morning.

The preacher was excellently reviving an old sermon of Reverend C.L. Franklin's, declaring that the congregation should let nothing separate them from the love of God. Tears burned at the back of Ronni's eyes as the reverend hit his stride, naming all the trials and tribulations a person would go through—the good times and the bad, when you were weak and weary. Nothing should separate you from the love of God. The choir came in slowly and built to a swelling crescendo with a song that touched Ronni and caused the tears to copiously spring forth. She was moved to stand up, just as many others around her were, and wave her hand in the air. Beverly stood with Ronni and held her around the waist, singing loudly as she reassured her daughter.

Ronni had been laid bare. As they took their seats and the reverend invited testimonials, she was hardly listening because she was leaning into the security of Beverly's arms and wiping her eyes. But soon, one woman's testimony attracted her attention. Ronni sat up and looked. She whispered to her mother.

"Is that Mrs. Winters?"

"Yes. Cathleen is a member, too," Beverly whispered back. Ronni turned her attention to Cathleen's words, punctuated by frequent "amen"s and "tell it"s from the other worshippers.

". . . and I was falling under the influence of the devil. You all know how Satan can look so good and say all the things you want to hear. Show you all the things you want to see. He can sneak up on you when you're weak. I have to admit . . . I was weak. I wasn't thinking right, and everything he told me to do—I did. You all know that the world sees me as successful. I am supposed to be a shrewd businesswoman. I allowed that vanity and ego— you see, not God—ego, go to my head. When I got to the point where I couldn't rationalize that I was doing what God wanted me to do, I turned my back on God.

"Now, listen, the reverend says let nothing separate you from the love of God. How right he is. When I turned away from God and forgot that His love was what had brought me this far in life, He gave me a wake-up call. God allowed me to follow the devil until he threatened my life's work. I almost lost my company following behind Satan.

You see, I'm hardheaded. It had to get to *that* point—the point where I had nowhere to turn—for me to realize what I was doing and turn back to God's love. Thank you, Jesus. I am here to testify today because I got out of the devil's grip in time to save my company."

Through all the clapping and praise following Cathleen Winters's testimony, Ronni sat stunned. Was she talking about Jeff? Her heart beat thunderously against her chest. In this context, if she were talking about Jeff, his actions were more terrifying. *She almost lost her company following behind the good-looking, syrupy-sweet-worded devil.* Ronni felt as if she were going to throw up. She reached in her miniscule purse for a peppermint. Beverly watched her daughter searching and instinctively pulled a few mints out of her handbag and placed them in Ronni's palm. Ronni thanked her and popped the candy into her mouth. The sweetness helped to alleviate the sourness in her stomach, and she felt a little better. She looked back to the front of the room, but she couldn't really concentrate as others bore witness.

Suddenly, Ronni had an overwhelming sensation to protect her father. She needed to forgive him for any perceived wrongs and help him escape from the grip of the devil, too. But even as she portrayed Jeff this way, her feelings fought that image. Whatever Jeff was, he was not evil. He couldn't have faked the emotion she saw in his eyes whenever he was with her. Could he? And why had he cut short his trip to San Francisco? He had been so excited about attaining a new client. *But he's a liar. He said he wouldn't represent Daddy anymore and he lied to me,* she reminded herself.

When the church service ended, Beverly wanted to talk to some of her friends and show off her beautiful visitor, but Ronni begged off.

"Mom, I'm not up to saying hi to everybody. You go ahead."

"Oh, come on. You had lots of advice for me to get back out there and *I* went through a *divorce*. You're just hurt over puppy love," Beverly chided her.

Ronni cut her eyes at her mom. It wasn't funny to characterize the most intense love she'd ever had in her life in this trivial manner.

"You enjoyed the services. At least tell the pastor how you liked his sermon."

"Mom, please. I still feel a little gun-shy. I don't want to talk to anybody," she confessed.

Beverly gave up and went visiting. Ronni sat on the bench and looked around at the exquisite stained-glass windows before her eyes settled on Cathleen Winters, who was also enjoying fellowship with others. When Ronni saw her conversation wane, she screwed up her nerves and crossed the room to talk to Cathleen, who was collecting her belongings from the pew.

"Hi, Mrs. Winters," she said, joining Cathleen at the bench.

She seemed happy to see Ronni. "Oh, hi, Ronni. How are you? You came with Beverly?"

"Yeah." Ronni looked at her hands, trying to get the courage to ask her what she needed to know.

"That's nice. Yeah, Beverly is a good member—involved in all the committees and stuff I'm too chicken to get on." Cathleen chuckled.

"You know, your testimony . . . it was really poignant." Ronni was beating around the bush.

Cathleen placed her purse on her arm. "Well, thank you, honey. Yeah, that's my story. Praise God."

"But . . . um, the devil whose influence you fell under . . ." Ronni alternated between glancing at her and looking down.

"Mm-hmm?" Cathleen could tell Ronni was struggling with something, and though she wasn't a patient woman, she waited.

"You almost lost your business and all, and . . . were you . . . were you talking about Jeff?"

"What?" Cathleen looked confused. "What do you mean, baby?"

"Was Jeff the reason you almost lost your business?" she finally spit it out.

Cathleen tilted her head and looked at Ronni strangely. "Aren't you seeing him?"

"Um . . . no. I mean . . . not anymore."

Cathleen stared for an instant. "Well, I can see why, if that's what you're thinking about that boy." She gave a mocking chuckle. Ronni felt her face burning and couldn't make eye contact. She felt Cathleen touch her arm. "No, baby, I'm not talking about Jeff," she said, amused.

Ronni looked up expectantly, hoping for more. Fortunately, Cathleen Winters was the type to take the lead in any conversation.

"Jeff, praise God, is the reason I *didn't* lose my company." Cathleen sat down on her pew and indicated for Ronni to sit, too. "Look, I don't mind telling you this because I know your family and y'all aren't prone to gossip." She gestured with her hands the same way Ronni saw her doing with Jeff that day at Navy Pier.

"The devil I was following after was gambling, baby girl. I would travel all over the world gambling. It all seemed so glamorous—and more fun than my everyday life. I would win sometimes, but most of the time, I would lose. I wasn't that good." She laughed at herself. "But it was fun in the beginning. I was getting into some major gambling *and* some major debt. I was making business decisions based on 'how much money can I get out of this for me?' Not my employees and my customers, but *me*. That was the vanity part. I couldn't admit that I was lying to myself and following the devil. Thank God I met Jeff, and he helped me to dig myself out of the hole I got myself into. He's sharp as a whip. And he knew where to make cuts and where to consolidate, and he analyzed my business strengths and got me back on track." Cathleen paused here because Ronni appeared to be lost in her own thoughts. She reached over and touched Ronni's hand. Whether it was to get her attention or to provide reassurance, Ronni didn't know, but she couldn't hide the remorse on her face.

"Look, baby, I ended up selling off the cosmetics line, but I got to keep the rest and, to tell you the truth, hair care and beauty supplies are really my thing. I had only been expanding out of greed, you know. Jeff got me a good deal in the buyout and I channeled that money back into the remaining arm of the company."

She stopped talking again and smiled. She seemed to be thrilled to have someone young interested in her tale, but she was also aware that Ronni must be going through her own thing. Cathleen saw Beverly approaching and stood up. "Hey, there, Beverly. I was talking to your girl." She kissed Beverly's cheek.

"Yes, I see that. You're the lucky one. She didn't want to greet anybody else," Beverly said with a chuckle.

"Well," Cathleen said, looking down at Ronni, "I suspect that she only talked to me because she needed to get some answers about something that's weighing on her mind."

Beverly looked at her child. "Well, I always taught her to seek advice from whomever God directed her to."

"Amen to that." Cathleen laughed.

Beverly touched Ronni's back. "You ready to go?"

"Yeah," she was barely able to say. As she stood to follow Beverly, who was already making her way out of the church; she turned to Cathleen. "Thanks so much, Mrs. Winters."

"That's all right, baby. But if you and Jeff broke up over this nonsense, then I think you have some apologizing to do."

Ronni only nodded and raised her hand weakly in reply.

"Your mother has my number. Call me if you need to know anything else," Cathleen called after her.

In the car, Ronni was very quiet while driving Beverly to her home.

"Why are you so quiet? What are you thinking about?"

"Mrs. Winters." Ronni glanced over to her mother. "Did you know what kind of trouble she was in? What she was talking about when she was testifying?"

"Oh . . . yeah. I did." Beverly waved a dismissive hand. "It's a terrible thing, but it could happen to anybody. You'd be surprised at the people who've fallen victim to gambling."

Now that Ronni had a better understanding of Cathleen's situation, she was beginning to put all the pieces of the puzzle together and she didn't like what it meant.

"Mom, is Daddy one of those people?"

Beverly fell silent and looked out her side window. She didn't turn to Ronni when she answered. "You'll have to ask your father about that."

Ronni didn't need to. She was pretty sure she already knew the answer.

Chapter Twenty-Three

Where's ice cream when you need it? Ronni thought as she entered her apartment well past ten o'clock. The test had been tough but Ronni thought she did very well. After class, she compared her answers with Theresa's. She was always self-effacing, but from what Ronni could tell, Theresa had also done well. Lance would use the results to see how well they were grasping the material and how much more information he would need to present to prepare them for the final exam. In five more months, they were supposed to be ready to get their certificates.

Since she hadn't stopped for chocolate ice cream, she would have to comfort herself with the next best thing— a steaming-hot herbal bath and a glass of wine. She had nowhere to go for the rest of the day, so she could allow herself to drink two glasses of wine if she wanted.

She looked at the caller ID. No calls from Jeff. She didn't want to think about why she always hoped the machine would read CONLEY, JEFF. Instead it showed that her so-called boyfriend, Tyler, had called. And her father. She would listen to their messages later.

She grabbed the wine from the kitchen and headed to the tub.

The water was nice and the wine and massage jets were taking her far away, but not far enough away from the previous week. Now that the preliminary test was

over, Ronni had nothing else to occupy her mind but
how she had treated Jeff. Because she was in the tub, she
tried to focus her thoughts on their first phone call. He
had been so sexy and masculine and determined to see
her. She gave a small laugh when she thought about how
he wouldn't get off the phone so she could answer the
other line. Her stomach flipped over when her next
thought was of the look on Jeff's face when she left him
with that security guard at the parking garage. She wondered if Jeff had to go down to a police station or spend
a night in jail.

At the time, she hadn't cared what happened to him.
But now she remembered the look on his face. He was
very tired. And he was very hurt. *He came back from San
Francisco to talk to me. Daddy must have told him I'd called
him upset . . . and Jeff must've come right back.*

Ronni tried to bury her regret in discomfort. She
turned on the hot-water tap. It was boiling hot and she
could feel her skin's temperature rising to a painfully
uncomfortable level. *He tried to explain everything and I
threw accusation after accusation at him.* Ronni winced
but kept the tap running for several seconds before
turning it off and lying back.

In their relationship, he had been so affectionate. Jeff
was the one who always expressed his feelings openly. *I
called him a snake and a liar.* She thought about his planning Venetian Night and how he needed to hear her say
she loved him before they made love for the first time. It
was supposedly the role of women to be so nakedly vulnerable. *He completely opened up to me. He allowed himself
to fully experience our relationship. How could I have believed
the worst?*

Cathleen had told her she owed Jeff an apology. She was
right, but it was pointless now. Jeff had moved on—no
doubt with someone who wasn't as full of suspicions and

unfounded fears. Yeah, the girl he was dating now looked very pleasant and cute and not such an uphill struggle. That's how Ronni assessed herself, as hard work, day in and day out. *She* even found herself to be hard work. Who was this person she was always projecting to the world? She had felt more alive and more her true self with Jeff than she had ever felt in her life. *And I said he looted family companies. Always second-guessing his motives and not accepting the fact that I had a good man.*

So he had lied about representing her father. So what. Why couldn't she have taken a moment and listened to his explanation? As loving as he had been to her, she at least owed him that. He was trying to keep her father's secret and almost certainly save their company. No wonder he was now with someone normal. He'd found one cuckoo in Ronni, but now he was free to shower his endless affections on someone who could appreciate him. Cute girls were a dime a dozen and Jeff didn't have to waste time with nutcases like her. *I believed he talked with Tamara, of all the stupid things.*

She drank more wine and determined not to think about it anymore. But her pain needed a scapegoat—and went to Cornell. Hadn't he planted that bug in her ear about Randy's father before she even got out of the gate with Jeff? And hadn't he left that paper in her car about Cathleen? She knew better than to listen to his catty gossip. He and his evil friends never wanted to see anybody happy.

Ronni reached for the phone to call Jeff. *Screw Cornell and his bunch. I'll call Jeff and beg him to give me another chance. Then, I'll show them. I'll end up happy and with the man I love, despite them.* She dialed his number except for the last digit. Her face suddenly crumpled and she hung up the phone.

Who am I kidding? This was not Cornell's fault. It was

all her. Look at her life. She was alone and had set up her entire life to function alone. Forever. Look at her cold apartment. Look at her little car. Look at her! In twenty-seven years she'd only allowed one man to get close enough to her to become intimate and now she'd even driven him away! As she ran all these things through her mind, her silent weeping became gut-wrenching cries.

When the phone rang, she wiped her face and tried to get some control before answering. It was her father. She couldn't deny her disappointment. She had to give up this thinking that Jeff would ever call her again. He dumped Stephanie for game-playing, and now he probably saw Ronni in the same category: a crazy, self-centered female. She remembered he'd had such high expectations for his relationship with her. Jeff had placed her on a pedestal and soon found that his statue was cracked.

"Hello," she said with barely any energy.

"Hi, honey. Please don't hang up," Benjamin said quickly.

"I'm not going to hang up on you, Daddy."

"Oh, good. I'm sorry to call you so late, but I know you have your classes and I haven't talked to you since . . . well, you know."

"Yes. I know, and I'm sorry I overreacted."

"Oh?" Benjamin hadn't expected this. "Oh, no. You have nothing to apologize for. I should've kept you in the loop about what was going on all along."

"I'm sure you had your reasons for not telling me."

"Yes, that's just the thing I called you about. I wanted to tell you why I've been so . . . been such a mess lately."

"Daddy, I'm sure it's a good reason and all, but I just don't feel like—"

"No, Ronni. Listen to me. I've hurt you and . . . I'd

rather do this in person, but it's been so hard to catch up with you lately that I want to get it all out in this call."

"All right." She didn't really want to hear his explanation, she didn't have the energy to protest either.

"Okay, sweetheart. Listen." He was having a hard time starting. "Where to begin."

"You've been gambling." She only said it for him because she was too exhausted to sit through his attempt to tell her about it delicately.

"Uh, yes. Jeff told you?" Benjamin sounded miserable.

"No, Daddy. I only wish I'd heard it from Jeff."

"Your mother?"

Ronni sat up, a little more interested. "Mom knows?"

"Well, yes . . . I told her recently. If you didn't hear it from either of them, how did you know?"

"I finally put two and two together and came up with four."

"Well, I always said you were a smart girl. I should've known you'd figure it out yourself after you found out about the Algonquin closing." Benjamin sighed heavily. "And, honey . . . I'm sorry for the way you heard about that closing. Believe me. I regret the day I ever laid eyes on that woman."

The way I heard it? Of course! Jeff had come home and heard the message—and since he wasn't in cahoots with Tamara, he must've been livid and wanted to see Ronni for immediate damage control.

Now she felt even worse. Grief-stricken, she could barely verbalize her next words. "Daddy, really . . . listen to me. I don't want you to go into that right now. I had a grueling test with NADA today and I'm pooped. You were right, let's do this in person. We can meet for lunch tomorrow and you can tell me all about it then."

"Aw, honey. I can't do that. I'm in Toronto with Benji right now."

"What? I was going to go with Tyler to see you get your award."

"I'll be back in time for the chamber's gala. I'll explain all this later. But I had to call you for another reason—"

"No more. Call me tomorrow." She hoped he would let her off the phone.

"No. I can't sleep on this. I owe it to Jeff. No matter what I've done to him, he always comes through for me. So if I can repair the damage I've done to him . . . to you . . . I'm going to try."

Ronni pressed the phone into her ear. Someone who knew Jeff was going to talk to her about Jeff. And better yet, it was her father, someone she could really talk to— about the entire situation. Although her feelings were sore and she was tired, she was very glad he had pushed her to listen to him.

"Are you there?"

"I'm listening."

"Okay. Good. Look, Ronni, it breaks my heart to hear you're going to the gala with Tyler. That really should be Jeff. I know I told you when you first saw Jeff that he wasn't right for you and that Tyler was a better choice, but that was only to hide my own secrets. I didn't want you to get close to Jeff and discover my gambling habits and how . . . how bad it had gotten."

Benjamin paused and listened. Only a small sniffle from Ronni told him she was still there.

"And you blamed him for continuing to represent me, when . . . it was *me,* honey. Jeff wanted to break it off with me once you gave him an ultimatum on the terms for your relationship. But I cursed him and accused him of horrible things to get him to continue to help me. Even then, he was going to tell me to go screw myself, I'm sure. But I threw it up in his face that he *had* to help me save this business for *your* sake."

"For my sake?"

"Yes. I told him you were preparing to take over the dealerships and if he didn't help me, there would be no more company for you head. I know I manipulated his love for you, but that did the trick. You must understand, Ronni, I was desperate. And you just don't know—Jeff is the best. In saving a corporation, he's shrewder than Tyler and a lot of guys twice his age. It's surprising that that's not the focus of his practice. He only does it for people he likes, but he would have an amazing career in corporate law if he wanted."

Benjamin was getting too excited in telling Ronni about how great a lawyer Jeff was. She had to rein him in. "Daddy . . ."

"Oh, yes. Sorry, honey. Anyway, he knew about your love for the dealerships and he couldn't imagine you not having those in your future or having to work your way up in someone else's company. So he hung in there with me to finish the job. But it was my fault he didn't obey your wishes."

"Was it that bad? Had it gotten bad enough for you to lose everything?"

"Well, if I continued down the path I was headed. You see, he was also my sponsor at Gamblers Anonymous. We became close before he offered to help me figure out the mess I was in."

"That must be how he met Cathleen," Ronni whispered, putting more of the puzzle pieces together.

Benjamin heard her. "Cathleen Winters? How did you know about her?"

"She *told* me, Daddy. After I asked her if *Jeff* was the devil she'd been following!" Ronni knew it wouldn't make any sense to Benjamin and she didn't care. All his secrets and lies had led her down this path. And the clincher was that *his* malicious wife had sealed *her* fate.

Benjamin was quiet for a moment, letting Ronni have her anger.

"I know. I know you're mad at me. And you're wondering how Cathleen could tell you and I couldn't, but you've got to understand, you mean more to me than you do to her. It's easier for her to talk about this with you than it is for me."

"Whatever."

"I started gambling with Tamara. She'd want me to take her to the boats, and later . . . gambling was my escape from an unhappy marriage. I didn't want to be seen around Chicago at the gaming tables, so I started traveling the world—to Monaco, Atlantic City, Vegas, the Bahamas. At my income level, I was getting into the high-stakes tables—"

"Daddy. Stick with Jeff. I don't want to hear about you and her—and I don't want to hear about how it all started for you. You've got a lot of nerve telling me you are in an unhappy marriage."

"Oh, okay. But I have something to tell you about that, too."

"I don't want to hear it." Ronni was finally confronting the true source of her mistrust and defenses: her father. But when she thought about how she'd shut Jeff out when he tried to explain, she softened her stance. "Not tonight. Not right now."

"All right, I hear what you're saying. But my point is, it's entirely my fault and I don't want you to hold my actions against Jeff. He loves you, sweetheart, and I couldn't ask for a better, more honest, more suitable man for my daughter."

"Did he tell you this?" She was hopeful.

"What? Tell me that he loves you?"

"Yes."

"Of course. He told me you were the only thing that mattered to him."

Ronni's pulse began to race. All was not lost. "Did he say this since we broke up?"

"Well, no, honey. He hasn't talked about it since he came back from San Francisco. But I'm sure he still feels that way. He was too crazy about you not to."

"Well, he doesn't love me anymore. He's moved on," she said flatly.

"I don't believe it. You should know by now not to believe gossip."

"It's not gossip, Daddy. I saw her with my own eyes."

"What? Are you sure?" Benjamin still was not persuaded. He knew Jeff pretty well, and knew how much he loved Ronni. They hadn't discussed her lately, but he couldn't accept that Jeff would be seriously involved with someone else so soon.

"Is it so hard to believe? I was a horrible, suspicious, fault-finding girlfriend. He has a new girlfriend and she's really cute and she's probably normal."

"How do you know it's his girlfriend? Jeff knows a lot—"

"Daddy! Stop it! It's over! He was holding her and they looked happy. I was as close to him as . . . I was close enough to touch him." She choked out a stifled sob. "It's hard enough for me to get on with my life and not trick myself into believing we could recapture what we had, without you doing the same thing."

"Then . . . I guess I'm too late." Benjamin sounded dejected.

"I guess so. And like it or not, Tyler is my rebound."

"Aw, honey, you never liked Tyler. You told me he made your skin crawl."

"But I never really gave him a chance, Daddy. I guess I just didn't like him because he worked with you."

"And you like him now?" Benjamin ignored the implications of her statement.

"Our first date will be the chamber's fund-raiser. But I am going to give it my all."

"I'm afraid to ask what that means."

"Just . . . that I'm not going to be so—so *thinking* all the time. If that makes any sense."

"Okay. I won't stand in your way if that's what you want, but let me just say this: since I feel it's my fault that you and Jeff broke up, I want you to at least give him a call and talk to him before you go any further with Tyler."

Ronni didn't saying anything.

"Ronni, call him."

"I'll think about it."

"Call him tonight. He's probably up late."

Ronni had an image of Jeff making love, intensely, slowly, passionately, to the new girl. She held the phone away from her ear and cried quietly before choking out a response. "No way."

"Well, call him tomorrow. Promise me."

"Good night, Daddy."

"Okay. Well, at least I tried. I'll see you when I get back in town. Good night."

She hung up and dropped the phone onto the bath rug. She couldn't face Jeff and she had no intention of calling his house. He never called her and he obviously didn't want to hear from her. Ronni decided not to shed any more tears and poured herself another glass of wine to strengthen her resolve.

Chapter Twenty-Four

The only light in the living room came from the illuminated clock behind the bar. *How apropos*, Ben thought, seething. At around seven o'clock that evening, when he'd first sat down on the white love seat, the room was full of the lingering light of daylight savings time. He hadn't planned on lying in wait for Tamara like a spider ready to spring its trap, but as the hours ticked by, this was exactly the position in which he found himself.

Even though the things Ben wanted to confront Tamara about were difficult, he'd prepared to meet her in a relatively calm mood. After all, he was no more in love with her than she with him. But now, staring vacantly at the glowing eleven-thirty, he couldn't suppress the anger that made his chest rise and fall. It was very apparent to him that Tamara had no respect for him and did little to hide her feelings.

He toyed with a small metal cassette player, absently turning it over and over in his right hand. Even sitting in this room was an act of defiance. Unlike Beverly's philosophy—that a house was meant to be lived in—Tamara had set aside this room as one for decorative purposes only. Benjamin and Benji were to consider it off-limits to themselves and their guests. Pure frustration caused Ben to raise the other hand to his forehead, trying to relieve his mind of thoughts insistent upon revisiting all the mistakes he'd made over the years. Sitting there in the dark, Ben not only vilified Tamara but also blamed himself for the way he'd let Benji down. He thought he'd given Ronni a pretty happy childhood. Yes, Ronni was marred by the divorce, but she was already in college by then. Benji, on the other hand, was involved in a daily activities schedule that rivaled that of a corporate executive, but he didn't really have the attention of his parents. Ben couldn't think of a time that the boy had any friends in for a sleepover. The last time he saw kids at the house was for Benji's fifth birthday party. Since that time, all his parties had been at someplace designated for children to get together, not Benji's own home. He was going to change all that starting tonight.

Benjamin was just about to give in to his impulse to call his errant wife's cell phone when he was spared the role of King Cuckold at the sound of Tamara's car pulling past the driveway into the garage.

After a few minutes, Tamara's heels clicked in the foyer. "Ben!" she called out. Ben noted that it was not yelled as convincingly as one who actually wanted to find her husband. "Ben, are you awake?" he heard her ask and her footfalls told him she was checking his office. He heard the rustle of shopping bags—her most popular excuse for getting out of the house—mixed with the other noises signaling her approach.

"Whatever," she said under her breath, turning on the hall light and entering the same darkened room as her husband. "Typical—gone to bed."

Benjamin could barely make out her silhouette as she dropped shopping bags on an armchair and crossed the floor in front of him, making her way to the bar. Just as she passed within touching distance, Benjamin spoke.

"No, I'm awake," he said quietly.

Tamara screeched and jumped, scared out of her wits. She nearly toppled off her high-heeled sandals. "What the—" Tamara struggled to regain her balance and find the closest lamp. "Benjamin! You scared me half to death. What are you doing sitting here in the dark?"

"No, don't turn on the lights," Benjamin instructed.

"I will too turn on the lights," Tamara said emphatically. Ben watched her outline as she went to turn on the dim light behind the bar. "What are you doing in the dark anyway?" she asked again. When Tamara finally saw him, she gasped, another fright delivered by his crazed appearance. His clothing was wrinkled, his shirt was half tucked in the front of his pants, and his hair was sticking out in all sorts of directions. But what really grabbed Tamara's attention was the wild look in Ben's eyes. He had an expression she had never seen before and she found herself hoping never to see again.

Ignoring the fixed stare that made her hands shake, Tamara launched into her prepared story as she fixed herself a Scotch and water. "It was packed at the mall today, and I was so absorbed in finding a gown for the chamber's gala that I completely lost track of the time. Come to think of it, I was probably the last one out. I went from store to store until I found the perfect dress— you'll love it. They had a brand-new line of fall fashions out at Versace. Can you believe it? Fall already? I was like, let us get in a little summer, could you? You know?" she snickered. Not daring to look at her husband during her babble, she finally glanced at Ben to see if her diversion had worked. "Honey, you want a drink?"

"No. Could you sit down for a minute? I need to talk to you," Benjamin said, gesturing to the couch next to him.

"I'm tired, sweetie, I think I'm going to hit the hay."

Tamara scooped up her drink and started to head for the nearest door.

"Sit down," Benjamin insisted. Tamara was surprised. In the seven years of their marriage, he'd never behaved this way.

"Okay," Tamara said, extending the small word. She smoothed down the back of her short orange dress, took a sip of her Scotch, and sat on the couch adjacent to Ben. She thought she spied something gleaming in his hand and a lump developed in her throat. Tamara wasn't sure which of her exploits had finally caught up with her, but she was sure she could find a way to smooth this over. "What's on your mind, baby?"

Benjamin's brow creased angrily at the term of endearment. It had been years since she tried to patronize him this way, typically followed by sex. He cringed at the thought of her trying to touch him now. "Did you know Ronni and Jeff broke up?"

"What? Oh, wow." Tamara feigned surprise. "Are you sure?"

Benjamin nodded, watching the theatrics closely. Tamara gulped some more of her drink, giving her a moment to think. She furtively glanced at his hand and was now fairly certain that he was in possession of the tape from Jeff's answering machine.

"So, you didn't know anything about this?"

Tamara lifted her shoulders faintly, placed her drink on the coffee table, and then shook her head as though she were really disappointed. "Well . . . truth be told, I knew Jeff long before he hooked up with Ronni. And I can tell you, sweetie, he's bad news. I should've warned Ronni, but she wouldn't have listened to me. Maybe I should have told you to tell her, but he's just not serious. Jeff can't commit. He dogs women and—"

"Oh? And what would be your characterization of

me?" Benjamin wasn't going to allow Tamara to fill his head with more lies until he got to the bottom of the ones she'd already circulated.

"What?" Tamara frowned, trying to remember what she'd said about Benjamin. She needn't have. Ben's thumb pressed the cassette player to let her hear her own malicious words. Before the recording was finished, Tamara unexpectedly stood up and began to defend herself loudly. "That's what I was trying to tell you—*Jeff* is the one who said you're old. You know I don't feel that way! *Jeff* is the one who pulls me aside after visiting you and tells me what's going on with you and your company." Her face crumpled and she managed to find tears. "Jeff is planning to take your dealerships."

"Tamara," Ben started, his tone measured as though he were talking to a child caught in a lie, "even if that were true, what does that say about *you*? My wife? It seems to me that if Jeff were plotting something as serious as you claim, you would've come to me. After all, it would affect your future too."

"But it *is* true. I—I wanted proof that you couldn't deny. That tape . . . I called him and made up that stuff about you being worried about Algonquin because I wanted to catch him on tape," Tamara said. She took her acting to the next level, wiping away the tears and pacing the floor. "Oh, man," she said, shaking her head. "I can't believe this. If I'd only got him on tape, saying all the things he'd say about you when you were out of earshot . . . then this would be a totally different situation right now." She sniffled.

Ben sighed, exasperated with her ability to be true to her lies. "Look, don't start." She was very convincing, and if he didn't have further evidence against her, he might even have considered her position.

"No, Ben, listen to me." She turned back to Benjamin,

desperate. "Jeff is very clever. He must've known I was on to him and gave you that tape to turn the tables on me." Wide-eyed, Tamara gestured innocently at her chest.

Benjamin reached behind his back for the manila envelope he'd been keeping, leaned to the edge of his chair, and dumped its contents unceremoniously—allowing numerous four-by-six inch black and white photos to flutter onto the coffee table and floor. "And what about these? Jeff have anything to do with these?"

Tamara's eyes widened at the array of pictures capturing her in very telling poses with men. They weren't lascivious, but the photos showing her snuggling in booths, bars, and other places, followed by images of Tamara strolling arm in arm with the men as they entered a hotel, left little room for doubt as to their intentions. Tamara became more enraged that the old man had evidence of her affairs than at his having hired a private investigator to follow her. She turned her rage to her advantage.

"You're always locked up in your office whispering with Jeff or Ronni, or whoever! And—and we never do anything anymore! You don't take me anyplace! You don't make love to me! And I know you've been calling Beverly," she finally ended with what she thought would be a zinger. She was right. Benjamin flattened his back against the chair and stared at her, shocked. He hadn't expected the shrieking accusations or for her to know about his frequent contacts with his first wife. He didn't know that his mouth was flopping open and closed like a fish out of water. Tamara caught his defenseless expression and pounced.

"Yeah! That's right," she said, pointing a manicured finger at Ben's face and leaning her body toward him from her hips. "I know all about you calling and meeting with Beverly. I'm no fool." Now on the moral high ground, Tamara dramatically jabbed at the air in front of him. She straightened her back and wrapped her arms around her own small body. "I'm a young woman. I'm starved for love and affection—that's what you see here." Releasing herself and picking up several of the photos, she held them out to Ben as though they were a winning hand of cards. "That's all this is—a desperate cry for your attention. Honey, I want our marriage to be the way it used to be," she said, her voice becoming lower and ending in choked-up sobs. She dropped the photos from her hand.

At that moment, Ben wished he had the steely nerve of Jeff, who probably wouldn't begin to feel sympathetic toward Tamara and wouldn't search his mind to assign fault to himself. Ben pressed his lips together and stared at the shaky, wrinkled hands on his lap. He looked back into her face. Then, as if given an aura of discernment directly from Jeff Conley, Ben noticed that as upset as Tamara was supposed to be, there were no tears. He stood up so abruptly that Tamara had to back up quickly to give him room.

"I want you to get out," Ben said calmly, showing her his back.

"Ben, do you realize what you're saying?" Tamara asked, her hand going to his shoulder. Her husband turned on his heels to face her, angrily.

"Get out!" he shouted. "Pack up your stuff and your lies and get the hell out."

It wasn't like her to grovel to any man when the relationship reached the point where he was yelling at her, but Tamara's eyes quickly scanned her luxurious home. She'd fought too hard to obtain this life to give it up without a fight. "Honey, I know I've done some bad things, but let's go to counseling or something, we—"

Ben cut her off. "There's nothing to discuss. There's

no need for marriage counseling. We don't even have a marriage. It's a farce," he said, casting his eyes at the floor and losing some of his passion.

Eyes narrowing, Tamara countered with what she thought was her trump card. "If I leave, I'm taking Benji."

"Benji's not going anywhere," Ben told her, crossing his arms over his chest.

"Oh, yeah? We'll see about that." Tamara turned from Ben and went into the foyer. She dashed up the stairs.

Benjamin followed behind her at a leisurely pace. As he watched her ascend the stairs with her chin poked out smugly, he called after her. "He's not here."

Tamara stopped on the stairs and shot him an evil eye. But even from his distance, Benjamin could detect a twitch.

"You're lying," she spat back at him, hoping against hope that it wasn't true. She dashed to Benji's room, and Benjamin waited patiently. Soon enough, Tamara appeared once again at the railing. "What have you done with Benji?"

"He's staying with friends. I didn't want him to hear or be dragged into our argument," Benjamin said, shaking his head sadly. "It's a good thing, too, because it seems that that's exactly what you had in mind."

High heels not withstanding, Tamara took the stairs at an amazing speed. She wound up standing in front of Benjamin, her eyes darting around like a trapped animal. She had to think fast. "Well . . . I'm not going anywhere. If you don't want to work things out between us, you can leave."

"It's my house, Tamara," Ben said hotly.

Placing her hands on her hips, Tamara tried to recover some of her pride. "Yeah, but I'm not the one who wants to separate."

"I don't want to separate. I want a divorce," he said. To

lend credence to his words, he took a few steps away from her.

"I—I'm not leaving," Tamara said uncertainly, clinging to the words for dear life.

Benjamin may have been surprised by her reaction to the photos, but he had prepared himself for Tamara to adopt this position. He walked a few steps down the hallway and turned to face her. "Fine. I thought you'd say that. But just so you know—I've let Angie go. I've frozen our joint accounts, and I've filed papers in court for a temporary custody hearing. So if you had it in your head that you would continue the lifestyle I've afforded you, you're sorely mistaken."

This time, actual tears streamed down Tamara's face and she sat down heavily on the stairs. Thinking about the loss of her lavish lifestyle caused her to cry into her palms. She turned a makeup-smeared face to Ben and carelessly wiped her nose on the sleeve of her dress. "Don't leave me, Ben. I may have made some mistakes, but we can work it out . . . for Benji's sake."

Sighing deeply, Benjamin removed his car keys from his pocket. "Tamara, it would be different if I loved you. Even given your affairs, I'd try to repair our marriage. But you and I both know that's not the case."

Tamara barely heard that for moving on to her next frantic tactic. "I want to talk to Benji," she blurted.

Benjamin glanced at his watch. It was well after midnight. "I'll have Benji call you in the morning."

As he turned to leave, Tamara became more honest about her real concerns. She jumped up from the step and faced Ben down the long hallway. "Ben, what am I supposed to do for money? And the bills and stuff?"

"You have your credit cards," Ben called over his shoulder, having reached the door leading to the garage. He was satisfied to know that Tamara's cards definitely had credit limits. "And you have your jewelry. Hock some of that."

Benjamin turned to her with his hand on the door. "Or you can always ask some of those men you were pictured with. Maybe they'll help you out."

He didn't bother to collect the photographs from the living room since he had copies of those and more in a safety deposit box. She would see the full collection when they met at court. Once in the garage, Benjamin climbed into his Cadillac, which had the appearance of someone who was moving their teenager off to college. The interior was filled with cardboard boxes containing his family mementos and heirlooms, paperwork, and suitcases of clothing.

Once he was on the road, Benjamin felt his body start to come down from the adrenaline high that made him able to confront Tamara. He yawned as he dialed one of his preprogrammed phone numbers.

"Hey." Beverly answered on the first ring, but sounded like she had been asleep. "That took a long time. Benji's asleep."

"I figured he would be. Sorry about that. I'll just let him stay there for tonight, if it's okay," Ben said.

"Of course. Of course. So . . ." Beverly waited a beat for him to share on his own. When it didn't happen, she prodded him. "How'd it go?"

"As well as can be expected, I suppose. She tried to lie her way out of everything," Ben explained. The sigh that followed was from genuine sorrow that he'd damaged so many lives in his self-indulgence. Now he'd have to add Benji to that list.

"And you're in the car, so . . . she thinks she's keeping the house?" Beverly asked through another yawn. It's not that she wasn't interested, it's just that it was well beyond her bedtime.

"I don't really think she has any hopes of being awarded the house in a settlement, but she just couldn't see herself being ordered out of the house. She insisted on staying, but I was ready for that."

"You know," Beverly said, stretching and trying to sound more alert. "You could stay here tonight, too."

Her offer was made innocently, but Benjamin's heart leaped without warning at the prospect of spending the night in such close proximity to Beverly after all these years. At the moment, he didn't need that kind of temptation.

"No, I'd better not. I'll come in the morning so I'll be there when he wakes up. But I'd better follow Jeff's advice and get a hotel room. Keep our relationship squeaky clean until the divorce is final."

"Huh! That's a change," Beverly said sarcastically. Benjamin could almost see his ex-wife's twisted lips.

"Okay. I'll see you in the morning, Beverly."

"Good night," she answered, sounding like her head had already reconnected with the pillow.

After he hung up the phone, Benjamin realized that if they got back together, Beverly was never going to let him forget that he'd interrupted their great love affair for seven years. And for some reason, he was just fine with that.

Chapter Twenty-Five

On this date, Ronni wasn't looking for a repeat of her first date with Jeff. When Tyler called to say he was in the lobby of her building, Ronni told him she'd be right down. The Metropolitan Chamber's awards dinner and dance was the season's biggest affair for the African-American business community and everyone would be decked out in their finest clothes. Ronni wore a Carolina Herrera strapless, knee-length red dress with matching shoes, a cream crepe wrap, and one of her mother's fancy necklaces.

Tyler was waiting in the lobby with a wide grin and an even bigger bunch of red roses. He was wearing a traditional black tuxedo.

"Hello, gorgeous," he said, leaning in to kiss her cheek. "These are for you."

"Hi, Tyler. Thank you. I guess I should've invited you up so I could put these in water."

"That's okay, I imagine they'll hold. Unless you want to go back upstairs."

"No. I think we can find a vase for them when we get back." She wondered if he'd really heard what she said; judging by the momentary shock on his face, she thought he had.

Tyler offered his arm and she wrapped hers around it as they walked to his black Mercedes.

"You look beautiful," he said smiling.

"Thank you. So do you." Ronni did notice that he'd gotten a haircut and his hair wasn't as conservative as he was typically wore it. It was short, but unlike Jeff's—whose hair was uniformly shaved—Tyler opted for something more like a fade. He held the door for her and she took a seat, thinking, *Here goes.*

By the time they arrived downtown at the Sheraton, Ronni had been bored to tears by Tyler's stilted conversation. He pulled into the line of cars waiting for a valet.

"It's a good thing we left early. We could end up in this line for ages." He chuckled. Ronni turned to him. She had to do something to make this better if she was going to continue with Tyler.

"Tyler," she said to get his attention.

"Yes?"

"While we're waiting, why don't you kiss me?"

He looked at her as though she'd suddenly turned into a space alien. "What? Right here? Now?"

She leaned toward him. "Just kiss me."

"All right," Tyler leaned over the armrest and pressed his lips firmly but briefly to hers. Ronni gently caught the back of his head and opened her lips slightly to him. Tyler's mouth registered surprise, then he relaxed and kissed her more earnestly, their lips closing together and opening together in small wet samplings. Tyler pulled back first, looking into Ronni's face.

"That was nice," he said dreamily.

"Yes," Ronni said. But she felt nothing. It was a decent kiss and his mouth tasted nice and minty, but it just didn't do anything for her. She turned from him to face the windshield.

Tyler turned back as well. "I wasn't expecting it, but it was very nice. Just how I'd always imagined it would be to kiss you."

Good heavens, is he going to analyze the kiss for the next hour? Ronni didn't realize she had shaken her head. No. She didn't think this was going to work out.

"As you know, I've wanted to—"

"Oh. Here comes the valet. I guess it's our turn," she said, pointing as a young man with a red vest approached the car. As Tyler rolled down the window to hand over the keys, Ronni got out of the car. She could hear Tyler saying, "Wait a minute," so he could get the door for her, but she was on the sidewalk by the time he came around the vehicle.

"You've got to let me do my gentleman's duties," Tyler said, offering his arm to her again. Ronni placed hers in his, though she thought arriving arm-in-arm was passé. But she imagined that Tyler took the phrase *having a beautiful woman on your arm* quite seriously.

The people at the reception table greeted them brightly. Tyler led her to the volunteer manning the list containing Hs. They would be seated at one of her father's two tables.

Tyler was playfully bantering with the woman behind the desk when Ronni tugged his arm and whispered in his ear, "Please make sure I'm not sitting next to Tamara. If we need to, switch with someone at Daddy's other table."

He listened and nodded. "All right." Pleasantly, he turned back to the woman.

Ronni would rather deal with the snide remarks of Terry, Ben's salesman, than to have to see that skank Tamara. She turned to get a drink for Tyler from the cash bar and passed the woman with the C names.

She stopped. "Hi, Tricia."

"Hey Ronni."

"Let me look at the list real quick. I saw someone I know, but I can't think of her name." Tricia was handing

Ronni the list even before she finished her feeble explanation, but Ronni continued with her trivial fib. "I think her last name begins with a C. Maybe this will jog my memory."

She quickly flipped to Conley and saw a table not too far from her father's, listed under *Senator A. Conley Family,* but not specifically to Jeff. So she had no idea if he would be here or not. In the past, he hadn't come to this event. But then again, maybe he hadn't attended because he lived in New York until just three years ago. She gave the clipboard back. "Nope, didn't help."

"No one wants to put on their name tags because it messes with their look," Tricia said.

"I know. Same thing every year, right? I know *I'm* guilty. I didn't lay down all this money on a dress just to put sticky paper on it," Ronni admitted with a laugh. She turned around, right into Tyler.

"You won't believe this." Tyler pulled her farther into the crowd, smiling.

Ronni didn't like surprises. "Uh-oh. What is it?"

Tyler saw the apprehension on her face. "No. This is good news." He leaned closer to her ear. "Tamara's not here."

"What?" Ronni smiled and leaned away from him to look into his face and see if he was kidding. He nodded his head.

There was no way Tamara would miss this. The chamber's gala was considered the highlight of the summer social calendar.

"And there's more," Tyler said with a huge grin. Ronni, still smiling, pushed his arm to encourage him to tell her more. He leaned into her ear. "You're sitting next to Beverly."

Her mouth fell open, uncontrollably shocked. "What! Tyler! Get out!" she whispered excitedly. He nodded again, smiling. "Are you serious? Is she here now?" She looked around the large crowd and couldn't see anyone who looked like her mother, but the room was packed.

"Yes. She already picked up her ticket. You going to go find her?"

Ronni smiled and tried to spy Beverly again. "Of course."

Tyler held out a name tag to Ronni and she waved it away. Tyler put it in his pocket. "I see Larry Porter. I'll be over there talking to him. What would you like to drink?"

"A merlot, please. I'll probably be at the table. That's Mom's general M.O.: she settles at the table early and lets all her friends stop by and talk to her like she's the queen bee." Ronni was so thrilled that her mother was finally out of the house that she gave Tyler's arm a quick squeeze before going to check out their table.

Jeff was standing far across the room, near the hallway toward the bathrooms. Ronni wouldn't have seen him hidden amongst a sea of black tuxes. *Especially if she's not looking for me.* He wasn't wearing a traditional tux anyway. His was a more contemporary tuxedo made by his tailor. But in her beautiful red dress, how could he miss *her*? Other women were wearing red, but in Jeff's eyes Ronni glowed as if a spotlight were shining on her. She was magnificent. She was happy and joking with everyone—and she and Tyler were sharing secret whispers and laughing together. He felt the blood rising hotly under his skin at the thought of her being intimate with Tyler, or anyone else for that matter. He nearly crushed the glass in his hand because he wasn't the man standing with her tonight.

There Jeff was, dateless. And there she was, radiant with that pretentious stick, Tyler. Jeff was convinced he shouldn't have come to this stupid event. He'd only agreed to present the award because his mother just couldn't imagine climbing the stairs to the stage with her arthritic knees. It had occurred to him when he accepted this responsibility that he might see Ronni, but he thought that might be good thing. The way it played out in his head, he imagined she would be alone and he could approach her quietly and talk to her for a minute.

Now that Jeff was actually in the same room with her, he knew it couldn't have gone that way. He was too emotionally invested. He still loved Ronni and watching her move happily through the world without him was killing him inside. He knew he couldn't play off his feelings for her the pitiful way he had at the tennis club. Jeff had the gut feeling that if he got close enough to Ronni, he would seize her arm and pull her away from the prying eyes of everyone, then demand that she sit down, shut up, and just listen to him. Thankfully, his schedule would keep him from making a complete ass of himself. He had already told the organizers he needed to leave once he presented the award.

It was true. Beverly was actually here. Ronni had greeted her with a kiss and settled down next to her. She was anxious to get the scoop from her mom but had to wait for her to finish conversing with one of her friends before she could really talk to her.

"Mom, what's going on?" Ronni leaned over, smiling at Beverly after Mrs. Thompson finally left.

Beverly smiled demurely. "What do you mean? Your father's being honored tonight."

"Don't play innocent with me. What's going on with you and Daddy?" Ronni wasn't going to fall for that. Her father had been honored several times in the past seven years.

"Well, all right. I guess I do owe you an explanation." Beverly adjusted in her seat to face Ronni. "We've been talking on and off for months, but in the last few weeks, we've been seeing each other a lot more."

"What!" Ronni was ready to laugh. "So you're the other woman?"

"Hey, two can play at that game. I can't help it if she can't keep her husband." Excited by Beverly's sudden upper hand, they both laughed at Tamara's predicament.

"So . . . is it serious?"

Beverly gestured to the rest of the table. "Of course. Do you see anybody else here?"

"Why didn't you tell me?"

"I didn't want to say anything until I knew it was real. You know I don't want to make a fool of myself over the same man *twice*."

Ronni looked hopeful. "It's real, meaning . . . ?"

"Oh, she's history. When he came back from Toronto, he moved out." Beverly whispered conspiratorially because one of her friends was approaching. She squeezed Ronni's arm before turning to her friend with a big smile.

"Beverly! I don't believe it!" Mrs. Cross took a seat on the other side of her and they began to talk. Ronni couldn't wait to hear the rest of this tale. She didn't even care about her mother keeping her in the dark for so long.

Ronni suddenly wished that Cornell were there so she could share this happy moment with him, but he had to work. Then it occurred to her that she could beat his gossipy friends with *this* news. She touched her mother's arm, saying she'd be right back, and went over to a quiet corner of the ballroom with her cell phone. She paged him and hoped he could call right back. When he did, she quickly filled him in on the little information she had. He asked lots of questions she couldn't yet answer, but he was just as excited as she was—except he had more choice words about Tamara that made Ronni laugh.

Ronni took her seat when she saw the attendees filing in from the cocktail reception area. It was nearly time for the program to begin. Everything was going so well, she didn't even mind when Tyler kissed her cheek as he joined her at the table.

Ronni repeatedly glanced at the Conley table. When everyone was seated, she didn't see Jeff or that girl. *Thank God,* she thought. But her relief was tempered by the fact that their table still had a couple of empty seats. Benjamin entered the room, conversing with one of his friends. He placed a soda in front of Beverly and kissed Ronni. He was pleasantly surprised when she also reached out to hug his shoulders. He hadn't been greeted with such enthusiasm from his daughter in years.

Ronni opened her program and glanced through it to find her father's name. He was receiving the Aaron Conley Award for Excellence and she read with some trepidation that Jeff would be presenting it to Benjamin. She got a sinking feeling in the pit of her stomach but was determined not to let it ruin her good mood. Sure enough, once it looked like everyone was fully seated, Jeff came to sit beside his mother.

The way he was seated, his back was to her. The Conleys' table was closer to the stage than theirs, so Ronni could watch him as much as she liked without raising Tyler's attention, especially when the lights went down. From what she could surmise, it appeared that he'd arrived stag, but she couldn't be sure.

One of the top local network news anchors emceed

the program. The audience was in the middle of their salads when Ronni glanced up at Jeff and he was looking over his shoulder at her. Her eyes fell to her plate. *Was that a mean look?* Whatever it was, she didn't think he looked pleased. In her nervousness, Ronni abruptly joined a conversation with some of the others at the table. When her eyes were drawn back to Jeff, he wasn't looking at her anymore.

As the first few awards were presented, Ronni thought her actions were ridiculous. She was a grown woman. With she and Jeff being in the same social circles, Ronni would no doubt have to see him at lots of events. She decided she would approach him after the evening was over and apologize, and at least they could be friends . . . or somewhat friendly, maybe.

But when it was time for her father's award, Ronni saw those plans dashed when the news anchor introduced Jeff. "We're going to bring up Jeff Conley to introduce the awardee for the Aaron Conley Award for Excellence. He's the son of Senator Conley and a successful attorney in the Chicago area. And, single ladies, when you get a look at him, you'll see why we've been trying to get him as the centerpiece of a bachelor auction. I think we could raise a lot of money with him. What do you think?" she joked and a lot of women laughed, playfully hooted, and clapped.

Tyler stole a quick glance at Ronni. She drank a big gulp of her water and tried to look unaffected. The anchor continued, "He's got to leave us early to catch a flight, so without further ado, come on up here, Jeff."

Standing at the edge of the stage, Jeff sprinted up the stairs and kissed her cheek as he took the podium. "Thanks for that introduction—you're going to make me blush. You all ever seen a black man blush?" he teased. "But I'm really pleased to present our next hon-

oree. Since my father passed, he's been somewhat of a
father figure to me and he's a great friend of mine. Benjamin Hampton . . ."

Jeff expertly read a bio and a long list of Benjamin's
accomplishments. If Tyler was watching her now, Ronni
wouldn't have noticed. Jeff captivated her eyes. She
thought he looked incredibly handsome. He was so comfortable and natural with an audience—something she
didn't think she could ever pull off.

"So, ladies and gentleman, I am honored to present
the Aaron Conley Award for Excellence to Mr. Benjamin
Hampton," Jeff announced enthusiastically. The audience clapped thunderously and the guests at Ben's two
tables stood, proudly applauding.

When Benjamin joined Jeff at the podium, they hugged,
patting each other's backs. It was evident to everyone
watching that the two men genuinely liked each other.
Benjamin started his acceptance speech by thanking Jeff
and talking about what a great guy he was and then moved
on to what the award meant to him, especially since he'd
known Aaron Conley very well. Watching Jeff return to his
seat, Ronni tuned out. Since she was a teenager, she had
been to dozens of these galas at which her father had accepted one award or another, and she knew the basic
premise of his speeches. Jeff was leaning over and talking
to his mother. He was sitting on the edge of his seat, so
Ronni could tell he was just going to stick around long
enough to listen to her father and then dash. She steeled
her nerves to try to catch him. It might be better that he
was leaving early so she would have him alone in the lobby
and their encounter would be mercifully brief.

Her father concluded his speech, the audience ap-
plauded, and the emcee began to move on to the next
honoree. Although Ronni felt a lump in her throat and
her stomach tightened uncomfortably, she knew she had

to seize her chance as Jeff rose and swiftly made his way through the ballroom doors.

"I'll be right back," she whispered hurriedly to Tyler. He didn't appear to like it but was immediately distracted when Benjamin returned to the table with his award. Ronni moved quickly across the room and pushed open the door. A few yards ahead, she saw Jeff's back moving away from her. She was about to call out to him when she saw him greet the same cute girl. She wasn't dressed for the gala, wearing blue jeans, a white shirt, and black blazer. He put his arm around her shoulders, leading her away, and saying, "Did you get your bags?"

Ronni's heart sank. *So he's leaving town with her.* Without Cornell there to stop her, her feet carried her closer to them as they separated and headed down the escalator. Ronni pulled her wrap closely around her body. They were engrossed in talking to each other, but Ronni thought the girl saw her. She must've said something, because Jeff started to look back just as their heads disappeared from her view. Ronni never saw his eyes.

They're gone. Ronni stood for a moment, stricken by what had just happened. She felt a tear trickle down her face and swiped it away. Now she had to admit to herself that she and Jeff were really and truly over. Somehow she found the strength on wobbly legs to return to her seat. Her face must have reflected her numb mental state because Tyler and her mother were alerted. On both sides of her they were asking if she was okay. She just nodded, unable to find her voice, and drank more water. She would have busied herself by eating her dinner, but she couldn't force a bite past her lips. She tried not to think about it, but she couldn't fool herself—she knew she was still in love with Jeff. If her mind lingered for another second on what she had seen, she wouldn't be able to go on with this evening.

Ronni decided to tell Tyler she wasn't feeling well. She *had* to get out of there. She just wanted to go home and collapse on her bed and cry to her heart's content. The more she considered it, she realized she actually *wasn't* feeling well. She leaned over to Tyler.

"You think we can leave early? I really don't feel so good."

"Oh. Certainly," Tyler said, surprised, "Do you think you can hang on a little bit longer? The program's almost over and I can say my good-byes to a few of my clients. We won't stay for dancing."

Ronni nodded. This was a great opportunity for Tyler to do some networking. Plus, he was her ride, so she didn't really have a choice. She could see now how life would be with Tyler as a husband. Work and social climbing would always come first. She turned to her mother and asked her if she could have a sip of her 7 UP; it might settle her stomach a bit. Beverly looked concerned, but Ronni waved it off. "I'm okay. Something just didn't agree with me."

Her cell phone rang and the people at nearby tables turned to look at her nastily. This was definitely a no-no. She'd forgotten to turn it off after talking to Cornell. She hastily stood up, grabbed her ringing purse, and went into the lobby.

"This is Ronni," she said, answering quickly.

"Aren't those things boring enough without you bringing your own windbag?"

"Jeff," she uttered, through a relieved, uneasy, and tearful laugh.

"Were you trying to catch me?"

"Yeah," she admitted, and cleared her throat. "Jeff, listen . . . I know it's too little too late, and I know you've moved on with your life . . . but I just wanted to apolo-

gize for the way I treated you. I'm really sorry. I also want
to thank you for helping my father, and—"

"Ronni." Jeff tried to interrupt.

"No. Please—just let me say this. I can't get through this
if you say anything, and I know you're with your girlfriend.
But please, just listen." Ronni's voice cracked before she
regained control. "Anyway, thank you for helping us keep
the dealerships and all. And I wanted to let you know that
I know *I'm* the reason we didn't make it. With my—with
my fears and suspicions and walls. . . ." She stopped again,
but she had to get to the end of this. She could hear Jeff
waiting. "You're a better person than I could ever be. I was
always thinking about myself and . . . you were always
thinking about others . . . and helping people. And I accused you of the worst things." Her words were now filled
with tears. "I know now that I was a horrible girlfriend. I
wish I could turn back the clock, but since I can't, at least
I can undo some of the damage I've done . . . to us . . . to
you. I hope if you ever think of me in the future, you don't
hate me. And maybe—maybe, at least, we could be
friends." Finally getting it all out, she was free to cry. Jeff
was free to speak now. She tried to control her whimpers
so she could hear his response. But she heard none. "Jeff?"
she listened. "Hello?"

From behind her, she heard Jeff.

"Hate you? I've been trying to convince myself that I
can live without you—with little success."

Ronni turned to face him, closing her cell phone as
he approached. "Jeff?"

"Moved on, you say? I'm stuck in one place, Ronni—
right back at that moment when you left me in the
parking garage. I ask myself, where did I make that
fatal mistake in losing your love and trust? After I got
over the sting—no, let me be honest—the pure heartbreak of losing you, I *did* blame you and I was angry,

thinking, 'How could she believe the things she said about me.'"

"Jeff, I'm so—"

It was his turn not to be interrupted. "No, I indulged you. It's only fair that you turn the floor over to me," he said, a small curl appearing on his lips as he moved closer to her. She wanted to touch him, but she wasn't sure what his return could mean. Instead she wrapped her arms protectively around herself. He took the lead by placing his hands on her arms. She nearly buckled against him but managed to stay self-possessed. "After I got over my anger, I knew I was the one to blame. Me. I was the one who didn't fully share myself . . . and tell you about my past. It's true that I couldn't talk about my clients' problems, but I could've told you about mine."

From the ballroom, they heard the emcee announcing that the evening was over, but guests were welcome to stick around and enjoy the great band. Jeff glanced at the ballroom door. He took Ronni's arm and led her down the escalator to his waiting limo. She hesitated at the opened door.

"What about your friend?"

"Liz? I'm sure she's on her way to the airport and couldn't care less about my drama."

"That's Liz?" Ronni knew Liz's name from calls to his office when they were dating, but she had never met her. "So she's not your girlfriend?"

Jeff shook his head at Ronni and indicated that they should get in the car before the crowd came. After he told the driver to hold on a minute, he settled on the seat and turned to his body to face Ronni. "No, Liz is not my girlfriend. Her fiancée would beat me within an inch of my life if I even looked like I was looking at her. She's engaged to Marc Peters—big burly dude who plays for the Bears."

Ronni looked at her hands. "Oh."

"I'm not even remotely interested in Lizbeth. I didn't introduce her to you at the club because I *did* want you to think I was involved with someone else. At the time, I was so surprised to just run into you like that . . . and I acted on my emotions. That was mean, and I'm sorry."

"No, I deserved that. Everything I did . . . and said . . ." Her eyes started to well up again. Jeff couldn't stand to see her so disconsolate. He reached to embrace her and she leaned into him and met his hug. He kissed her forehead. Ronni laughed but the release turned into a small cry. Jeff was holding her and kissing her forehead. Like he always did. Like they had only left each other yesterday.

"Oh, baby. I missed you," he said quietly, rubbing her hair. Emotion was evident in his voice and Ronni could feel a trembling in his body. She looked up into his face, intending to repeat the sentiment, but their eyes caught each other's and their mouths soon followed. This was no kiss like they'd only recently parted—their kiss was deep, hard, and hungry. She remembered that that mouth was her favorite to explore, and their tongues fell easily into their furtive, persistent language. Jeff hugged her tightly around the waist.

Their hearts beat heavily against each other's and Ronni wrapped her arms securely around his shoulders, vying with him to get closer. Ronni—yearning for this embrace even while she was heartbroken over him—knew where their simple kiss could easily lead. The intensely pulsing throb in her lower body told her she would have to let him go or climb on top. She mustered all her feeble strength to rein in her tongue and simply kiss his wet lips. Jeff couldn't conceal his amazement that Veronica Hampton was back in his arms and peppered her mouth, cheeks, nose, and eyes with loving presses of his lips.

"I love you," Ronni said at last, speaking from the heart. "I never stopped loving you."

"Veronica." He said her full name as if there were only one person in the world with it. He caressed her face. "I love *you*, baby girl. I don't even know how you could think there could be someone else."

"I thought . . . you might hate me," she said quietly. Her chest hurt at the memory of their bitter parting.

"Oh, no. No way is that even possible." Jeff shook his head. "I didn't blame you. It was my fault. I should've told you how I got into this business of rescue."

"Daddy told me he made you—" She stopped talking when she saw Jeff shaking his head.

"It wasn't just him. It was that I didn't know how to tell you my story." He considered her face. "Do you know about Gamblers Anonymous?"

Ronni nodded. "Daddy said you were his sponsor."

"Well, you probably wondered how I got there." Jeff rubbed her arms. Ronni looked over his shoulders out the window.

"Wait. There's my parents." She separated herself from Jeff and waved in their direction. Jeff turned to see them, with Tyler, looking around anxiously.

"They can't see you," he said.

"Oh, right." She placed her hand on the control to roll down the window and waited a second. As she expected, not finding her outside, Tyler went back inside to look for her. Finally, she rolled down the window and called out to her worried parents, waving her hand. "Mom!"

She saw Beverly get her father's attention and watched as they crossed the street to approach the car window.

"Well, hey!" her father said, reaching in to shake Jeff's hand.

"Hi, honey, we were looking all over for you. Hi, Jeff."

Beverly leaned in. "Feeling better now?" Beverly twisted her lips sarcastically at Ronni, then smiled.

Ronni laughed. "Yes, ma'am."

"I thought so. Here's your gift bag." Beverly handed Ronni the decorative bag filled with goodies from many of the black businesses.

"Mom, tell Tyler I wasn't feeling well and took a cab home."

Beverly nodded and waved an agreeable hand.

"Okay," Benjamin answered, beaming. "We'll make up something. I'm so happy to see you two together."

"The feeling's mutual," Jeff said and winked at Ben. They all laughed easily.

Beverly pulled Benjamin's arm. "Come on, we better get away from here before Tyler gets back."

"Bye. Thank you. I love you guys," Ronni said as Jeff rolled up the window. Ronni fell back into his arms and they both smiled giddily. "I love you."

"Oh? So what's up with old stuck-up pants?"

"He was my consolation prize," Ronni teased and wrapped her arms around Jeff's neck.

Jeff swallowed. "Really? How consoling?"

She gave him a look that said *get real*. "Please."

"I need to know." Jeff's eyes were vulnerable. He couldn't stop his mind from going down that rocky path.

"Jeff, *really* . . . that was our first date. And as you can see, it didn't end very well."

"For Tyler. It ended just right for me." He rolled down the window separating them from their driver before quickly consulting Ronni. "My place, okay?"

"Naturally." She forgave his jealousy, kissing his chin and remembering that there was male blood pulsing through his veins.

"Take us home, please—on Woodlawn," he clarified,

and closed the intercom. He kissed Ronni's lips. Ronni looked at him, cocking her head.

"And what if the answer had been different?"

"Then . . ." Jeff considered the question, leaning his head to one side, ". . . you'd have to wait in the car while I went back and kicked his ass." Jeff pointed a finger in all directions, looking out the windows. "Up and down these streets here—for hours. As a matter of fact, you might've had to take the car on to my house and wait. I'd have been home late."

Ronni laughed. This was the truthful, silly, and totally masculine Jeff she had missed terribly. She poked out her lips sympathetically. "Poor Tyler. It wouldn't have been his fault."

"Oh, yes, the hell it would." Jeff gave her a shrewd look. His large hands engulfed her back and he pulled off her wrap. He placed his lips to her shoulder.

She sat up alert, suddenly remembering something. "What about your flight?"

"Oh, that was actually Liz's flight. I just told the organizers it was me because I knew I wouldn't want to stick around. Plus, she needed my keys to get in my office down here. She forgot to get the contract."

"She's going to see that new client you were talking about?"

Jeff laughed at the thought of Liz meeting Tony. "Yeah."

"What's funny?"

"The dude is a bona-fide nutcase. But he'll meet his match in Liz. She'll cut to the chase and wrap it up with him, get him to sign the papers without getting caught up in his nuttiness." Then Jeff thought of something. "I wanted to talk to you about that. This client could be a new beginning for us, Ronni."

Us. She was an *us* again. And it didn't escape her notice that he'd been planning to talk to her, even while they were apart. She was comforted to know that Jeff had been intending to get back together with her at some point. Ronni smiled at the thought and relaxed into his arms.

"Tony Maldonado, the client she's going to see, is a baseball player. I'm changing my practice into entertainment law. I know you didn't like my handling cases like your father's and I don't ever want us to go through something like this again."

"Jeff, it's all right. I understand now what you were doing. Besides, my father says you'd have a brilliant career in corporate law."

"Yeah, but it was just a way to atone for my past. After I met you, I wanted to give it up for myself, too. Let myself off the hook for being young and stupid."

"You mean the gambling?" Ronni said, looking worried. "How bad was it?"

Ronni could feel Jeff's body tense up. He glanced out the window and spoke as if to himself. "I've started to tell you so many times, and then I would just . . . I didn't know how you would take it. And you're so perfect . . . and so innocent." Jeff's mouth curled easily as he looked into her clear eyes.

"I'm not so innocent, and by no means am I perfect," Ronni said with a frown.

"Ronni, please. "This is Jeff you're talking to." He released a nervous chuckle. "You were trying to guess what kind of a scoundrel I was in college and your mind couldn't conceive of anything worse than cheating on an exam."

"Well, knowing you, I couldn't imagine anything really horrible . . . in college," she amended, aware that she'd thought worse things of him as an adult.

"Well, this was really bad." Jeff took a deep breath. "I left in my junior year at Columbia because I had to, to avoid a scandal." He felt Ronni stiffen at the word. He rubbed her shoulders to comfort her for what he had to say next. "As a state senator, my father smoothed everything over so that it didn't get in the papers and I wasn't prosecuted. But . . ." He felt a knot in his throat and his eyes couldn't connect with hers. He'd never shared this with anyone outside of his family, with the exception of the people at his meetings. "I was betting on the games. Our games."

Jeff finally found the courage to look at her and saw a confused frown on her face.

"I don't think I understand. You were expelled?" She tried to grasp its significance.

"That, and I was investigated extensively to see if I had thrown any games . . . and stuff." His words faded out, thinking back on that unpleasant time in his life. "You're gambling on the team you're playing for. You get in deep with bookies and it's only a matter of time before you're tempted to make the outcome . . . what they expect."

"Oh." The full impact of what he'd experienced was dawning on Ronni. "And did you do that?"

"I had been approached to and, honestly, I was thinking about it." Jeff's face reflected sincere pain and remorse. "Thankfully, a teammate turned me in and told the coach. He didn't know I was betting on the team, but he knew I was a serious gambler and getting into some scrapes with the bookies." He looked out the window, remembering the incident. "Of course I was pissed at the guy at the time, but by turning me in, that dude might've saved my life. The way it turned out, I was able to transfer to another college without anyone really knowing what happened to me, but I was banned from playing collegiate sports."

He looked at her intently as their limo pulled in front of his house. "Before we go in there, and go back to being Ronni and Jeff, I wanted to lay all my cards on the table and let you know who you're getting involved with—or not. The choice is up to you." Now the ball was in Ronni's court and Jeff steeled himself for her possible rejection.

Ronni moved away from him and stared at him, annoyed. "You know, Jeff, I think I'm really insulted by your and my dad's assumptions that I'm so naive and thin-skinned that I couldn't handle the truth. No matter how bad it was or what impact it had on your lives, I deserved to know. It impacted my life, too." She folded her arms in front of her chest. "It was all the deception and secrecy that really drove a wedge between us, not the gambling. Sure, I might have been momentarily disappointed in Daddy or surprised at you, but if I had known from the beginning what you and Daddy were going through, I could've been part of the solution. I wonder . . . is it some sort of male thing? Are you thinking that we women are too stupid or fragile to grasp the complexities of your male world?"

Jeff couldn't have been more stunned if he had been slapped. She was right. The entire time he and Benjamin had worked so hard to conceal their past gambling habits, they were assuming that their disclosures would be greeted with hostility and harsh judgments. Ronni was also right about his having lived a life almost completely engrossed in a man's world. When his father was alive, he was very much a daddy's boy and they were always together. Then, being in sports all his life, he'd never really encountered anything female, except dates and girlfriends. And none of them captured his attention enough to dig deeper into the female psyche. He just honed his skills as a man and a gentleman in their presence. Since his father's death, he'd shared more intimate thoughts with Benjamin than he had with his mother.

"If you love somebody, you agree to support them in the good times and the bad. While we were apart, I heard a sermon. The pastor made it clear that we should never let anything separate us from the love of God. You know—he was talking about how it's easy to love God and accept His love in the good times, but the challenge was to turn to Him during the moments when you feel like your life is crumbling around you. I want you to be able to seek *my* love when your life is crumbling around you, and I hope you would also accept me at my lowest. You were wrong to characterize me as perfect. If you think that, then we're really headed for trouble." Ronni shook her head sadly. She could see from Jeff's eyes that the depth of her words stung him, but she had to deliver him her ultimatum.

"You're right," she continued. "If we're going to go in there and continue our relationship, I need to know that you won't turn away from me when you're going through hardships—no matter how bad. Yes, I want to be your lover, your friend . . . your woman. But that means *in all things,* Jeff. I'll tell you honestly: I love you and I could spend the rest of my life with you, if that's what you want, but I won't set a foot in your house if you're going to continue to treat me like some fragile object to be placed on a pedestal and never jostled."

Jeff was quiet for a moment.

"I do want . . ." Jeff's voice splintered from the emotion behind his words. He could feel something releasing inside him that had been pent up all these years. Ronni's words hit home with him in a way he hadn't expected. He was always the strong one. He was Jeff, the ultimate problem-solver. He now had to admit that it was all an act, a persona he'd adopted—he couldn't even remember when—to protect himself from letting his guard down.

With Ronni, he had been as emotionally vulnerable as he could ever recall. He hadn't cried when he'd gone through that horrible time in college, transferring schools, facing clandestine hearings on his fate. He hadn't allowed himself to cry when his father died, convincing himself that he needed to be strong for his mother. The only time he could remember fully experiencing his emotions as an adult was over the loss of this woman beside him. That he was in this emotional state again could only mean one thing: she was the real deal. She was his rock.

"Ronni, trust me when I say this: I need you, baby. Until I met you, I was going through life jovial to the outside world, but kind of dead inside. I want to share everything in my life with you, including the bad stuff. I'm sorry and I promise I will never *ever* keep you in the dark again."

The back of Ronni's hand touched the wet trails on his cheeks before she pulled his head toward her to kiss him lightly. "Then . . . let's go inside, Jeff," she whispered. She lightened the mood, jerking her head in the direction of the driver. "I'm sure this man wants to get home to his family."

Jeff opened the car door. He reached for Ronni's hand before he set foot outside the vehicle to confirm his promise that she would be his partner in all things, and led her into his house. Hannibal slowly came to greet them, wagging his tail swiftly and sniffing their shoes. Once he closed the door behind him, Jeff turned to Ronni and wrapped his arms around her waist. He'd wanted to feel her full body against his ever since he saw her appear across the room in that red dress.

"So now begins a new phase of 'The Jeff and Ronni Show'?" Ronni asked.

"Not quite yet." He pulled her backward and led her into the living room, taking her to the spot on the couch where she'd settled when she first came to his house, and gestured for her to sit down. Ronni looked amused at whatever he was up to. He reached into the drawer beside the couch and found the small velvet box he'd brought back from San Francisco.

Jeff fell to his knee in front of Ronni, and she immediately started to cry. She placed a hand to her mouth to keep herself from wailing like a baby, but she was deeply affected. Earlier today, she thought she would have to get used to the fact that he was out of her life, and now . . . This couldn't be real.

At one time, Jeff thought he would pull out all the romantic clichés when he proposed to Ronni, and fill the chosen place with dozens of red roses and live violins and the whole nine. Right now he found all that to be an unnecessarily flamboyant display. This moment dictated that his proposal be true. It was real and heartfelt, not some fancy production. He opened the box to reveal a platinum ring with an emerald-cut diamond stone.

"Ronni, sweetheart, you know I love you. Since I met you, my every waking thought has been you. When we were apart, I couldn't breathe. I couldn't figure out how I used to go about my days before you were in my life. You're the only thing that really matters to me. You told me, just now, that you want me to share everything with you, the good times and the bad. Now I'm asking you to share something very important with me—my life. Please share my life with me, baby. Please make it official that you will be my partner in all things . . . and say that you'll marry me."

Ronni was crying, sniffing and choking back her sobs in such a way that she couldn't answer. She nodded her head with her furrowed forehead and reached for him. She firmly pressed her mouth to his and then stared into his eyes, caressing his face. "Yes, Jeff," she finally choked out. "Yes, my love."

"Thank you," Jeff was barely able to say over the lump in his throat. He'd almost lost Ronni and now she was going to be his wife. He hugged her around the waist and buried his face in her chest, relieved. Ronni wrapped her arms around his shoulders. They clung tightly to each other for a long while, both rocking slowly together. Jeff finally looked up into her face and his lips found hers again. They kissed intensely, their mouths expressing all their deepest feelings. They broke their kiss and stared at each other and then kissed deeply again. Jeff pulled away from her to pull the ring from the box and place it on her finger. He held her hand and kissed it. They both stared at the new declaration of their love and nervously and tearfully laughed. "We're going to be man and wife," Jeff said in disbelief.

"I know. It's incredible, isn't it? I couldn't in a million years imagine that this day would end this way." Ronni reflexively kissed his head.

"I know," was all Jeff could muster, still staring at the ring on her finger.

"So, if we weren't together . . . when were you planning on giving me this?"

"I don't know." Jeff started to laugh at himself from somewhere deep in his belly. "I don't know, baby." He shook his head.

"Maybe it was providence. If you hadn't seen me tonight, you would've just taken it back."

"That was *not* an option. I've never bought one before, and I'd be damned if it wasn't going to be worn by the woman I planned to give it to." Jeff's face showed Ronni the determination he must have had when he was considering this plight. "All I knew is that I was going to muster up the courage to face you again and try to patch things up. I figured if Benjamin and Beverly could get back together after all the crap they'd been through, then our stuff was small potatoes—just misunderstandings and stuff. I hoped that your heart would soften toward me at some point. But after I saw you with Tyler, I knew I'd better get a move on that plan."

"You knew that Mom and Daddy were back together?" Ronni looked at him with a frown that reflected confusion and admiration.

"Mm-hmm. Ben and I talked about it. He never meant to leave Beverly in the first place."

"What? That doesn't make any sense." Ronni raised an annoyed eyebrow.

Jeff shook his head sadly. "It's a long story . . . and I promise I'll fill you in. But I'll give them a chance to tell you first. Let me just preface it by saying this: you have *no idea* how treacherous Tamara can be."

Ronni's raised eyebrow indicated the level of her curiosity, but she decided to drop the subject. If it had to do with that witch, Ronni didn't want to know—not tonight, anyway. She suddenly stood over Jeff and reached for his hand, feeling playful again. "Okay, mister, you bought the cow. Now you're stuck with her no matter how lame she is."

Jeff took her hand and rose to his feet. "She was in prime condition, from what I recall. And I believe I negotiated some extra perks." He raised his eyebrows at her. Ronni laughed and threw her arms around his neck, crushing him snugly. She looked into Jeff's piercing brown eyes, with their little smile lines in the corners, and could see that the sentiment was mutual. She also saw someone she wanted to look at for the rest of her life.

"You certainly did," she said and kissed his cheek softly. Ronni ran her hands over his back and brought them around to grasp his hands before pulling him in the direction of the upstairs bedroom.

Chapter Twenty-Six

As they relaxed in the glow of their passionate love-making, Jeff spooned with Ronni, wrapping his arms securely around her waist. The dark room made it easy for him to tell her the entire story of how he'd gotten involved in the whole "rescue" business.

To Ronni's surprise, Senator Conley had been quite a big-time gambler himself. His game of choice was the really restricted high-stakes poker tables. These games were usually held at some place so secretive and obscure that the average gambler wouldn't know about them. Jeff made clear that difference between him and his father was that four times out of five, his father would win. Aaron Conley had built such a fortune for his family at the poker tables that Jeff didn't really think of gambling as dangerous when he became a young man and was ready to dabble. But he had neither the gift nor the unrestricted funds of his father.

Jeff hadn't considered himself really addicted. He just thought that if he kept trying, he could beat the old man on his turf—not necessarily with poker, though Jeff did host a few games on campus—and impress him by creating his own financial resources at a young age. Senator Conley didn't know Jeff was gambling or he certainly would have put a stop to it.

When it was all over, Jeff had been so relieved to get

out of his scrape that he continued with the Gamblers
Anonymous organization for years after he'd been deterred from his problem. Tired of sharing his story with
mostly whites, he started a chapter on the South Side
when he came back to Chicago. He was surprised the
day George Marshall, someone from his social circle,
walked in. Everyone could tell that despite what George
said in meetings, he was still out there, struggling with
his addiction and threatening his family's carpeting business. Jeff pulled him aside one day and offered to be
his sponsor.

His big mistake with George was loaning him a lot of
money to keep him from losing his business. Jeff had
come into his inheritance by then and he couldn't bear
to watch an upstanding brother, a pillar of the community, lose everything he'd worked so hard to achieve. As
fate would have it, George put some of the money into
the company, but he was too tempted by the new figures
in the bank to stick with the plan Jeff gave him to turn
things around. George ended up liquidating his business, and most of the money did wind up with Jeff, but it
was the only way for Jeff to recover some of his losses.
He'd learned from that mistake by the time he helped
Cathleen and later Benjamin: Never loan them money.
Give them a financial plan out of their mess, but it has to
be based on the resources they're working with or able
to create through corporate restructuring.

"But I don't understand why Daddy would take money
from the company when he has loads of money in his
personal accounts," Ronni said into the darkness.

"With Benjamin, he must've had a great financial ad-
viser. Most of his private funds were locked up in trusts
for you and Benji and in investments and the founda-
tion. He used a lot of his liquid cash, but the other stuff
was almost untouchable without the signatures of several

other people . . . and he wasn't going to go there." Jeff sighed. "So the most readily available funds to him were in the dealerships."

"Oh." Ronni felt miserable at the thought of Benjamin being addicted to anything. It didn't sound like her father.

"But, baby," he snuggled her closer to when he felt her shoulders droop unhappily, "I have never seen someone so committed to turning his situation around like Benjamin. He did everything I suggested, and he came up with even more aggressive strategies for repairing his damage. He made progress in record time—better than Cathleen, and, needless to say, better than George. Gambling is not in his true nature. He only started by taking that woman to the boats and then just got in deeper. At his level of wealth, you get approached to join some really serious tables. Be it poker or blackjack or whatever."

"Well . . . thanks again for helping him."

"He was going to tell you. You'd have figured out something was wrong anyway, after we closed the Algonquin site. But he was making such great progress, he figured he'd tell you when it was all over so the sting of your disappointment wouldn't be so severe."

"You're really close to my father, huh?" Ronni nudged him with her elbow.

"That's right. You've never really seen us together, have you?"

"Nope. Except at the gala."

"Well, if you saw the way we interact, you might not think so, but we really love each other. Your old man is the only thing that kept me sane a lot of days, and I think he would say the same about me. He reminds me of my dad."

Ronni chuckled and rubbed the hair on Jeff's arms. "They were kind of alike, weren't they? That sharp, straight-talking, old-school kind of black man?"

Jeff laughed, too, thinking about their characteristics.

"Then Daddy will be happy to have you as a son-in-law," she said brightly. She could feel Jeff nodding.

"And Mom will be thrilled with you. I didn't have the heart to tell her we broke up. She's been pressing me to bring you over for dinner ever since we met."

"What? You never told me!" She slapped his arm, scolding. "I swear. I'm going to have my work cut out for me, whipping you into shape."

He gave her a little squeeze and placed a kiss on the back of her neck. "Don't be too hard on me. I wasn't ready to share you with anyone else yet. Besides, she'll be even happier, now that we have something to announce."

"That's right. We do have happy news to share with everyone, don't we?" She struck out her hand to try to see her ring in the dark. It caught a little bit of the moonlight from Jeff's bedroom window.

"We certainly do, baby. We certainly do."

Jeff's arm guided Ronni's body to turn and face his. He could see her onyx eyes shining in the darkness. He pressed his mouth to her forehead, her nose, and, finally . . . her lips.

Dear Reader,

Thank you for allowing me to tell this tale. We all read fiction to escape our everyday lives and sink into another time and place. I hope you found this book an enjoyable place to visit for a while. I had fun writing it and following along, myself, as the characters revealed their story to me. Next, I'll tell you about another couple who went through trials and tribulations before finding true love.

Sincerely,

Crystal Downs

I hope you enjoyed *All or Nothing*, the debut novel from emerging Arabesque author Crystal Downs. For your reading pleasure, we've provided a sneak peek at this author's upcoming novel, *The Proposition*, which will be in stores February 2006. Enjoy!

Tracy Middleton blew out a ragged breath and allowed the weights to slam back into place on the machine. She snatched up her notebook from the floor and jotted down the number of repetitions she'd just completed. As she wrote, she caught the swift movement of the woman she had come to identify as her stalker.

On sore legs, Tracy moved from the weight room to the locker room, noticing the woman she'd caught staring at her several times over many days. The old woman was following her. Again, Tracy's mind raced as she heard a second pair of footsteps behind her on the stairs.

Tracy wasn't sure how long the woman had been watching her and dogging her movements. On Wednesday, she noticed that when she left her aerobics class ten minutes early to nab a treadmill facing the windows, her follower left, too, and occupied a treadmill behind her. Tracy also noted that when she ended her run forty minutes later and moved on to the weights, the lady also moved, choosing a weight machine not far from hers. Ever since that day, Tracy had been monitoring the woman's movements and they always, uncomfortably, coincided with hers.

She was an attractive woman who appeared to be in her early fifties, with pretty honey skin and a floppy pageboy haircut. She was incredibly fit, except for her thighs, and she was shorter than Tracy.

Just a year ago, Tracy wouldn't have given the older woman a second thought. But after her now-defunct stint at Chicago Metro Television, Tracy had witnessed the darker side of human nature. Her work buddy, Vivien Marsh, an occasional weekend anchor, told her about some of the disturbing mail attractive female anchors received from men *and women* who were fixated on them. In Viv's usual cool manner, she laughed it off, saying, "There are some real kooks out there, girl." But it was one disturbed guy who had created a full fantasy life in his head about Vivien that changed her attitude from amused to frightened.

Vivien received all sorts of strange mail and gifts from him. She ignored the packages until the tone of the letters started to become increasingly threatening. The station manager was finally alerted and called the police when the guy arrived at their building, waiting in the lobby to confront Vivien about her recent engagement. He had read the announcement in a community newspaper and came to ask her why she was breaking up "their family." Fortunately, the man was arrested and Vivien had a restraining order issued against him.

Tracy cut a commanding presence at five feet, nine inches, but she knew she had no real defense against a crazy person. Working out was her favorite pastime, but she did it to accentuate her full breasts, impossibly small, tight torso, curvaceous hips, and long shapely legs, rather than to build bulky muscles. She had a figure of model proportions, but with a bit more meat on her bones—and she wanted to keep herself that way. With her remarkably striking looks—rich chocolate brown skin so radiantly poreless it appeared to be velvet, a heart-shaped face set off with big brown eyes, thick eyelashes, and a prominent cleft in her chin—Tracy had become accustomed to strangers occasionally taking a second glance . . . but this was ridiculous.

Tracy wanted to take a shower before heading home, but the woman was creeping her out. Out the corner of her eye, she could see her staring and she certainly didn't want to take off a stitch of clothing under this kind of scrutiny. This really sucked, too, because she liked the ritzy downtown health club, and now that this creep was there, she was going to have to finagle a way to get a premium membership somewhere else. She was already overextended financially, and high-end health clubs cost a lot—even if they'd been bought second-hand. Vivien, who received all sorts of first-class gifts from companies eager to list her as a patron, had handed over her membership to Tracy, and once she tried it, she'd vowed never to go back to the Y.

Tracy opened her locker, removed her street clothes from the hook, and stuffed them into her gym bag. She slammed the locker, turned to leave, and nearly jumped out of her skin. The woman was standing at the end of her aisle.

"Hi," the older woman said, staring at her curiously.

Tracy looked around her. No other people were in the locker room. She had at least twenty years of youth on the woman, but Tracy mentally plotted an escape route anyway. The sister was in good shape, and you could never tell how strong another person was until you got into a scuffle with them. "Oh, hey. You scared me," Tracy said, quickly turning to go down the other side of the aisle.

"Uh, Tracy, wait. I want to talk to you for a minute," the woman called, rushing up behind her.

When Tracy turned around, walking backward, the woman was awfully close. "Whatever you're thinking— wait, did you call me Tracy?"

"Yes, Tracy. I wonder if you would join me for a coffee or something." The lady advanced on her, smiling, and Tracy backed farther away. Now she was certain she was dealing with some sort of crazed middle-aged stalker. She stared at the woman, horrified. The woman, sensing that she wasn't getting any closer to achieving her goal, stood in place and offered an even larger smile. "I'm Elaine Newell. Please, it'll only take a minute of your time." She extended her hand, but Tracy just looked at it.

"Look, I'm not into women, if that's what you're thinking," Tracy said.

Elaine clasped her hands in front of her and laughed. "It's nothing like that. I assure you."

A true city girl, Tracy knew that nuts came in all shapes, sizes, and sexess. And just because this Elaine chick looked fairly wealthy, sharp, and sensible didn't mean she was any more normal than the kook who was yelling expletives on the corner every morning as Tracy left her house. Tracy slung her gym bag over her shoulder. *Is she lonely? Looking for girlfriends?*

Tracy turned away from the woman again. "Hey, maybe some other day. I've really got to get to work."

"But you're not going to work. You lost your job, Miss Middleton. Surely you have time for coffee."

Tracy turned back, stunned. She'd been unemployed for three weeks, but it wasn't the kind of news—and she wasn't the kind of person—to make the papers. How could this stranger know her name and know that she was no longer employed? She stared at her incredulously and Elaine looked back at her with the demeanor of a kindly old grandmother.

Tracy squinted at her. "Now you're just freaking me out. Who are you again?"

"I'm Elaine Newell, CEO of Cathy Booker Foods, and I might be able to offer you a position with my company." When Tracy still stared at her skeptically, she elaborated. "You'd be *very* well compensated." Elaine's eyes drifted toward a group of women returning from their aerobics class. She cautiously took the few steps toward Tracy and took her elbow. "Please, let's talk in the juice bar."

Tracy was too perplexed to resist. She knew of Cathy Booker Foods, whose chief product was a popular line of canned and frozen soul dishes. Since Tracy was in no position to turn down a job that appeared to have fallen into her lap, she let her legs carry her along with the woman.

As they boarded the elevator, Elaine made general conversation about the unseasonably warm weather Chicago was experiencing in late September. Tracy could only utter monosyllabic answers in response. Her thoughts were still occupied by the strangeness of the entire situation, but she didn't see a reason not to at least hear the woman out. They got off the elevator at the floor of the stylish cafeteria and juice bar.

Elaine approached the counter and turned to Tracy. "What'll you have?"

"Uh, nothing for me, thanks." She wanted to make this as brief as possible.

Elaine turned back to the counter girl and handed her a credit card. "Two chai teas, please, and a bran muffin. We'll be over at that table."

Tracy followed Elaine to a table that was by the windows, but far from the few other patrons who were in the bar. It was only eight-thirty on Friday. This early in the morning, very few members had the luxury of idly hanging around the health club after they finished their workouts.

"Well, this is nice. I finally have a chance to sit down with you," Elaine said, settling into her seat. Tracy placed her bag on the floor and looked at the woman expectantly. The server dropped off their drinks and Elaine quickly signed the credit card receipt. She started to drink her tea. "You should try this. It's really good."

Tracy still wasn't sure that the woman wasn't mining for girlfriends, so she pushed her to get to the point. "You mentioned something about a job."

Elaine chuckled and broke off a piece of her bran muffin. She sat back in her chair, smiling. "I can see you're the direct type. That's good . . . good. Smart and direct. Just how I was hoping you'd be."

"Um, Mrs. Newell is it . . . ?"

"Please. I insist that you call me Elaine."

"Well, Elaine. Do I know you? How do you know I—"

"Was fired from your job at CMTV? How do I know your name? Etcetera etcetera?" Elaine drank more tea as Tracy nodded slowly. "Well, Tracy Middleton. Don't be alarmed. Or should I say, don't get any more alarmed than you already are." She chuckled. "But I've been watching you for quite some time. I've also had a private investigator look into your background."

Tracy's brow wrinkled angrily. "Who the—"

"I know, I know. It sounds pretty crazy." Elaine waved a dismissive hand at her. "But listen—I own a multimillion-dollar corporation and I can't have just anybody work with me as my personal assistant."

Tracy sat back and crossed her arms over her chest. "I know you think you've searched extensively into my background and stuff, but apparently you didn't look hard enough. I'm not the personal-assistant type. I'm a journalist."

"I'm well aware of that . . . and you're pretty smart, too. Top of your class at the University of Missouri. I thought you produced some great segments on the news, and, to top it off, you're very attractive. You should've been in front of the camera. Trust me. You're exactly what I'm looking for." Elaine ate more of her muffin.

Tracy took a sip of her tea, allowing herself time to study the woman across from her. The tea turned out to be a spicy mix that was quite tasty. But she didn't think she could trust Elaine's judgment about everything. "Well, honestly, I don't think *you're* what *I'm* looking for. I think I'll just look for another news job."

"That pays nine thousand dollars per month? Plus expenses in the form of your own company credit card? Plus a bonus of half a million dollars if you work out?" Elaine raised her eyebrow and gave her a sly smile.

Tracy was once again astonished. The producer's job at CMTV, though short-lived, was the highest salary she'd ever made in her twenty-nine years. She was thrilled to have negotiated $72,500 with them. Now this woman was offering her so much more to be an *assistant?*

"So let me get this straight. You're offering me more than one hundred thousand dollars a year to be your personal secretary? Plus another five hundred thousand as a bonus if I work out?" Tracy asked, making quote marks in the air. She sat up straighter in her chair and frowned at the woman, trying to get a better understanding of her motivations.

"That's right," Elaine said without a hint of irony. "But it's not a secretary. You'd be my personal assistant. That involves more than secretarial duties."

"Oh," Tracy said with sudden understanding. She sat back and looked at her coldly. She curled her lips. "I get it. And these *duties* involve the bedroom, right?"

Elaine laughed and shook her head. "You young people are so jaded with life. I am *not* a lesbian. I am not interested in pursuing a relationship with you, other than, uh, a professional one."

"'Uh, professional one'?" Tracy mimicked Elaine's words. "So what's the catch? One hundred thousand is already a generous offer for a secr—personal assistant, or whatever. Why would you also throw in an additional half million dollars?"

"Okay, so I admit, there is a catch." When Elaine saw Tracy's big brown eyes become guarded, she hurried to explain. "But it's not what you think. It's that I have an immediate assignment for you, should you accept my offer."

"And it's not sex, so it's illegal." In her mere seven months in the news business, Tracy had seen a lot of scandalous acts committed by people who looked as clean-cut and wealthy as Elaine Newell. CEOs were dragged away in handcuffs just as frequently as common criminals these days.

"It's not illegal," Elaine said, avoiding Tracy's eyes and twisting her lips. "It might not be ethical, but it's certainly not illegal."

"All right, Elaine, spit it out. What is this covert assignment you're really offering me? Because I'm getting the distinct impression that the secretary-assistant thing is just the stick and this little project you're throwing in is the actual carrot." To prove to Elaine that she was completely unimpressed by her, Tracy reached over, pulled a piece off Elaine's muffin, and popped it into her mouth.

Elaine amiably pushed the plate with the muffin to Tracy's side of the table. "That's why I like you. You're a smart cookie."

Shrewd move, Tracy thought. This woman was a smart cookie herself, and an adherent to Dale Carnegie's *How to Win Friends & Influence People.*

Elaine leaned forward on her elbows and crossed her arms. "Okay, here it is. I really do need a bright assistant. This person would have to stand in for me at meetings and attend some of my committees in my stead, help me organize my schedule, and manage my staff. You would get to use some of your journalism skills by ghostwriting some things for me and making sure the external relations staff is on their toes. Plus, you've got the connections to get Cathy Booker some prime media placements."

Tracy drank more of her tea, relaxing a little. "Sounds good, but why not advertise for such a person? I'm sure every girl with that kind of experience would be chomping at the bit to grab that job."

"That's the second part." Elaine swiped her floppy hair out of her eyes and touched Tracy's arm. "The part where you earn half a million. She has to be smart and beautiful and confident—like you—if she's going to catch the eye of my son."

Tracy set her cup down and really started to laugh. She saw Elaine looking annoyed at her, but she couldn't control herself. Tracy finally settled down, shaking her head as though she'd just heard a great joke.

"Find something amusing, Miss Middleton?"

"I insist—call me Tracy." She smiled, noting Elaine's angry look at the mock. "Isn't this a lot of trouble to go through to fix up your son? Kind of expensive, huh? He must be a real looker," she added sarcastically.

"As a matter of fact, my son Sean is quite handsome," Elaine insisted. "He has no problem meeting women."

Tracy smirked. "They say a mother's love is blind."

Bristling, Elaine reached for her wallet and opened it to a photo of her son. She held it out to Tracy irritably. Tracy took the wallet and stared at the photo.

"Ooh, cutie pie. He's almost a double for Blair Underwood."

"Who?"

"Ever seen *LA. Law*?" Tracy handed back the wallet. "So if he's so fine, how come his mama is out trying to find women for him? He won't settle down?"

"It's *whom* he wants to settle down with that's the problem," Elaine said, relaxing.

"Oh? A hoochie-mama? And you don't approve?"

Tracy ate the muffin unconcerned. This obviously was not her problem.

"Just the opposite. He's engaged to—she's a nice enough girl, but the wrong woman for him," Elaine said, looking down. For a woman who, Tracy could tell, prided herself on speaking her mind, Elaine was tripping over these words. Something was up, and this woman still wasn't leveling with her. "You are exactly the type he used to date. His type . . . until she came along. And I can't have my company fall into, um, the wrong hands."

"Your competitor's daughter? A real-life Romeo and Juliet?" Tracy eyed her, but Elaine didn't respond. "Whatever. I'm not into pretty boys; I go for the more masculine type. Besides, I'm all for love, and if these two are in love, who are you to split them up? This really doesn't sound like the job for me." Tracy reached for her bag and frowned when Elaine touched her arm to stop her.

"Tracy, don't be foolish! I'm not asking you to marry him. This would only take a year out of your life, and imagine the money you'd make." When Elaine saw Tracy's steely face, she tried another tactic. "Maybe less than a year. Once you got there, you would turn his head. Just think, six months of work and you could be a very wealthy woman."

Tracy stood. "Sorry. No deal."

Elaine rose to her feet and gripped Tracy's arm. "Please," she whispered desperately. "All you have to do is come and work as you normally would. I really could use you as my right arm. You've got everything I'm looking for. And if, in the course of your work, Sean sees you and has doubts about this impending marriage, what's the harm?" She spread her hands open as if to show how easy it would be.

"First of all, I don't think your stupid plan would work

unless your son is some sort of cad or womanizer, and secondly, you need to find somebody else to do your dirty work." Tracy slung her gym bag on her shoulder and headed for the door.

Elaine caught up with her. "One million dollars." She grabbed Tracy's arm again, whispering, "I'll give you one million, but our arrangement would have to be absolutely confidential."

Tracy pried Elaine's hand off her arm. "Lady, you really need to get a life. Good-bye." Tracy headed toward the elevator. When she boarded, she was relieved to see that Elaine hadn't followed her. She blew out a breath. *Whew! Talk about your nutcases.*

Tracy stepped out of the health club and onto Michigan Avenue. She was sorry she didn't have that shower. Although the weather was unseasonably warm for September, the underlying breeze from the lake was incredibly cool. It caught the dampness on her clothes and chilled her body. Tracy walked quickly to the parking garage to retrieve her car. She tried not to think about it, but it really rankled her nerves that a total stranger could readily get as much information on her as she wanted. At least Elaine's ludicrous proposition had one positive effect on her—it strengthened her resolve to stop dawdling and find another job.

About the Author

Crystal Downs was born and currently resides in Chicago. She has worked as a business writer, marketing consultant, and grant writer. Crystal publishes a consumer magazine highlighting African-American films and filmmakers. Though she's been writing short stories, plays, and fiction since she was a little girl, this is the first time she has published her work in book form.

BOOK YOUR PLACE ON OUR WEBSITE AND MAKE THE ARABESQUE ROMANCE CONNECTION!

We've created a customized website just for our very special Arabesque readers, where you can get the inside scoop on everything that's going on with Arabesque romance novels.

When you come online, you'll have the exciting opportunity to:

- View covers of upcoming books

- Learn about our future publishing schedule (listed by publication month and author)

- Find out when your favorite authors will be visiting a city near you

- Search for and order backlist books

- Check out author bios and background information

- Send e-mail to your favorite authors

- Join us in weekly chats with authors, readers and other guests

- Get writing guidelines

- AND MUCH MORE!

Visit our website at
http://www.arabesquebooks.com